Dear Catherine,

I hope you enjoy the story!

Alexander Olson

MARCH OF FIRE

March of Fire

Rattle Their Bones
Volume One

CHARLOTTE STORM OLSEN

Huldra Studio

ONE

Scotland and England, late in the year 1628

The British Isles in ca. 1642, adapted by the author from
Willem Blaeu's Atlas Major, 1634 - 1672
Public domain, via Wikimedia Commons

~ One ~

The Outskirts of Edinburgh, November 2nd of the year 1628

He rode, hard and fast, through the howling wind and driving snow, thundering hooves beneath him beating away the time, time he could not afford to lose. Through the thicket he saw the forest clear to the open fields of the Pentlands, and beyond, the granite spectre of the city appeared, the castle on the hill emerging in the frosty mist: Edinburgh. He could almost hear the tap-tap-tap of the slow death drums as the procession would be pushing her towards the waiting fire, throngs of people jostling and heckling the executioner and the condemned, a trepid anticipation for most, and a gleeful sight for the more deranged: the burning of a witch.

We must make it in time, Dealanaich, the rider urged his mount on, with his heart almost in his throat at the prospect of failing in his mission, *we must make it before it is too late...*

But time, as was her habit, would wait for no one; and the gut-wrenching stench of burnt flesh and the horrific spectacle of cindering bones assaulted him with every sharp gust of wind when he, Jack Lyon, pulled up his steed at Castlehill, the last, and now a lone, witness of her burning. Utterly disbelieving, his heart torn, he stared at the smouldering pyre, ash and cinders all that remained, save a few charred bones and teeth that peeked through the smoke and lingered in the last of the glowing embers.

So absorbed in his failure, and his grief, was he, that the sound of a voice behind him echoed only distantly in his mind, until

Dealanaich, who recognized the stranger's voice, whinnied softly and nudged her master back to the world of the living.

"My Lord," the young voice repeated, "I am so glad you have come!"

The boy could almost not recognize his master when he turned to face him; the confidence and courage he remembered of Jack Lyon, Lord Glamis, now gone, instead before him a broken man, bloodshot eyes, pale as death and body so beaten with worry and exhaustion he would have fallen to the ground had the boy not caught him first.

"My Lord!" the boy said again, anguished at the sight, but Lord Glamis brushed him off dismissively, too ashamed to face the boy.

"Aye, I came, Hamish, but too late," he almost sobbed.

"Aye, sire," acknowledged Hamish. "but you'd not have been able to stop them- the forces were so strong against her!"

They stood silently for a while; above, a buzzard and a crow circled and spun, one around the other, taunting each other, competing for their prey somewhere below. It seemed like night, but it was only late afternoon; the sun still lingered some way above the horizon, peering through the clouds, and in the distance, the cacophony of sounds and overwhelming smells of the market crowds slipped in, between the smoke and the low, slow gasps of crackling embers and dying flames.

Hamish paused for a moment, considering his words somewhat first, before he broke the silence.

"My Lord, I never saw a lady with such courage in an hour of such darkness; she neither flinched nor cried as the flames took her! She spoke, until she could not speak anymore- she cursed them all, my Lord! The King, the Bishop, the General....and even her brother!"

Lord Glamis felt a sharp jolt in his heart.

"She was alive, Hamish? Alive, when they lit the fire?"

The boy replied with a barely noticeable nod; it had been an ordeal so horrific to witness it was beyond imagination, beyond description.

"No poison first, Hamish?" persisted Lord Glamis, his voice trembling, "no long, cold, iron grip around her neck to hurry her death before the flames consumed her?"

"Aye, my Lord, she was alive," were all the words Hamish could find to reply. He knew his master well; and he knew his anger was beginning to fill the hollow grief he felt. And the young lad was not wrong, for Lord Glamis began to feel the hatred, and thirst for vengeance, flood his senses.

William Douglas....Lord Glamis thought and bitterly cursed the man responsible, *even if it drains the last drop of my blood, I promise, you will pay dearly for this! I shall have my pound of flesh and you will rue the day you dared to anger the House of Glamis!*

Images of her in a sea of flames flashed into his dark thoughts, and the grief returned, when he suddenly remembered: what of his niece?

"Balgaire," his voice, now frantic, shook slightly, terrible thoughts of the little girl's fate entering his mind, "where is my niece, Hamish? And why did McAdam and Alastair not come with you?"

"I beg pardon, my Lord," his servant answered carefully and cautiously, "I thought she had told you! McAdam took Balgaire to safety....they sailed to Germany, to stay with your cousin, Robert Douglas!"

Hamish waited to continue, hoping his master too distracted to pursue his inquiry about Alastair; but Lord Glamis, although he was plunged into sorrow, and so consumed by guilt and hatred, was gathering his reason, and insisted so strongly that the poor boy had no choice but to answer.

"And Hamish," he asked again, now looking directly with piercing bloodshot eyes at the boy, a hardness from his master the young lad had not felt before, "where is my steward, Alastair?"

The snow had eased, and the clouds gave way to the orange glow of the late afternoon sun, the wet and cold cobblestones glistening a bright russet as the light struck the streets; they seemed cleansed, renewed.

"Master Alastair...pardon, sir, I thought you knew!"

"Knew what, Hamish? Has something happened to him?"

"I dunno know, my Lord....but, er, we cannot find him anywhere after all the murders! The sheriff is searching for him as we speak!"

Alastair, thought Lord Glamis, *you fool, what have you done this time?*

He looked past Hamish towards the city; everything was as it always had been, the burning of innocents as common and routine now as the bloody spectacle of a cockfight and it truly horrified him. He turned his gaze towards the dying fire once again.

"Gather the bone and ash, Hamish, or what remnants of those you can," Lord Glamis muttered. The snow had begun to fall again, thick tufts of white descending gently onto the pile of ash and bone before him, dampening the last few breaths of the fire.

"The embers are almost cold."

"Yes, my Lord," nodded Hamish, and not feeling his question impertinent, he asked, "but who will bury her, my Lord, as a witch?"

There were few who would bury a woman condemned to the fire for witchcraft, even those of higher birth did not escape the curse of superstition that came with such an association.

"I will bury her, Hamish; she will return to Glamis and rest there, where she belongs."

The young lad, himself weary of the constant flavour of death he had been forced to taste in recent weeks, scavenged the bones and ashes, and amidst the debris, he found a jewel; it was a ring.

"My Lord, did this belong to her?" he held it out in his bony, blackened hands, carefully shaking the ashes away; his master took it from him, curious.

"Aye," he smiled, for the first time in a long while, "aye, a gift from me; it belonged to my mother."

It was not lavish, but beautiful, nonetheless: a thin, gold band carved with flowers and leaves, and inscribed on the inside were only two words: *salus mea*- my salvation.

"I will keep it with me for now," he decided, and slipped it into his mantle pocket; the wind was picking up, and the light was beginning to fade.

"Let us be rid of this godless place, Hamish; we have a long ride home."

"Aye, my Lord; but you have come far today already: do you not wish to rest here in Edinburgh, and continue tomorrow, instead?"

"No!" Jack Lyon snapped at Hamish so sharply, the boy jumped a little. The thought of remaining in the city that took her away too much for the wounded heart of Lord Glamis to bear.

"If I never see this city again, Hamish, it will be too soon!"

Her ashes and bones by his side, wrapped in a cloth in his satchel, he and the young lad began their journey home. They passed through Newgate, along the markets, at one point almost unaware of straying missiles in the form of rotten apples assailing them, turning to see another weary stranger and his horse contending with a rabble of child vagrants, before they passed through the city gate and found the road to Glamis. Hamish and his master were both exhausted, the horses weary, and so the journey was slow. They did not reach Glamis until after midnight, the dim light of the waning crescent moon fading with the last hours of Allhallows Eve, the Day of the Dead.

Into your hands, O merciful Saviour, we commend our sister, Margaret.
Acknowledge, we humbly beseech you,
A sheep of your own fold,
A lamb of your own flock,
A sinner of your own redeeming.
Receive her into the arms of your mercy,
Into the blessed rest of everlasting peace,
And into the glorious company of the saints in light.
Amen.

*

The City of Portsmouth, England, about two months earlier, on August 23rd, 1628

"Villain!" he screamed, spluttering, stumbling, awkward and disbelieving into the crowd, as if he had encountered the Devil, a flood of crimson seeping through his torn shirt, and he, George Villiers, the 1st Duke of Buckingham, trying in vain to pursue his killer; but he fell down dead, on the cobbled stones outside the Greyhound Inn, and the gathered crowd cheered at the death of the King's favourite.

"The Duke is dead, and we are rid of strife
By Felton's hand that took away his life!"

The hero, for so he was to almost everyone who had witnessed the assassination, was Felton, and he, barely interested in an escape but more in knowing that his final mission had been accomplished, was able to flee down only a few of Portsmouth's streets, until the King's guards tracked him down. He knew he would die in prison, or worse, but that was irrelevant. Felton had achieved what he set out to do- and brought justice to all the soldiers who had died under the careless protection of the villain Villiers; he knew the resounding infamy of his crime would live beyond his death, and that, to Felton, was all that mattered.

*

Southwick Park, St Mary's Priory, Portsmouth, the same afternoon

In a spacious chamber fit for kings two men appeared to languish in its sombreness; one was in repose on a comfortable bed, for he was, in fact, the King. It was not, at that moment, a place of lighthearted discussion; neither the dark curtains, filtering out the intermittent light from the sun, nor the teal stone walls with the somber-faced oil paintings encouraged a feeling of hope or happiness. The stern demeanor of Archbishop Thomas Cromwell and smug imperiousness of King Henry VIII, both ardent dissolutionists, had been left as a final insult to what remained of the Priory after King Henry's act of vengeance against the Church.

"My soul-mate," began the King, hesitating, and drawing in a wounded breath, "the most devoted friend to this Crown..is dead....," he moaned, "dead!"

He, King Charles I of England, Scotland and Ireland, was not usually one of such naked sentiment, and threw himself back onto his bed; he had barely ventured from his chamber since the news of the Duke of Buckingham's death.

His head half buried in the goose down blanket, he turned a little to look at the only other person in the room. William Laud, the Bishop of London, was about to speak, but the King paid no attention.

"Murdered by one of our own. Murdered!" he shrieked; grief had taken over his senses, it pierced his skin, cut his flesh, and gnawed at his bones without mercy. He was unable to form rational thoughts in his mind; oh, how he wanted his dear, dear, handsome friend, instead of this ugly, pompous figure standing condescendingly before him, forgetting for a moment the true loyalty the Bishop had always offered the young King, and his father before him.

A tear formed in the corner of the young monarch's pale brown eyes, collecting momentum before it rolled reluctantly down his cheeks, blending unobtrusively with the saliva and mucus trickling from his nose, and clinging on to his thin moustache. The Bishop could only look away; he, too, was deeply grieved by the death of one of his own favourites. But, he was the Bishop of London, and must hold his composure, and banish thoughts of the flesh- at least when he was in the company of those whose favour he wished to uphold in order to advance his own ambitions.

Apart from the faint tapping of a wind that had picked up against the windows, there was a hollow silence. Neither of them moved. One was too grief stricken, his mind appearing to have temporarily left his body to find some relief in another dimension; the other was too uncomfortable and apprehensive to be seen as weak, and thus, for him to offer any gesture of comfort, or words of solace, were not an option.

It was late afternoon, and the daylight began to fade across the skies. Beyond the fields and gardens of St Mary's Priory- or, what was left of it- that were visible through the windows, the light of the on-setting evening crept across the sea, the first shadows closing in on the silhouettes of the naked trees and woods, cloud-shaped forms of grey sweeping over the water with the late summer winds. Only the last glowing embers in the enormous fireplace of the King's chamber offered light and warmth in an otherwise bleak moment. It was the loud crack from the wood yielding under the heat of the fire that forced the King to rouse himself. He cleared his throat, and, removing himself from the warming comfort of his pillow, he turned to the window. His own reflection horrified him, and while attempting to tidy long curly strands of dark hair, he asked:

"And what have you to say of this.... utterly heinous business, William Laud, as Bishop of London, keeper of the faith?" the King suddenly had found interest in his fellow chamber mate, or perhaps he was tired of feeling like he was talking only to himself, or God, who appeared not presently to be inclined to listen.

The fire in the hearth had begun to diminish, and the chill of the late summer clung to the great, thick stone walls of the Hall. The Bishop felt the slight cold, too, and tended to the glimmering logs, pushing them about to stir the flames, as if they would perhaps offer some answers or arguments for the King.

William Laud was a tall and intimidating figure, eyes and brows permanently raised in a look of haughty suspicion, even more so as he stood, feet firmly apart, in his long, blue bishop's cloak, with the high and stiff white frilled collar, and the flat black cap. The gilt and yellow tunic and black trousers he wore made him, in his opulent presence, all the stuff that archbishops were expected to be made of, at least in his own opinion, and he now formulated in his clever head an answer to the King's question, which he, the Bishop of London, hoped would help his own cause for advancement, feeling himself the only cleric worthy of becoming the next Archbishop of Canterbury.

"Your Majesty, I am at a loss for words," he began, very well aware that he was in fact rarely in such a situation, stroking his thin grey tuft of a beard, "the Duke..." he stopped briefly, composing himself again as he thought of that beautiful figure of a man, now pale and dead and utterly lifeless, whose soft touch and mellow voice had been sent to the vast eternity above, and was now beyond his reach forever, "was a man of state, of greatness, and his murder is a crime so vile, those responsible will feel the violent wrath of the law, of this I may assure you!"

It was not Laud's own voice, raised and shaking in anger and grief, that had surprised the King, who had only half-listened, somewhat distracted; rather, only two words the Bishop had spoken had caught hold of him, and, becoming inquisitorial, he turned a sharp tongue to the Bishop.

"Those responsible?" he asked, releasing himself from the comforting softness of his bed, his red-rimmed eyes almost matching the deep red of the velvet curtains that surrounded his four-poster bed, which, in the vastness of his chamber, seemed quite small, almost ridiculously so for the grand status of a King of three countries.

He left his bed and moved closer to the Bishop, who had not flinched from his resolute stance by the fireplace.

"Do you mean to tell me, Bishop, that Felton, curse him!- did not act alone?" he pressed for an answer, clenching his fists, deep grooves furrowing his pale brow as all manner of dark thoughts entered his disturbed mind.

The Bishop was once again too slow in replying, while the King continued his rant, a mixture of deep wounded sorrow and fiery anger, barely able to keep control of his reasoning.

"The Spanish- a curse on them, too!- they always despised George, after the business with the Infanta Maria- which was the fault of their blundering, not my dear, most excellent George! And now that we are at war with them, they would do anything to destroy my image- anything!" He paused, a darkness coming over his pale, worn face, eyes narrowed and lips pursed as his resentment grew ever deeper.

"Philip and his so-called Prime Minister, that oaf of a man Olivares, have never shied away from committing the foulest of crimes to save their pathetic empire from further ruin!"

Laud, who had in exasperation tried to intervene on several occasions, could, to his extreme irritation, not find a gap in the King's tirade in which he could successfully interject his opinion, which in his own humble opinion, was in fact much more important, and actually far more interesting, as the King, now thoroughly worked up, spilled his mind's contents to the chamber.

"Or Richelieu- that blaggard! He, who calls himself a Cardinal, a Man of God, interlocutor of higher wisdom- hah! He would sooner see George dead than anyone else, even sooner than Philip, after the treacheries of the Isle-De-Re and La Rochelle!"

Seizing a vital second of silence, the Bishop, who had in his mind moved swiftly onwards with his self-serving plan while the King had moaned, replied forcefully:

"Majesty," he flattered, "although I cannot deny the shrewdness of your interpretations of the political treachery of our foreign enemies, I fear the treachery is rather more close to the heart of your own Crown lands....you may have heard that there is talk that the Devil's work is afoot in Scotland?" He paced deliberately slowly back and forth in front of the fireplace, the flickering flames lighting up the one side of his face; he looked, thought the King, rather ridiculous, reminding him of a court jester he had once imprisoned for mocking his mother.

"Scotland? The Devil?" the King asked, confused and irritated; he had never had much time for the Scots, his almost complete lack of interest in that place, save the country's questionable stance on religion, preventing him from visiting his birthplace since his father's accession to the English crown had moved them all south of those borders.

"Scotland?" he said again, with great vexation, wondering what other political maneuverings he had failed to see in the recent calamities that had befallen his kingdom.

"Yes, Majesty, Scotland- unfortunately, in addition to the usual troubles we are faced with in that heathen-filled place- although the border reiving has mostly come to an end, thank the Lord," he crossed himself theatrically, "more recently, there have been discoveries of witches- powerful witches, who do the Devil's work with great cunning and deceit!"

The King was disappointed. He had hoped there were some more rational and intriguing explanations, to do with matters of higher state and complex politics, that could have appeased his conscience; unlike his father, he had no great belief in the ability of witches, and how, even if there was some connection, would witches in Scotland have anything to do with the assassin Felton, an English soldier, or his dear, beloved, dead friend?

"Witches, Bishop?" he murmured, deflated, "Does that not seem unlikely? What is your evidence for this?"

Laud had been accustomed to the frequent obsessions with witches and witchcraft of James I & VI, the King's father, whose own work on the subject, *Daemonologie*, had been published a few years earlier; the Bishop therefore found Charles' lack of interest, which almost reached the extreme opposite of his father's unrelenting passion, unsettling, and replied with an attempt at patience:

"Sire, witchcraft is not a matter to be trifled with; and we do have evidence that a witch in Scotland- one of noble birth, at that!-

had influence in the death of the Duke of Buckingham, God rest his precious soul!" He crossed himself again, and continued quickly:

"This lady of noble birth had been under suspicion from her half-brother, the 7th Earl of Morton, William Douglas, for some time; and he has himself witnessed her deceit and sorcery. It may interest you, Majesty, that the Earl of Morton's own son is married to a niece of our dear, departed friend, the Duke of Buckingham....so you see, the familial connections are strong."

This new information was beginning to take a hold of the King's interest, but he was not wholly convinced.

"But why, Bishop?" Charles, still unconvinced, attempted to paint a picture in his mind of the situation, but all that entered into his mental visions was an angry and bitter old crone, who for whatever reason was sitting in her rocking chair in a remote half-ruined castle in Scotland, casting spells over a brewing cauldron and muttering curses on George. He had heard his father speak of the subject often, and had been forced to read his work, and although it had been thoroughly studied, Charles had never believed as fervently as his father of the influences of witches; to the current King, a witch seemed to be nothing more than an aggrieved old woman who had upset her family or fellow parishioners about some small trifling matter; they, in turn, wanted their revenge, or to get their hands on some part of her fortune.

Knowing he could not provide a satisfactory answer to the King's rational question, Laud replied in an overly sinister manner:

"Witches need no other reason, my Lord, than the uncontrollable desire to practice that dark magic to satisfy the whims of their master, the Devil."

"Hmm," grunted Charles; he had hoped for a more sensational political argument, one which he could use to punish Parliament, which was an increasingly sharper thorn in the King's side as the days went by. Try as he might, he could not muster up the enthusiasm for the sinister idea of the witch, even less so in connection with the death of his friend.

"And who is this lady you speak of?"

He had moved to the window again; the rain had started to fall, small drops sliding rhythmically down the glass, blurring the shapes of the trees and hills below him in the distance, and blending with the vast iron-grey sea beyond.

"Lady Margaret Douglas, my Lord; she is a Douglas, for whom your grandfather had great enmity- their treasonous past is well-known to the Stuarts."

Charles frowned, dismissively waving a hand to an unknown recipient.

"Her brother is also a Douglas- why should he be less treasonous? How do we know that he does not have some selfish interest in persecuting his sister, Bishop? It sounds nothing more to me than a trifling family squabble!"

The King remained hopeful that a treacherous Parliamentarian plot was behind the death of George, and that Felton was merely a small pawn in a vast political conspiracy that sought to bring about his own downfall; for he knew that such a conspiracy was real and ever present.

The Bishop replied soothingly, as if speaking to a small child:

"Sire, the Earl of Morton is the *right* sort of Douglas; he has only ever been a loyal supporter of the Crown, and yourself, I assure you! His only interest is to serve and protect you, and the future of the Stuart line."

Thunder rolled in the distorted hills beyond, an invisible assailant from the skies, and her inevitable companion, lightning, flashed in thin irregular streaks across the teal clouds. *Tears from Heaven,* thought the King, lamenting the death of his trusted friend, *rage from God against the evil that has beset my own household. Evil; the work of the Devil.*

Feeling the King still lacked conviction in his explanation, the Bishop continued:

"Her mother, you may have heard from your own father, was Jean Lyon, Countess of Angus, herself daughter of the 8th Lord

Glamis; she was also accused of witchcraft by your own great father. Furthermore, the 8th Lord Glamis was the grandson of Janet Douglas, Lady Glamis, burned at the stake for witchcraft by your own great-grandfather, King James V.....so you see, my Lord, the history of Douglas treachery along the female line against the Stuarts is a long and deeply rooted one; and one which I, as Bishop of London, and your spiritual and political advisor, would implore you not to ignore!"

The embers in the fireplace began to burn down, and Laud, being tired of having the task of stoking the fire, rang a bell, after which a young and nervous-looking steward swiftly appeared to tend to it. He reminded the King of George- dear, beloved George!- tall, and dark, and lean and charming. He could not help but stare at the boy, who in reality had no resemblance to the Duke at all, save perhaps his noticeable height, and the boy, conscious of eyes burning into his back, he hurried his task, and once finished, bowed deeply out of the door, and hoped he would not have to return again soon. Once the boy had left, Charles, saddened, considered a short while, and asked, half-mocking:

"And, Bishop Laud, if the tragic death of my dear, dear friend is indeed a plot by the Devil, what plans do you have to deal with the matter?"

Pleased that he had finally gotten through to the confused muddle of thoughts in the King's head, Laud replied confidently:

"I have two men in mind, sire; one is an expert, a witchfinder general by the name of Matthew Hopkins with a most stellar reputation for successfully prosecuting a large number of witches here in England, and he is one of my most ardent followers. The other is a priest...a Catholic from Spain...", but before he could finish Charles threw him a suspicious glance and interrupted.

"A Spaniard? We are now to trust the treacherous Spanish?"

"He is the Head of the Order of Christ, and well-practiced in the Inquisition," the Bishop reassured, "his loyalty lies with the Catholic faith, and not with the Spanish King. I would keep his name and presence a secret for now, though, but I have asked them both to await my instructions- with your permission, I will dispatch them to Scotland immediately to deal with the matter. The Earl of Morton knows of Master Hopkins and his work, and is eager to be of aid in bringing an end to the Devil's work, now so rampant in Scotland!"

"Even if this means bringing about the end of his own flesh and blood?" inquired Charles, astonished that even a half-sibling would wish the death of a child of one of his parents.

The weather had now taken a turn for the worse, the lightning and thunder raging violently, rain lashing hard against the window, a stark contrast to the calm and quiet of the King's chamber. *God's wrath*, he thought; *He is asking for vengeance, vengeance for my friend.*

Charles moved away from the window to face the Bishop; the two men were about the same height, tall in stature, but where Charles' slender and slight frame belied the hardness of his ambitions, Laud's big and broad form hid well the delicate feelings he harboured towards men in particular, and he, to an outside observer, would have appeared to be the dominant stronger man, a physical symbol of masculine might and power, as the fixed norms of social perceptions had required.

Sighing reluctantly, but exhausted at the thought of who his friend's band of assassins might include, the King nodded feebly.

"Very well, Laud, if you think this will avenge George- do what you believe you must do. But involve me no further with the proceedings until you have reached a verdict- or if you discover a wider conspiracy against me, as I know there must be behind this horrible business! And keep an eye on the Spaniard- I will hold you personally responsible if he betrays us!"

He waved a dismissive hand at the Bishop, who bowed deeply as he backed away to the door.

As soon as the large oak doors had shut, the King could do nothing but succumb to intense grief and began to weep again. His soulmate, his friend, his rock and mountain, lay dead in the morgue, cold and statuesque, and there was nothing he could do to bring him back.

But he could take back his pound of flesh; and he swore to himself, if it was the last act he would perform on earth, that he would make those who murdered his most ardent confidant and beloved companion pay for what they had done- *blood for blood*, he thought, as anger and sorrow strangled his bleeding, suffering heart.

~ Two ~

Aberdour Castle, Fife, in Scotland; about two months later, on October 1st, 1628

"I was very surprised to receive your invitation, brother."

Margaret Douglas confessed this sentiment with a tone of some irony, sitting in one of the grand reception rooms, opposite William Douglas, 7th Earl of Morton, now the owner- through legal trickery and cheating- of her childhood home, the beautiful Aberdour Castle.

"I was given the impression that our friendship- and certainly our filial bond- was at a decidedly unegotiable end, since our quarrel over my father's estate."

Margaret was about forty years of age, small in build with long, auburn hair, surrounding an oblong face with deep brown eyes and a short, thin nose. She had not seen her half-brother since she had left to live with her cousin at Glamis; he remained just as she had remembered him: the stern brow and accusing brown narrow-set eyes, the thick moustache that curled up at each end and contrasting thin and pointed beard, and the long, bumped nose that separated his sunken cheeks. The only change to his appearance was the slight greying at the temples of his elaborate, wavy black hair, and the deeper creases in the skin around his mouth. In his black, knee-length tunic and dark breeches he would have resembled an executioner, had it not been for the enormous, frilled collar that assailed his neck, and the high-heeled silver-buckled shoes adorning his feet. Margaret thought he looked rather ridiculous, although the fine cotton and silk cloth with which his garments were made gave his appearance at least a few redeeming qualities.

The Earl had given his sister a similar evaluation while she had spoken. She looked, in his view, more tired and frail: the pink in her cheeks had gone, and the green-brown eyes he had remembered once to be so lively now seemed to have lost their shine. Her apparel, too, was not as fine as the gowns he remembered she had worn those long years ago; the silk dress in which she presented herself to him now, a pale yellow colour with gilt embroidery, seemed plain and worn, with unassuming sleeves, more akin to the dress of those ladies who aspired to be in the higher classes of society, but were unfortunate in their situation in that respect.

"In the past few years, since we last saw each other....", he began, his tone calm, but Margaret abruptly interrupted him.

"It has been more than ten years, brother," she corrected him sharply.

"Aye," he hesitated, irritated at being cut off, but maintaining his composure, "so it has; and as my age advances, dear sister, I regret to live a life filled with quarrels, particularly with those members of my family who are very dear to me."

Do you threaten all those you hold dear with their life, if they do not give you what you desire? she thought bitterly, and, tempted to continue the argument, she withheld instead; it was a pointless expenditure of her energy, and she, knowing William, was aware that her invitation to Aberdour was not because of his feelings of guilt, and certainly not the result of fraternal love, but because there was still something from her that he desired.

William, who had summoned the steward for refreshments, rose from his seat without speaking to retrieve some documents from a finely carved oak writing desk which stood in the far corner of the vast room. Slowly pacing back to Margaret, he looked her over once again, slightly disapproving, before sitting down, and replied:

"Although we may have quarreled in the past, sister, we are still of the same flesh and blood," he smiled at her in the patronizing manner only an elder brother could. *Only partly of the same flesh and blood*, she thought to herself, as William continued.

"..... And, whether you choose to believe it or not, I have always held your best interests at heart in our dealings!"

Margaret looked up at her brother; he had never cared for her or her father's side of the family- and not even particularly for their mother's side, at that- but in his eyes she saw that he tried to believe it himself.

"I have here," he waved the document in front of her, "a *precept of sasine*, which proposes to equally divide the remainder of your father's estate between us."

He placed it on the small table that stood between them; Margaret, who had suspected her invitation to be a disguise for her brother's real intentions, picked up the document and began to read it.

"And who, William, made you heritor of my father's estate?" she asked, with a combination of amusement and bitterness.

William sighed; he really did not wish to quarrel any longer, but he was frustrated at his sister's lack of sanguine sentiments.

"Your father left no male heritor, my dear sister; however, as we share the same mother, I assume such responsibility. It is, I am certain, what she would have wanted."

Margaret remained silent; her knowledge of legal affairs was limited, but the document before her did not convince her of her brother's rightful status as heritor.

"I confess I am not familiar with the intricacies of the law, William, but I do know that a woman may hold the status of heritor as well as any man; my mother was so, as you know."

Neither of them uttered a word for a while, and the silence of the room was only interrupted with the arrival of the steward and the parlour maids, who laid out an opulent table of refreshments.

The Earl was the first to break the silence.

"Will you not have some food, sister? I must admit," he added, rather judgmentally, "I find you looking thinner and less vigorous than when we last were together!"

When you last saw me, thought Margaret, *you threatened me with an attainder; and that I should look less youthful or 'vigorous' after ten years of life has passed by me, evicted from my home, is the usual crime for which a man would condemn a woman!*

"I thank you," she replied politely, helping herself to pasty and beer; she was thirsty after the carriage ride, and although her Fionnsgoth, her lady's attendant, had brought with her enough provisions for the journey, the exhaustion from her nervousness had dried her throat and increased her hunger.

"It was most regrettable to hear, sister, that your husband was killed in Germany.... this war, my dear, is long and cruel, and there appears to be no end in sight!"

Margaret nodded faintly. *I suppose you will want my husband's property next as well,* she thought, and was disappointed to see that ten years of life's lessons, or her absence from his life, had not changed William at all.

"I suppose the Baron Eythin's property...in Orkney, I believe it is?- will fall to you, now that your son is also....".

She flinched, and shot a hard, cold stare at him.

"That is not confirmed," she interjected bluntly, "and my husband's properties remain in my stewardship until it is!"

She was getting weary of his constant attacks, and so she fired back at him.

"I hear, brother, that you were forced to sell Dalmahoy not long ago?" Her tone was mocking, self-satisfied.

"That must have been such a wrench for you, and particularly for Lady Anne! Do you have plans to do the same with Aberdour, William?"

They were like cat and mouse now, and as hard as they had both had wanted to try, another soul gutting quarrel was now inevitable.

"I was not *forced* to sell Dalmahoy, sister; I chose to, so that I could help our King to fight the French!"

His voice shook slightly with anger. This visit had gone completely awry from what he had intended; he had planned to appease Margaret, to soften her, so that she might agree to his proposal, and after so much time had passed, he thought her bitterness might have passed with it. Instead, he understood, it had grown, and it angered him.

"Ah yes, the King; the English King.....there are those who say Scotland is not Scotland with an English King!"

Margaret knew of her brother's undying loyalty to the King and could see in William's eyes that his blood was beginning to boil in anger. A rumble of thunder in the distance rolled across the sea as if affirming his malcontent, and, waving her translucent hand dismissively towards him, she feigned a light, condescending laugh.

"Politics have never interested me, as you know, dear William, and what you decide to do with your *rightful* property is your business," she smiled, taking a sip of beer and nonchalantly finishing her venison pie.

Had there been a freezing snowstorm, it would still have been warmer outside than in the icy air that had risen as the two siblings baited each other's antagonism into deeper and darker realms of resentment.

"It is a pity, sister, that no suitor at all has come forward since the news of your husband's death! It must be difficult for you, being who you are, to be without a male guardian; the uncertainty of your own future must rest like a dead weight on your mind!"

Amused at seeing her face darken, watching her hands shake with anger as she took a long sip of beer, he continued his assault.

"Although I did hear that your cousin, Jack Lyon, perhaps had such feelings brewing for you, but he has obviously had second thoughts, or I imagine he would have made a proposal of marriage to you by now!"

She was angry; angry for having to listen to the condescending opinions, and angry for not finding the right words to put him down.

"Unlike some, brother, Jack Lyon has honour and decency, and understands the need to respect a widow's grief!"

William rose and paced about the large room, stopping by the window to watch the incoming storm in the distance. Margaret remained seated, wishing above all that she had never come back.

"Well, sister," continued William after a while, "I believe you must be tired after your carriage ride; I have prepared for you a chamber which I think you will find most comfortable. Mistress Fionnsgoth will have a cot in the servant's wing."

She nodded in feigned appreciation; she had placed the 'proposal' her brother had handed her on the seat next to her and did not give it further attention. Should they both wish for a reconciliation of a kind between now and Margaret's departure the day after tomorrow, then she would have to ignore the insulting and hurtful proposal William had handed her, and the horrible attacks on her character. Slightly irritated, William said:

"And, sister, I have arranged for an evening of entertainment tomorrow to be held here at Aberdour, with a few friends who you may remember, and one or two guests from England, who may be interested in gaining your acquaintance."

She looked at him, unnerved. There was something about his manner now that appeared different; it was as if he knew he would win this game.

"Dear sister, you do look tired and worn!" smirked William. "Perhaps an early night would be best today- I will arrange for a timely evening meal so that you may rest early tonight."

He rang a bell, and as if by magic, a steward appeared; the stewards of Aberdour, noted Margaret, had certainly gained importance since her last departure, the fine dress and cloth in which they were fitted not the same as the plain and unremarkable servants' garb she remembered from a decade before. *William must be doing well in his business; I wonder why he is so fixed on taking what is mine.*

"Donaldson, please fetch Mistress Fionnsgoth so that she may show Lady Margaret to her chamber."

The young steward bowed, and Margaret, feeling slightly light-headed and sleepy, followed him, like a lamb, curtsying to her brother as she went out of the door, with a cold smile. "Thank you, brother, for your kind hospitality."

William grinned falsely, eyeing with a piercing glance the proposal she had pointedly left behind on the settee.

*

Margaret slept surprisingly well that night. William had, either by design or coincidence, given Margaret her old bed chamber, which had remained much as she could remember: her old four poster bed with the same bed curtains, the window seat overlooking the gardens still comforted by that big cushion which, on a bright sunny day, was the colour of the sea beyond, and the beautiful small maroon Turkish rug, with flowers and creatures of all different colours, to warm the cold stone floor.

Fionnsgoth had arranged everything neatly for her, as always, and rather than sending for her maid, Margaret dressed herself that morning, although fixing the stay properly had been a challenge, as had tying her dress in place. Fionnsgoth appeared nonetheless, tutting, and clucking at Margaret's feeble attempt to arrange herself properly, putting everything to rights before she fussed over her misstress' hair.

"My Lady, I do think we should forego the plain look as you are back in your mother's home! I packed a few alternative hair arrangements- permit me to try them this morning, my Lady?"

Margaret rarely had patience for the elaborate hair styles some women preferred and thought of a compromise.

"Not this morning, Fionnsgoth," she replied, noting the look of disapproval, and quickly adding, "I would rather put on my hat, as I will take a turn about the garden; the weather is bright today! But this evening," she smiled encouragingly, "for the entertainment my brother has arranged, I would like to try one of your arrangements very much!"

Satisfied with the job of fixing her Madam's appearance and the forthcoming chance to show her considerable talents with hair fashion, Fionnsgoth nodded in agreement.

Margaret took the familiar winding stairs down alone to the great hall, where the breakfast table had been laid out with food and drink as fine as that of any royal household. *My brother can certainly afford to spare no expenses*, she observed. After waiting some time for him and Lady Anne to join her, she understood that William would not appear at breakfast, and so she took it alone, rather uncomfortable in the feeling, before she ventured through the large double doors that led into the garden. A group of dogs, three greyhounds and two spaniels, were chasing each other and having games of rough-and-tumble, which delighted her greatly. They bounced up to her excitedly as they saw Margaret, and leapt around her like little children, and stayed with her throughout her tour of the garden, which to her disappointment, had changed markedly. She had always liked some of the wildness of the gardens when her mother had been alive, who preferred to see it as nature had intended, without too much fuss or fanciness. But now, the garden had been divided into sections arranged by types of trees, flowers and other plants. The symmetry was appealing, and she enjoyed the faint remaining fragrance of the plum and cherry trees, she admitted to herself, but felt something was missing: the soul of the garden had vanished or had been torn into several parts that longed to be together again in their wild freedom.

It was a chilly morning, but the sun shone, and the Forth glistened calmly in the distance. She had missed this place, and the sea; and she missed her mother. Margaret sat, with her five companions surrounding her, on a bench that overlooked the beach and the water in the distance. It was warmer in the sun, and the intermittent heat she felt amidst the peaceful quiet briefly brought back the tranquility she had remembered here before.... before the world had been turned upside down for her.

Aberdour Castle was not large- and not nearly as grand as Glamis, certainly- but she felt a belonging to it, a feeling she could not explain in words; and the sea, the sea was in her blood, somehow, it made her feel free, and not to see it every day now that she was at Glamis made her feel as though she had left behind a long-lost friend.

"How do you do this beautiful morning, Lady Margaret?" a thin, cold voice spoke behind her, as she jumped a little startled, the dogs running away at the familiar but unwelcome sound of the high-pitched tone. She turned around to see William's wife, Lady Anne, with her maid behind her, holding a parasol to keep the weak sun from her mistress' fragile pale skin.

"Good morrow, Lady Anne," Margaret replied, apologizing, "pardon, I was lost in my own thoughts, and did not hear you coming. How do you do?"

The ladies curtsied respectfully, if not meaningfully; neither of them had ever taken any liking to each other, and years of absence had not changed their resentful feelings.

"Will you permit me to join you?" asked Lady Anne, pointing to the bench.

"Of course, it should be delightful," lied Margaret, with as broad a smile as she could muster.

"Fetch my hat, Christian," snapped Anne to her maid, who looked a rather nervous soul and promptly curtsied and ran off to attend to her instructions.

Anne lowered herself gently onto the bench, careful to keep her long blue silk dress away from the grass, sighing slightly as her snugly fitted stay dug even further into her tightly bound waist. She looked and played the part of the noble lady; her elaborately groomed appearance- from her fashionable dress, styled in the French fashion, to her white painted face and rosy cheeks, and the long, blond ringlets of hair and strands of pearls that fell around her shoulders, told Margaret that Anne was someone who closely followed the tastes and fashions of her royal counterparts.

"My husband, the Earl," she spoke haughtily, emphasizing his title, "tells me that you will stay for our entertainment this evening, and return to Glamis tomorrow?"

"Aye," Margaret confirmed, "he has kindly invited me; it is a pleasure to be back at Aberdour, after being away for so long!"

Anne's eyes narrowed slightly, and as her maid, who had returned with a wide-rimmed feather hat, fixed it to her mistress' hair, Anne continued.

"And how is Glamis in these days? How does Lord Glamis do? I hear he is mostly away on some variety of business and has left the castle in your hands...now that his marriage is no longer."

Margaret did not wish to give details of her cousin's personal affairs, and merely nodded.

"He is away now and then, aye, but it is he, not I, who has charge of the estate; but he has kindly allowed me to remain in my mother's childhood home."

"And what will you do when he marries again, and will no longer wish you to stay?" Anne asked abruptly, with an acid, accusatory tone that took Margaret by surprise; but she would not be drawn into a petty squabble to feed her sister-in-law's domestic paranoia and changed the subject.

"May I ask what the entertainment will be tonight, Lady Anne? Will it be a large gathering? I notice you have one or two other guests staying in the new east range, although I have yet to make their acquaintance."

Anne was enormously vexed at the change of subject; she had a burning desire to know if Margaret was a threat to her current comfortable style of living. What if Margaret were to find a way to reclaim Aberdour? Now that William had been forced to sell

Dalmahoy, they had few options of living elsewhere- at least, few options that were acceptable to Anne's status in society.

She rose from the bench, calling over her maid, ordering her brusquely to remove her hat, and to bring back her parasol, all the while glancing at Margaret suspiciously.

"I believe my husband, the Earl," she enjoyed this emphasis of title, "has arranged for carolers and a play." Her reply was haughty, and annoyed, as she intermittently slapped away the maid's hands in irritation, scolding the poor girl for trying to help, and reprimanding her when she did not. "There will also be a banquet, of course.... do you hold many banquets at Glamis, Lady Margaret?" she enquired in a tone that assumed the contrary; it was extremely vexing that someone like Margaret, who, in Lady Anne's fixed opinion, was below her own rank in society, should live in Scotland's finest castle, and have the support of one of Scotland's most influential families.

"My cousin holds a banquet when it suits him," replied Margaret, trying to match Anne's cold tone, "and when he feels the expense of it would be of benefit to those for whom he holds it!"

Margaret rose from the bench, and the three ladies strolled back to the great hall in silence, the maid fussing over her mistress but doing nothing right to please Lady Anne. When they had reached the Great Hall, Margaret curtsied as she took her leave from her hostess.

"I will be delighted to see you again at the banquet this evening, Lady Anne, for I am certain it will be a feast to remember."

Anne inclined her head ever so slightly in acknowledgement, and they parted ways- Margaret returning to her chamber, angry and insulted, and Anne seeing to the preparations of the banquet, shouting orders at the servants, ill-tempered with the duty of having to host a sister-in-law who had the power to determine the security of her future.

*

The Long Gallery, a grand chamber in the newly built east range of the castle, was to be the venue for the evening's entertainment at Aberdour. The east range had been built in quite a different style than the older central range. Rather than turreted stairs, small chambers, and narrow hallways, space in the east range was wider and more open, with high ceilings, of which the Long Hall had a magnificent example: painted with vibrant flowers, floral motifs, and heraldry the wood ceiling was the new pride of Aberdour Castle. To add to the grandness of the Long Hall, the Earl displayed his fine collection of art and furnishings in this room, with paintings by Dutch masters gracing its walls, and furnishings from as far away as Japan and China arranged majestically in every corner.

The evening was cold but clear and bright under the moon. A large group of guests had already assembled by the time Margaret entered the gallery. She had kept her promise to Fionnsgoth, who had fashioned her hair neatly around an elaborate velvet-covered wire frame, with pearls and diamond pendants that tingled gently as she moved among the crowd. Her gown was not as opulent or fashionable as some of the ladies around her; Margaret had always preferred a sobre appearance, which many in what one might call higher circles would mistake as a lack of wealth. Rather, it was a modesty she preferred to uphold.

Lady Anne- or rather, her frightened maid- had informed Fionnsgoth that the banquet would be masked, although this was not an obligation; most of the guests had donned them, but for now, Margaret preferred to carry her own mask beside her, in the hopes that long forgotten friends might recognize her and welcome her back.

By the time her brother and Lady Anne arrived- about an hour later- only one person had spoken to her, an old friend of her mother, but while engaged in conversation, his wife had dragged him away after a frosty greeting. *My brother has done well to blacken my name,* she thought, *I wonder what lies he has told of me.*

"Welcome, dear friends," her brother shouted jubilantly, with a sombre note that followed, "to this banquet, a celebration in honour of the late and very great George Villiers, 1st Duke of Buckingham, and most trusted and loyal servant to His Majesty King Charles! This night," he continued, spreading his arms wide as if embracing the room, "we show our loyalty to the Crown with this mighty feast, music, and a play that was a favourite of the Duke. Let us be merry, for that is what he would surely have wished!" he clapped, as the guests cheered.

The banqueting table was one of the most opulent Margaret had ever seen. In the centre of the long bench, which stretched nearly the entire length of the gallery, stood the crowning dish, an enormous peacock pie, complete with the fully stuffed version of the bird sitting on top of it, long, gilt-edged tail fanned out, as if guarding its nest. To the left was a large plate of venison, and to the peacock's right lay a tray with a boar's head. The apple in its mouth, and the wide, glassy eyes, gave it the horrific appearance of a creature that looked like it had not had time to finish the apple before some cruel individual had cut off its head. Large china bowls of fruits and nuts- lemons, oranges, apples, plums, figs and every other exotic fruit imaginable- and fine pewter trays with sweets and cakes, cheeses and pasties, countless jugs of wine and flagons of whiskey crowded the table. So much food and drink was laid out on the table one wondered how there would be room for anyone to sit and eat.

The music began. A group of minstrels played the tune of Greensleeves, as William beckoned his guests to the table. He sat with his wife at one end, closest to the fireplace, while Margaret- who thought she might be seated next to him, being his sister- was ushered to the other end of the table, nearer to the door, allocated for the less important guests, with two couples at either side of her. She was not acquainted with them, but they seemed pleasant enough company once the wine began to flow into their cups.

"Poor Master Robert," slurred one of them, a gentleman who had introduced himself as James Ferguson, "to have to contend with a death in the family so soon after his betrothal; I do not see them here today- I think they must be away to London, to console her father!"

He frowned and shook his hairless head, scratching his greying moustache as he looked longingly into his empty wine glass.

"I beg pardon," asked Margaret, who had been silent for most of the conversation, "what has happened to my nephew? Is his mistress unwell?"

It was James Ferguson's wife, Euphemia, who answered before he had a chance, never one to miss an opportunity for gossip and scandal.

"My dear, do you not know?" she asked, her grey eyes wide open, "the Duke was her uncle!" She continued in a low whisper. "There are some who say that his murder was not committed by one man alone, but is a conspiracy against the King, a plan hatched by the Devil himself!" Her whisper was now almost inaudible, and Margaret strained to hear her over the music and the echo of chattering voices.

"A conspiracy?" repeated Margaret, "but whatever for?"

It was James Ferguson this time who jumped in before his mistress, rather peeved, could reply.

"Parliament! They are difficult, the members. The King is not satisfied by their lack of support- they will not allow him funds to conduct his business properly!"

"I would hardly, my dear," sniffed his mistress, "call 'war' a properly conducted business!"

Ignoring her impertinence, and seeing Margaret smile, he continued haughtily, as if speaking to a child that did not understand the basic rules of life.

"You see, he needs the agreement of Parliament to fund his army, but they will not have it; it should not surprise me at all," he burped, "that the Devil has a hand in this- most members of

Parliament certainly behave as though they have a pact with him!" He laughed at his own amusement, and waved his wine cup at a passing servant who promptly filled it to the brim.

"Well, I should not wonder if there were more to the death of the Duke than a soldier with a grudge," decided his mistress, casting a sideways glance at her husband, "and whether some trickery or such to conspire against the King were the real reason he was murdered!"

Margaret smiled and nodded and was grateful when her brother finally announced the start of the play. The singing minstrels were to perform an act of *The Pageant of the Shearman and Tailors*, apparently one of the Duke's, and the King's, favourite plays. Servants rushed about to ready the far end of the gallery, where the performers set up their makeshift stage, and servants arranged rows of chairs for the guests, with William and Anne- as hosts- separated in the front row. Margaret observed them from the last row, where she was seated; in their opulent finery- Anne fanning herself with an elaborate gilt swan-feather creation, her brother weighed down by a heavy gold chain around his neck- she wondered whether they were trying to appear as grand and important as the King and Queen themselves.

Although most guests had now removed their masks, feeling less inhibited after the flowing drink and food, some had kept them on, but one, in particular, had caught Margaret's attention. The figure, a man, dressed in black in a long mantle, had remained apart from the crowd throughout the entertainment, as if scrutinizing every single individual, and she wondered who he could be. She had noticed him particularly because of the beak doctor mask, but also because of the peculiar and grotesque skull-shaped pocket watch he caressed, as if it was a cherished rosary.

"This is a fine pageant, is it not?" a voice asked nearby, and startled out of her thoughts, she turned to see the other couple she had sat next to at supper sitting once again beside her for the play.

"I have seen it performed a few times, and I can never tire of the beautiful lullaby at the end!" the lady remarked, beaming with delight.

It was clear the guests found the pageant entertaining, laughing and gasping throughout, until a hushed quiet descended for the final song.

Lully, lullah, thou little tiny child, Bye bye, lully, lullay.
Thou little tiny child, Bye bye, lully, lullay.
O sisters too, how may we do
For to preserve this day
This poor youngling for whom we sing,
"Bye bye, lully, lullay"?
Herod the king, in his raging,
Chargèd he hath this day
His men of might in his own sight
All young children to slay.
That woe is me, poor child, for thee
And ever mourn and may
For thy parting neither say nor sing,
"Bye bye, lully, lullay."

Clapping and cheering ensued after the last line had been sung, and the minstrels took turns to bow to their audience before they disappeared in an excited flurry up the stairs to their borrowed chambers.

"How beautiful but mournful- such a tragic story!" sniffed the lady. "I could not imagine having to bid my children farewell for all eternity!" she continued, tearfully, as her husband put a consoling hand on her arm, patting it soothingly, until she calmed.

Yes, Margaret thought, thinking of her son Duncannon, *it is a cruel fate to have to part with your children too soon.*

The reverie went on without the minstrels or the music. Margaret, feeling weary in the late evening, gathered her mantle to leave, but not before Euphemia Ferguson and her husband intervened, red-faced and glassy eyed with drink.

"Lady Margaret, take another glass of wine with us- the night is yet young!" they spluttered, and to her dismay, as if controlled by a spirit, she was ushered away from the door, being forced to be entertained by their drunkenness, substituting as serving maid when their wine had run dry and no servant was free to oblige. Euphemia Buchanan returned to her views on the murder of the Duke, and her husband offered ever darker opinions about the sinister workings of the English Parliament, until Margaret, having poured them the last of the wine she could find, finally was able to wrench herself away and escape the noise and clamor of the lively long gallery.

As she stepped through the doors onto the courtyard, she thought of catching some air and took a turn on the new terraces her brother had recently commissioned. She was glad to have left the noise and thick air of the banquet, but disappointed that her brother had not attempted to offer her company; William had not even offered her a single word or glance in her direction, and she felt wounded by his coldness. *But,* she thought, *why should I believe he had any other motive for inviting me here than to gain an inheritance that is rightfully mine?*

The moon lit up the night, the frosted grass a silvery carpet beneath her feet and crackling softly as she walked along the terraces. It was still, apart from the distant noise of the entertainment. Suddenly a sharp sound in the shadows behind her made her jump; looking into the moonlit night, between the shrubs and the trees, she could see nothing.

"Hullo! Who goes there?" she asked, trying to hide the shake in her voice; apart from the very faint sound of someone breathing, she was met with silence. Her heart started to beat furious and fast, but she forced herself to stay quietly where she was for a few minutes to see if someone- or something- would appear.

It was completely still, apart from a gentle breeze, but the lingering feeling of someone watching her stayed with her. She thought her heart might stop when as if out of nowhere, she heard slow footsteps nearing and a hushed, thin voice whisper:

"*So Witches who their Contracts have unsworn, By their own Devils are in pieces torn...*"

"Who's there?" she shouted, agitated, but all she could hear was the heavy breathing of an invisible enemy, and remained still with fear until out of nowhere, a raven crashed through the trees, shrieking a last farewell and knocking into her face before it fell at her feet, dead. Frightened, heart beating in her throat and blood running cold, she hastened as fast as she could back to the central hall, looking over her shoulder all the way, certain she would be caught by whatever ghost was out there; but there was no one behind her. She reached the hall, out of breath and almost crying, and was relieved to find Fionnsgoth waiting for her in her bed chamber.

"How did the evening go, my Lady? How do you do? You look out of sorts?" she asked, as she began to undress Margaret.

"Fine, Fionnsgoth, 'tis nothing," she lied, "although I had no chance to speak with my brother- but he is who he will be, as you yourself well know."

Fionnsgoth frowned, with pursed lips, her nostrils flaring slightly, as she silently folded her mistress' garments, and offered her a nightgown.

"Aye, my Lady, that I do know very well!"

Margaret had now become very sleepy, the long days and uneasy turn in the garden catching up with her mind and body.

"Fionn, would you do me a last kindness before you go to your bed? I feel rather parched after the evening; I confess I did not drink much. Would you fetch me a jug of beer? I think I may sleep better less thirsty."

Fionnsgoth nodded and disappeared to the kitchen. Margaret sat down in front of the mirror on the dressing stand and studied herself. She had not forgotten her brother's words about her appearance, and it still made her angry. *I would not look beyond my age if you had not betrayed our blood bond*, she lamented, and suddenly remembered the proposal he had given her the previous morning. William had shunned her at the banquet, and it was because she had not agreed to his request; she sighed, tired, and unsure of what she should do.

But Fionnsgoth distracted her from her thoughts when she appeared with a jug of ale, and after a glass or two of drink, she crept into bed. She slept soundly, waking only to some commotion in the hallways a few hours later, but feeling too tired to rise to see what it was all about, Margaret promptly fell asleep again.

*

McAdam, the carriage master of Glamis Castle, had prepared for Margaret and Fionnsgoth to leave soon after breakfast. The morning meal was an awkward affair, with William and Anne attempting polite conversation about the evening's entertainment, but both looking tired and ill-humoured. Margaret pretended to ignore their state and tried to engage in light banter.

"I heard some commotion during the night," she mentioned, with a smile, "did the revelers extend to the castle corridors, as well?"

Her lighthearted tone produced a frown from both her hosts, and lady Anne sniffed proudly:

"Certainly not!"

She took a bite of bread and cheese, snapped orders to bring more ale and honey to the waiting servant, and added:

"In fact, Lord Ferguson was taken ill in the early hours; a serious case of colic, or some other stomach problem, I gather."

"I am very sorry to hear it," offered Margaret, with genuine concern, trying to refrain from offering her opinion on the reasons for James Ferguson's current condition, which she believed were probably due to a large amount of wine, and too much peacock pie.

William did not speak until Margaret rose to bid them fare well.

"I must be away after breakfast," she said, looking at her brother, "I believe my cousin returns this evening, and I should like to be back at Glamis before then!" She smiled, and thanked them both for their hospitality.

The Earl and Anne rose, curtsying and bowing, and Wiliam finally spoke.

"Allow me to see you to your carriage, sister."

As she left, Margaret remembered the sad affair of her nephew and his mistress' uncle, and turned to them both.

"I am sorry for Master Robert's predicament- I hear the Duke was his mistress' uncle; it must be a difficult time for her family, and for you."

Anne did not speak, instead returning a cold smile, before reverting her attention to the ale she was sipping, and her half-eaten breakfast plate.

Fionnsgoth was waiting with Margaret's hat and mantle, and deftly arranged them on her mistress. McAdam lowered the carriage steps, and held the door open, and it was only then that William offered the smallest token of affection, as he gave Margaret his hand to help her into the carriage.

"Fare well, sister," he spoke quietly, with sadness, with what Margaret thought, although perhaps wishfully, was a look of affection, "I do not hope it will be too long until the next time!"

William bowed as McAdam closed the door, and he remained by the castle entrance, hands behind his back, contemplative while he watched the carriage move out of the gate. Margaret waved, but he merely stared back, and as they drew away from Aberdour Castle, she looked up to see Anne, with a face like thunder, from a window glaring, not at her, but at William.

She was sad to leave her childhood home, seeing the sea move further and further away from her, and felt a longing that was leaving her. *Glamis*, she thought; *that is now my home, or my home at least until I am no longer welcome*, for she had not forgotten Anne's cruel words in the gardens; they had cut like a knife through her heart.

~ Three ~

In one of the many rooms of Glamis Castle- for there were more than anyone could count on several hands- Margaret sat in her bed chamber by the dim light of a candle, reading a letter. She had hoped to find her cousin Jack when she had returned from Aberdour, but instead, this letter had waited for her.

"Dear Margaret,

I write to you in haste and with great concern. I regret I am yet unable to return to Glamis, but I have received word from a trusted source that you may be in danger of being out of favour with the King. I fear it is a conspiracy against you that is led by your brother William, so that he may confiscate your estate to raise monies for the King. An investigation has begun by the Bishop of London, William Laud, which implicates you in a most vicious plot; but I will not go into detail here, for fear that it will only add to your predicament. I will only say that you will, almost with certainty, be visited by a person who has interest in seeing your reputation ruined, if not worse; when he should come, I urge you to comply with his wishes as far as the law allows- and you have my consent to send for the Constable if this visitor should exceed the proprieties of your gracious hospitality as a Lady of Glamis.

I regret I am not able to tell you more, but please have trust in me when I say that I am doing this to keep you safe.

I hope to return to Glamis within the fortnight but will write again before I journey.

Your devoted cousin, Jack L.

She scanned the letter several times as she sat at her dressing table by the large window which looked over the vast castle grounds. It was a still night, the cold of winter showing its hand with frosted ground and a biting breeze, but the snow had yet to greet the days.

Glams Castle, the seat of the Clan Lyon and home of Jack Lyon, Lord Glamis, second Earl of Kinghorne, lay peacefully in the valley with the Sidlaw Hills to the south, and to the East, the sea, although not in the near vicinity, shone in the moonlight. The majestic snow-capped peaks of the Grampians rose to the north behind it, further in the distance, showing its faces to both Lowland and Highland dwellers.

The Castle was, many claimed, the most beautiful castle in all of Scotland, and the current occupant was in the process of extending the building with a new east wing. The original building, square, turreted, and sinister, was one steeped in legend and stories of murder, politics and plots, ghosts and monsters. There were even those who said she, Margaret Douglas, had an uncanny resemblance to the ghost of Janet Douglas, Lady Glamis, Margaret's great-grandmother. Known in legend as *The White Lady*, it was said she walked the dark and long halls of the castle, unable to rest her soul after being condemned to the fire, branded a witch, less than one hundred years earlier.

Jack Lyon had given Margaret some peace by offering her a home at Glamis, and it had saved her heart and soul, after years of quarrelling with William and the unexpected death of her husband, Baron Eythin of Orkney. She had left Aberdour with a heavy heart but utterly exhausted from life and grief and found some tranquility at Glamis.

William, she thought, bitterly, the same knot in her stomach which time eventually had been able to undo now returning, twice as tight, *he never gives up; to think that we share the same blood in our dead mother!* She shuddered, pulling the woolen plaid over her shoulders as she moved to the window. A stag and his mistress grazed among the tall trees, ambling peacefully in the moonlight, casting faint shadows as they wandered further into the dark woods.

The deer and stag, like herself, did not know what fortune or calamity of fate may come their way; both to be hunted, perhaps, in a world where only the strong and the cunning might survive. She sat back down in the armchair, spreading the plaid over her like a blanket; she felt the bitter cold, and she would have no sleep that night.

*

Glamis Castle, October 6th, 1628

They came in the night; a troop of five or six. There were only men, as Matthew Hopkins, who held the rather questionably named office of 'Witchfinder General', was renowned to have a deep fear of and intense loathing for women, instilled in him by his Master, the Bishop of London, William Laud. Some, or even most, would describe the General, as most to his own childish delight referred to him, as an utterly detestable being, both in appearance, as well as in his gross manner, from which emanated a distinctly inhuman air. He was not tall in stature, but overbearing in his physical appearance. He carried a well-fed belly, the tell-tale sign of wealth procured through the parasitic infliction of his cruel beliefs on the royal court, who had appointed him to "fell the devil's work that is done through the weak ladies of our otherwise wholesome society", or some similar claim, and posted by royal decree in every city, town, village and hamlet across Scotland.

The portliness of the belly had not in itself been loathsome, were it not for his pitiful attempt to hide it by wearing trousers that were too small, unsuccessfully concealed by a slightly loose waistcoat, from which dangled a grotesquely designed skull shaped pocket watch. The General caressed it tenderly, lovingly, with long, thick fingers that ended in yellowing nails. Remnants of encrusted food and other questionable debris shone through them in repulsive silhouettes. Underneath his large black feathered hat protruded strands of yellow hair shiny with grease, almost matching the deep yellow spots staining the whites of his eyes, and from his breath, as he spoke, emanated a putrid odour perhaps so powerful the more wholesome in society might believe he himself was possessed by the devil.

Matthew Hopkins stood opposite Margaret Douglas in the Lower Hall of Glamis Castle which led, through a series of hallways and stairs, to the Crypt. Margaret rarely visited this part; she felt afraid, and unsafe, a feeling of terror always hovering over her when she did, out of necessity, venture there. She observed her repulsive visitor in silence. *The pocket-watch*, she thought, *it was you dressed in the doctor's beak, at my brother's house; you, no doubt, who followed me into the garden....and you who threatened me!*

The intruder, for that was what he was, stood before her, passively indifferent to the fact that it was far into the late night, a time when most were asleep in their beds; but feeling irritation at the fact that Margaret, who would not be intimidated, appeared unmoved by this disturbance, he persisted with his mission.

"I am to convey to you a message from the Earl of Morton," he began, finally removing his hat, "regarding a proposal he made to you during your last visit, and one that he hopes you have now had ample time to consider."

Margaret did not reply. She had not yet made up her mind about how to proceed with her brother's astonishing proposal and had waited for her cousin to return to obtain his advice on the matter.

But he was still away, and she still undecided and uncertain as to the best course of action.

Met with a silent stare, which dug further into his already lacking patience, particularly with females, he changed the subject, continuing in a slow, thin, deliberate tone.

"I am also to relate to you that an unfortunate incident occurred during your last visit....one of the other guests, a Master James Ferguson, was taken gravely ill- poison, the doctor believes- and is yet to recover. It is understood," he carried on, as if bringing a case forward in a prosecution, "that both you and your maid.... Fionns-goth, I believe her name would be?....brought the man food and drink before he was taken ill; we have," he smiled condescendingly, "several witnesses to this fact!"

William, she thought, her face dropping, unable to hide her astonishment, *this is a new low, even for you! I see you have not changed after all in your cruel and selfish tendencies...will you stop at nothing to take what is mine?*

"Well," Master Hopkins went on, pleased at finally having made an impact with his presence, "methods were used to poison Master Ferguson which appear to be similar to those who choose to prac-tice dark magic!"

She laughed, loud and condescending and utterly disbelieving.

"You accuse me of poisoning a man I had not known until the day of the revelry?" she replied, attempting to stay calm. "And more," she almost chuckled in incredulity, "of performing some kind of sorcery, like a witch? Why would I endeavour to do such a terrible thing? What good would it do me to harm a stranger?"

His reply was quick, sharp and accusatory.

"I see you acknowledge the possibility of witch's work at hand! The Devil's work needs no purpose other than to spread evil, and," he smiled, a gold tooth glistening in the light of the fire, "as we both know, he has many a following in Scotland!"

Every word this supposed defender of the faith, standing a few feet away from her, made her feel physically unwell; but then again, he was an Englishman, dishonest and deceitful in her own experiences. If she had had a dagger to hand at that moment, she would not have flinched for a second in using it. Fighting to keep her mind clear and heart cold, despite the anger and rising loathing inside her, she replied, as indifferently as possible:

"The Devil has no place in this House, Master Hopkins, whatever my brother and his 'friends' may believe." Margaret offered a cold stare directly at her odious visitor and continued:

"And while I am not familiar with the proprieties of English manners, I feel obliged to tell you that in Scotland unfounded accusations of a crime against those of noble birth may carry un-desirable consequences for those who perpetrate them- especially, perhaps, if they lack the grace of nobility, and even more so, if they are English."

He narrowed his eyes, frowning and pacing, as if confronting an unreasonable child, uttering a short "hmm", when something caught his eyes and forced him to stop, as if he had very suddenly come upon a miracle. He had stopped in front of a tall metal statue.

"Do you know," enquired the Witchfinder General, circling slowly around its rounded form, his hands, greasy from a recent feast, moving along the bulges and bends of its surface, "what this is?"

The maleficent intruder stood directly in front of this ghastly instrument of torture, his mouth agape as if in awe of the genius of the craftmanship that had led to its wondrous invention.

Margaret could smell the faint nauseating waft of the General's breath, although she stood some distance away from him; he was slinking and hopping around her like a circling fox, trying to in-timidate her. But Margaret, having withstood battles and raids to defend her home in the absence of her husband, was not easily intimidated. Since his death, she knew she had lost protection from the Crown, and since her mother's death, she had gained enemies in both her half-brothers, both fervent loyalists to the King; and so, she had found herself, along with her young son, in the position of having to learn to defend herself and her family, at whatever cost.

Margaret did not reply to his question She had read a little about the methods of witch hunters, and how they favoured a long, drawn out process of wearing down their prey until she- for it was nearly always women who were accused of witchcraft- exhausted from the waking torture, the ducking, the thumbscrews, the leg weights and the pricking, guilty or not, confessed, and he, a champion of Christian salvation and sole beacon of hope in all humanity against the works of the devil, would be crowned a hero, in his own eyes a prophet of God like Jesus Christ himself, only with all the riches and nefarious spoils that came with such self-proclaimed fame.

"She is....magnificent, is she not?" he marveled, as the metallic melody of his ringed fingers echoed against the hollow shape of the form. It was as if he was begging it to open up, and reveal itself and the horrific acts it was capable of executing.

"Such ingenuity, such beauty...," he continued, "the cruel brilliance of the magnificent mind that was able to devise such a contraption is-", he let out a deep breath, eyes glassy with reverence, "simply, almost...God-like!"

God, thought Lady Margaret, certainly had nothing to do with this, no matter how terrible a judgement God may pass on the weak and ephemeral flesh of which we are all made.

"The Iron Maiden, they call her," he continued, caressing the statue's face lovingly, as if she would be an angel in disguise, "but I confess it a rather unjust designation, wouldn't you agree...my Lady?"

Without turning to Margaret, and certainly not expecting a reply, he continued in his mesmerized fascination, slowly unlatching the hinges on the side of the metal figure, as if undressing an unwilling participant in a sordid play of carnal gratification. He hesitated, ceremoniously and melodramatically, as he prepared himself to meet the organs of his object of desire. The crank rotated and creaked, objecting to the unwanted intrusion, old, rusted metal resisting as well as it could as he slowly opened the device, and the long sharp spikes that lined the inside retreated into the shell with the turning handle.

A hollow silence followed as it stopped, and the persecutor stood goggle-eyed at the contents afore him, gently touching the spiked ends with his fingertips. His long, dirty yellow nails caught the tips as he moved along them, as if to make certain they were still able to fulfill their duties. To his delight, it seemed that they were, streaks of red liquid trickling into the palm of his hand as he moved away, but Matthew Hopkins, either not noticing or not caring, paying no heed to his own blood being drawn.

Margaret watched him, beyond disgust at this repulsive being. She had, for the first time, noticed the face of the Iron Maiden. Although she had walked past this hideous monstrosity every day since she had lived at Glamis, she had never stopped to take a closer look at it, and until now had not even realized that the device had a face, with the irregular and imperfect facial features of a human being. But these features had been distorted, the Iron Maiden's eyes wide open in fear, and her mouth agape and twisted to reflect the cruelty and suffering she was inflicting on whoever she had reluctantly been forced to consume. Ironic, thought Margaret, that a female form had been chosen as the symbol of such a horrific instrument, as it had certainly been designed by a man. Perhaps a man whose hatred for women was so profound that he had to turn this into an item of unspeakable horror- someone, for example, like the General, who, forgetting himself, and thinking aloud, mumbled, " I cannot wait to see this restored to use when...", he paused, catching himself, as if he were a naughty boy peeking through the keyhole of a lady's dressing chamber, and drew himself tall again. He gently shut the cover, carefully reattached the hinges, leaving drops of scarlet fluid on the dull metal surface, and paced around to the back of it to face his unimpressed hostess. She had remained silent and unmoving throughout the entire disturbing and ridiculous spectacle of his over-performance, and now, as he fixed his small, hard eyes on her, she merely stared back.

"Well," he finally spoke, greasing his long fringe back behind his ear, "His Majesty should be very interested in this contraption! I am certain her ladyship," he uttered the words as if she had been an impostor- "would not object in presenting His Majesty with this as a gift...not in person, you understand," he cackled, as if even the mere idea of it was so preposterous it could only be a far-fetched fantasy, "but I would be delighted to oblige your ladyship and take the...item with me at my earliest convenience, and I shall, of course, convey to His Majesty the generosity of your nature- or should I say your cousin's, who I imagine could have no objection!- and your wish for His Masjesty's best health and prosperity....".

He drew his lips upwards pretending to smile, but the result failed, and he reminded Margaret of one of those court jesters with such badly painted faces they looked like they had escaped from Bedlam. But he gleefully continued:

"If she were to agree to Sir William's proposal, I am to understand, it will also without doubt heighten her ladyship's esteem in the eyes of the King, which, as I am certain she, as the wrong kind of Douglas, is aware, currently does not stand at a great height, but rather more close to the ground, if not already entering into a deep and very dark abyss, since the unfortunate demise of her keeper, the Baron Eythin, God rest his soul!"

Hopkins did not wait for a reply, but continued in his monologue, feeling perhaps a need to explain his visit further, for he did not feel that the gravity of his presence, was, at present, having the suitably detrimental impact he had anticipated.

Margaret pointed to the Iron Maiden, still baring herself to the chamber, and complied resolutely, "Of course, sir, you may take this instrument away; I am certain the Earl of Kinghorne would have no objection to ridding this House of this instrument of torture. In fact, it would give us great pleasure, for a week at least, to offer the King such a gift; it is certainly befitting of a man of his character." She smiled at the General's darkened face and went on matter-of-fact.

"Perhaps now is as good a time to take this ....item....with you, as any other? The six *friends,*" she uttered the word with a low smile and high irony, for three of them had fallen asleep, one was picking his teeth, and the remaining two had left the room to stand guard outside, "you brought with you appear to have nothing to do at present and seem to be more than capable of arranging for its transport....do you go far this night?"

But looking out of the window and seeing the orange light of the sun reflect below the horizon, she continued.

"Or should I say, this morning, sir? We seem, once again, to have had unsociable interactions throughout the night, as the sun now greets us."

He attempted to speak, but she ignored him completely.

"And as for the Earl of Morton's proposal," she teased, "I am afraid I cannot recall its particulars, but if Sir William would present them to me again, I may consider finding a moment to review them a second time!"

Margaret grinned in such a self-satisfactory manner at the Witchfinder General that he became all heated at her daring forthrightness. But underneath her confidence, she was angry, the dagger she wished she had to hand still on her mind, but the one had now become a thousand more.

~ Four ~

That night, with all the commotion the unexpected night visitors brought with them, there had been another nocturnal spy afoot in Glamis. Effie, a young maid of no more than sixteen years of age, had been entirely captivated by the band of strangers who had woken the entire household demanding to speak to Lady Margaret. She had followed them to the crypt but had not been able to listen to the conversation through her usual spying methods, with that horrible little nosy girl Bal, Lady Margaret's niece, discovering Effie's perfect observation point. So, Effie had been forced to sneak behind a small cabinet by the oak door that led to the crypt, and strain to hear the proceedings through a slither of a crack in the wood paneling. She had not been able to understand much, as the bitter Highland wind had howled and whistled, rattling the windows throughout most of the night, but she had heard enough to understand that the Mistress had been accused of a crime: witchcraft! The young maid could not believe it; Margaret Douglas, Baroness Eythin, a witch! That explained a few things, thought Effie; she had always wondered how her own tricks were so easily discovered without Her Ladyship ever being in sight of the maid. *Finally*, thought Effie, *I will have my revenge!*

She, being impressionable in her young age, and particularly so in the presence of older men, had paid particular notice to the master of the gang of six strangers. He spoke so well and had such authority and power; he was English, yes, but Effie had no interest at all in understanding the animosity between the Scots and the English, and had already found an attraction in the first few minutes of seeing him pass by her in the entrance hall, as he cast a long glance and wicked smirk her way. Blind to his utterly repulsive appearance, Effie could only see a spellbinding confidence and authority.

The visitor, Effie was certain, had found an interest in her, too, asking her genially about her work and her Mistress, for whom, at that time, she had only had kind words to offer, while the visitor complimented herself, Effie, on her excellent housekeeping methods and gracious hospitality. *There,* thought Effie, *is a great man who can truly appreciate me!*

Effie had been with the House for three years, and after all that hard work, she deserved better terms for her loyalty, a deep bitterness growing inside her as the days had gone on: rising every day before daybreak, sometimes hours before dawn broke in the winter, to light the fireplaces, prepare hot water, ready the breakfast room, and everything else, so much that it often seemed as though she was the only one doing any work at all! And all this under the watchful eyes of the steward of Glamis, Alastair; cold, mean Alastair, who had had his way with her whenever it pleased him! And what was she to do, poor Effie, but let him? After the third or fourth time, anyway, the expectation had not become so unpleasant, and she was getting to the point where she, being young and perhaps not beautiful but fresh and kempt and clean, and he, aging and lustful, could manipulate him to her advantage. And she would rather take to bed with him- or the larder, or the outbuildings, or the folly if the weather was nice in the summer- than get a beating, as the steward had given her, whether she had deserved it or not in his eyes, in the last House she served. But Alastair, noted Effie to herself, had become so weak with lust that he now only seemed to be able to beg for her favours, rather than demand them with any authority at all.

All her life she had only been loyal to those she served. Her father, after his third or fourth jug of whisky, had repaid her by punching and whipping her, sometimes so senseless that Effie had blacked out and woken up, much later, somewhere cold and dark, and often naked and bleeding. And she found no refuge in her mother, who had insisted she give favours to visitors in exchange for payment, not minding the physical pain or emotional torture her own daughter suffered, as long as mother got her crowns and ducats. And when Effie, with beaten body and weary soul, had finally been able to escape that horror and eventually arrived at Glamis, she had felt such relief, a safe comfort, and such happiness.

Fionnsgoth, Lady Margaret's personal maid, had first been so kind to her, and forgiving, until those visitors had come, and Her Ladyship's necklaces had disappeared. And Effie had only borrowed those silver sewing scissors to mend her dress, which she had torn in the larder as Alastair was not one to take care once the passion took hold of him; the Mistress could not know that she had not meant to return them! It was that horrible little girl, Bal, who had told Fionnsgoth; she was always spying on Effie! And Effie had promptly made certain that the other items she had borrowed indefinitely were well hidden under the larder floor. She had managed to loosen a floorboard, and wedged them between the joists- a silver porridge spoon, a sweet little gold brooch which Fionnsgoth had dropped one day, and a little figure of St Christopher. That Fionnsgoth, cursed Effie, airs above her station, she had; telling on an equal to advance her own position, and no right, no right at all had she, a visitor in this House, to tell her, Effie Campbell, who served Lord Glamis, how to conduct her tasks. Curse her!

As the light of dawn had begun to creep in through the windows, and she heard movement in the crypt, she realised that the visitors were about to leave. *If I'm discovered, it's the end*, she panicked, irritated, squeezing past the cabinet, and hurrying along the long corridor that led to the servant's passage. She had slipped back into the breakfast room, but not unnoticed; Fionnsgoth had woken earlier than usual to find the maid absent in her duties, and with a temper already frayed, she had given Effie an earful, shouting so loudly the other staff had stopped to listen.

Effie was furious when Fionnsgoth had done with her; she had found the scolding entirely unfair, especially in front of the other servants. Such humiliation! She had always been treated as though she was stupid, and the tricks that little girl Bal played on her every day, for which she, Effie Campbell, constantly got blamed, had only made her bitterness grow, day by long day. But she knew more about the comings and goings of this House than any of the other servants, and if her Mistress would realise that, then she would surely think twice about treating poor Effie in such a lowly, demeaning way. Secrets, she knew of, that could bring great shame to this House, and would certainly see Lord Glamis banish Lady Margaret for good, even if she was his cousin!

"Get back to your duties, you lazy whore!" bellowed a voice, followed by a low chuckle, as she felt a hand run around her waist, gliding down her lower back and reaching further and further down, then up again, lifting her frock with it as she felt Alastair's sweaty palm between her legs. Soft bursts of his breath touched her neck, and made the little hairs stand up in goosebumps, as they always did when he came near. But she had never been able to decide whether the little hairs stood so erect out of a pure disgust which brought back memories of all those leering men her mother used to call to the house, or if they rose from an honest lust for his flesh.

"Master Alastair," she said, coyly, "I'd be done with my work long ago if you'd not keep distractin' me...!" She returned his touch by sliding her smooth, young hand slowly along his muscled thigh, to his crotch, until he grabbed her, violently, and threatened, almost pleaded.

"Do not tease me! Or I will drag you to the milking shed by your hair in front of all to see!" His green eyes were so wide and dark, Effie observed, she thought they might pop out of their sockets; and no wonder, for she could see from the bulge in his trousers that he had lost control over his sexual desires. But she was used to his lustful outbursts, and said calmly, "Now, Master Alastair, what would the servants think?"

Smiling meanly she added, "And sure you must know by now that I'll not be able to give you anything of myself if you don't keep our secret...I'll be forced to stop our meetings, and who'll you be able to complain to?"

Alastair, beads of greasy sweat forming above his lips, which he was slowly licking, turned a wry smile to her; she was devious, this one, he thought, and gently let go of her soft hand. Devious, and so desirable, he thought he must go somewhere private to compose himself. Effie looked at him, amused.

"The milking shed in an hour," she said, business-like, "and light a fire, for I'll not be cold in there!" She continued in a matter-of-fact way to lay the breakfast service, as Alastair backed away, in a half-stupor, and disappeared.

"I do hope he will return," she thought to herself, thinking dreamily of Master Hopkins, fancying wedding bells, expensive silk frocks, and a life of riches in her near future. She smiled, her encounter with Fionnsgoth and Alastair a mere fleeting distraction that was now completely forgotten.

Gathering the cups and plates from the big silver tray, she placed them around the far end of the long breakfast table and paused for a moment; she had always liked these cups- they were ornately forged tin and pewter creations with delicately decorated flowers and birds, no doubt worth a handsome sum. Reconsidering the practicalities of taking one or two to her room unnoticed, she sighed, and carried on setting the table for breakfast. When she was finished, she returned, silver tray dangling indifferently from one hand, through the back door that led to the passage and stairs down to the kitchen.

One day, she mused bitterly, dark thoughts from years of violent abuse of body and soul returning, and a bitterness that had defeated her kind nature clouding her mind, *I will be the one drinking from such cups, eating from such luxurious finery! And you, Lady Margaret, shall not be telling me to serve you!*

It had been a long time since she had seen her work as an enjoyment, but this chilled early autumn morning, Effie felt as if the world was about to change; and she, Effie Campbell, deserving of reward after years of hardship, and scolding, and violent abuse, would soon find her status in society elevated beyond that of maidservant. She was certain of it. So confident of this was she that she almost skipped into the kitchen, to the surprise of her fellow servants, who had recently never seen Effie anything but sour-faced and ill-humoured.

But as the dark skies gathered above Glamis Castle, heavy with snow-filled clouds, and the bright morning light waned, obscured by the fog, little did they all know that a terrible, unspeakable tragedy that would change the fortunes of all at Glamis would be sent upon them before that ill-fated day would end.

*

Matthew Hopkins had taken Margaret up on the offer of taking away the Iron Maiden that very morning, much to the distress of his henchmen, who struggled to find a way of maneuvering the monstrosity through the many long corridors of Glamis, and up, and over, and down the many staircases of the vastness that was the castle. Margaret had instructed Alastair to call for a cart, for the General and his men had only brought their horses and had no other means of transporting the metal beast back to Aberdour, the only place Master Hopkins could think of storing his grotesque acquisition. Margaret thought scornfully how appropriate it would be for an instrument of torture to end up at the home of her brother. *I am certain, William, that you will find ample ways to entertain yourself in the presence of the Iron Maiden!* she mused, imagining one of his lavish banquets in which the Iron Maiden would be the focal point of conversation among his guests, and he, no doubt, proudly proclaiming that there was none other like her in all the Crown Lands.

The young boy Hamish had been dispatched in search of a suitable vehicle, and, being fortunate in finding an unused cart on the estate itself large enough to carry the Iron Maiden, it was not long before she lay there, as if being carted off to her own funeral, stretched out and tied down, two of the henchmen's horses harnessed and ready to pull the poor lady off to her next life.

Not forgetting her duty to hospitality, Margaret had instructed for the kitchen to prepare breakfast for the men before they departed. Matthew Hopkins sat in the grand breakfast room, alone. His men, who he considered vastly lower in status than his own, remained in the rather less comfortable and infinitely chillier stables, getting drunk on the beer and whisky, while he, the General, admired and enjoyed a delicious array of food; there were cheeses, boiled eggs, butter, cream and honey, ham and venison pasty, wheaten loaf, and to wash it all down, whiskey, and brandy.

The General contemplated his encounter with Margaret, satisfied that he would soon return for her arrest, and a fervent excitement rose within him at the thought of having accomplished his mission to please the Bishop and the King. Only when Effie, having realized that her chivalrous knight would be staying for breakfast, appeared under the pretense of having forgotten to bring up a flagon of beer for his journey onward, was he brought back to the present moment. Effie had been determined to see him before he left, to try to seek a way of keeping him in her life; this could be her last chance.

Hopkins smiled graciously when he saw the young girl as she set down the container of drink before him. He had no interest in her at all, other than seeing afore him a rather plain and unremarkable female of no special character except, he calculated, some enviable ability for deceit. This was not unusual for women, of course, in his humble opinion, but at least here was one he could exploit to his own advantage.

"I bid you a good morrow, young mistress," he murmured, rising from his chair and bowing theatrically, smooth and slick as a silver-tongued snake.

She blushed slightly, bowing her head with a quick curtsy.

"Good morrow, sir," she replied, and boldly added without looking at him directly, "'tis a pleasure to see you once again, sir."

He was successfully ensnaring her, he thought, relishing in his abilities for manipulation, and drawing himself up authoritatively, he began to talk.

"Thank you, young lady....it is Effie, is it not?" he marveled, his cold black eyes fixed intently on her.

"Yes, sir," she smiled coyly, her heart almost leaping when she heard her name slide so smoothly and invitingly off his lips.

"And Effie, I must say, I can see that you are the most hardworking of all of Lady Margaret's servants! She must hold you in high praise," he ventured, knowing he would press a sore nerve, her previous ill-humour and dark countenance at the mention of Margaret not having escaped his attention.

She hesitated slightly, considering how to reply. She despised the Mistress, and Fionnsgoth now, and that child, and although she did not really believe in witchcraft or witches- for why did they always accuse women, and hardly ever the men?- her anger and hatred betrayed her into believing the Mistress deserved punishment for the way she had allow Fionnsgoth to treat Effie.

"The Mistress chooses those she favours, sir," she offered, with wide blue downcast eyes, and brushing a few strands of blonde hair from her cheeks, she continued with lament, "and I am not one of those!"

He raised his eyebrows in feign surprise, the half-mocking and false appearance of concern once again taking over his facial expressions.

"My dear, I am most distressed to hear that! And most surprised, for I had considered Lady Margaret an honourable and decent servant of God....", he tutted, in his familiar manner, puckering his

lips slightly, screwing up his eyes in an effort at pity and commis-
eration.

Effie, having entirely forgotten her frequent and calculated
promised assignations with Alastair, kept her eyes to the floor in
dejected woe; any external observer would have thought a most en-
gaging theatrical performance, rather than a real conversation, was
being rehearsed for a later audience, the two actors so overplaying
their parts it was almost amusing.

"Pray, tell me, young lady, if I was wrong about Lady Margaret,
which I cannot for one moment believe?" he continued to lie, eyes
wide in disbelief, a soothing fatherly tone infiltrating her weakness
for power and desire for status.

Goading her, he invited her to eat, but she quickly refused.

"Oh, sir," she replied, a hand against her pink flushed cheek
feigning distress, "the Mistress would never allow it- we're given a
week's ration of milk, bannocks and pottage, and if she's in a benevolent humour, we may have some cheese; but never, ever this," she
gestured to the richly laid out table, and cried.

"She would say 'tis too good for us lowly servants; she's cruel,
sir, so cruel! And never a kind word if she's took a dislike to you!"

She managed to squeeze out a tear, which trickled down her face,
hanging onto her chin stubbornly before she wiped it away with
her neat, clean apron, attempting an angry and lamenting sob.

"My dear," Master Hopkins said, "I am aghast at such allegations!
Perhaps you would tell me more?"

She hesitated, glancing into the garden; it was quiet and although the clouds had blackened, the rain had not yet begun to fall.
Master Hopkins followed her thoughts.

"We could take a turn about the garden- I saw a pretty folly in
the distance; no one would hear us there," he whispered, rolling
pieces of meat pie along with some cherries and cheese into a nap-
kin. "These will give you comfort; and," he carried on, picking up
the flagon of beer, "as long as I may take this with me, which you
so thoughtfully brought, I give you my word," he crossed himself

dramatically, the silly spectacle of sinner in one hand, and saint in the other, "that I will keep all of your secrets!"

He mellowed his brow and smiled encouragingly, and Effie, who could feel that she would finally get what she wished for- without so much as a single prayer! - smiled inside herself, and nodded.

"There, there," he silver-tongued, placing a large, greasy hand on her shoulder, brushing briefly against the naked skin showing where her plaid had slipped down her shoulder, "it will all be put right, you will see."

But throughout their theatrical interchange, neither of them had noticed a spy by the door. It was Alastair, and he was furious, clenching his fists so hard the white of his knuckles stretched the skin so tightly on his hands it seemed it would split and give way to his crimson flesh and the white of his bones.

*

Bal, the curious little girl who Effie despised so much, had been vexed and excited by the number of visitors the castle had seen in the last few days, none of whom she had been allowed to meet; she had been ushered away by Fionnsgoth on every occasion, either to play in her room, or if the weather had been fine, to throw sticks for the dogs in a remote corner of the maze of castle gardens that surrounded them.

Visitors had always stirred a curiosity in her; the excitement of someone travelling from far-away lands to see Glamis Castle had only recently entered into her imagination as mysterious and exotic events, particularly with her discovery of an enormous globe atlas tucked away in a corner of the library, to where, with Lord Glamis' frequent absences, she had secretly escaped more often.

The two sets of visitors who had come, Bal had noted and methodically analysed, were quite different. The first, Bal knew, had come a week earlier, and her aunt had expected them; maids and stewards had rushed about, preparing the best bed chambers, arranging the finest cloths and carpets in the grand reception room, where they set out the finest cups and plates around a large table with mouthwatering meats, sweets and cakes. There had been only two of them: the man was tall, not handsome but striking, with deep-set and piercing, yet kind, blue eyes under a stern brow; a long, thin face, was surrounded by wavy long brown locks, with a short beard that made his mouth look like it was constantly amused by something. He was taller than any man the little girl had ever seen; despite his somewhat forbidding presence, he did not make Bal feel afraid.

The tall man's attire was also different to anything the little girl had ever seen; there was no plaid in sight, and the cloth that made up his trousers were almost shiny. They were a dark green, tucked neatly into tied ends below the knees, with snow-white stockings and black, shiny leather shoes with enormous silver buckles, which looked as though they had only recently seen the first light of day, so crisp and clean, they were! A blue and yellow embroidered waist coat held in place a white and yellow embroidered tunic, whose collar was unceremoniously plain, unlike the extravagant ruffled monstrocities she had observed in the current visitors. What was more, noted Bal, this visitor also had no other jewellery than a signet ring on his left little finger, and a somewhat plain blue enameled pocket watch, the subtle gilding of its edges catching light from time to time as he moved about the room, calmly but deliberately; *I wonder what they are talking about*, the little girl had mused.

His companion was the most beautiful woman Bal had ever seen, and a marked contrast to the man: she was of smaller stature- about the same small height and slight frame as her aunt Margaret- with a soft glow in her cheeks and pale green, forgiving eyes. But the most mesmerizing feature was her hair- almost white in hue, which was turned up into the most elaborate braids which twisted around her head, almost like a crown, ending in an almost perfectly shaped small dome on the top of her fine head. Bal, whose hair had always been managed in the same unimaginative

way- her long, brown hair neatly bundled up and tied by a ribbon-
had never seen anything like it.

The lady's clothes were as finely made as those of her fellow
traveller; modest in design, but not in expense. She wore a long,
red gown, without a modesty collar, but a wide yellow shawl, embroidered in a similar fashion to the tunic   that her companion
wore, provided adequate modest cover for most of the lower part
of her neck. The sleeves of her dress were short, but her arms were
 kept warm by fine, long, translucent yellow gloves; the little girl
could not see her footwear, but imagined it, like the man's, to be
equally luxurious.

All this, the little explorer had observed through the far window into the grand reception room, as she balanced herself carefully on the branches of an obliging garden bush, trying with great
difficulty not to be seen. Possessed with a mind that was methodical and analytical, the girl observed her aunt's attire in comparison: she wore a silk plaid, which, unknown to Bal, was of the Douglas clan. But, in comparison to the glamour of her visitor, Bal
thought her aunt looked rather plain; her auburn hair was tied
back with a simple ribbon, a few pearls to adorn it, but otherwise
she looked reserved and unassuming, to the girl's disappointment.

And now, only a week since the last visitors had come and gone,
a second group of visitors had woken them all in the night- a group
of men who had arrived in the darkness, had appeared unexpectedly to her aunt; Bal had watched them through a secret observation point that took the shape of a small hole just above the floor of
the hallway near the Great Hall, created when the castle was built,
so that the lord could spy on the conversations of his visitors, and
be warned of any betrayals that were planned against him.

The visitors, all dressed in black, all men with large bellies and
even larger feathered hats- or so it had seemed to the young spy-
had frightened her, even more when she could see that her aunt
had also been so afraid, underneath the cold exterior to which Bal
was accustomed. These men had remained through the bitter

night, until the light had begun to appear over the horizon. That morning, Bal had noticed her aunt's absentmindedness, and short temper, being told to stay out of the way and play with the dogs in the garden. Only when, through a garden hedge, she had observed the sheriff's men appear, to Bal's excitement, and they instructed the visitors to leave Glamis, was she forced to abandon her investigations, when a stern and disapproving voice demanded:

"Isobel Balgaire Douglas, come away from that window immediately!"

Fionnsgoth, accompanied by Lilias, a young girl of fifteen who had only just arrived at Glamis as a parlour maid, had stood on the lawn, hands on her hips and brow stern as she admonished the little delinquent.

"Young ladies," she emphasized, "do not spy on visitors, or anyone else they are curious about; it is unseemly and ungodly!"

Bal sighed, sulking, as she maneuvered herself down from the obliging branch that had been her viewpoint into the breakfast room, and slowly shuffled over to Fionnsgoth.

"I was not spying," she insisted, "I was investigating; no one tells me who all of these visitors are, so I must find out for myself!" The little girl was not about to apologise, which Fionnsgoth was very well aware of, so the maid replied:

"Isobel, if you do not apologise and admit that your activity was unbecoming of a young lady, and assure me that you will not do it again, I will set you extra lessons in good behaviour!"

Bal hated lessons more than anything; she would rather spend time exploring the inside and outside world of Glamis, and considered for a moment.

"I apologise." Her concession, although curt and rather less meaningful than Fionnsgoth had hoped, was, the maid knew, as well an apology as she would get, and nodded.

"I hope you will amend your 'activities' to exclude any further investigations in future, young lady," Fionnsgoth admonished, but Bal simply grinned, knowing that was highly unlikely.

"When will uncle Jack return, Mistress Fionnsgoth? He has been away so long, and I want to hear of his adventures!"

Bal had always found uncle Jack very mysterious; he came and went so often, and was away for so long, her curiosity burned about what he could be up to when he was away.

"I do not know, dear; we had hoped he would be back by now, but his business still keeps him away."

"What business, Mistress?" persisted Bal, but the maid was losing patience, and had duties to attend to with the visitors.

"Young ladies, I should also mention," she said, frowning sternly at Bal, "are taught to mind their own business, and not ask too many impertinent questions!"

She had ushered the little girl, who was hurt and resentful at her mistress' lack of interest in these events, towards the games room, where Bal, never interested in the frivolity of play, pulled out the big cartograph of the world she had claimed from the library, and dreamed herself away on exotic adventures in faraway lands. But her curiosity about the night visitors burned so strong, she was determined to find out the identity of the mean looking man in the enormous feathered hat, and the terrifying scull-shaped pocket watch.

~ Five ~

"Where is that dreadful girl?" shouted Fionnsgoth, seeing the breakfast room was still to be cleared, with Effie nowhere to be found. At least Alastair had done his duty, and not abandoned the household; he had understood that the arrival of Master Hopkins was an ill omen, and dispatched young Hamish to fetch the sheriff, who had, with his own small troop of men, eventually arrived as the sun came up, and taken a firm stance at the front gate, to see Mr Hopkins and his men off the castle grounds. So finally, that horrible man and his gang had departed, and peace had returned- at least momentarily- to Glamis; but Fionnsgoth knew he would be back, and it worried her greatly.

She had not been told what his conversation with Margaret had been about, and she did not dare to ask; but seeing Lady Margaret's pale and worried face- and had she gotten thinner over the last two weeks? - she herself began to feel afraid. Lady Margaret had taken to her room more, furiously writing letters which she had asked Fionnsgoth to dispatch with great haste. Not feeling it godly to spy, she had, however, glanced at the names to which the letters were addressed, and almost all had been to Margaret's relatives in Germany and Sweden, mostly to her cousin, the man who had visited the week before with his wife.

Oh, if only Sir Jack would return to his castle from his dubious adventures! Fionnsgoth felt unsafe without him, but his adventures- which she knew would serve no favour with the English King- also frightened her. Such troublesome clans, the Lyons and the Douglases; and such troubling times brewing around them all. She sighed.

"Mistress Fionnsgoth, what troubles you?"

She jumped in fright as she heard the cold, uncaring voice of Alastair, who had appeared as if out of nowhere, offering a dutiful concern. His manner was perfunctory, rather than genuinely concerned, as he tried to hide the bitterness he bore towards a woman he saw as a usurper of the castle's household servants, who were rightly his to command, and no one else's!

"Oh, nothing...", she breathed, distracted but aware of her own dislike of the house steward and his lascivious ways, and changing the subject, she cruelly asked him.

"Where has that Effie got to? I imagine you, Master Alastair, will know where she is?" With a biting tone and sharp eyes, she stated:

"This room needs clearing so it can be ready for the afternoon."

She looked at him; he was not a particularly handsome man, but had a coarse charm that even she, to begin with, had found attractive, until she had become aware of his frequent and lust-filled assignations with Effie. Although they had never spoken about it, Fionnsgoth knew that Lady Margaret, to her dismay, had also found them together on several occasions, and admonished them both quite harshly that if they did not cease this display of loose morals, she would have to inform Lord Glamis who, she had threatened quite adamantly, may ask both of them to leave before they should disgrace this House entirely.

Alastair was not stupid. He knew that if he wanted to keep his affairs discrete and stay in favour with the ladies of the house- and more importantly, to keep his position, for it would be difficult for him to find another elsewhere- he would have to at least show partial honesty, and replied with feigned indifference:

"I saw Effie with that dubious visitor; in here, in fact, while he was breakfasting. I believe they went for a turn about the gardens."

Irritated, Fionnsgoth replied, shaking her head and frowning angrily:

"What business does she have taking a stroll with a strange visitor? That girl," she snapped, "is more trouble than life is worth!"

Alastair did not reply; his earlier anger at Effie and Hopkins had dissipated slightly, but he still wanted his revenge, and so he offered, with feigned innocence, his help.

"Perhaps this visitor wished to interrogate her....he has been asking a lot of question of the servants about Lady Margaret's affairs," he added, to his secret delight; Fionnsgoth's frightened look did not escape his attention. She nodded dismissively in agreement.

"I will seek her out, Mistress," he bowed, and went on his quest; he did not know what he would do if he found them together, his heart beating hard and fast at the thought of that greasy intruder taking sordid pleasure in Effie's soft white skin and plump crimson lips.

Fionnsgoth looked out of the vast windows across the green, frost-bitten grass and over the rows of tall fir trees. They looked as though they were guardians of Glamis, and she suddenly realized that the day felt strange, almost otherworldly. She could make out a figure, dressed in black, moving between the trees. *One of the General's men,* she wondered, and felt the fear deepen in her heart. In the skies above, a falcon circled repeatedly, as if following her future feast along the ground below. She swooped, a sharp dive, low and quick as lightning, upon her unsuspecting victim, before ascending back into the clouds above, her prey writhing in hopeless desperation as it was taken away into the distance to an almost certain end. There was a sense of foreboding that made Fionnsgoth shiver in fright, and she wrapped her plaid tightly around her shoulders for comfort, but the warmth she sought still did not come.

*

It was Hamish who, after taking the Iron Maiden all the way to Aberdour, had returned to Glamis late in the evening, to find poor Effie, naked, cold and dead in the icehouse beyond the folly. He had finished clearing out the straw and matting the day before, and seeing the door ajar, had ventured to close it, but looking inside, the boy, who was only fourteen, had vomited at the horrific sight that met him. Effie had been strangled and cut open, trails of intestine and whatever else left spilling from her insides, her eyes popping out, large and disbelieving, as if she had turned into a broken doll, an arm and a leg half-thrown over the walls of the empty ice-pit, the big blue eyes staring back at him like those of a ragged and lifeless puppet.

Hamish had run back to the Castle as fast as his long, spindly legs could carry him, scared out of his wits, for the killer, or whatever evil spirit had done this to Effie, could still be around him, and he might face the same fate!

"She's dead!" he screamed, eyes wide open in fear, tears streaming down his red cheeks, as he burst through the coach house door, meeting McAdam's angry frown.

"Murdered! Someone has butchered poor Effie!" he spat, breathless and so anxious from fear he might faint, leaning into the doorway.

"What?" answered McAdam irritably. He knew Hamish was prone to exaggeration and fanciful thoughts.

"In the icehouse!" he gargled through a knotted throat and choked sobs, tears still rolling down his apple-red cheeks in disbelief.

"She's there- she's dead! Her eyes popping from her head and guts ripped out!"

The boy vomited again, and the yellow-green sludge spewed onto the stone floor as he doubled over, clutching his stomach.

McAdam grabbed the poor lad and shook him, slapping him, as if this would make sense return to the boy, but Hamish continued breathing deep sobs, choked by swallowed, vomit-muddled words.

"You are not making sense, lad!" barked the coachman.

"Effie- she's in the ice-house! Dead, I tell you, Master McAdam! Murdered!"

He put his hand over his mouth, worried the vomit would come up again, but managed to gag himself. McAdam could now see and understand that whatever it was that had frightened the boy so much was real, and not a figment of his often vivid and ridiculous imagination.

Taking on a more fatherly tone, he attempted some words of comfort, and replied calmly:

"Take a deep breath, or two, Hamish, there's a good lad, and try to calm yourself."

He took a glass and filled it from a nearby jug of whisky, sitting the shaking boy down on the stone window seat. Hamish poured the contents down his throat in one go, and although his stomach perhaps did not appreciate the burning liquid, his senses became more sedate, and he began to breathe more regularly, sobs abating and tears starting to dry.

McAdam pulled out a stool from behind the door and sat down in front of the boy.

"Now, lad, will you tell me what you saw?" he asked gently. "Or we can go together to the ice-house and see how it looks; what do you think, Hamish?"

The young boy's eyes widened in horror at the mention of visiting the ice-house, and his breath began to quicken again.

"No, sir, please, I cannot go back there!" he pleaded.

"Alright, alright, lad; you do not have to go. I will ask Duncan."

Seeing Hamish relieved, and less hysterical, he poured another large dram and handed it to him.

"Take this; it will sort your senses. Will you be fine here, while I fetch Duncan?"

The boy shook his head violently, tears welling up around his red eyes.

"I'll wait in the kitchen, Master McAdam, if I may! I don't want to be alone here! I'm afraid, sir, so afraid!"

The coachman nodded, and the boy, throwing down the drink, departed for the kitchen, stumbling and clutching his stomach as if it might fall out, while the coachman, worried and weary, went to look for Duncan so they could embark on their dark journey to the ice-house.

*

Night had now settled in, deep and dark and so cold the frost had formed long, thin ice crystals on the great tall fir trees that surrounded the castle. The ice-house had been designed to store ice from the nearby lake for cooling food and drink in the summer months and had been cleaned and cleared of the straw and matting only a day or two earlier, as was usual for the time of year. Built by the previous Lord Glamis a few years previously- he had wished to imitate the lavish tastes of King James at Hampton Court- the ice-house was, in fact, connected through an underground passage that led back to the Castle, serving the additional purpose of a secret escape route for the family in case of danger. This, however, was not known to any servants, who accessed the ice-house over ground, through the thick of the woods.

Duncan and McAdam appeared as two insignificant figures moving between the giant trees, only the flicker of their torches being witness to their presence, as they made their way back through the forest from the ice-house. Poor, dead Effie, covered only in straw and dirt, a mess of bone, dried blood and flesh, was laid out on the cart that Hamish had abandoned in panic by the ice-house entrance, her lifeless remains trembling as the wheels of the cart moved along the rough and rutted grounds.

They brought her back to the castle, and not knowing where to put her, kept her on the cart which they left by the coach house. McAdam was not able to stomach the sight of the young maid, not least because she was naked but mostly because the sight of the mutilation was too much to bear. He fetched an old horse-blanket and threw it over the girl. Practical by nature, he had absentmindedly considered how the ground was already too frozen for burial, so he could not think how they could give the poor lass a proper funeral until the thaw in spring.

It was Fionnsgoth who told Margaret of the maid's horrific end. Sitting in her bed chamber by the fire, Margaret was more in shock than grief.

"I....", her voice broke briefly, "I do not know what to say, Fionnsgoth," she stated, shaken but calm.

"I did not like the girl- she was a thief and loose in her conduct- but such an awful end as this....".

Margaret shuddered, covering her mouth as if to prevent a sorrow from entering.

"I cannot believe anyone here would do such a thing! It must have been an intruder- surely that! God knows we have had many of them here in the past few days!"

I am a coward, she thought to herself, *but I must take a last look at Effie, dead; it is the decent thing to do, no matter ow much I disliked her!*

She rose from her chair, wrapping her plaid around her several times, for the late October freeze was setting in, seeping through the thick stone castle walls, where it would remain for the long winter.

Turning to Fionnsgoth, who had been crying and sobbing quietly since Effie's discovery, Margaret disregarded her emotional state and demanded with an almost callous authority:

"I would like to see Effie, one last time; then, we must fetch a doctor, and notify the Constable, and my cousin- if he is anywhere to be found!"

She considered the situation, now thoughtful and matter of fact.

"I do not think Hamish will be up for this task- poor boy, what a terrible shock for him! - but perhaps McAdam or Alastair would send word to the Constable!"

Fionnsgoth nodded, but replied with notable worry:

"My Lady, I do not think it wise for you to see the girl- she is-", but she was not allowed to finish.

"I *will* see her, Fionnsgoth, whatever ungodly state I may find her in! You do not have to accompany me. I know this is difficult. Now, do as I ask of you!"

Margaret hesitated briefly and continued with a renewed concern.

"We must let her parents know....I do not know that they will care- they sounded cruel, heartless. No wonder Effie turned out as she did, poor lass! But we must let them know their daughter is dead. They may well demand restitution, which we will have to pay. And do not tell Bal of this; no doubt she will discover the events herself, but the longer she is oblivious of this horrific affair, the better!"

Fionnsgoth curtsied as Margaret led the way out of her chamber and made her way towards the coach house. A horror beyond her imagination awaited her, but the awful sight of Effie's mutilated body was only to be the beginning of a long and fateful nightmare.

*

Sir John Scrymgeour, Constable of Dundee, received word from McAdam about the tragedy that had occurred at Glamis that same night. An hour's hard riding had brought McAdam to Dudhope just past midnight, and Sir John's servant had reluctantly woken his master, understanding the seriousness of the matter after some negotiation by McAdam.

The Constable was a tall man with a kind face, short, dark hair greying at the temples surrounding an oval face. A thin, tidy moustache and neat tuft of a beard on his chin exaggerated his high sunken cheekbones, which framed a long, straight nose. His posture and demeanour suggested him to be a person of command and respect, perhaps well-fitting for the court of King Charles. However, unlike the popular impression among his peers that Sir John had an unwavering loyalty to the Crown, he was inwardly disinterested in politics, and even less so in the King and his activities. As Constable, he wished only to maintain law and order in this part of Scotland, as far as social and political circumstances allowed.

McAdam had explained the reasons for his unsociable visit as concisely as possible, and visibly disturbed, the Constable immediately summoned two deputies to join them on their journey back to Glamis. The four men arrived at the castle in the early hours of the next morning, a faint light of dawn beginning to appear over the distant Highland hills as they made their way down the long avenue to the castle gates.

Soon after Effie's discovery, the servants had been sent to bed. The cook, Geilis, and the three other maids- Agnes, Lilias and Morag, had stayed together, taking solace in their company. The grounds keeper Duncan had taken in his two assistants, along with the boy Hamish, who was still uneasy and terrified, into his cottage, and the rest of the castle servants had, under the direction of Alastair, remained together in the servants quarters, while he, trying hard to repel his feelings of grief for Effie, had stayed awake in the kitchen, drinking, until he had been dispatched to fetch the doctor.

Only Fionnsgoth and Margaret had remained vigilant during the night, terrible thoughts racing through each of their minds in waking nightmares. It would have been impossible to sleep, anyway, the horror of it all was there to keep them awake. Despite the dreadful sight in front of her, Margaret had stayed with Effie alone through the night, and only left the dead girl when she heard the thudding sound of hooves and the murmur of distant voices nearing the coach house.

"Sir John, how kind of you to come! I wish I could bid you a *good* morrow....I apologise for asking McAdam to summon you in the wee hours of this cold morning!"

The Constable bowed, shaking his head in dismay as he took off his large, feathered hat, and waved his hand dismissively.

"Lady Margaret, do not trouble yourself unduly; this is my duty as Constable- it is a calling that requires my attention at all hours of the day or night. And I am very sorry for you, to have to bear this stain against humanity on behalf of your cousin, Lord Glamis."

Dear John, thought Margaret, *always so kind and obliging- a true friend in times of need.*

"You must be tired and hungry from your early start, and the hard ride; shall we have breakfast first?" she hesitated momentarily, before continuing:

"McAdam may have related to you the horror with which poor Effie met her end! I am, to be honest, not certain if you will be able to stomach any food once you have seen her in the...*condition*...she is in!"

The Constable agreed after a short pause.

"Aye, let us eat- we are all in need of refreshment," he said, and ordered his men to see to stabling their horses.

She ordered Fionnsgoth, who had appeared quietly in the background, to see to the breakfast. Fionnsgoth had wakened the cook and maids when she had heard the sound of horses in the distance, and Geilis and her assistants now busied themselves in the kitchen, welcoming the distraction of having something, anything to do other than to face the constant reminder of the young maid stretched out grey and dead, as near a vision from hell as one could imagine, on the cart by the coach house.

*

The surgeon, whose name was Arthur Johnston- a small-statured man perhaps in his late forties, thin and pale with a solemn demeanour- arrived at Glamis with Alastair shortly after Sir John and Margaret had finished their breakfast. It was not yet eight o'clock, the light of day barely skimming the horizons, when, after brief introductions, the three agreed to view the body of Effie together. Alastair had explained in brief detail the state of the poor maid, to prepare Sir John and the physician for what they were about to see, for Margaret, with visions of the horror still fresh in her mind, needed no reminder.

The cold of the autumn had prevented Effie's body from beginning its natural process of decay, and, apart from a faint, sour odour that had started to surround her- so unbefitting, thought Margaret, for although she had not liked the girl, Effie had always been clean and tidy with a faint scent of lavender about her- she looked no different than the night before, when Hamish had found her.

Sir Jack started violently, turning away and covering his mouth, as the physician pulled away the blanket, met with Effie's bulging eyes and her naked body for all to see, drying trails of intestines, flies buzzing around her as if she were a novel attraction. It seemed that Arthur Johnston, too, was shocked at the utterly appalling sight; although, Margaret imagined, he had surely seen many horrors of equal proportion, or worse still, in his profession.

"She was strangled," he noted, examining her neck and throat, "by a pair of strong hands, it appears."

He pointed to large dark purple bruises evenly spaced like a necklace of horror around Effie's neck, which, against the white translucence of her skin, looked almost as if they had been painted on by a skilled artist. The physician then gently lifted her hands, first her left, then her right, and inspected her nails, manipulating each of her fingers with his own against the faint morning light.

"Her nails are clean for a servant," he commented, rather surprised. "She does not appear to have resisted her attacker. There appears to be no debris under her nails, and there is no other bruising," he murmured, quickly adding, "other than the...cut to her abdomen."

He leaned closer to Effie, gazing at the large open wound; the cut flesh was smooth, almost surgical in precision, but the organs had been hacked into a mess as if in a frenzy, and he struggled to differentiate the various organs in their present mutilated state.

"Interesting," he muttered, then raising his voice, stated, "I shall have to examine her further at the morgue, but I would suggest that she died of strangulation, and....", he frowned, puzzled, "I assume, she was mutilated sometime after she died; for who would disembowel their victim, and then strangle her when she was already dead?"

He replaced some of his instruments, and closed his medicine bag, and Sir John still recovering from the shock of Effie's gruesome spectacle, spoke, his voice shaking gently, for the first time.

"Was this the work of a madman, Mr Johnston? It is truly horrific!"

Arthur Johnston mused, with sharp eyes fixed on Margaret.

"A madman, yes- perhaps;" he paused briefly, "or a madwoman."

Margaret snorted in contempt.

"A woman would never do this- to any living creature!"

"Aye," he agreed without hesitation, and a glint in his eye, as if a bright idea of some genius had suddenly appeared before him, "but she might, if she were possessed by the Devil, my Lady- a witch, perhaps; and we are close to Kirriemuir!"

"I do not believe in witches or witchcraft, Mr Johnston, and I am surprised that a man of learning, such as yourself, entertains the idea so willingly!"

"If you believe in God, my Lady- as a woman of your standing in society no doubt does- then you must also believe in the Devil; and the Devil will possess those who let him. Those who let him do so, my Lady, are those whose moral fibre has been worn by the black seeds of bitterness and envy; and to such a weakness only women are prone."

Smiling faintly and somewhat condescendingly in Margaret's direction, morbidly amused at her apparently naïve innocence with regards to her own sex, the physician covered up poor Effie. Sir John sensed the tension in the atmosphere and intervened in his trained diplomatic habit to avoid a quarrel between the two. There was a murder that needed to be solved, and time would wait for no one.

"Perhaps it is best not to conjecture too greatly on the possible culprit of this poor girl's death, until we have conducted further investigations," he suggested in a practical tone.

"Aye," the physician once again nodded in agreement, "the magistrate will decide how to proceed once the facts concerning Effie's death have been established, and that may take some time. I shall begin a thorough examination of the body as soon as I return to Dundee."

Indignant at the blatant hatred of women this doctor possessed, Margaret was reminded of Matthew Hopkins. *Perhaps they are friends,* she thought, *that should not surprise me!*

Aware that she was displaying the bitterness and contempt that Mr Johnston had so pointedly attributed to the general character of all women, she attempted to compose herself; her face softened in sadness as she glanced at Effie's remains.

"We owe it to Effie to bring her murderer to justice! I thank you, Mr Johnston, for aiding us in this endeavour; I know that my cousin, Lord Glamis, will also be most grateful for your help."

The good doctor bowed, in a manner that was perhaps a bit too discrete for some- considering the differences in their social standing -but an act that did not surprise or anger Margaret. The world belonged to men, for the most part, and although this might, with the passing of time, slowly ease in the favour of her fellow sisters on earth, the balance of power would never change. With a parting glance at Effie, they left the dead girl for the last time. Margaret excused herself, thanking Sir John for making the necessary arrangements as she disappeared back into the castle. *Bal,* thought Margaret, *I must know that she is safe!*

And Bal was indeed safe in her room; Fionnsgoth had entertained her with stories, and they had looked at the large atlas and gone on several adventures across the world by the time Margaret appeared. The little girl had only paid a fleeting attention to the commotion outside, but had thankfully taken no interest, to Margaret's relief. She looked out of the window, which had a view of the long drive up to the castle. Sir John was directing one of his men to remove Effie and the cart, and to follow Mr Johnston back to Dundee, and within a short while, the train of men and horses, with Effie, a mess of flesh and bones quivering under the old torn blanket as they pulled her across the uneven ruts and holes in the road, the poor girl once again the last in line.

*

Kirriemuir Town, October 14th, 1628

It was late in the evening, and the *Three Bellies Brae* was crowded with loud, boisterous and drunk Kirriemuir locals, beer and whisky flowing like liquid gold, to the absolute delight of the Inn's owner, Master Craig Tulloch, whose coffers of silver and gold grew ever fuller as the autumn days set in. Although he recognized most of the men- the regulars, some gently behaved, and others which he frequently had to throw out- there were that evening three faces that he had never seen before, who, observed the Inn keeper, had found a table near Alastair, steward of the house at Glamis. One of those faces was certainly not English or Scottish, hair and skin too dark for these climes, in his opinion, and Master Craig took notice of the large gold cross, Jesus prostrate, that hung around the stranger's neck; *a Catholic*, he mused at the stranger's bravery, before turning his attention back to the steward of Glamis.

Alastair, knew Master Tulloch, had been hit hard by the death of the young maid Effie a week past- what a terrifying end to have met, poor lass!- and had been drowning his sorrows more frequently, and more thoroughly than was his habit, ensconced in his usual corner pew by the window. Occasionally, he would stare out to the street, but mostly into his glass, where he would lose himself until the closing bell chimed for the last time.

The weather had turned bitter in the last few days; it was not yet November, but frost had appeared in the nights, and stayed well into the morning, even in the brief and intermittent light of the sun. The villagers of Kirriemuir, the innkeeper had noticed, were beginning to wind down the year's work ahead of the coming winter, darker days and slower toil taking over, with little but the comforting warmth of the inn and sense-dulling tranquility of its drink to keep their spirits high.

Rory Dalmore, a steward from nearby Drum Farm and a regular customer of the Inn, had made his way over to the sorrowful corner table that hosted the steward of Glamis. Dalmore's interest also appeared to be stirred by the strangers only a few tables away from Alastair, and a keen observer would have noted Rory's faint nod and fleeting smile in the direction of the stranger with the gold cross as he passed his table.

If not a friend, Rory Dalmore was at least a close acquaintance of Alastair, and he wished to enquire about his health, particularly after the news of Effie's death.

"Evenin', Master Alastair," he tipped his cap lightly as he sat down, not waiting for an invitation, and was greeted with a short, almost scoffing, snort.

"How goes the search for Effie's killer?" he wasted no time in asking, completely indifferent to the uncompassionate tone in his voice, even at the obvious pain the mention of her name caused to his companion.

"I hear there is talk of witchcraft, dark magic, and all sorts," he whispered slowly, in a low, dramatic voice, "and that a Witchfinder General- from England, no less! - has been to visit his Lordship! What scandal!"

He shook his big, round head, long brown greying locks quivering as he spoke with glee, a burning curiosity lighting his bright green eyes.

"Nonsense!" slurred Alastair, red in the face from drink and anger. "Dark magic- what utter rot! My poor Effie was murdered out of revenge....".

He began to sob quietly, and Rory who felt uncomfortable knew only to respond by pouring his companion another large dram of whiskey.

"Revenge?" Rory inquired, a little surprised. "But what for? And by who?"

Alastair, whose emotions wavered between deep sorrow and violent anger, although he was too drunk to act on either, spat out his thoughts between large gulps of whiskey.

"Ahhh....don't know....but that Fionnsgoth always hated Effie...Effie was right, my poor lass, that hag only wanted to be the head of the household- take my place!- wi' no right to it, comin' with Lady Margaret from Aberdour, she'd no rights in my household!"

Rory considered, slightly bemused:

"You mean, Fionnsgoth is not a part of Lord Glamis' household? That is interesting....". He delighted in being able to fan the flames of his friend's burning grief and anger so easily, and added:

"Well, she has no right to your station- you must be careful! And," he continued more matter-of-fact, "if this talk of witchcraft has a ring of truth in it, my friend, you must be extra watchful! For who knows what further misfortune she could conjure up!"

They sat in silence for a while, Rory with a furrowed brow, a feigned concern for his distressed table companion, and Alastair's mind in a flurry of chaotic thoughts and violent feelings, suggestions of dark magic flowing into his hateful visions of Fionnsgoth, who he was sure had taken his beloved away from him.

Breaking the silence, Rory put on a jesting tone, and asked:

"What if we were to play a trick on mistress Fionnsgoth, Alastair?"

He was whispering again, although there was no need, as the crowd in the inn had now become so rowdy and noisy, it was difficult to hear oneself speak even at a normal pitch. But talk of witchcraft in Kirriemuir was never open; the town had been stained with it before, and was eager to remove itself from such blasphemy, and whenever anyone dared to mention it, it was in hidden company, and only with a low whisper.

"A trick? What kind of a trick?" mumbled Alastair. He had begun to form his own dark plans in his mind to avenge Effie.

Rory shifted, perhaps slightly uncomfortably, his broad frame overshadowing the small and wobbly table they sat around.

"Well, nothing terrible, 'course, just a trick to make her understand who is the rightful keeper of the house at Glamis....I can help you think of something...".

The relatively calm conversation they had endured up util then was suddenly disrupted by Alastair's large, clenched fist banging the table, drink spilling and glasses clinking as he did so.

"Let it be humiliating!" he blurted out, through gritted teeth and with narrow eyes. "So humiliating she will want to leave and never come back to Glamis!"

Rory, satisfied that he had fulfilled his mission, nodded eagerly in agreement; he looked calmly over to the table where the stranger sat, acknowledging him with another nod and a furtive smile. Amidst the rancorous drunkenness and merry singing of the Inn crowd, it never ceased to astonish Rory Dalmore how easy it was to earn a living from the misery of others.

~ Six ~

Master Hopkins had felt a seething anger at being escorted off the lands of Glamis by a troop of men charged by the Constable of Dundee to remove him for trespassing. But, on returning to Aberdour, where his host, William Douglas- although rather puzzled at the additional arrival of an instrument of torture that he found utterly ghastly- had counseled him on his possibilities, the General gradually became more at ease with the options that lay before him.

The Constable of Dundee, Sir William assured him, had only been discharging his proper duty in safeguarding the Estate of Lord Glamis. But there was no more loyal servant to the King than Sir John himself, William had emphasised, and if the Constable were to become aware of the serious accusations that were brewing against Lady Margaret, he would be less likely to interfere with the Witchfinder again in future. However, Sir William cautioned, if Margaret's reluctance to agree to his terms on the presept of sasine, the complicated nature of local loyalties and strong sentiment of resentment against the English would undoubtedly obscure matters for them in their attempts at arresting a cousin of Lord Glamis. And so, Master Hopkins had been advised that the most prudent course of action would be for him to travel to Edinburgh to seek the aid of the Lord Advocate, Sir Thomas Hope, who could bring forth charges on behalf of the Crown to the Lord Justice General, without the more common and drawn-out judicial process entailing hearings at the court of sessions. If Margaret were brought directly in front of the Lord Justice General in Edinburgh, the process of charging her with crimes would be quicker, and the threat of a conviction more assured, the outcome of which, hoped William, would lead to his sister seeing reason, and to her finally agreeing to his proposal.

Furthermore, the Lord Justice General was Lord Graham, the 7th Earl of Menteith, a most fervent supporter of King Charles, who had also a Commission of Justiciary. This, explained William Douglas to his ignorant English guest, meant that the Lord Justice General, as well as being the highest judicial appointee in Scotland, additionally had the right to exercise regional prosecutions, particularly relating to accusations of witchcraft. So, felt Matthew Hopkins, the pieces were finally falling into place for his plan; and how pleased the Bishop of London, and thus the King himself, would be to hear of his swift and successful actions! The rewards, imagined the General, would be too numerous to fathom; riches, status and renown beyond his wildest dreams!

A week after his return to Aberdour from Glamis, with Sir William's reassurances and the good news in mind, Matthew Hopkins had made the journey to Edinburgh, where he currently found himself in the spartan comforts of an office in the College of Justice.

"But do you have any evidence, Master Hopkins?"

Sir Thomas Hope, Lord Advocate, was known for his successful prosecutions and defenses, all the cases he had won being on good merit due to his unrelenting adherence to the particulars of the Law which required the establishment of facts and a thorough examination of evidence, rather than hearsay or conjecture of the accused's guilt. The General, however, had no such inclinations, of course; if God had shown him the Devil's work was at hand, then that was all the fact he needed. But he would find this approach a dead end when faced with the unyielding Sir Thomas.

"I admire the Earl of Morton, and his loyalty to the Crown- it is a most enviable quality," Sir Thomas offered, "but I am uncertain on what basis he makes the accusation of witchcraft against his own sister? It is unusual- not in lower circles of society, of course, for they are known for their petty quarrels and vengeful antics- but both the Earl and Lady Margaret are of reputable noble birth, Master Hopkins, and I am hesitant to proceed with any judicial procedures unless a crime has in fact been committed, according to evidence that is indisputable."

He paused, studying the rather loathsome man in front of him, and wondered whether the law was actually ever practiced in England, or merely there as an occasional tool of reference for the higher born, who could refer to it according to their whims and moods, without obligation to its proper enforcement.

Master Hopkins sulked openly at the negative reception he had received. He had been given such high hopes by Sir William regarding his visit to the Lord Advocate that he had not even considered the possibility of opposition. Languishing in a large armchair, he sat, legs splayed apart, as if in a drunken stupor. The foul odour emanating from his entire being did not escape the Lord Advocate's senses, who promptly opened a nearby window.

"Sir Thomas," began Hopkins, "I have no doubt that your meticulous approach of gathering facts and evidence is an admirable past-time and appreciated by all those who practice the Law here in Scotland!" he frowned in doubt at his own words, "however, it is God who has shown me that the work of the Devil is at hand in Scotland, and that the Devil was helped by Margaret Douglas, who conspired with Jack Felton to murder the Duke of Buckingham! The plot had been brewing for some time, Sir William tells me; and he, being his sister's brother, must surely know."

Sir Thomas was a man of reason and considerable intellect, with no measure of endless patience, and yet he could feel the irritation of what was undoubtedly to be a long, tiresome conversation rise within him. What was even more tedious was that this hideous man was English, and in the employ of the Bishop of London, and thus indirectly, the King himself; it would be difficult to avoid any kind of investigation into this loosely brought accusation. It irked him to think of the time and moneys that would be wasted on attempting to procure an unlikely and unjust conviction, not to mention the injury and insult to a lady of noble birth who was no less than the cousin of the Earl of Kinghorne.

"And what is the connection between Lady Margaret and Jack Felton? I understood him to be a soldier in England, never having set foot in Scotland; nor has Lady Margaret, I believe, ever ventured further south than this very city, from what I understand."

Master Hopkins merely sighed, as the justiciar continued.

"How are they to ever have met to plan this…er…conspiracy, as you call it?" Still, giving no opportunity for the General to reply, Sir Thomas persisted further:

"Is it not possible, Master Hopkins, that Jack Felton acted out of his own will? I am told he had some personal objection to the Duke's method of administering his troops, and that Felton was a member of some troops serving under the Duke, having suffered fatal losses in France, at both Isle-de-Re and La Rochelle."

Matthew Hopkins was beginning to understand that he would have to work harder to find something that would convince this over-zealous legal peddler to act on his own wishes, and that this journey would not be as easy, or rapidly concluded, as he had first thought.

Unsticking himself from the deep armchair he had conquered, and rising slowly, the General smiled, almost facetiously, and pretended to consider the words of Sir Thomas for a moment. In his mind, however, he was calculating how to gain the Lord Advocate's confidence, and from experience, he knew that flattering the intellect of people in high office often worked towards this aim. Feigning interest, he asked innocently:

"I confess, my Lord, that I am somewhat ignorant in the ways of Scottish law; perhaps you could explain to me some of its basic principles and procedures, related to, say, criminal acts such as witchcraft and murder?"

Sir Thomas never liked men who believed they could win their case through any form of flattery, but he was pleased he had been given the opportunity to explain to his loathsome visitor the proper procedures of Scottish law, even if it was entirely insincere on the General's behalf.

With a slight frown, Sir Thomas replied coldly:

"Certainly, Master Hopkins; Scottish law differs from English law in various ways."

He sat down behind his broad, wide oak desk, folded his hands in front of him, and began to explain.

"First, let me assure you that, contrary to the general belief by English lawyers that torture is widely accepted in Scotland, this is most certainly not the case; torture," he emphasised sternly, "may only be used in the most exceptional circumstances, by approval of the Privy Council, which is extremely rare, if not non-existent."

The visible look of disappointment on Hopkins's face prompted Sir Thomas to explain further.

"That is not to say that, unfortunately, torture appears to be common in provincial burghs and towns; you understand," continued the Lord Advocate, knowing quite well that there was actually no reason at all for Hopkins to understand, "in order to extract any relevant information from the accused, which is necessary to obtain to enable criminal proceedings to begin in the first place, torture is believed by many to expedite the release of such necessary information."

In other words, thought Hopkins, feeling more at ease now, *torture does not officially fall within the bounds of legality, but is practiced, nonetheless.*

"Interesting," he replied, "and what does the process entail once the relevant information has been, er, *obtained* from the accused?"

Sir Thomas had not enjoyed being interrupted, and snapped impatiently:

"Yes, yes, I was just coming to that.... while in England the law requires a jury to come to a unanimous consensus on the verdict that is to be served to the accused, here in Scotland," he paused slightly, for he felt that what he was about to confess to was a serious failing in the Scottish legal system- and he abhorred the idea that the English and their barbarian ways carried moral superiority in this regard, "in Scotland, the jury requires only a majority to agree in order to serve a verdict."

This was like music to the General's ears, and once again that self-satisfied grin of someone who would soon get what he wanted appeared across his mean countenance.

"Ah," he mused, "that is very interesting to learn, indeed."

He waved his hand with an overly exaggerated authority, the pomposity of the action nearly forcing Sir Thomas to laugh.

"I thank you, Lord Advocate, for these snippets of enlightenment! I will confer with Sir William, Lord Advocate, for further details, and when I return," he sniffed, his nostrils flaring in contempt, "which will be very soon, I shall present to you the 'evidence' you require. I shall waste no more of our time here today, Sir Thomas, and bid you good morrow."

He bowed ceremoniously, and was met only by a cold stare and a faint nod from Sir Thomas, before he disappeared through the door, but not without almost knocking over Sir Thomas' clerk, Angus, who was rushing in, slightly out of breath and rather excited.

"I beg pardon, sir," said the young clerk, bowing, and screwing up his face at the pungent odour that met him. But he received no acknowledgement other than a pointed glare from Matthew Hopkins as he pranced imperiously down the long corridor and out of sight, the feathers from his large hat flapping about him like a flock of bewildered birds.

"My Lord," the clerk hurried, "there are some news from the Constable of Dundee!"

He placed a letter in front of Sir Thomas, who, almost as soon as he began to read it, furrowed his brow in concern. News had travelled far and fast of the grim occurrence at Glamis, and he wondered at the coincidence of the connection between the various events that were starting to unfold in his charge. Uneasy, and with an ill feeling, he sat down at his desk, and read the letter again. Dark events had always hung over the history of Glamis Castle, like a shadow that would never fade. Not long ago, he had attended a play whose plot was set in Glamis Castle, and, reading this letter, he now remembered some words that had haunted him since:

By the pricking of my thumbs
Something wicked this way comes......

~ Seven ~

Glamis Castle, October 21st, 1628

"Of what, precisely, do I now stand accused?"

Margaret was still in her night dress, and this time, she abandoned any pretense of politeness.

Matthew Hopkins had returned to Glamis exactly two weeks after his first nocturnal visit, and now, after a thoroughly educational sojourn in Edinburgh in order to torment Lady Margaret further, he faced his prey again, this time in the Great Hall of the sprawling castle.

The flames in the enormous fireplace of the Great Hall had almost extinguished, and the night was bitter with a deep frost. Margaret shivered slightly; she had barely had time to find her dressing gown when the night visitors had forced themselves in, bewildered guardsmen and servants not knowing whether to fight or take flight, without the direction of her absent cousin. Her feet were bare in her delicate cotton slippers, through which she could feel the ice cold of the stone floor creeping into her body, a slow, unrelenting conquest of her flesh, bones, and soul.

"Do you quiver from fear, my Lady?" the odious invader asked, mocking; he pulled his lips apart in a gleeful grin, under which appeared blackened and yellow teeth, like a row of old, rotten chess pieces. "You need not be afraid of me, my Lady; I am known as a most benevolent and forgiving man, like God himself! Those who confess and repent shall find me a most warm recipient of those who seek the path of spiritual virtue!"

A smile, self-satisfied, as if he were in awe of his own God-like qualities, passed over his shiny face. He licked his food-encrusted lips in delight at believing to have achieved his goal of intimidation, but Margaret, who was not one to be easily moved, retorted calmly:

"It will no doubt disappoint you to hear that it is the cold, rather than your presence, that is making me shiver."

Her voice was almost indifferent, without fear, and she could see his irritation surfacing, as his eyes narrowed, and his eyebrows formed a frown. Again, she asked:

"Would you be so kind as to let me know what offence I may have committed that has resulted in you gracing us with your second visit to Glamis, so soon after your first attendance?"

But he did not answer; instead, he continued his questions.

"Where might your cousin be at this time, my Lady? Is he still away? As the Lord of the Castle....", he looked around the room with an air of superiority, noting the fading curtains, tattered cushions and worn furniture, muttering, "such as it is...", and strode to the window, "I would have thought the Earl of Kinghorne would be present to keep safe his estate during such...uncertain times."

He stroked a fur blanket hanging on the back of an armchair, the sorry remains of a former fox, carefully caressing it as if it were a beloved pet.

"You- or should I say more precisely, your cousin- has beautiful possessions, my Lady, despite the worn and decrepit state of some...many would say they would once upon a time have been fit for a King!"

He turned his face, and staring directly at her, as she stood trying to ignore the intense cold that was overcoming her, reiterated:

"Your cousin, my Lady- and your son? - as your protectors- where are they?"

Margaret began to feel an irrepressible irritation creep through her bones, along with the bitterness of the biting cold; but she attempted to hide it, and replied with swift and sharp conviction:

"My son is fighting in Germany, sir," she answered, emotionless, "and my cousin is still away on some business."

Having had no understanding, even since birth, of compassion or empathy, brought up by loveless parents, Matthew Hopkins knew only how to indulge his own narcissism, where he and his work where all that mattered in the entire world. He queried in a matter-of-fact manner, with apparent amusement:

"Your son- fighting, my Lady?" he drew his mouth downward into a false show of pity, tutting softly.

"How so? I received information that he, in fact, is dead?"

She did not know if it was a convincing lie, but still unflinching, she answered:

"As a man of God, sir, I would think you disinclined to accept rumours so easily."

He drew down one side of his mouth and contorted his face into such a ridiculous caricature it reminded Margaret of those figures she sometimes would laugh at in the humour section of a daily pamphlet. He persisted.

"And your daughter?"

The chill of the night, or early dawn as it was now, emanated from the stone walls like an invisible assailant, and Margaret could see the remaining warmth of her breath meet the cold in a cloud of grey, dancing, smoke-like, into thin air. At the mention of a daughter, she struggled to keep her cool composure; only she and Fionnsgoth were supposed to know the truth about Bal! While thoughts raced through her mind as to how he could know, she struggled with the fear of it. For herself she was not fearful- she was not afraid of dying, perhaps only the manner in which it came about- but her children...her son was safe, she believed, her cousin Robert giving her hope that he was yet alive, but Bal....she must do everything to protect her.

Her feet were now so frozen she could not feel the floor, and the damp of her perspiring skin caused her to shiver uncontrollably, and as hard as she tried to hide it, she began to shake gently.

Her inquisitor, who had found another object on a cabinet by the window to fixate on, was highly amused by the spectacle of misery he saw in his company. He was not alone, of course; he had his men with him, ready to obey any command he might give them, and they stood, poised, by the heavy oak doors of the Great Hall, ready to leap as if their lives depended on it, expecting her ladyship to attempt an escape at any moment.

Margaret, weary of the tiresome conversation Matthew Hopkins was having, mostly with himself, decided to move closer to the window in the corner of the room.

"I do not know what gossip the office of the General takes for fact, good Sir, but I can assure you, I do not have a daughter."

The Inquisitor drew up the left side of his mouth in a half-smile, the few rotten teeth that had been capped in gold gleaming as they caught the faint candlelight. He let out a short snort and paced slowly over to one of the grand armchairs, casting his eyes around the room. It was the same chair with the fur shawl he had found so interesting only a few minutes before, and he eased himself into it with great ceremony, groaning and whining as if his age had outgrown the years he had actually lived.

"It is arduous and dangerous work, this, my Lady," he commented, attempting to address Margaret respectfully for the first time since he had entered her home, "the Devil's work is everywhere; we may not see it in the clear of daylight, but it is among us prevalently, like the plague. In fact, the plague is also one of his many works, and it has been allowed to prevail and spread only because of the many deviant souls he has employed to do his work!"

He closed his eyes, and put his hands together, fingertips touching in a semi-meditative pose, while he continued his monologue.

"I recently came from Bamberg, in Germany," he mused, pausing to question her in mid-sentence, "have you been?",

"I have not." Margaret impatiently shook her head.

"Ah, well....", he regretted, "it is a pleasant enough city, in fairness, an excellent destination for tourists- very good beer- were it not for the misfortune of the deeply pervasive and persistent evil that has possessed it!"

The Inquisitor shifted slightly in his seat, a mask of faint regret hiding his total disinterest in the potential qualities of Bamberg as a destination of leisure and beer-tasting, for there was only one issue that concerned him, one single objective in his life that he wished to pursue: the presence of witchcraft, its defeat, and the punishment of those who engaged in this foul work of the Devil. It was this obsession he woke to before dawn on every day, and what he lived and breathed even after the light of the last candle had given way to night, and sleep.

"I visited the *Malefizhaus......*," he went on, eyes still shut but wide open to the frozen and numb atmosphere of the room. Faint puffs of condensation appeared in regular rhythmic intervals from his nostrils, which, to Margaret, appeared yellow and putrid, like the rest of him.

"Are you familiar with it, my Lady, the *Malefizhaus* in Bamberg?"

She was beginning to feel sleepy, as if her mind was leaving her body, standing in the corner, half frozen, her blood running colder by the second. But she did her best to remain calm and appear unaffected by the sheer mental and physical torment to which the Witchfinder General relished in subjecting her. She answered bitterly, fighting to keep her teeth from clattering too noticeably.

"I am not. But I have no doubt that you will momentarily spare no details in explaining to me what this.....what did you call it?" she asked, dismissively.

"*Malefizhaus.*" He spoke the words slowly, and condescendingly, in syllables, emphasizing the first especially strongly, as if trying to explain something to a child who had yet to learn how to comprehend simple words.

'*Ma-le- fiz-haus.*"

"Yes...", she continued, trying not to laugh at him as he spoke the words in such a ridiculously theatrical manner that it reminded her of a comedy scene in a play she had attended in Edinburgh not long ago. Hopkins tried to hide his irritation by beckoning her to sit in the armchair opposite to the one he had sequestered; the whole scene was a reversed and perverse version of the proper rituals of court. It was *she* who was the Lady of the castle while her cousin was away, *she* who should invite *him* to sit on their furniture; *she* who should be able to ask *him* to leave their estate.

Although Margaret would have preferred to stand- she had no desire to submit to any of her inquisitor's whims- she longed for the warmth of a chair, and to be able to take her frozen feet off the icy stone floors. Hesitantly, she moved to the armchair and sat down, watching him- his eyes closed but observant- and as she did so, lifting her feet from the floor, she leaned back and grabbed a wool blanket covering the back of the chair. When she had finished covering her feet and legs, the intruder remarked, eyes still firmly shut:

"'There is a chill in here, my Lady; I will have one of my men light the fire."

He snapped his fingers as if summoning a dark spirit to perform the deed, and one of his henchmen sprang into action as if his life depended on it, which, Margaret assumed, it quite probably did. *Where is Alastair?* she wondered, slightly afraid. *It is his duty to see to lighting the fires within Glamis! Why has he not come?* The servants had all disappeared, it seemed, as if by the means of some dark magic.

Within minutes, a slow warmth began to pervade the room like a veil of comfort, and Margaret, annoyed at the intruder for once again taking advantage of her cousin's home as his own, felt a mixture of hatred and gratitude as her body, limb by limb, began to thaw from the cold, feeling a tingling in her feet now as the icy flesh gave way to the warmth that gently returned to her bones. It left her feeling even more drowsy, as if someone had given her a strong medicine for sleep. She longed for the soft cocoon of her bed; she felt exhausted.

"Now, that is an improvement, is it not, my Lady?" his voice had gone from an attempt at menace to the false, slippery-smooth tone of pretense fatherliness, which did not have the effect perhaps desired, not least because the Inquisitor was some years younger in age than Margaret.

"Your cousin has an excellent and comfortable home, my Lady! Such trinkets and objects and furnishings of riches I have rarely seen anywhere else, outside of His Majesty's possessions, that is! And from foreign parts, too, I see....".

He mused, now open-eyed, taking measure of the large Ottoman rug that spread majestically before them, covering most of the central part of the room.

"Have you had the pleasure of travelling to Ottoman lands, my Lady? This is a particularly fine rug; so fine, in fact, I believe the King himself has in his possession only one or two such exemplars!" He imagined this, for he had never actually seen them, or even been invited to an audience with the King; but staring straight at her, and seeing her struggle to keep awake, he suggested:

"I am certain His Majesty's displeasure at your ladyship could be softened to a more benevolent demeanour if this rug could be added to his current collection of carpets from foreign lands!"

Margaret, having again briefly succumbed to her exhaustion, started slightly. Her anger had reawakened, and changing the subject, she replied sharply:

"How does the Iron Maiden fare at Aberdour, Master Hopkins? Has it been put to good use by my brother, or has the poor lady already made her journey to the King?" Her tone was mocking, acidic, and feeling no desire for a reply from her interrogator, she continued, utterly carefree of the consequences her tirade against an officer of the Royal Court might bring.

"And speaking of the King, is there a need for His Majesty to feel such particular displeasure towards my cousin, or myself, sir?

I do not believe that either of us have had the honour of an audience with His Majesty, and I am yet to be told of your accusations, which, I assume, you present on behalf of His Majesty, through the direction of Bishop Laud, I understand?"

She had surprised even herself at her ability to maintain such coherence in her utter exhaustion, but it was her anger that had brought her back to her senses; no, it was her hatred of this disgusting being sitting opposite her, making mental tallies of all the possessions that were not his own which he wished to take to the King to gain favour.

The General, displeased with the impertinence of his victim, was reminded of his own hatred for women. He studied her more closely: she had been described as a beauty, but beyond the fine, long auburn hair and pale, almost translucent skin, he found no extraordinary features in her. She was not tall, and too skeletal for his taste. Her eyes were small and a dull greenish-brown, though her teeth seemed whiter than those of most women with which he had been forced to acquaint himself. Looking, by aid of his vivid and perverse imagination, beyond her gown at the naked skin it hid, he could see all sorts of witches' marks appearing as he pricked her with his imaginary selection of bodkins and needles; he smiled inwardly, for these witches' marks would no doubt be revealed in good time. For now, he decided to hide his wrath at her rudeness, and bluntly answered the question she had posed.

"Murder, my Lady," he paused to see what reaction that might provoke, but Margaret remained stone faced, "murder, by means of a dark magic."

Margaret remained unstirred; in the distance she could hear an owl, its rhythmic *two-hoo, two-hoo* echoing in regular intervals as the General delivered his charge.

"You may have heard that the King's most trusted friend and ally, the Duke of Buckingham, was murdered some two months ago; in Portsmouth."

She shifted momentarily, as if uncertain as to her answer, but replied confidently:

"Yes, it was announced at my brother's banquet when I last saw him." Not hiding her annoyance at the nature of this questioning, she asked:

"Why do you mention this affair?"

"Well, my Lady," Master Hopkins' tone was condescending and accusatory, "the Duke was stabbed several times by one of his former soldiers, a lowly devil-possessed creature named Jack Felton...", again he stopped briefly, waiting for a reaction, before adding:

"You may know of him, my Lady- Captain Jack Felton? No?" The witchfinder raised an eyebrow, in disbelief.

"No," insisted Margaret, "I have never been to Portsmouth, nor do I know anyone by the name of Jack Felton." She smiled, knowing well that she was fanning the flames of his zealotry even further.

Master Hopkins chuckled, self-satisfied, for he knew she had no evidence to contradict him, and went on.

"Jack Felton, my Lady, was known to your husband, the Baron Eythin, and so connecting him to you; and, the Earl of Morton's daughter-in-law was a niece of the most unfortunate Duke, tying you further into this devilish business!"

Pausing, not for any other reason than to effect a moment of drama, slowly looking her up and down in the hopes of making her feel uncomfortable, he continued.

"And you, my Lady, come from a long and unsavoury line of witches, most recently, your own mother, the Countess of Angus. According to your brother William, the Earl of Morton-", but he was swiftly cut off as Margaret snapped.

"Half-brother!"

Bemused, he apologized.

"I beg pardon, my Lady- *half*-brother.... according to him, you appear to have inherited many of your mother's qualities," he frowned condescendingly, "regrettably not the good ones, if these indeed ever were present in the Countess."

With the hot anger rising inside her came a slow and cold realization: this was her brother's revenge, conveniently placed in a time when he disputed her inheritance of the estate of her father, the Earl of Angus, of which he had already taken more than his share. Whatever she had thought of William- his undying support for the English King, selling Scotland to the English cause, his greed, and his envy- she never thought he had the empty cruelty to sell his own flesh and blood for the paltry fortune of a near-derelict manor and a small parcel of land to raise money for the King.

But she would not be scared by this opportunist accusing her; he had no proof of such ridiculous claims, and Margaret knew he would have trouble taking his complaint further, especially as an Englishman.

"As for my mother, God rest her soul, the claims of witchcraft were so ridiculous even King James did not feel he could proceed against her, as I am sure you are aware, instead encouraging my mother to marry again. I am sure you know of Lord Spynie, a loyal friend to the Crown and the Stuart line?"

Despite the fire now raging furiously in the large fireplace her thin blood ran cold and slow through her veins; she knew what was coming now.

"That, my Lady, may be so, but it would not prevent me from accusing you of conspiring through witchcraft to commit the murder of George Villiers, the 1st Duke of Buckingham, with the aid of your ally Jack Felton."

Hopkins raised himself up, as if directly speaking through God.

"And I am charged by William Laud, the Bishop of London, to bring the perpetrators to justice. Furthermore," he added before Margaret had a chance to reply, "there has been an unexplained death here- the parlour maid, Effie Campbell, who confided in me only the day she suffered her untimely death, of her suspicions of your trade in witchcraft and your acquaintance with Jack Felton-

and, after having reviewed the facts of her... *demise*... with Doctor Johnston in Dundee, it is indisputable that acts of witchcraft caused poor Effie's death! Murder by witchcraft, here on your cousin's estate, with you and Mistress Fionnsgoth resident; are you to tell me that it is a mere coincidence that you both happened to be at your brother's estate-".

It is mine, she thought, *not his!* "-when poor Master James Ferguson was poisoned, and that you were by chance at Glamis when poor Effie Campbell was murdered? The evidence connecting you to this web of violence," he claimed, pausing as he shook his head regretfully, "speaks for itself!"

Daylight had now appeared above the hills, a faint shimmer of orange fire nipping at the fading black darkness, as Margaret realized that she had been awake the entire night, and sleep now appeared a distant, beckoning but unreachable friend. All argument and reason having left her as her exhaustion grew, she answered calmly:

"I understand."

For now, she knew she was safe and had time on her side, as the General had as of yet no special permission to exercise his authority on her cousin's estate, or anywhere else in Scotland. She rose from the chair, her nearly thawed feet once again feeling the biting cold of the floor, and capitulated.

"Then, I look forward to you returning with your warrant for my arrest, Master Hopkins! But for now, as you are trespassing, I must ask you to leave the estate of Lord Glamis, or I shall be forced once again to ask the Sheriff of Angus to assist in your removal."

Without fear, or waiting for an answer, Margaret turned her hand to the door, half expecting to be abused in some way by the General's men, for she had sensed he was a man who enjoyed both torturing the soul as well as the body; but they, having understood the limits of their jurisdiction, obeyed, almost like lambs, filing through the great doors and passing down the stairs with only a final remark by the Witchfinder.

"Enjoy the protection of the few friends that you still have, Lady Margaret!"

A bitter smirk darkened Hopkins' face.

"Until we meet again; a time that will come soon enough, of that you may be assured!"

He bowed ostentatiously, the buttons of his close-fitting coat almost popping, and the yellow-pink skin of his scalp showing beneath his grease-filled hair as he lifted off his enormous black hat. It reminded Margaret of the ones that the witches wore in the pamphlets that had recently been printed, and she shivered again slightly, this time at the irony and the horror.

~ Eight ~

The sheriff's men took Fionnsgoth away only two days after the General's visit, by order of Doctor Johnstone. The warrant for her arrest stated first that the deputies had a right to search her possessions for any incriminating evidence that could point to Effie's murder, or engagement with witchcraft, which they had done with little opposition from the maid, as she vehemently professed her innocence of both. Fionnsgoth was shocked and horrified when they returned with what they had found- a poppet in a maid's dress, with a knitting needle impaled in her belly, and her neck torn and twisted. When they had shown it to her, she had violently denied any knowledge of it, nor had she been able to tell them how it had ended up among her things, but despite protests from both Lady Margaret and Fionnsgoth herself, she was taken away. Such shame and humiliation came over her as they marched her through the castle, for all servants to see, that she could not even face her mistress to protest her innocence.

Lilias, who was the most recent addition to the household servants, was most profoundly affected by Fionnsgoth's arrest. The young maid, who had been an orphan, had seen her almost as a mother, and Fionnsgoth had responded in a maternal way, treating Lilias as the daughter she had once had, but who was long dead and buried.

"What will happen to her, my Lady?" Lilias asked Margaret through tear-stained eyes and heaving sobs, her usual rose-red cheeks now pale with fear and worry, "what will they do to her?"

Margaret did not dare to answer truthfully; she knew what horrors awaited those accused of witchcraft.

"I will ask for the Constable's help- with his, and my cousin's, influence, all will be well! Try not to worry, Lilias; Fionnsgoth will be back at Glamis soon. All will be put right!"

But of that, Margaret was far from certain, and retreating to her bed chamber, she hastily wrote two letters. One was for her cousin, the other to Sir John Scrymgeour, which she dispatched with McAdam as soon as she had put the quill down. And he, faithful servant, rode as hard and as fast as he could to Dudhope, snapping at the heels of Fionnsgoth and the sheriff's men as they took the confused and distraught maid to Dundee's gaol.

*

Sir John returned with McAdam, this time alone, the morning after Fionnsgoth's arrest. The weary and worn look on his face, Margaret knew, did not bode good news.

McAdam left them in the Great Hall, and went off to search for Alastair, but not finding him, he asked Lilias to fetch some food and drink for Margaret and Sir John, who observed with concern how Margaret had gotten thinner in the last few weeks. She waved it away, despite eating or drinking very little, while he, ravenous from another early rise, ate heartily.

"Have you had word from Fionnsgoth? Do you know where they have taken her?" Margaret asked, trying to keep her emotions subdued.

Sir John finished chewing, took a large swig of beer from his mug, and frowned.

"I am afraid I know very little, my Lady; the sheriff tells me that they returned with Fionnsgoth to the city goal, but when they arrived, he was ordered to hand her to a warden acting on behalf of the Earl of Morton, and they took her away to Aberdour, then and there!"

"My brother? She has gone to Aberdour, Sir John?" she retorted with surprise and fear, now worried. "But why?"

"It appears that there is also a charge on his behalf of...", he stopped, taking a deep breath, "witchcraft against her, which she supposedly practiced while you last visited his estate a few weeks ago."

His estate, thought Margaret; *everyone knows it is not his estate, but mine- and that this is what this horrible state of affairs really concerns!*

"I cannot believe it," she sighed, disbelieving, staring not at him but at his empty plate, for she felt ashamed; he, it seemed, was powerless to do anything to help, and she suddenly realized that her circle of friends and allies was slowly but surely beginning to diminish in size. At least she still had her cousin- he would be able to help, she was sure of it!

"I am sorry to have placed you in a difficult position, Sir John," Margaret finally said. "You have been a kind and trusted ally, and I am most grateful."

He bowed his head, as if in shame, regret furrowing his brow, bringing out the greying temples and crinkled skin that came with age.

"Margaret, I will still do what I can to help; I have dispatched one of my men to Aberdour to search for allies who may have some influence in releasing mistress Fionnsgoth," he offered, un-convincingly, and then confessed, "although, I admit, the Earl's influence is such that this may prove to be difficult- but we will try, nevertheless!"

He rose, holding his hat ready for departure, and tried to re-assure her further.

"I will let you know what I find out as soon as I have news from Aberdour- you have my word!"

Margaret did not reply but smiled as he bowed. She was left alone in the Great Hall, with only the company of a warm fire and the soft crackling of the logs as they burned. She looked out of the large window next to the fireplace; snow had begun to fall, and winter had finally announced her arrival.

*

McAdam, after searching everywhere, had not been able to find Alastair anywhere on the castle estate, and so, when his day of duties was finished, he rode to Kirriemuir to search for the steward at the *Three Bellies Brae*.

Alastair had, in fact, retreated to his usual corner in the Inn soon after Fionnsgoth's arrest. This was not how Rory's trick had meant to turn out! Arrest for witchcraft was serious, and Alastair was beginning to feel afraid. Staring once again into a glass full of amber-coloured comfort, he began to think. There were things that had not made sense; Rory's trick of placing the poppet among Fionnsgoth's possessions was meant to frighten her a little, but nothing more. How did the sheriff come to know about it? The only person who could have told him was Rory- but what would Rory gain from that? He had to find Rory; Alastair might himself be implicated, and that would lead to his own arrest, and God only knew whatever else. He shuddered and took a few slurps of whiskey. Looking out of the window, he could see the snow now falling, a mass of thick flakes gently gliding through the night, the Mercat Cross in the middle of the square a ghostly shape through a fog of eerie calm, until a figure he recognised appeared out of the frozen mist: McAdam.

The coachman was so tall he had to lower his head as he entered into the tavern, stamping his snowy boots on the straw and sawdust floor, bits of both sticking to them instead, to his frustration, for he was a particular and meticulous man when it came to his appearance. After exchanging news with Innkeeper Tulloch, he spotted Alastair, and having ordered his drink, ambled over to the steward and sat down opposite him. It seemed to Alastair that no one ever took the time to be polite anymore, everyone and anyone apparently inviting themselves to sit at his table with or without his leave.

"Well met!" greeted McAdam, half-jesting in response to Alastair's deep frown.

"I looked for you at the estate, but you were nowhere to be found! But here you are," he said, without surprise.

"You are troubled," McAdam added, with a slight question.

Alastair grunted in reply; he had no inclination for chat, and certainly could not speak of his troubles without being untruthful, and did not wish to lie, at least not to McAdam.

"What news of Mistress Fionnsgoth?" the steward asked, instead, as unperturbed as possible.

McAdam looked at him; he had always been grumpy and unpleasant, a lecher partial to the drink, but there was something unsettled about him that was not in his usual character, and he wondered if it had to do with the murder of Effie, or the arrest of Fionnsgoth- or, perhaps both.

The coachman took a small sip of beer. Unlike his companion, he enjoyed the taste, rather than the effects, of his drink, and so he took his time with it when he could afford it.

"Sir John Scrymgeour has been to see Lady Margaret," McAdam replied, looking at Alastair for a reaction.

"I do not think it was a good meeting; I hear Fionnsgoth has in fact been taken away from Dundee, to Aberdour, by the order of the Earl of Morton!"

This prompted a sharp reaction in Alastair, as the words had felt like a sharp knife stabbing his gut; what was supposed to have been a harmless trick was turning into a mess of more serious accusations by the hour. What if they found out his pact with Rory, and he was next?

"Aberdour, you say?" he replied, feigning disinterest. "Whatever has she been taken there for?"

McAdam shifted his thin, bony frame on the hard stool, took another sip of beer, and continued.

"I am not entirely certain, but I hear that the Earl of Morton has accused the mistress of witchcraft during their last visit with him-something about poisoning one of his dinner guests!"

Alastair raised his eyebrow; his heart quickened, as he tried to hide his growing panic. *I must find Rory! This is his doing!*

"What a load of shite," he muttered, gulping down the last of his drink, slamming the glass on the table as if in contempt of the world.

"Another?" asked McAdam, pointing to the glass, but Alastair had already gotten up to leave, and mumbled, "Nay, must be off!"

He stumbled awkwardly out of the Inn, knocking into an equally drunk customer whose friends had to restrain him from giving the steward a swift punch to the gut.

McAdam wondered, as he sipped his beer and looked through the dirty window at the falling snow, what Alastair could be up to, seeing him ride into the night on his horse, away from the long road back to Glamis, instead heading in the direction of Drum Farm.

*

A letter from Dudhope arrived by express messenger the same night, and Margaret now sat, in a disbelieving stupor, by the window in her bed chamber as she read it.

Dear Margaret,

I write in haste, as I received some news at last regarding Mistress Fionnsgoth when I returned to Dudhope; but prepare yourself, what I am about to relate to you is most grave.

One of my men, for the exchange of money, obtained information that Mistress Fionnsgoth has been in custody, and under torture has confessed to the murder of Effie Campbell; I admit, the medical evidence and whereabouts of Fionnsgoth at the assumed time of the murder leave me in doubt as to the honesty and truthfulness of her confession, and rather that she has made such claims to ease further prospects of torture.

However, one Master Matthew Hopkins, a Witchfinder from England apparently sent by William Laud, the Bishop of London, has therefore expedited criminal proceedings with the Kirk in Aberdour, although how the jurisdiction has been shifted from Angus to Fife, I do not know. I can only conclude that, under the patronage of the King and Bishop Laud, this has been approved, though it is highly irregular. What is more puzzling is that the Earl of Morton as of yet shows no opposition to Fionnsgoth's imprisonment and torture, to the accusations against her, or the unusual decision to proceed with a trial in his county.

If I were to convey to you that this were the end of the trail of criminal accusations, I would be untruthful, for my man also informed me that, although Fionnsgoth confessed to the murder, she claims to have acted on instruction from one or more witches. I am certain your acquaintance with me is good enough to understand that I believe that to be complete non-sense- but other events, particularly a visit by yourself and Fionnsgoth to your brother's estate recently, where a guest suffered a mysterious poisoning, and the allegation that you by some means had a hand in the murder of the Duke of Buckingham- add to the incriminating allegations, although credible evidence of this has yet to be presented. But, I must tell you that you must prepare yourself for a charge soon. The Witchfinder will return to Glamis, and his mission is to arrest you.

I am aware that your brother would gain from your imprisonment by obtaining your fortune, which you would have to relinquish; his bargain, I am told, is to withdraw all charges in connection with the Duke of Buckingham's death, and Effie Campbell's murder, and to release Fionnsgoth, should you return the proposal he offered you with your signature, and hand over to him your estate.

I beg of you to take my assurance that no trial for you or Fionnsgoth would proceed seriously without evidence for any of these far-fetched accusations, and such evidence currently has not been presented.

You will have my continued aid and loyalty, Margaret, until Lord Glamis returns- I promise you, the Scottish system of justice will not fail you.

Faithfully yours,

John S., Esq

She read the note again, and again, until each of the letters flowed together into a series of words that made no sense. The tight knot in her chest returned, and she felt dizzy, her thoughts unable to form in a coherent manner.

So, thought Margaret, *it comes to this; I am to bargain for my maid's and my own life with my fortune so my brother may advance his political cause to sell our faith and our ways to the English King!*

She looked out of the window and peered into the night. The stag and his companion had returned, peacefully grazing on patches of grass that cropped up between the blanket of snow that had fallen around Glamis Castle in the last few days. They had still escaped the hunter's bow, she thought, heartened, and it gave her a sense of peace in the lonely stillness of the night. Suddenly resolute, Margaret went to her writing desk, took her quill and paper, and, considering only for a moment, she began to write.

My dear brother William, she scribbled, and after hesitating briefly, the words poured onto the page as easily as if she had been preparing them all her life.

*

McAdam had returned late from the *Three Bellies Brae* the night before, and it was not until the next morning the coachman realized once again, to his utmost vexation, that Alastair could be found nowhere on the estate.

He's probably sleeping off his drunkenness in the company of an unfortunate lass, he thought, knowing his fellow servant's desires in that direction, which often were so uncontrollable that the women he dragged to bed, willing or not, often had no other choice. It had so been up to McAdam to inform the second steward, a young man named Callum, to perform the usual duties in Alastair's absence, a responsibility that Callum appeared to be delighted with, perhaps in the hopes of a more permanent promotion should Alastair never return to Glamis.

There had been no instruction from Lady Margaret, who was equally vexed as to Alastair's absence without her leave, for the need of her carriage that morning, and McAdam therefore took it upon himself to look for the missing steward. As he rode towards the road that would lead him to Drum Farm it was clear where he would begin his search.

Drum Farm was an hour-long ride from Glamis, and, although it was a cold and snowy morning, the sun had appeared, and the ride was pleasant. He thought he would find himself alone on the road, but along the way- less than a half hour from Drum Farm- a group of men, one who McAdam recognized to be from the Constable's office, thundered past him, barely slowing to greet McAdam, as they raced on into the distance. Wondering briefly what they could be doing so far from Dundee, he dismissed his thoughts when he saw an inviting apple tree that had still escaped the pickers and the cold. He stopped briefly, and tore off a few tasty-looking examples, feeding one to his horse and saving the rest for the return journey to Glamis. The sunlight streamed through the leaves and branches of the tree. He looked out over the vast fields and rolling hills before him, and McAdam wished he could stay there forever; it was such a tranquil spot, away from the strife of the intrigues of Glamis, which, by the day, seemed to become more and more complicated and dark.

A falcon swooped down in silence nearby, and somewhere, a shot rang out, causing a rush of smaller birds that had conferenced in a tall oak tree to flee into the skies. *We are either predator or prey,* thought McAdam, *with nothing in between,* and he swung himself back into the saddle, urging his mount onwards towards Drum Farm.

He had almost forgotten about the troop of sheriff's men he had encountered a short while before, when to his surprise, he saw their destination had also been Drum Farm. The farm was recently built, with a large main house set slightly away from the outbuildings, stables, and animal sheds. It was a sizeable estate owned by a cousin of Lord Glamis, the Earl of Angus. As they saw him approach, one of the sheriff's men stopped McAdam, and tipping his hat, he asked politely but sternly:

"Good morrow, Master McAdam, what brings you to Drum Farm?"

Returning the greeting, McAdam dismounted, and tied his horse to a nearby pole.

"Good morrow to you, sir; I come to see Rory Dalmore on some business I have with him."

The sheriff deputy's interest was kindled immediately, and he continued his questioning.

"And what business might that be, Master McAdam?"

McAdam hesitated; he saw a maid weeping as one of the sheriff's men questioned her, awkward in the face of her emotions, while the others conducted a search.

"Has there been an incident, sheriff?"

"One might call murder an incident, aye!"

McAdam, completely dumbfounded, almost stumbled over his words in disbelief.

"Murder? *Murder?* Who?" he demanded.

The sheriff studied him briefly, and having concluded that McAdam's surprise was genuine, and knowing the coachman was an honest and pious man, he relaxed a little.

"Rory Dalmore has been murdered, Master McAdam. And now," he continued matter of fact, "might I again ask what business you had with Rory that brought you all the way to Drum Farm? It is not a short ride from Glamis, so I assume that the business was not of a trifling nature?"

McAdam had to take a minute to absorb the news; another murder, which in his mind rapidly became connected to Effie, and Alastair, and the recent troubles that had beset Glamis.

"Err...," he began to reply, trying to compose himself as his thoughts, now racing through his head, caught up with him, "aye; you are correct. I came to ask him if he knew the whereabouts of Alastair, Steward of Glamis Castle."

The sheriff became more interested now.

"And why would Rory Dalmore have knowledge of Alastair's location?"

McAdam had no wish to cast Alastair in a suspicious light- at least not without good cause- and so replied quickly:

"I saw Alastair at the *Three Bellies Brae* last night... we spoke briefly, and then he left. But instead of returning to Glamis, I saw him take the road to Drum Farm. I assumed it would be to see Rory, unless he had some other...", he paused, slightly embarrassed, "meeting here."

"I see," mumbled the sheriff, thoughtfully. "So, in fact, no one is aware of Alastair's whereabouts?"

McAdam shook his head.

"Unless he has, since I came away this morning, returned to Glamis."

Hesitating again, he asked, almost afraid of the answer:

"How did he die, sheriff?"

The sheriff wrinkled his forehead slightly, frowning as the horrific memory of seeing Rory's body jolted his mind.

"It is a sore sight, McAdam; his throat was slit- not across, but vertically.....and his tongue pulled out through the cut. Next to poor Effie Campbell, it is the most vicious attack I have seen in a long time!"

So, thought the coachman, *the sheriff has made the same connection as I have; two murders that lead back to Glamis Castle!* He shivered.

Seeing McAdam's discomfort, the sheriff, with a kindlier tone, suggested:

"It would greatly help me if you returned to Glamis as soon as possible, McAdam, and send note post haste to let me know if Alastair has returned; and if he has not," he sighed, "we shall have to order a search for him, as it appears that he may have been the last person to see Rory Dalmore alive!"

Without another word, McAdam nodded, untied his horse, and took to the road as fast as his steed could run. The light had darkened, and the sun disappeared, replaced by grey clouds heavy with snow. As the wind picked up in speed, a deep, stinging chill tore at his eyes, and the snow began to fall again.

*

Alastair had not returned to Glamis, to McAdam's dismay, and after enquiring with Duncan and Hamish who also had no clue about the missing steward's whereabouts, McAdam had sent word to Dundee to inform the Constable's sheriff. There was no doubt that a search party would be organized to find Alastair, who was now the prime suspect in Rory's murder, but McAdam could not help an ill feeling in his gut that there was more at work here than Alastair's hand alone could be responsible for. Reluctantly, McAdam had told Margaret about Rory's death- sparing the gruesome details- and she, to McAdam's despair, had appeared distant and almost unresponsive. Feeling restless and uneasy, the coachman had busied himself with repairing the carriages, noting which horses needed a visit from the farrier or horse doctor, and attending to Hamish, whose tasks he supervised from time to time.

By the late evening, Lady Margaret had sent for McAdam in the main hall. She appeared, in an elegant silk button-down gown in deep crimson with a grey trim, a translucent collar covering her chest and neck, so matching her ghostly paleness that they almost seemed one. The dark grey shade under her eyes were evidence of seemingly countless nights of no sleep, and gave her the look of the forlorn maiden waiting for rescue that one sometimes read about in poems and stories. Her bony fingers- which had always been so- seemed even more skeletal, as she slowly descended the main staircase, almost ghost-like, where McAdam stood, waiting. The apparition reminded him of the legend of the ghost of Janet, Lady Douglas, who, after her execution, was said to roam the halls of Glamis in restless anticipation of acquittal. So finely dressed was Margaret that the carriage master wondered if she was expecting a visitor, or had plans to visit someone herself.

"How fare you, McAdam," she attempted with authority but sounding weary instead, inclining her head slightly, and he returned the greeting with a bow.

"Good evening, my Lady. I regret to inform you that I have yet been unable to locate Alastair...I sent word to Dundee, and I expect they will gather a search party to find him. With your permission, I would like to participate, if they require my assistance.... but perhaps you will be in need of the carriage, my Lady?"

She nodded, absentmindedly; between the translucent fingers of her right hand, she held a letter, which she tapped against the wrist of her left hand, as if in anticipation of something.

"May I assist you in sending away the letter you are holding, my Lady? I can fetch Callum for your service, my Lady?" McAdam asked, trying, in vain, to reach her through her thicket of thoughts. But she shook her head and looked at him, with a strange reply:

"No, I thank you, McAdam," she mumbled slowly, "the letter is still being written."

Then, without looking at him, she abruptly placed the letter on a small table by the foot of the stairs; and turning, without further words, she walked slowly up to the landing again, disappearing into the maze of corridors that sprang from all corners.

McAdam was puzzled and curious. *Why did she send for me?* He looked to the table; the letter was addressed to her brother, William, but not sealed. As soon as she was out of sight, he unfolded it, and as he read it, his heart sank heavily, and an anger he had not felt since his wife had been taken from him a few years since rose within him so fiercely that he almost felt, momentarily, that he had gone back to that dreadful moment in time when he had seen his beloved draw her last breath. *William Douglas*, he thought, *if ever the opportunity affords me in life, you will find your final reckoning by my hands!* So angry was he that he almost crushed the letter in his hand; and, worried that another servant would find it, and call for the post, he tucked the letter into his coat pocket, before returning to the stables, a violent and vengeful fury festering beneath the constant appearance of calm and reason for which McAdam was known.

*

McAdam and Hamish worked late into the evening, completing most of the day's chores, before the coach master gave the boy leave for the rest of the night, and he himself, tired from toil and weary with worry at the day's disturbing events, turned into his bed, and fell into a heavy sleep. Although it was deep, it was not restful, his vivid nightmares were so alive and palpable it was almost as if he was still awake in a haunting parallel world.

He woke, almost with relief to be released from the horrible sequence of images that had plagued his slumber, to a rumbling sound, a few hours into the night. At first, he thought it was a distant thunder, but seeing the night was clear and lit by a bright round moon, he realized that it had to be something else. The sound came closer, became louder, a deep, constant rolling murmur until it stopped abruptly. McAdam's bedchamber was on the second storey of the coach house, and the window looked out over the long, tree-lined approach that stretched from the woods up to the castle. The night was freezing, and he pulled his plaid over him as he moved to the window to see what had woken him. In the light of the moon, he could see a cart, driver-less, its horse nervously moving about the driveway, as if lost, or abandoned.

That is not one of our nags, he thought to himself, puzzled. He pulled on his boots and breeches, threw his cloak over his night-shirt, and grabbing a lantern on his way, he went out into the cold night to investigate.

McAdam had been right; the horse, a black mare, was not one of his. She was restless, fearful, the white of her eyes showing, and she breathed hard, the gray plumes of breath spilling from her nostrils in short bursts as the coachman approached her carefully. His heart began to beat faster.

"Steady, lassie, steady, easy does it," he soothed in a calm tone, gently taking her by the reins, and stroking her neck. It was damp with sweat, but her breathing slowly became more regular, and she calmed at the coachman's touch.

"Where is your driver, lass?" he whispered, looking around him; but he neither saw nor heard anyone in the shadows of the bright moonlight. *Something has frightened you,* he thought. He looked over to the cart; a dirty horse blanket covered it, but as he moved closer, he began to see uneven bulges, as if something was hiding under-neath. Holding his lamp up with one hand, he pulled the cover away carefully. The sight that met him was so terrifying it forced him to vomit violently; doubling over, retching at the shock of the smell and the sight of his discovery, he nearly dropped his lantern. The mare whinnied softly, her fear returning as she smelled the rotting, mutilated naked body of Fionnsgoth, her face so distorted it was almost beyond recognition, and what remained of her flesh and bones barely kept her hanging together in one piece. The soft call of the falcon circling above broke the screaming silence, as McAdam stumbled back towards the coach house, half-witless and ill with despair, in search of Hamish, and help.

~ Nine ~

The Office of the Lord Advocate, Edinburgh, on October 25th, 1628

Sir Thomas, looking out over the college green from his office window, wondered if the weather would turn to snow that day. The clouds appeared heavy and grey, and the biting chill of the past few days seemed to be easing a little, although the sun had not yet come out from behind the thick of the fog. The Lord Advocate seldom shrank from any duty, nor was he intimidated by individuals purported to be of higher rank than he, but today, he did not look forward to entertaining the visitor he was about to receive. If only King James had not taken up the offer of being King of England as well as Scotland, Sir Thomas was certain, this religious and political mess- which seemed to spill into all areas of society- would not be on his mind that day, and he would be free to conduct the proper business of the law.

His imminent, and eminent, visitor, Patrick Forbes, Bishop of Aberdeen, was predictable in his anti-popish sentiments, a strict firebrand and upholder of the Kirk's principles to whom the Five Articles of Perth recently endorsed by King Charles had been as close to entertaining blasphemy as possible. The Bishop was also, however, not equally predictable in his willingness to oppose royal decree directly, and so Sir Thomas wondered, amidst his distraction by the persistent interference of that so-called English Witchfinder, about what Patrick Forbes was so eager to speak with him.

An unassuming knock at the door dispersed his perturbed thoughts, which had brought him unexpected irritation.

"Enter!" he said, in a rather more sharpened tone than he had meant, for his young clerk Angus seemed scared as he carefully peeked in from behind the door.

"Beg pardon, Sir Thomas; the Lord Bishop Patrick Forbes has arrived to see you."

With a sigh, Sir Thomas nodded and smiled faintly with guilt at his acidic tone.

"Thank you, Angus; show him in."

A brief moment later, Patrick Forbes entered. He was a tall man with kind brown eyes, a high forehead and oval face surrounded by diminishing grey hair which was completely overshadowed by the large grey beard and moustache that warmed his chin and upper lip, with dark sideburns completing the hairy frame around his face. The Bishop was dressed all in black, save the modest white frilled collar that protruded from under either side of his beard. His cap, also black, covered the remainder of his head, which quite possibly was entirely hairless. Being a man in his late fifties, he was not young but only slightly older than Sir Thomas, and his spirit exuded a youthful energy when he spoke that could match anyone half his age.

"My Lord Bishop," Sir Thomas flattered, "it is a pleasure to have you grace us with your visit!"

The two men bowed in respect; there was an air of tense formality in the Lord Advocate's office that Sir Thomas had hoped to avoid, so he attempted to lighten the mood.

"You have journeyed far, my Lord- may I offer some refreshment to you? I can ask my clerk to bring beer and some food."

But the Bishop was not inclined to be hosted that morning and waved his hand in dismissal.

"I thank you, no, I would rather get to the business at hand, if I may- I must get back to Aberdeen tomorrow, and in addition to this particular visit," he frowned disapprovingly as he spoke, "I have other matters to attend to while I am in Edinburgh."

Disappointed, Sir Thomas agreed.

"Of course, my Lord; as you wish."

He beckoned to the chairs by the window- one of which had hosted the corporeal greasiness of Matthew Hopkins only a few days since- and the two great men of state sat down, postures upright and eyes alert. Sir Thomas noted with relief how the Bishop's manner of comporting himself with the proper posture was so markedly different from that of Master Hopkins' utterly arrogant, disrespectful, sleazy, and quite frankly, disgusting, comportment.

"How may I be of service to you, Bishop?" Sir Thomas asked genially. "I am not certain what matters of the Kirk I may assist you with, as Lord Advocate, but I will certainly help if I am able!"

Patrick Forbes, although polite and diplomatic in his approach, was not shy of being direct, and launched into his problem without reserve.

"I have been informed, Sir Thomas, that we have been plagued with an Englishman who refers to himself as the 'Witchfinder General'," he scoffed at the word bitterly before continuing, "who has taken it upon himself to bandy about accusations against some of our finest nobility, not to mention take actions that are not in his jurisdictional privilege, a gross insult to those of us," he nodded to include Sir Thomas, "who are tasked with properly upholding the regulations of the Kirk and the law!"

So, this is why you have come, thought Sir Thomas, surprised and a little puzzled, *to complain about the presence in Scotland of the irritating Matthew Hopkins!*

The Bishop did not wait for Sir Thomas to interject, but continued forcefully in his speech.

"I am to understand that this 'Witchfinder' is here at the request of the Bishop of London, William Laud," he sniffed, "which, if true, is an even graver problem than I had imagined, Sir Thomas; do you confirm this to be the case?"

Sir Thomas saw no way to answer his question truthfully without being direct himself, and replied:

"Aye, Bishop Forbes, that is indeed the case; the Bishop of London has sent Matthew Hopkins to us, for good or ill."

"Good or ill!" cried the Bishop, now animated and almost angry, only his status as clergy holding him back from pouring out his true, and unyielding disparaging emotions.

"Do you know what further interference from England means for Scotland and the Kirk? *Popery-* that is what it means, Sir Thomas! In addition to kneeling for communion, we shall all soon be forced to make our pilgrimage to the Vatican, desecrate our churches with garish statues of the Virgin and Child, declare the King as the head of the Church, and tell our bairns and grand-bairns that the holy sacrament is in fact the real blood and flesh of Christ!"

He rose, and paced about, continuing his tirade passionately.

"We shall be subjected entirely to English politics and the King's misguided fondness for Catholics, which he has already shown to favour through choosing a French popish woman as his Queen!"

Sir Thomas, who had, admittedly, had similar concerns, nodded sympathetically, but could think of nothing helpful to offer consolation. As far as he knew, unfortunately, there was little power they had to combat these misfortunes; if the King wished to enact his religious and political will on them, they must bear it as well as they could.

"Would King James had never accepted the English Crown- we would not be fearing for our great Scottish way of life! Was the Declaration of Arbroath all for nothing, after all? Robert the Bruce would be turning in his grave!"

The Bishop was now solemn, his fiery youthful enthusiasm taking on the resignation of accepting the inevitable that often came with older age. He had moved to the window, the same that Sir Thomas had opened to relieve the stench of Master Hopkins during his visit, and the clergyman said wistfully:

"Edinburgh is a beautiful city; I have often wished I might be Bishop here, instead of Aberdeen!"

"Aye," replied Sir Thomas, "it is a fair city."

"Let us hope," replied the Bishop, "that it will not be overrun with the English! We must find a way to placate the King, but also keep our systems, Sir Thomas; we must. And what I hear," he went on, in an offended tone, "is that the cousin of the Lord Glamis has fallen under suspicion of some lunatic conspiracy to murder the Duke of Buckingham, a ridiculous accusation which has been brought forth with no apparent shame on behalf of this so-called Witchfinder. It is disgraceful, and we must fight it!"

A ray of light from the sun pierced the window, throwing a sharp white beam across the floor. It looked almost as if the room had been split in two, with the Bishop on one side, and the Lord Advocate on the other.

Sir Thomas agreed, although hesitantly; he feared, as the days went on, that this persecution fell further and further out of their reach and control.

"Aye, Bishop Forbes, I am in agreement there; but," he ventured further, knowing what he was about to say would prompt a backlash from his visitor, "I fear very much that we will be forced to go through the legal procedures surrounding the accusations against Lady Margaret Douglas. I believe the actions of Matthew Hopkins- although abominable in every possible way- are at the direction of Bishop Laud, and indirectly, the King himself!"

"Pah!" snorted Patrick Forbes, once again enraged at the thought of such interference by the English, who, in his mind, would be best left to tending to their own turbulent affairs south of the border.

"I expect any day now, Matthew Hopkins will return with his version of 'proof' and 'evidence' against her," continued Sir Thomas, ignoring his visitor's outburst, "and we shall no doubt have to assemble a jury, and commence with the trial!"

Bishop Forbes almost barked his response, so furious was he at the thought of an Englishman directing a trial against a Scot.

"I dare say I shall offer no assistance in procuring jurors, Sir Thomas! It is an outrage that we have even reached such a low point in our constitutional activities!"

Sir Thomas would also have been more at ease if it had in fact been up to himself to select the jurors, but that task was in the hands of the Lord Justice General, who, knew Sir Thomas, would have in mind his own high favour with the King when he considered who would be most appropriate to serve in the jury.

"I shall be grateful, Sir Thomas," asked the Bishop, now calmer, "if you would keep me informed of these developments; and if the accusations- for whatever preposterous reason- lead to any trial, I should like to know. I am not without influence, and I will not let the craven self-interests of a zealous Englishman defile the hallowed institutions on which this great country of *ours* was built!"

He stuck out his chest and chin in defiance, and his kindly eyes flashed with the glimmer of revenge as he paced past Sir Thomas, his black cloak hissing as it swished with fervour when he stopped by the door. Sir Thomas, understanding that this was the end of their conversation, followed him, replying:

"Of course, my Lord Bishop; I will keep you informed of any activities. I must add, as a matter of personal opinion," he went on, attempting to display a detached tone, "that the evidence presented so far in the case has been feeble, to say the least; I do not expect a conviction, and hope for a speedy acquittal of Lady Margaret."

The Bishop frowned suspiciously, but nodded.

"Aye; this I have also heard. But, Sir Thomas, this plot is devious, and relates to far more than the purported sorcery and wickedness of a woman; there are politics at play, material self-interests, and I fear if those games are played deceitfully, that the veracity of any evidence presented will not have much significance or relevance when it comes to a conviction!"

The Bishop's page had now appeared, ready to attend to his master, and Sir Thomas and Patrick Forbes bowed once again as they bade farewell. The air in the Lord Advocate's office had suddenly become heavier and thicker. Sir Thomas, trying to ignore the dark thoughts Bishop Forbes had left with, wearily sat down behind his desk, for he had a mountain of paperwork to get through. Another knock at the door would, however, prevent him once again from getting back to what he wished to do most, as Angus entered on his command.

"Two letters arrived a short while ago, my Lord; another message from Dudhope, Sir Thomas," he said carefully, placing the letters in front of his master, "and one from Aberdour." The downcast look on the Lord Advocate's face was familiar to the young man, who promptly left his master alone with his thoughts.

Sir Thomas stared at the unopened letters, wondering which to read first. He had no particular desire to know the contents of either of them, for he had a feeling they would not bear good news. *I suppose it makes no difference,* he thought, and broke the gold wax seal of Sir William Douglas.

Lord Advocate, it began,

I write with excitement as I have procured the evidence necessary to bring forth accusations against Lady Margaret of the most heinous crimes of murder and witchcraft. I have a number of witnesses, not least the parents of Effie Campbell, who have confirmed that their daughter professed fears of dark magic at Glamis Castle after the arrival of Lady Margaret Douglas and her servant, Mistress Fionnsgoth. The latter is in custody here at Aberdour, and we are confident that she will soon confess; she has already confirmed that her actions were led by a witch, whose name she has yet to reveal, but, given her situation at Glamis, we can only assume that witch to be Lady Margaret.

I have also procured a letter from Jack Felton, addressed to Lady Margaret, asking for instructions detailing the plot to assassinate the Duke of Buckingham. These three revelations must surely be considered sufficient proof for a conviction, although I have little doubt that more evidence will present itself as I investigate further. Sir William and I hope to travel to Edinburgh tomorrow to discuss with you the necessary procedures.

Matthew Hopkins, Withchfinder-General

By appointment to William Laud, Bishop of London, advisor to His Majesty King Charles I

Sir Thomas had no doubts that the 'evidence' Matthew Hopkins had mentioned in the letter was a result of forged letters, forced confessions under torture, and information obtained through bribery; but he could not prove this, and neither, he feared, could Lady Margaret. Bishop Forbes had been wise in his foresight on this occasion.

He put the letter aside, still open and in view, as he reluctantly broke Sir John Scrymgeour's seal, and, as he read, felt his hopelessness begin to deepen.

Dear Sir Thomas,

I have more grave news from Glamis, and write in haste yet again, as we have not a moment to lose.

Not two days ago, there was another murder; this time, not on the Glamis estate, but at Drum Farm, land owned by a cousin of the Earl of Kinghorne. One of his stewards, Rory Dalmore, was found dead, murdered in a most gruesome fashion, details of which I will relate when I have a report from the doctor. This may seem unconnected to the rest of the sordid affairs that have come to pass at Glamis, but in fact, a witness had seen Alastair, steward of Glamis, in the vicinity of Drum Farm shortly before the murder. Furthermore, Rory and Alastair had been conversing at the Three Bellies Brae in Kirriemuir only a day or two previously. They were overheard speaking of witchcraft, mentioning Effie Campbell and Mistress Fionnsgoth. Although I am not one to engage or believe in hearsay, I believe this warrants further investigation, particularly now, as Alastair has disappeared.

I also write with concern to you, as I was informed, even while penning this letter to you, that the dead and mutilated body of Mistress Fionnsgoth had arrived back at Glamis last night, in mysterious circumstances. I can only assume that she did not survive the torture the Witchfinder General and his men had subjected her to; but as she is now dead, we have only the word of Matthew Hopkins as to what her last words to him were, and I fear that he will claim she accused Lady Margaret of orchestrating this string of crimes, with no one able to refute this statement. I have been told that he will soon make his arrest and have sent word to Lady Margaret to warn her of this prospect.

While I have already begun to make enquiries regarding a suitable lawyer for Lady Margaret's defense, I would be grateful if you could offer help to do the same, as I am not as knowledgeable about the best lawyers in Edinburgh as yourself.

I hope to visit Edinburgh, and if I may, to discuss these serious injustices further with you, in the next day or two; I will send word post haste before my departure.

With respect,

Sir John Scrymgeour, Esq., Constable of Dundee, Dudhope Castle

The nightmare which he had feared since the day Matthew Hopkins had visited him was unfolding with menacing speed, and he, Sir Thomas Hope, Lord Advocate, was at a loss for how to end it. The snow had now begun to fall in thick, regular flakes, coating the green below him and the hills beyond in a soft white blanket; the superficial tranquility, thought Sir Thomas, of a world turned upside down.

*

Glamis Castle, October 27ᵗʰ, 1628

They buried Fionnsgoth the day after she had been returned to Glamis. It was a quiet affair completed early in the morning, at St Fergus. The church stood at the entrance of the Glamis estate, and faced the village, but no villagers paid their respects. Had Lord Glamis been in attendance they would have come out of duty to him, but he was still away, and Fionnsgoth had never been liked in the village, a result of the constant maligning she had been subject to by Effie and Alastair. So, it was McAdam, Lilias, Hamish, Geilis and Margaret who bade the maid her final farewell, as she, covered only in a mortcloth of embroidered velvet, which Lady Margaret had chosen, an expense she had insisted on bearing herself, was lowered slowly into the ground.

By the Spirit of God and through our keeping to godly rules, sin is benumbed and kept in subjection by the faithful during their life, but it always remains working on us, and is never banished or rooted out except by death. Sin is so rooted in our flesh that it never dies until the flesh itself dies: when the corpse dies, sin departs. So by death we are delivered and made free from sin...

The minister motioned for the rest of the funeral party to join him.

Christ, for your might and majesty,
That for our sins shed your blood,
Grant the faithful live and die,
After which receive our souls to you.
Amen.

Lilias wept and wept, Geilis trying to comfort the poor girl as well as possible. Hamish and McAdam stood by, heads lowered, as Lady Margaret took a handful of soil, and threw it over Fionnsgoth, before she nodded to the minister, and began the walk back to the castle, alone. *Blood for blood,* she thought, bitterness rising within her, *that is to what this must come.*

It was the Iron Maiden that had finally killed Fionnsgoth. Lady Margaret recognized the deep, evenly spaced punctures, too large to be from the pricking of a bodkin, amidst countless other horrifying injuries her dear friend had suffered. Now sitting in her bedchamber, she wondered: if she had not consented for Matthew Hopkins to have taken the dreadful device away with him, might Fionnsgoth still be alive? *What if all of these events are a result of my actions, after all? Would any of these deaths have happened, had it not been for my resistance to give in to my brother's demand for my inheritance?*

No! She took herself back; this was not her doing: this was the work of evil, manipulation and greed by her brother, whose only interest in life was to advance his status with the King.

Margaret suddenly remembered the letter she had begun to William some days earlier; where had she put it? She scrambled around her desk but found nothing; she wished she had not taken that potion to calm her nerves which Mr Johnstone had prescribed for her- she had lost her memory from that day, or most of it. *Think,* she encouraged herself- she remembered seeing McAdam by the stairs, the letter in her hand; but then, what did she do with it?

"Lilias," she shouted, frantically ringing her bell, not thinking her new maid would not be back, "Lilias!"

A parlour maid finally appeared, and Margaret asked her to fetch McAdam to the Great Hall.

The coach master appeared not long after Margaret had sat down by one of the windows in the Great Hall. McAdam bowed as she walked over to him, but she did not greet him, instead demanding haughtily:

"The letter you saw me with the other day, on the stairs- do you know where it is? I cannot find it, and I am certain I did not ask for it to be sent!"

McAdam hesitated slightly, rapidly trying to think of a reply that would not make him seem untrustworthy.

"Yes, my Lady," he replied, taking the letter out of his pocket, and handing it to her, "you had left it on the table, and fearing someone would take it before it was finished, I kept it safe."

She snatched it from him, and read it again, almost feverishly, as if she had never read it before; then she sat down in her chair by the fire. Without looking at him, she asked:

"Did you read it, McAdam?"

Giving no consideration to whether it mattered if he told the truth or whether he lied, he nodded.

"Yes, my Lady; I confess, I did. But I did not mean to intrude on your privacy. I-", but he was not allowed to finish.

"I am glad you did, McAdam; there has been no one other than my cousin, who is always away, that I have found I could confide in about my – predicament."

She glanced at him, and saw for the first time a man, a good, honest man, who had found loyalty over greed; and she understood why her cousin had kept him in his service all these years.

"And what did you think of my decision, McAdam?"

The coachman felt the air in the Great Hall suddenly to be thick and a little suffocating; he regretted his curiosity at having read the letter.

"I cannot judge your actions, my Lady; how you live your life is your privilege."

For the first time in a long while, she smiled, and almost laughed.

"But is it, McAdam? My brother would have it differently; he takes away what my privilege- all I love and hold dear- would be until I have only my own flesh and bones in my possession!"

The letter was still in her hand, and she began to read it out loud.

William, I have thought long about your proposal, and in honest, your methods at attempting to take from me what you know to be rightfully mine so you may increase your favour with the King have offended the deepest of my sensibilities. Our mother, God rest her, would be ashamed at your greed and manipulation; my father, were he still alive, would have banished you from the estate long ago.

Unlike you, however, I value my friends and my family above my fortune or ambition, and it is for this reason that I agree to your proposal. I will sign any deeds once Fionnsgoth has been returned to me safely, and once I have assurance that you, and Matthew Hopkins, have withdrawn your accusations against me. Beyond that, I will have nothing to do with you, and shall call you my brother no more.

The two stayed silent for a moment. Margaret peered out of the window for an answer, and McAdam, uncomfortable and hot, stared at the intricately decorated carpet under his feet.

"Well, McAdam, what say you? Was I right, under the eyes of God, in writing this letter?"

"Only God can judge, my Lady", he answered, and seeing his discomfort, she sighed, took a last look at the letter, and threw it into the fire.

"If my brother believes he will have even a single handful of soil from my estate, he is mistaken! He can do his worst! He already has," she exclaimed. She was angry, and flushed, a colour returning to her cheeks that McAdam had not seen since the first visit of Matthew Hopkins.

Reaching into a pocket inside her breast, she held out another letter, this time sealed with her initials, and offered it to him.

"Please, McAdam, make certain that the Earl of Morton gets this letter as soon as possible; and then, we must prepare for his retribution."

She sighed. "He has murdered Fionnsgoth- perhaps not with his own hands, but he is responsible! And," she continued, almost a little frightened, "if he is capable of that without scruple, then only God knows what lengths he is prepared to go to in order to achieve his ambitions!"

McAdam gently took the letter from her, bowed, and did as she had instructed.

She looked out of the window again. In the gardens, Margaret could see Bal running about with the dogs, teasing the poor creatures, who, gentle as they were, did not seem to mind, as she pulled their tails and ears, and they nipped her heals and licked her face in return. *There are things I must arrange,* she thought, *before it is too late,* and she hastened back to her bed chamber, and her writing desk.

*

My dear Canagan,

As I sit here, holding your favourite book, I hope and pray that you are safe. I have had no other news, since your father's death, and maintain my faith that you still live.

My days are coming to an end- I will not recount to you here the long and terrible injustice I have faced but beg you to please accept that I am ready to face our Maker, and endure whatever difficult journey that will take me to Him.

There is a task you must take upon yourself, but first, you must understand that what I am about to tell you is as much a confession of a sin, as a plea for your aid.

The news of your father's death destroyed me; my grief was then, as it still is, beyond any sorrow I thought I could ever feel. I found myself longing for a feeling that would bring me back to the glorious love that he and I had, and so, I confess to you, I found a brief respite from my grief in another man's arms. He was a visitor from another land, one who brought the news of your father's death; here one comforting day and night and gone the next. But he did not part without leaving me with the most beautiful gift- your sister, Isobel, now seven years of age, and a likeness of you I cannot describe! She has been a secret within this household and does not even know herself that she is my daughter.

Visits from His Majesty's Witchfinder General began only a month ago, and I feared she would be taken from us. He is a cruel man, blinded by greed and zeal, and plays mercilessly on the Stuart hatred of the Douglas name. To protect her, for I know that they will come for me any day now, I will send her away to Germany. You must promise me to find your sister, and to protect her as you would protect me; I fear that the General's persecution of me will not end his or the King's thirst for Douglas blood.

Fare well, my son, and although we will not meet again in this world, your father and I will see you in the next; in pastures greener, under a brighter sun, and cloudless skies.

Yours ever loving,
M.

Margaret stared at the letter for a brief moment, before she sealed it with her ring. She could not quite believe that she would never see her son again, and a deep and sudden pain twisted her heart, as she clenched her tightening chest amid sobs and slumped briefly over her desk. But she composed herself quickly before slipping the letter into a secret panel in the binding of the book. It was the first printed copy of George Buchanan's *De Jure regni apud Scotos*, which had been passed down to her from her father, Archibald, who she had hardly known. If only he had lived beyond her childhood, and her mother still lived, life would now have been quite different.

*

In the deep and dark of the night, through the thick of the falling snow, Margaret could see the caravan of lanterns approaching along the long avenue, orange and red flames dancing in the pitch black of night like a great march of fire, as if carried by a magical spell: they were coming.

The boy, Hamish, had been good to warn Margaret; he had spotted the trail of wardens on his way back from Kirriemuir, and she knew that time was short. Most of the servants were on their leisure day, and so, only Lilias and Bal remained. Seeing the men approaching, Margaret hurried to Bal's room; the child was sleeping so peacefully, unaware of the torment and upheaval the innocent girl would soon be put through. Gently, Margaret pulled out the child's trunk and hastily, and as quietly as she could, began to fill it, throwing in clothes and toys, and other necessities. A long and tiring journey was ahead of them, but Margaret had no other choice. She jumped slightly as she heard a low voice behind her.

"My Lady, what are we to do? They are coming over the horizon!"

Margaret whispered softly, as soothingly as she could in her state of panic:

"They are almost here, Lilias; they are coming for me- I cannot escape now, but you can, and you must! Take Bal with you- there is so little time!" she whispered.

"The carriage is ready for you- all is arranged. McAdam will take you- he has instructions. He and Hamish will look after you until you are on the ship!"

Lilias began to weep, softly, aware she might wake the child; where were they to go?

"Ship? Where do we go to, my Lady? And why do you not come with us? You will be doomed if you stay here; they will send you to your death!"

Margaret shook her head violently.

"They will find me- the General has spies everywhere, and he is a determined man. If I go with you, we are all for the fire- and

I will not allow you to be taken with me! You must go and save yourselves and Bal!"

She grasped Lilias by the shoulders, and pleaded:

"Please, do this for me!"

Bal stirred gently, waking, aware of the commotion; Margaret did not soothe her, but began to dress the half-asleep child, while Lilias finished packing her trunk. Hamish appeared, eyes wide with excitement, out of breath.

"Take the trunk, Hamish, good lad!" she demanded; Margaret could feel the time pressing on, against them, and, taking the tired child by her arms, began to lead Bal and Lilias down the stairs through the Lower hall and the crypt, Hamish following not far behind. They stopped briefly at the end of it, and to Lilias' wonder, her Mistress had suddenly unlocked a secret door! Down, down, and further down more stairs they went, as if looking for a dungeon, but as the air became colder and wetter, suddenly another long, low passage appeared. Margaret was almost running now, dragging Bal and Lilias behind her, until they reached an arched opening. They were in the ice-house, the dark stains of Effie's blood still tainting the floor, and by the entrance, McAdam was waiting, as Margaret had promised.

Hamish appeared a few minutes behind them; he was excited, scared.

"They are almost by the front gate, my Lady!" he warned. "And there are so many of them- at least twenty! I think the General would bring the entire town with him! Most hate him so much, but he still found so many followers!"

His young face was flushed, and his eyes narrow in fear.

"Why is Sir John not helping us and where is Lord Glamis?"

Margaret stroked his arm to calm the boy; she would miss him. Hamish had a true and kind heart.

"This is beyond the Constable's power, Hamish; he has done all he can .... and my cousin has been detained elsewhere, but I know he will help us; I know it," she tried to reassure him.

She clasped both her hands around his and shook it warmly.

"Thank you, Hamish; thank you for everything you have done for us! And I am sorry- truly sorry- for all of this!"

Holding onto Bal, who was still half asleep, Margaret pushed some notes into the coachman's hands, and said:

"McAdam, my undying thanks to you, also; I owe you a debt of gratitude that I will never be able to repay. When you return, Lord Glamis will be waiting for you, and he will reward your unwavering loyalty! But now you must go- go, while there is still a chance they will not come after you!"

Lilias attempted to keep calm but cried, and gave her mistress a warm embrace. Bal, who was now more awake, was stirred by the commotion, and asked:

"Aunt, where am I? Where are we going?"

"My dearest," replied Margaret, "you must go with Lilias- you are going on a big adventure to see your uncle in Germany- you remember him!" She kissed the child, a hot cheek meeting her cold lips, and handed her to McAdam. The gentle giant placed her in the carriage, with a cushion to ease her, and Lilias followed.

A throng of voices were carried over the strengthening wind, and Margaret knew that her jailors had arrived.

"I must go," she said, "fare well, and God's speed!"

As the coach drew away Bal began to scream, her matchstick arms flailing as Lilias tried to calm her, tiny fists banging against the window, red, tear-torn eyes staring at Margaret in fear, and hatred.

Not looking back, Margaret disappeared along the passage, not running now, but walking, the sorrowful song she had heard at her brother's banquet haunting her at every step.

That woe is me, poor child, for thee
And ever mourn and may
For thy parting neither say nor sing,
Bye bye, lully, lullay

~ Ten ~

Edinburgh Castle, in the goal, October 29th, 1628

Margaret woke in a darkness. The air around her was thick and musty and only a thin ray of light slowly began to appear through the narrow slits posing as windows under the low vaulted ceiling. It caused her eyes to adjust only slowly to her surroundings as she squinted to focus her obscured vision. A sharp and blinding ache at the base of her neck shot through her temples and pierced her eyes whenever she tried to move. Raising herself up from the hard wooden bench on which she lay was nearly impossible without feeling excruciating pain over her entire body. She remained motionless, lying on her back facing the ceiling, and tried to collect her scattered and fragmented thoughts to piece together memories of how she had come to end up in this place made only of nightmares.

The memories came in flashes of horror. They had used methods of torture the terror of which were beyond imagination, the most insufferable being the waking treatment; but for now, at least, it seemed she had escaped the horror of the rack, or the Maiden.

She had lost track of all time. Days, perhaps, had gone by; she could not know. She felt sharp, short bursts of hunger pierce her stomach, and her mouth was dry with the taste of iron and blood. Her tongue, still pierced by the scold's bridle, felt like an old piece of bloody cotton. The cold of winter swept through the windows above her, haphazardly dusting the walls with a fine layer of powdery frost, and although there was a large, grand fireplace in her

131

cell, it had not been lit, and the firewood now lay in a heap next to it, black and white and musty with rot.

Her body was so cold, her blood so frozen, she wished she had remained unconscious, unfeeling; her head was throbbing with the metal spokes of the bridle digging into her neck and the inside of her mouth, but at least her tongue was now numb from pain.

The irregular, rectangular room of the vault was large, with only one entrance by a set of stairs. The door was an old, heavy gate of oak and iron. A small opening with a shutter was located at the bottom of it, by which a tray with some water, a bowl of foul-smelling stew, and a bannock had been left. A mouse or two had already helped themselves, but Margaret, so frozen and hungry, needed some kind of nourishment to fend off the icy cold. She mustered her strength, and staving off the pain, gathered the the food and returned to the hard bench.

She managed to pour some of the foul stew into her mouth through the metal grid of the bridle, and although most of it spilled onto her dirty shift, it was welcome nourishment. It was still lukewarm, despite it being so utterly vile she nearly vomited. She was still in disbelief that on her head she had the scold's bridle. She, once a Lady of consequence, would-be Countess of Angus and Baroness Eythin!

She looked over through the slit that posed as the window. It faced the city, Edinburgh, below and beyond, the seemingly endless North Crags, sharp, ragged snow-covered rock stood guard over vast oceans of green, beige and brown lands, with the iron-grey waters of the Firth in the distance. In the early morning light, the orange and crimson flames of the sun flooded the autumn landscape, interrupted by a long grey or white cloud, here and there. In the distance, the unknown and the unseen, safety beckoned her. But she had no means of escape; there was no one who would, or could, help her now for fear of risking their own lives.

The door opened slowly, but Margaret was so exhausted she did not care. *Should you be a visitor or executioner, I will welcome you both.*

"Lady Margaret!"

It was the voice of Sir John Scrymgeour, and on hearing it, her heart leapt as if she had been reunited with a long-lost beloved. Still, she did not move from the window, her back turned to him, rather in embarrassment at her hideous appearance, than in indignation or fear.

"Sir John."

She had not meant it to be so, but her tone was stiff, unfeeling, mechanical; a polite exaggeration of courtly propriety.

'What brings you to this.... exclusive part of the castle? I hope," she smiled wryly, awkwardly, as far as the bridle would allow her, when she finally turned to face him, "that you have not come to offer your help or consolation?"

She had to work hard to sound as though the burning sores in her mouth were of no consequence, and imagined herself at Glamis, in a silk gown, clean-smelling and presentable as a lady of her status should be, rather than the horrific apparition that now stood before him: back slightly bent in agony, her mouth encrusted with dried blood and yellow puss, as she moved closer to him, away from the window.

"I require neither."

Her pale eyes rested briefly on his; there was an aloof calmness which John Scrymgeour, his own eyes wide open at the horror of her injuries, had great difficulty in comprehending.

"Lady Margaret," he asked in open despair, "what have they done to you?"

"What they do to all women who are branded a witch," she swiftly retorted, and gesturing with her arms to her own appearance, "as you can see, no methods have been spared!"

He moved closer to her, thinking he could make her understand the desperate nature of her situation.

"You must think of yourself and your family! Do you not understand? There is still time to negotiate with the Earl of Morton- if he sees you, and the abominable treatment the General has cursed you with, he will surely withdraw his claims against you!"

Margaret sighed; she was so weary. She did not move, but only retained her fixed gaze.

"Death will come to me, today, or another," she almost whispered, for her tongue was so swollen and painful, the words came out in parts rather than in whole.

"All I had dear in my heart I have lost, and whether I live or die is of no consequence; as long as my brother is denied what he wants, and those I love are safe, I will meet death with courage, in whatever form it comes!"

Sir John paced around the room to release the negative energy of his anger, agitated, with his hands behind his back, staring at the floor, and then out of the window. It looked to be a bright day; it was bitterly cold, but the clouds had lifted, and the skies were blue.

"Do you know what they will do to you? It is much worse than what they have already done to you; the scold's bridle and the ducking chair- those are only instruments of humiliation, Margaret!"

She did not react, other than flinching slightly as the memory of that humiliation revisited her.

"You forget the waking torture, Sir John; that is their favourite method," she added, matter of fact and cold, "or it may perhaps be the leg weights."

He shook his head in disbelief.

"The pain," he almost swallowed the word as he tried to contain his emotions, pausing slightly to compose himself, "the *pain*, that is yet to come; the fire, Lady Margaret! They will send you to the fire! And I have heard rumours that they will dispense with the usual courtesy and subject you to the fire while you are still alive ...", but he was not allowed to finish. Margaret laughed, contorting her face in agony as she pulled her torn lips upward, smiling at the ironic stupidity of such rules; justice did not have a meaning when it came to witch trials. Anyone accused was as good as dead or banished, either by drowning or by burning, after a long stint of the waking torture and a stretch on the rack.

"Please, Margaret!" Sir John pleaded; his normally resolute and forbidding countenance had softened into a deep desperation.

"If you admit to some wrongdoing there is still a chance that your noble birth will spare you! Make peace with your brother; I am certain he will spare you if you agree to his proposal!"

Margaret, not being able to laugh for the pain, chuckled hoarsely instead, pulling up one side of her mouth before relaxing it as the torment caught up with her.

"Do not make a mockery of my intelligence or my emotions, my dear Sir John! *I* have done nothing wrong! The Stuarts have always had a hatred for my side of the Douglas blood; since the days of my great-grandmother has the royal family persisted in our persecution. My judgement is now in the hands of Master Hopkins and my brother- you know as well as I that this can only end in one way!"

As she uttered the last words, the heavy oak doors creaked open, and two prison guards entered with a third man. He was taller than the guards, gaunt and serious but with a kind eye; his dark skin and raven-black hair, slightly greying at the temples, suggested he had come from a place far from the Crown Lands.

"My Lord," grunted a guard, ignoring Margaret entirely, as if she were of no consequence at all, "the physician is here to attend to the prisoner."

The physician bowed to both of them, but Sir John's anger was so hot that he, in a manner so unlike his usual self, barked back at the guard without hesitation.

"Guard, it is not *I* who need attending to! And address a lady of nobility in the proper manner a stinking lowly creature such as yourself is expected to! What fools the courts appoint to do their guarding these days! I wonder who gave you this duty, guard, for I cannot believe it was Sir Thomas! You," Sir John snarled, "are fit for nothing more than the gutter!"

The guard said nothing but pulled a cruel smile. A white frock and chains were presented to Margaret by one guard, and a sharp barber's knife fell out of the pocket of the other. She, who had been trying to stand as upright as possible, began to feel weak at the thought of what would come. The guard quickly retrieved the knife before replying coldly, but with a tone pretending to mimic the tone of the upper classes:

"It is time to prepare Lady Margaret for trial, my Lord."

Throughout the interchange, the physician had remained quiet. Margaret had shot a glance in his direction; she could see that he was distressed by her appearance, but no doubt felt unsure, as a foreigner, about his place and did not dare to speak.

Sir John laughed sardonically at the guard.

"Lady Margaret is hardly fit to stand trial in her current state, you fool!"

"I have my orders, my Lord," returned the guard, smiling now, "orders from above!"

"Above?" Sir John was determined to beat him down, but the guard remained as fixed in his manner as when he had first stepped into the chamber.

"The Lord Justice General, sir; but," the guard offered, knowing that Sir John would have no such recourse in reality, "if you wish to take the matter up with him, I will be pleased to show you the way to his good office!"

The physician stared at the floor but seeing Margaret nearly doubled over, he offered her his arm to steady her.

"Allow me to help you, my Lady," he said quietly, gently easing her into a chair.

"What has Scotland become," lamented Sir John, still angry, shaking his fist at the guards, "if we are to leave our fate in the hands of those who condemn others so easily to advance their own prospects!"

He grabbed his hat and moved towards the door, pushing the guards out of the way, one nearly drawing his sword, but the other holding him back with a scornful look.

"Margaret, I will seek to delay the trial; but I beg of you, for the sake of your House, consider what I have said to you! It does not need to end here!"

The guard, who could not resist a final insult as Sir John departed, snorted with a half-smile:

"Nay, it does not end here, but with the fire!"

Both guards laughed, slapping each other on the shoulders as if they had cracked a hilarious joke. Margaret felt as if something dear had been torn from her with Sir John's absence; she wondered if she would see him again.

The physician, himself feeling exhausted by the brief commotion, bowed again to Margaret, who smiled faintly back at him.

"I am Galenius, my Lady, at your service. Would you please allow me to attend to your health?"

She nodded, only gently; she could feel the spikes of the bridle digging into her neck. To her disappointment the numbness that had comforted her before had gone.

"May we remove this.... contraption, guards? I wish to inspect her mouth and her head before you take a knife to it," he asked politely, but sternly; but they declined, neither of them having the necessary instrument to remove the branks.

"Very well," uttered Galenius, who gently dabbed a cloth with some foul-smelling potion on the areas of her face and the parts of the inside of her mouth that he could reach, Margaret flinching at the odour and the stinging touch.

"What lands have you travelled from, sir?" she whispered as he attended to her wounds.

"I am from Syria, my Lady," he replied, half-truthfully; she did not need to know his true origin. His expulsion from Spain, although fifteen years earlier, was a memory still so fresh to him it seemed like it had only been yesterday; and the pain of that memory was still too raw.

She spoke softly and in short bursts to spare her tongue.

"I hear it is beautiful there," she said, pausing for strength. "I met a man from Syria some years ago.... he travelled with my husband's regiment in Germany... he came here," she mumbled, "with some other soldiers, to tell me of my husband's death."

Galenius looked up briefly but did not reply.

"My condolences on the death of your husband, my Lady," he offered, "that is a difficult burden to bear."

She went on, ignoring his sympathies.

"There are not many Syrians in Scotland, as I am sure you are aware, but perhaps you would have heard of him? I am afraid I can only remember his first name- my memory has failed me so in the last few weeks. His name was Noureddine."

Galenius continued quietly for a short while, before replying:

"I do not think I am acquainted with him, my Lady," he lied, finishing the last of his tasks; but he could see that she did not believe him.

"I would speak with you alone, physician," she whispered, so low he could almost not hear.

He glanced briefly at her face; her eyes were desperate, but why should they not be? She was here, in a prison, no doubt her last abode on earth; she would be sent to the fire. Galenius shuddered at the thought, his own memories haunting him; he could not ignore her plea.

"Guards, for the sake of propriety, please leave us for some moments; I need to perform some very intimate examinations in private."

"Orders are to keep an eye on you and the prisoner!" one of them replied harshly.

"Of course," the physician agreed in a calm tone, "but I also have my orders, jailor; and I am unable to fulfill these if I cannot examine the prisoner in full. And," he continued, as if speaking to a stupid child, "social proprieties, as they are, will not allow me to conduct a complete examination of the prisoner in your presence. So," he finished as the jailor was about to reply, "either you will leave me alone to perform my duties properly, or I shall have to report to my superior- who is none other than the Lord Advocate- that the prisoner is not fit for trial," he smiled, "in which case, good sirs, we may be here some time!"

The guards looked at each other, skeptical of the physician's intentions, but not appealed by the thought of a long wait, or a harsh rebuke from the Lord Advocate, they agreed.

"Five minutes, then, physician- no more! We'll be waiting outside!"

"You have my gratitude," Galenius nodded feigning appreciation, and they plodded, still hesitant, out of the door, the great chains of the keys clanging as the key turned in the lock.

"Yes, my Lady, how can I help you?" he asked, once he was certain they were out of earshot.

She got up from the chair in which he had attended to her, and slowly walked over to a small desk in the corner of the cell. Pulling out the drawer, she felt for something, and eventually drew out a small parcel.

"There are so few people I can trust, physician. I need to send this parcel to Germany- can you help me?" As she spoke, she felt dizzy again, and Galenius helped to lower her back into the chair.

"But you do not know me, my Lady; why do you trust me?"

She smiled briefly, forgetting there were sharp metal bars that kept her mouth shut, and winced softly.

"Your eyes," she replied, "they have truth and honesty; please, will you help me?"

He looked at her, and the parcel she was holding; there was no risk for him, as such, as he had never been searched when leaving a prison, only when entering one. But he still felt uncomfortable.

"May I ask what it is, my Lady?" he asked, nodding to the parcel.

"It is a book- my son's favourite book, sir; there are many who say he is dead, but I know he is not! I feel it in my heart. There is a letter with the book- if you can help me so that it reaches Germany, I will be able to go to the fire in peace!"

Galenius looked at her; such resignation before death, almost a welcome prospect of tranquility after days, or perhaps weeks, of enduring such horrors. He nodded.

"It would be my honour, my Lady, to help you, if I can."

Relieved, she took his hand.

"I thank you, Galenius!"

The sound of chains clinking at the door warned them of the guards' return, and Galenius managed to slip the parcel into his medicine bag unseen, just as the two soldiers appeared.

"I have tended to her wounds as well as I can," he remarked coldly, "but I would like to stay for the shaving," Galenius insisted, as one guard grabbed Margaret by the hair, pulling her head about as he scraped the knife across her scalp, beautiful long auburn hair sliding to the floor, blood spilling from her thin white skin and spattering the stone and the white frock she wore.

"Must you be so harsh?" snapped Galenius, angry at seeing the blood spill from the long cuts as they slashed the skin.

"They say you are a Jew," the jailor sneered aggressively. Brandishing the blood-stained knife, and spitting at Margaret, he threatened, "I could leave you in here with her, if I wished! So, shut your trap and keep to your work, Jew, and I will keep to mine!"

Galenius, with hard eyes fixed on the guard as he continued his work, remained silent. *You will get what you deserve*, he thought, *God will see to that!* As they left the chamber, Galenius glanced back at Margaret, her hands and feet in chains, and the scold's bridle now loose around her shaven head; she looked a figure from a terrifying nightmare. An owl had settled by the window, watching as they left, peering mournfully at the auburn hair and small, rust-red pools of blood that remained scattered on the cold stone floor.

*

"What has she got on her head, Master Hopkins?"

Justice Gordon MacDonald, an old hand on the bench of the Court of Justiciary, was irritated, but the General, looking rather pleased with himself, took no notice, and responded enthusiastically, and somewhat too condescendingly:

"It is a scold's bridle, or the branks, if it please the court-", but he was not allowed to finish as the Justice interrupted him bluntly.

"I know very well what it is, Master Hopkins; my question was posed in a manner which I had hoped you would understand to be rhetorical. Have it removed from the accused, immediately!"

Matthew Hopkins did not understand.

"Removed, my Lord?"

A long and loud sigh echoed around almost the entire court chamber as the judge realized he might as well have spoken to a witless child.

"How, if she wears a contraption that suppresses her tongue, Master Hopkins, will she be able to present her case, so that the members of the jury might be able to pass judgement on this ludicrous affair?"

"But, my Lord, if she is able to speak, she may put a spell upon you, upon all of us, and I c-", but again, he was cut short. Raising his voice slightly, Justice MacDonald uttered in clear, sharp words:

"This court is losing patience, Master Hopkins; remove the implement around the head of the accused, or this court shall hold you in contempt!"

The General, now so accustomed to gaining favour from almost everyone- at least in England- as a purported member of the King's most inner circle of advisors, with eyes now narrowed in disapproval, approached the accused reluctantly. There was a stuttering silence as he produced a set of keys and fobs at the end of a long chain, fingering them in a familiar way until he, reluctantly, found the correct one. He unscrewed the bolts first on either side of Margaret's mouth, then proceeded to unfix those on top of her head, which released a spiked metal brace that was digging into her neck. No blood appeared, but deep crimson impressions appeared in a regular pattern around her throat. Finally, he loosened the screws around the mouth guard, releasing the tongue depressor, which was made of a metal bit with a sharp edge; as he yanked the device off her head with no pretense of caring, dark blood trickled down the side of her mouth. They stained her teeth as she gulped silently, though she uttered no sound of pain. She merely stared defiantly into the crowd; some spectators cheered, a few fainted, and most gasped in horror. The release of pressure around Margaret's head caused her to feel dizzy, everything around her swaying as if she was on an unsteady ship in a wild storm. She had worn the device for four days now, and, unable to eat or drink much, her senses had been so numbed that she had almost forgotten it was there. Almost, but not quite; only the previous day, the General had paraded her around parts of the city in the ducking stool, before gathering a large crowd of supporters at the water of Leith, where he had attempted to drown her. She could still feel the water as she was plunged into the sea, gagging her mouth and strangling her lungs as the freezing liquid bit her naked skin. The only warmth she had briefly felt was the small gush of urine that had escaped from her at the shock of her body meeting the ice-cold winter sea. She wished she had drowned; then her innocence would have been proven, and she would be spared from this disgusting and humiliating ordeal, this horror of a so-called trial, this ridiculous theatre performance disguised as justice.

"Other than the branks, Master Hopkins, has the accused been subjected to methods of torture?" MacDonald snapped, disapproving; he had become increasingly exasperated with the General's supercilious bullying and arrogant ways. The judge was a puritan in the interpretation of Scottish legal writings, and strictly adhered to the realms and limitations of the law as it had been written. Any deviation he would frown upon, and if egregious enough- as he supposed was certainly the case with the complaint against Margaret Douglas - the judge would even use it against the plaintiff's council. Even more so than the flexible application of the law, he abhorred violence, in any form, for whatever reason, particularly the use of torture.

Hopkins was, his character taking the reflection of Narcissus in almost every aspect, at this stage, unsure of his status in the eyes of the judge. But once again, his unwavering self-assurance got the better of him, and believing himself to have impressed the judge favourably- for who but the lowest of the low would consider the General anything but a learned and respectable man who wished only to rid the world of the devil's work?- he stated:

"The *prisoner*," he stressed the word particularly, "as is customary with those accused of the most heinous and blasphemous of crimes associated with witchcraft, has been the subject of *testing* means!"

He paused dramatically, scouring his audience with a raised eyebrow, authoritatively waving a quill in the air which served no particular purpose. No one spoke or uttered a sound in the large chamber, and he took a moment or two to savour the power he held over his captive crowd, before he went on.

"To determine the truth, such measures deemed necessary may perhaps have shown so forceful as to be penetrable not only to the soul, but also to the flesh!"

He had gotten well into the diatribe he was delivering, as if preaching in front of a congregation of devout believers, and continued. "With success, I might add, as the prisoner has confessed.....", he claimed, triumphantly; but Margaret interrupted him with a loud snort and half-laughed, as far as she was able to without feeling the need to vomit with pain. But Justice MacDonald, observing both accuser and accused, had become intolerant of Hopkins' childish display, and cut him off violently.

"I will not be lectured to in my own chamber of court, or listen to unproven nonsense! Sit down, Master Hopkins, and curb your tongue, and do not speak again until you are addressed by me; council," he nodded toward the General's lawyer, "instruct your client in the proper ways of the Scottish courts, and remind him that excessive torture of the accused, whatever he may have been told, does not put him in a favourable light in my chambers- or I shall with my own bare hands throw you both into the Tollbooth for wasting the Court's time!"

He sniffed angrily, and despite his advanced age, his acidic tone could still command a respectful silence in the court room.

"This is not the Bedlam, Master Hopkins; and we are not in London, where your brutal ways may be mistaken for some notion of justice! We are in Edinburgh, and this is the Court of the Justiciar-true justice, where proper procedures, through facts and evidence, shall determine the guilt or innocence of anyone accused; *our* God," he spoke slowly and loudly, looking down at Hopkins, "is very particular about this!"

The council bowed deeply; the General, deflated, but seething with anger, stared narrowly at the judge, before taking his seat in silence in his allocated pew, unfeeling of its hard discomfort. Only the sound of a clerk of laws nervously shuffling papers somewhere in the recesses echoed quietly over the pale and cold walls of the chamber, and only a single daring spectator dared to utter a muffled and unassuming cough.

*

The Office of the Lord Justice General, Edinburgh, October 30th, 1628

Lord Graham, 7th Earl of Menteith, was not a man who invested unnecessary sentiment into the predicament of his fellow human. Having that year been appointed the Lord Justice General, his seat on the Privy Council of Scotland had also been extended by King Charles to the Privy Council of England; so, he, Lord Graham, believed himself to be sufficiently elevated in society to be exempt from caring for the needs of those he deemed to be below his own status.

It was this thought that occupied his mind when Sir Thomas Hope, with who he had demanded an audience, arrived, in Graham's opinion, rather weary-looking and downbeat.

"My Lord," said Sir Thomas, with an overly deferential bow that was perhaps insincere, but which his host reveled in, for Lord Graham was fond of all deference towards him, regardless of which form it took.

The Lord Justice General's mean and utterly heartless outlook on life was not reflected in his outward appearance. He had deceptively kind brown eyes and an average nose that presented a symmetrical centre in an oval face, and bore long, receding hair the colour of honey. A modest, pointed beard and upward-turned moustache surrounded his chin and thin, pale lips. A collar of the finest lace covered his neck and spread across the shoulders of his dark blue doublet, which in their expense matched his breeches and stockings. The enormous fine silver buckles that adorned his shoes were perhaps the most obvious symbols of his vast wealth.

"Ah, Sir Thomas, I am glad you have come," he stated with a warm smile, motioning to a chair opposite a large, neat oak desk, as Thomas obediently sat down.

"I am sure you can be in no doubt as to why I have called you here this morrow, Sir Thomas," the Lord Justice General began, now casting a disapproving frown at his visitor. Sir Thomas, who knew the ways of his master too well, remained silent, as he continued to speak.

"This unsavoury business of the Duke of Buckingham and the disturbing events in connection with Glamis have cast a dark shadow over us, Sir Thomas, and the King is not pleased," he complained, shaking his head. "I have asked you here to ensure the trial is quick and a result is guaranteed, Sir Thomas; can you give me such assurance?"

So, thought Thomas, sighing gently, *they have got to you, too; the long arm of greed extended by the Crown has held its grip.*

"The trial has only just commenced, my Lord; the justice in question is hearing the arguments, and I believe the accused shall give her statement today," he continued bitterly, "if she is well enough to do so."

Lord Graham grunted, dissatisfied, and abruptly got up from his chair. A few papers strewn on his desk quivered as the air caught them, and one fell to the floor, landing at the feet of Sir Thomas. He picked it up; glancing quickly at it as he replaced it on the desk, his heart jumped. Lord Graham, fortunately, had not noticed, and instead launched into a condemnation of Thomas and his process.

"Sir Thomas, as Lord Advocate, it is your duty to ensure this trial is conducted in such a manner that the result is in the best interest of the Crown; we cannot afford to fall out of favour with the Royal Court- it would mean the end of us! The King has been most generous to Scotland, as was his father, and we owe him our loyalty and allegiance, even if there is a price to pay for it."

Sir Thomas struggled to keep his calm composure, and retorted politely, but sternly:

"My duty, Sir, and oath as Lord Advocate, is to uphold the laws of Scotland and her constitution, and to ensure criminal proceedings are afforded due process, and defendants a fair trial. I cannot think you would disagree with the remit of my duty, Sir, or that I should abandon the oath I took!"

Lord Graham had never liked Sir Thomas, and had it not been for his impeccable record as Lord Advocate, and his favour with the King, he would have had him replaced with someone more accommodating to his own aspirations long ago.

"Sir Thomas," smiled Graham falsely, "I understand your son, John, has high hopes for the bench; and that he is currently clerk to Justice MacDonald."

He sat back down into his cushioned chair, folding his hands in front of him, as he studied Sir Thomas, whose sharp glance at the mention of his son proved that the tender nerve Lord Graham had hoped to prod had been reached.

"It would seem a great shame, Sir Thomas, if your son's promising prospects in the courts were hampered by his association with Justice MacDonald, whose age and frailty are hardly suited to the trial of Lady Margaret, would you not agree?"

Thomas shifted uneasily; he loathed Graham even more than he had done before, and it brought out a rare defiance in him that he did not like, but which he took advantage of in the heat of the moment.

"My son's merits speak for themselves, my Lord," he replied, "and as for Justice MacDonald, aye, his age may be advanced, but you will have difficulty finding a judge with sounder judgement, greater experience of human nature, or a fairer mind. What is more-", but he was not allowed to finish, Graham cutting him short abruptly.

"There, I disagree with you," he fired back; his superficial benevolence had disappeared entirely, the meanness in his eyes, the pursed lips and hard tone of voice bringing out the true nature of his character.

"And I would suggest that, for the sake of your son's future, you would most seriously consider MacDonald's speedy retirement."

Sir Thomas was too angry to reply, not just at the Lord Justice General, but also himself; how had he not seen this betrayal coming?

Graham once again got up, but this time remained standing behind his desk, looking down on Thomas; it was a pose he enjoyed with those beneath him, for he knew that the intimidation often caused his victims to bend to his ways of thinking. His expression was now neither angry nor disappointed, but resolute.

"I have discussed the matter with members of the Privy Council, and we have agreed that we should appoint Senator Seton to conclude the remaining affairs of Lady Margaret's trial."

Sir Thomas stood up now, too, and the men faced each other, as if they were about to enter a duel.

"Lord Graham, I must object; the trial's fairness is in question if we are to exchange the sitting justice for a new one, when the proceedings are almost at an end!"

Graham laughed, only briefly, but it was a hollow sound that sent a chill down Thomas' spine.

"The matter has already been decided, Sir Thomas; and if you would, in future, like to see your son on the same bench, I suggest you will raise no objection to Senator Seton's appointment with the Privy Council," he waved his hand dismissively, "though that is, of course, a decision only you can make."

With no words left to say, and not caring if his master had finished with him or not, Sir Thomas bowed curtly, and left the cool palatial surroundings of the Lord Justice General's office. The few words he had read on the letter he had picked up made him wonder what the purpose of the law was, if it apparently was neither to be fair or just: *a jury that will ensure a conviction...* The trial was nothing but theatre; Lady Margaret's fate had already been decided, but he, Sir Thomas Hope, still had one card to play. As soon as he had returned to his office, he began a letter.

Honoured Bishop Forbes, I have no time to spare in relating to you the grave turn of events regarding the trial of Lady Margaret, and am asking for your assistance, which you kindly offered during your last visit....".

*

Twice, the trial had been adjourned, while Justice MacDonald increasingly lost patience with the petulant manner and childish antics of the General, who dragged the court proceedings out as long as he could with unreliable witnesses and long-winded speeches about God and the Devil, the notion of presenting facts or evidence completely escaping his fancy. MacDonald secretly lamented what he saw as the misfortune of the Union of the Crowns between England and Scotland some twenty-five years earlier; *would the crowns have remained separate*, he moaned to himself, the Court would not inflict upon him such irritating and black-hearted persons as Matthew Hopkins, who was clearly in great favour with His Majesty the King, a King who, unlike his father had been, was himself not Scottish, but English.

Justice MacDonald hoped that this day, the day of Lady Margaret's speech for her defense against the ridiculous accusations she faced, would be the last, and that this extraordinary matter would finally be laid to rest. He had considered long and hard if this should be his last case as Justice; he was of an age in which there would be no shame in retiring and did not relish the prospects of his court being riddled with the likes of Matthew Hopkins in future sessions, if this was to be the new fashion in the legal world.

MacDonald deliberated thoughtfully in his chamber on the current case. The family of Margaret Douglas had been long and loyal friends to Scotland, despite the many political entanglements- which some had deemed "treasonous"- the family had faced. He could not help but think that Lady Margaret had fallen victim to a malicious plot driven by William Douglas' desire for revenge against his sister, and for whose family the Stuarts had a long-seated hatred. And Matthew Hopkins' loathing for women was well-known by now, even in Scotland, not to mention his abhorrent passion for power within the King's court.

A knock at the chamber door caused the old man to start, and he responded with a sharp, slightly irritable, "Enter!"

It was his clerk, John Hope, the young son of Sir Thomas. Aged about twenty-two, tall and thin, with long dark hair and bright green eyes in a round, pale face flushed with red cheeks, there was something almost child-like in his appearance.

"The court is ready for you now, my Lord," he said, dutifully gathering the Justice's robes and placing them around the old man's shoulders.

"Do you think," asked the Justice, uncharacteristically wistfully, "that I should retire, John? Do I seem weary to you? Has my judgement left me?"

John had become accustomed to the Justice's occasional melancholy musings, and replied as gently as he could:

"No, my Lord, you do not seem weary! But, is it not God's will that one should feel enthusiasm for one's work ebb away with the passing of the years?"

"Masterfully put," smiled the Justice, "you are good at choosing the right words, John. Your father has taught you well; I have high hopes for the future of Scotland with you in place!"

He paused; his demeanour suddenly changed, and he became irritated.

"It is the insufferable likes of Matthew Hopkins that endear me to an early retirement; it is he who should be locked up, in my opinion, and not this poor lass he has chosen as his victim!"

John remained silent.

"Well, the sooner this is done, the better! Lead on, John, to the courts- it remains my first home, at least for now!"

The two began to walk slowly, reluctantly down the long corridor in the direction of the court chamber, passing offices and waiting areas, an almost reverent silence surrounding them as they talked quietly. They had almost reached the court entrance when suddenly, without warning, three guards appeared before them, swords drawn.

"What is the meaning of this?" exclaimed MacDonald, angrily. "Weapons are unlawful here- as guards, you should know better!"

The captain of the three guards smirked and chuckled, replying with an air of satisfaction:

"We are on duty, Justice, to arrest you!" And without warning, his two subordinates took hold of the old man and began to drag him away.

"What do you think you're doing?" John tried to push them away from the judge, but a soldier struck him hard on the side of his head with a baton, and he fell to the floor.

"Arrest? Me? For what? This is an outrage! I demand you fetch the Lord Justice General- he will put this right!" MacDonald was shouting, but his voice cracked slightly with fear, for he had been afraid it would come to this one day.

But the captain only laughed.

"It is the Lord Justice General who has ordered your arrest, *Sir!*" He pushed him further along. John, dizzy, pulled himself to his feet and tried to stop them, but this time, he was met with the sharp end of the sword at his throat; he was forced to back away. They hauled the poor old justice along the corridor, the old man's feet scuffing the uneven floor as he tried in vain to resist, unable to keep up with the pace of three stronger and younger lads. John shouted, not intimidated, but panicked, as loud as he could; if he could cause enough commotion, someone might come to their aid. People began to appear from offices along the hallway, to see what the upheaval was all about, many gasping as they saw the familiar figure of Justice MacDonald being carried away by armed guards, but none daring to intervene.

The soldiers only continued laughing, as the frail old man, weaker than them, stumbled along; his judge's robe had loosened and became entangled in his feet.

"This is treason!" he croaked. "You will hang for this!"

The Captain snapped a short reply.

"Hold your tongue, old man, for it is you who shall hang for treason!"

John, now desperately trying to distract the soldiers to slow them down, demanded as he ran after them:

"Where are you taking him? Tell me where you are taking him!"

A soldier stopped abruptly to block his way; he raised his sword against John once again.

"I should mind my own business, if I were you, or you may find yourself in company with the judge before you know it; as his clerk, that is very likely!"

John ignored him, and instead shouted to the old man, "I will see my father, my Lord; we will put a stop to this, I promise! Do not worry, sir!"

John, entirely helpless to stop them, could only watch as they pushed the judge down the stairs, his robe ripped off him now, before they disappeared completely into the grey darkness of the maze of corridors that was Parliament House. John picked up the robe in disbelief; what was happening?

Father! Suddenly it dawned on John that his own parent might be in equal danger, and he ran as fast as he could to the Lord Advocate's office.

~ Eleven ~

Thomas Hope stood by one of the windows in his office, motionless, staring out over the distant hills. The snow had ceased and turned into an icy rain as the afternoon drew into the evening. The days were getting shorter and darker, it seemed, and it felt like the light and hope of spring and summer would never return. He had begun to formulate in his mind a conversation with Justice MacDonald that would not wound the old man's intellect, or insult his years of service to the Law, to gently coerce him into retirement, but Thomas had still found no words that felt appropriate. He had viewed the court schedule for the day, and knew that time was running out. The evidence was still being heard and argued, and then there would be adjournments- during which time, he also knew, the Lord Justice General would take the opportunity to replace the old judge with the notoriously severe and habitually merciless Alexander Seton, Lord Kilchreuch.

Lost deep in thought, he felt a brutal shock when his clerk and his own son both violently burst into his office, breathless and agitated, each speaking over the other in panicked words.

"Be silent, you two- I cannot understand a single word you are telling me!" His tone was ill humoured and harsh, but when he realised his son stood in front of him, afraid and distressed, he softened a little.

"John, why have you come? Is the court not in session?"

John shook his head, and began to ramble.

"Father, they have taken him away- they have arrested him! They say he will hang for treason!"

"What are you speaking of? Who? Who will hang for treason?"

Wishing above all, but knowing it unlikely, that Matthew Hopkins' motives had finally been discovered, Thomas hoped that it was he who would be silenced forever.

"Justice MacDonald! They have arrested Justice MacDonald!" Angus explained feverishly; his voice was trembling and his face flushed with worry.

Sir Thomas stared at the two young men, speechless. *This cannot be true*, he thought, *not so soon!*

"What? That is impossible!" he muttered in disbelief. "Who arrested him? When?"

John had calmed slightly now and replied, attempting to be methodical in his account of events.

"Justice MacDonald and I were on our way to the chamber to hear arguments, and suddenly three guards stopped us- I do not know who they serve, but they claimed to be there on the order of the Lord Justice General. But, father, I do not believe them- why would Lord Graham have cause to arrest Justice MacDonald?"

The rain and wind had picked up now, and they lashed against the windows of the Lord Advocate's office, so loud that Sir Thomas had to raise his voice momentarily to overcome the loud howling and the hard patter of ice knocking on the windows.

"Angus," he said, as gently as possible, "would you leave me alone with John?"

The clerk, somewhat hurt at being excluded, bowed, and closed the door as he left.

"Sit down, John," commanded Sir Thomas, "so I can explain."

John sat down, while his father remained standing, hands folded behind his back, thoughtful.

"I was summoned to Lord Graham this morning," he began, still looking at the floor as if searching for the right words, "who wished to discuss the case of Lady Margaret Douglas and the Justice MacDonald's presiding over the proceedings."

"You knew this would happen, father?" John asked in disbelief.

"Let me finish, my son," asked Sir Thomas. He sighed softly before continuing.

"Lord Graham and the remaining members of the Privy Council decided that Justice MacDonald should retire....," he paused, and took a deep breath, "....and they have appointed Alexander Seton to take his place!"

"But why? The process is almost complete- why replace him so close to the end of the trial? And why Seton?" John shook his head, puzzled. "He will condemn Lady Margaret, without a doubt!"

Sir Thomas raised his eyebrows in uncertainty and now looked directly at his son.

"I believe the reasons are political, John; but we have no power to stop them!"

"You can raise an objection, father; that is your right, is it not?"

"Yes, that is my right- but I cannot do that."

"But why not? I thought you had respect for Justice MacDonald! Why will you not defend him?"

John was now shouting at his father, standing square in front of him, angry and disappointed.

"John, do not raise your voice against me! I have a reason!" He paused, and repeated quietly, "A very good reason."

"What reason could you possibly have to allow this to pass, father?" John was screaming at his father now, losing all his own reason; his emotions took over and darkened the ideals of his young age, as he, almost spitting at his father, mocked him mercilessly.

"Or have they paid you off, as they have so many others, to keep in step with our new King's criminal acts?"

But that was too much for Sir Thomas, and as if another being had taken over his senses, he struck John across the face with a blow so hard that it split the boy's lip. Crimson blood spilled from the cut, large drops splashing onto the cold grey stone floor of the office. They stood in silence for a few seconds, both in shock. Sir Thomas had never struck anyone before in his life, let alone one of his children. A few tears ran down his cheek as he reached out his hand towards John's face in consolation, but the boy turned away, the shock and anger in his eyes unmistakable.

"Forgive me," choked his father, "please, my son, forgive me! Lord Graham told me only to ask MacDonald to retire- I did not know the Privy Council would arrest him! Please believe me," he whispered.

John was still holding his blood-covered hand to his lip, eyes flashing with anger.

"But why will you not object, father? It is your right!"

Sir Thomas shook his head vigorously.

"No, no, my son, do you not see? I cannot because of you! He threatened your future as an advocate and judge- if it were my own future, I would not have waited a second to object, but you- you have such promise, I could not allow your future- or the fate of our justice system- to be ruined because of me!"

The old man sobbed now, a mixture of anger and despair in his heart, wishing he had never been involved in the affair of this trial, that he had excused himself somehow from its process.

John sat down, still furious, but now not certain at who or what he was angry. After a minute or two, he spoke, calmly and quietly.

"I regret, father, that you have been forced to choose the fate of my future over your duty as Lord Advocate. I do not know what to think," he added, "other than that if my future as an advocate and judge also includes having to break my oath to appease someone as cruel and malicious as Lord Graham, then I would rather choose a different profession!"

Without looking at his father, he got up and left, Sir Thomas staring after him, the right words yet again failing to help him. He remained unmoving for a few minutes, when a soft knock at the door forced him to compose himself.

"Enter!"

It was Angus.

"A letter has come, my Lord, post haste; it is from Bishop Forbes."

Sir Thomas snatched it from Angus and waved him away, the boy once again hurt at the uncharacteristically dismissive manner of his master. *At last*, thought Sir Thomas with relief, *some good news!* But as soon as he began to read, his heart sank even deeper.

Sir Thomas,

I write in response your recent request regarding my assistance in the procurement of jurors for the current trial of Lady Margaret Douglas.

I have no recollection of having made such an offer of assistance to you, and nor do I wish to involve myself in these affairs of local politics, particularly in a time when my days as Bishop of Aberdeen are coming to an end. I have been advised that my duties as Bishop will be transferred to the City of Edinburgh upon the request of the Lord Justice General, Lord Graham, the 7th Earl of Menteith, and that I shall assume these duties forthwith.

I shall pray for Lady Margaret Douglas in her hour of need.

Patrick Forbes
Bishop of Aberdeen

Thomas began to weep, his sobs almost at one with the irregular sounds of the storm raging outside, a sore contrast to the calm and silence that now had returned to his office.

*

Alexander Seton, Lord Kilcreuch, was a man who, upon entering any chamber, commanded fear and silence over those who had the misfortune of being in his presence, a sentiment he often mistook for respect, of which he had none- neither towards himself, nor anyone else- save, perhaps, the King, should it suit Lord Kilchreuch's purpose in that moment.

As he entered the court chamber that morning, his notorious ability to evoke intense fear in those around him had not waned. His reputation for exceptionally harsh and cruel sentences, usually with no room for leniency, made the prospects of any lawyer acting for the defense of securing a fair trial or acquittal practically impossible. Lord Kilcreuch cared little for justice if it did not serve his own goals in life, which almost solely centred around advancing his own power in society, and above all, his favour with the King. In that, he, William Douglas and Matthew Hopkins were entirely alike. With this knowledge in hand, the Witchfinder General entered the chamber in a particularly good humour that morning, for he was certain that his toil to rid the world of the devil's work would finally be recognized by those who mattered most in society.

The hush of standing members in the chamber pleased Lord Kilcreuch, who took his time to arrange himself and his documents slowly and methodically at his pulpit, before finally uttering a curt "Be seated" at which the entire population of the chamber, not daring otherwise, sat down in synchrony, only the creaking of hard wooden pews disturbing the deathly stillness of the room.

"Justice MacDonald is-", he began in a booming voice, pausing briefly, "indisposed indefinitely; it is I who will preside over the case henceforth, although," he added indifferently, "I gather the matter is almost at its conclusion. Bring in the defendant," he commanded to the bailiff, who bowed deeply before disappearing into the antechamber.

A few moments later, two guards appeared with Margaret. Someone in the chamber gallery dared to gasp on seeing her shaven head, the long blade-shaped cuts and russet-stained white tunic she wore revealing the brutality of that action. Margaret looked up to see William, mouth agape and horror-stricken. Next to him stood Anne, entirely unaffected by her sister-in-law's horrific appearance, as ice-cold and stone-faced as a statue.

"Margaret Jean Elizabeth Uan Douglas of Glamis Castle, daughter of Archibald Douglas, 8th Earl of Angus, and Jean Lyon, Countess of Angus, both deceased," spoke Lord Kilcreuch, almost with glee, his voice echoing against the bleak chamber walls, "you are present today to be judged for the alleged crimes of murder and witchcraft to conspire in the murder of George Villiers, 1st Duke of Buckingham," he continued gravely, glancing at the papers in front of him, "the attempted murder by poison of one Sir James Ferguson, and murder by witchcraft of Effie Campbell, servant in the House of Glamis. You have entered a plea of not guilty. Is this correct?"

She nodded, rather than spoke, afraid that if she opened her mouth the wounds on her tongue would burst. But the pain she had suffered until then had rendered her almost numb in her whole body, so perhaps it mattered little.

"Speak when spoken to by a justice of the Court!" Lord Kilcreuch thundered, almost apoplectic at the disrespect by the criminal before him, and a woman, at that.

Margaret, too exhausted to feel the wrath of his abusive outburst, replied as forcefully as she was able.

"I am not guilty."

With narrowed eyes and sharp grin, the judge nodded.

"That is for the jury to decide," he snarled, slowly. "I believe the prosecution has put forth its case. Present your statement to the court."

A clerk, brave enough to face the mercurial temper of Lord Kilcreuch, whispered in his ear; the judge responded, eyes rolling at the inconvenience.

"Remove the branks from the defendant, Master Hopkins."

The General, feeling confident now that he had gotten rid of old Justice MacDonald, protested.

"My Lord, I cannot allow that; she is dangerous! Her tongue can put us all in the Devil's house!"

But Lord Kilcreuch, even less so than his predecessor, had no interest in, or patience for, Matthew Hopkins and his ridiculous theatrical performances.

"You will do as I say, Master Hopkins," he commanded, his voice so slow and cold it could have frozen the still air. "Remove the branks."

The two men, not dissimilar in manner in many ways, both being cruel and wholly without feeling for their fellow humans, stared at each other for a few seconds, and, had Hopkins not given in at the moment he did, he may well have been sent to his own end that day.

"As you wish, my Lord," and the General, having no choice to do otherwise, did as instructed. He removed the bridle from Margaret's head as unceremoniously and roughly as was his custom.

"Speak, Lady Margaret, for I do not have all day!" barked Lord Kilcreuch, ignoring the blood and yellow pus trickling out of her mouth and down her chin, and like him, she paid hardly any attention, only faintly wiping her mouth with the back of her hand. The chamber fell into complete silence.

"Those who believe in the merit of my brother, the Earl of Morton, are encouraged because he is in their power, and convinced that he might fall a sacrifice to me. And they now discharge their bile on me, because of my rejection of his proposal to sacrifice my inheritance to advance his cause with the King; and to gratify their revenge with my blood, they accuse me of crimes which, if true, deserve the severest death. But seeing it is only the prerogative of God to punish men or women for the faults of others, which belongs to no judge on earth, you ought not to punish in me the actions for guarding what is rightfully mine at the wish of my dear father. Above all, you ought to consider if those things I am accused of have the least appearance of truth imaginable; for what gives the greatest evidence either of the guilt or innocence of an impeached person, is their former life. What fault could any hitherto lay to my charge? Did any ever reproach me with anything that is scandalous? Examine, I entreat you, my former conversation; vice hath its degrees as well as virtue, and none can attain to a perfection in either, except by long use and practice; and if you can find nothing reprovable in my conduct, how can you believe that I am arrived all of a sudden to contrive these murders, which are the very height and perfection of impiety? I protest I would not deliberately injure the most despicable wretch alive; could I then make the murder of my sovereign's favourite, whom I never encountered and who never did me any wrong, the first essay of my wickedness? None are capable of such damnable and unnatural actions, except two sorts of persons: those of desperate fortunes who are weary of their lives, or those who are hurried into them by revenge, such as my brother. My birth and manner of life put me beyond the suspicion of the first kind; and for the latter, seeing I was never injured by the King's favourite, how can I be suspected to thirst for any revenge? I am here accused for purposing to kill the Duke, by an elaborate plan involving a person I had never met; and to make my pretended crime appear more frightful, it is given out, that the way was to be by witchcraft, and adding the heinous murder of a serving-maid. With what impudence can any accuse me of such wickedness, who never saw any such actions, nor know I anything about the person who is the murderer? Can any say they ever saw me speak with him, see him, send him letters? Let them show me the evidence. It is well known, that since the death of my husband, I have lived in the country, and never once did I visit London; what opportunity could I ever have then to murder the Duke? You may see by those circumstances, which give great light in such matters, that I am entirely innocent of those crimes I am charged with. It is the office of you judges to protect injured innocence; but if the malice and power of my enemies be such, that whether innocent or guilty I must needs be condemned, I shall die cheerfully, having the testimony of a good conscience; and assure yourselves that you shall certainly find it more easy to take away my life, than to blast my reputation, or to fix any real blot upon my memory. This is my last desire of you, that I may be the sole object of your severity, and that those other innocent persons may not share in my misfortunes. Seeing my chief crime is, that I am descended of the wrong sort of Douglas, there is no reason that they should be involved in my ruin; for my cousin is neither of that name or family. I shall end my life with more comfort if you absolve them, for the more of us that suffer by your unjust sentence, the greater will be your guilt, and the more terrible your condemnation when you shall be tried at the great day by God, who is the impartial Judge of all flesh, who shall then make yon suffer for those torments to which we are unjustly condemned!" *

The speech exhausted Margaret, and she slumped sideways against the pulpit, no soul, even if willing, daring to come to her aid. Lord Kilcreuch's anger had doubled as she read out her statement, his face now so hard and cruel an observer might wonder if, given a sword, he would not entirely dispense with the ceremony of the fire and put cut off her head himself.

The hush of the chamber was broken when he finally spoke; his words were calculated and methodical.

"The jury will now deliberate," he said, waving his hand in their direction, and the bailiff promptly guided the members to an antechamber.

"I expect a verdict in no more than an hour!" He slammed the gavel against his pulpit so hard the sound block bounced onto the stone floor, missing the nearby clerk, who jumped in fear, by a hair's breadth.

Throughout the deliberation, Margaret was forced to stand, barely able to find her strength, in the box, as if a grotesque spectacle of curiosity on display in front of an audience who had paid good money to see this show of horror. Few spoke, mostly for fear of upsetting the judge, until finally, after what seemed to Margaret another lifetime, he gestured to the bailiff, snapping impatiently, "Bring them in!" and the clerk of courts hastily obliged, returning swiftly with the jurymen.

All men, most who have my brother's ear, thought Margaret, *most who favour the English King above their country; and most who would find some grievance against my father and mother.*

"Lord Montrose: has the jury deliberated on the facts and evidence....", but he was interrupted by Margaret, who dared to let out a laugh. To her surprise, the judge merely glared at her, and continued, repeating a little louder, "The facts and evidence presented to them, and based upon these, reached a verdict in this case?"

Lord Montrose looked uncomfortable, peering at Margaret apologetically, awkwardly, for he had argued for her acquittal, but had been outnumbered. His voice trembled with hesitation as he began to read out the verdict.

"Aye, my Lord; the majority of the jury has found the evidence against the defendant to be overwhelming, and therefore, on the charges of murder and witchcraft, find Lady Margaret Douglas..... guilty!"

The room, disregarding their fear for Lord Kilcreuch's volcanic temper, erupted in protest and cheer, some arguing and shouting at each other, and it looked as if violence would take hold. But Margaret did not flinch. *This is not the end,* she thought, *blood will be let; and blood will avenge me!* Her eyes remained emotionless and fixed on William as the judge called order for sentencing.

"Order!" he boomed. "Order! I will have order in my court!" The gavel, having lost its better half, hammered the pulpit furiously, splitting the tired wood, and the room soon settled, as deadly silent as it had been before the verdict.

"Call in the dempster!" Kilcreuch ordered, and a tall figure appeared shortly afterwards, cloaked, and hooded: it was the executioner. Those in the audience who favoured Margaret again began to rumble in anger at his sight. She looked at her brother; he was shaking his head, shouting for Matthew Hopkins, while Anne, embarrassed at her husband's outburst, hid behind her large silk fan. Margaret recognized it; it had belonged to her mother.

"Silence!" shouted Lord Kilcreuch, feeling for the first time in his long time as a justice that he might lose control of his court. "I will have silence in my court!"

But the rumble, although quieter, continued, and Lord Kilcreuch could do nothing to stop it entirely.

"Dempster, pronounce the sentence for the crime of murder and witchcraft!"

The dempster cleared his throat; his voice was so deep and booming it even outperformed Lord Kilcreuch in its ability to intimidate.

"Lady Margaret Douglas, on the charges of murder and witch-craft, the jury has found you guilty. You will be taken at once to a place of execution, where you will be condemned to the fire....", he hesitated for a second, slightly perplexed, before finishing the sentence, "condemned to the fire- alive!"

No strangling, first, then, thought Margaret, *no poison, no mercy at all! Lord Kilcreuch has outdone even himself this time....*

The crowd erupted once again, some- including Matthew Hopkins, who was almost giddy with excitement- relishing the prospect of a burning, but most appalled at the act being committed while the guilty was still alive. The cruelty of it was unthinkable, unbeliev-able. Lord Kilcreuch, who had finished his mission and no longer had any interest in the proceedings that would follow, and feeling unsure of his own safety, hurried away through the antechamber, whistles and shouts of abuse following him as he did so.

Ordered to leave, the crowd began to congregate as Margaret was led out. The hecklers pushed and shoved each other, and she saw William, fighting his way through the commotion. Her blood was burning so fiercely she forgot the pain in her mouth and shouted to him:

"My lawyer has some news for you, dear William; fare thee well, brother, and may you forever dwell on this day as one where you became a murderer of your own flesh and blood!" she spat, sneer-ing at him.

She almost relished her fate, feeling as though she had finally won, and went on as the dempster dragged her along the corridor.

"Will you not watch, brother? See the flames consume my flesh until I am gone? Is this not what you have been waiting for all of these years, my dearest William?" she mocked, the bitterness taking complete hold of her.

"Remember this, dear brother, from Macbeth, that we saw together, when we were still friends?

The time approaches that will with due decision make us know what we shall say we have and what we owe!"

Seeing Anne, so delicate and clean, still waving her mother's fan, she scoffed:

"My dear Anne, I am so glad you could come! I pray of you; will you fuel the flames with my mother's fan to quicken my end as you watch the fire consume me? That you revel in your new-found fortune, if one should come to you, for you shall not have mine!" she hissed, spitting blood through her white teeth unable to feel anything now but hate and an overwhelming thirst for vengeance.

William looked genuinely confused and distressed. The guards dragged her on, down the stairs, onto the cold damp streets, her bare feet shuffling alongside, tearing at her thin skin, leaving trails of blood on the freezing snow beneath her, but she no longer felt anything. William ran after her, while Anne, caught in the crowd, shouted after him.

"My dear, where are you going? You cannot leave me with this....rabble! They might do anything to me! My dear!" she screamed amidst the crowd, who jostled and pushed, some so violently that fights broke out. But William paid no attention to his wife; this had not been the agreement! The maid, Fionnsgoth, was an unfortunate accident, but his sister was to be spared- that was the accord between them; why had he been betrayed by Matthew Hopkins?

"Master Hopkins," he screamed again, half angry and half afraid, seeing the wretched creature that had condemned his sister follow the crowd out of the building. "You have betrayed our agreement! You promised me that nothing would happen to Margaret! You must put an end to this now!"

Hopkins, drunk on his feelings of vindication and the prospect of favour with those in the highest circles of society, merely waved him away dismissively, commenting:

"I have got you what you wished, Sir William; the inheritance you so desired!" He turned his mouth down in mock-pity and continued, "'tis a pity the judge was so harsh; I had in honest thought she would merely go to jail. But," he clapped his hands together, "there we are!"

William would have gladly himself committed murder at the sight of that man, who he regretted bitterly ever having brought into his life.

"My dear," demanded Anne slightly irritated, who, having freed herself from the crowd, had now caught up with her husband, "why do you work yourself into a fret so? It is not as if you were fond of her," she went on, already having killed Margaret off as she spoke, "and now we are safe at Aberdour; we need worry no more to be turfed out of our home!"

He would have slapped her, or worse, had they not been in public, and was about to give her a piece of his mind when Margaret's lawyer approached.

"Sir William Douglas," he said coldly, "I am to give you this letter on behalf of Lady Margaret." With no other words to offer, he bowed, and headed for his private chamber.

"Well, open it, my dear," urged Anne, exuberant at the idea of obtaining the fortune she had finally desired, "it is bound to be the deed for the estate you coveted- it will be yours in a matter of an hour or so; they are taking her now to the fire!"

But William's face dropped even further as he read the lines in front of him, with a sharp knot in his stomach and a deep pain in his heart.

"No," he said, in a low voice, "no, no.... This cannot be!"

"What is it, my dear?" Anne, who was so wrapped up in the fantasies of her new future, had not sensed his disappointment. "Is it even greater than we could have wished? Oh, William!" she burst out, hands clasped together in anticipation and joy.

William looked at his wife, and for the first time, he hated her, and what she had become, but more, what she had made him become: a traitor to family and to country.

"We are not safe, Anne; There are rumours that Margaret's son is still alive. She has left her estate in the trust of her cousin, Lord Glamis. It is his now, not ours; and he may well turn us out, if he wishes...."

Somewhere, a bell tolled; it was the bell of the executioner, the call to the march of fire.

* *Margaret's speech is an adaptation of the speech by Janet Douglas, Lady Glamis, her maternal great-grandmother, who was condemned to the fire in 1537 on the order of James V of Scotland, as recorded in Fittis, R.S. Heroines of Scotland, Alexander Gardner, 1889, pp. 123-126.*

~ Twelve ~

The City of Edinburgh, on November 2nd of the year 1628

It was the last eve of Allhallowtide, *El Dia de los Muertos*, as the stranger on the horse remembered from his now distant homeland. Making his way through the suburbs of the West Port of Edinburgh, the chilled dusk was warmed only by the lit jacko-lanterns, flames spilling out of grotesque narrow eyes and toothless grins, as beggar children of all ages hopped from house to house, knocking on doors that sometimes opened, but mostly did not, hoping for a morsel of bread or a coin that probably would not do much to make their desperate lives any easier.

The lone rider, who, it was apparent- not only from his appearance but perhaps also his dress and demeanor- had a home in another part of this world, slowly passed by the old and new houses as he made his way along the road of the West Port. The Castle rose in a majestic assembly of stone towers, parapets and walls above him, and the thick black plume of smoke from a recent burning within its walls did not escape his attention. "Another poor soul condemned to the fire," he lamented, as he entered the horse market, a cold shiver creeping down his spine at the thought of burning flesh. The streets were busy, shops and travelling merchants still eagerly selling their goods, some stopping to stare at the dark stranger in the exotic apparel on his white horse as they passed through the crowds, one opportunistic horse courser ignoring the strangeness of the Stranger and shouting: "Sire, I'll give you 50 Scots for that willowy horse of yours!" He chuckling with glee at the prospect of fortune for pandering an unusual creature to those craving an exotic pet, for this was no ordinary horse; she was small and dainty, with a finer head and elegant gait.

They turned left and upwards along the winding Straight Bow, and right upon reaching the imposing Weigh House at the top of the hill, where all manner of merchants crowded in to have their cheese and dairy goods weighed under the scrupulous eyes of the weigh masters, who wanted their taxes, and to make certain no goods were sold above the designated price to those innocent buyers who knew no better. Before the mysterious Stranger lay the long stretch of the High Street leading to the Nether Bow, where the road would take him left again down Leith wynd, and towards the Trinity Hospital, his destination for the evening.

The stranger, and his steadfast horse, were weary; their journey had been a long and troublesome one when they had touched the shores of the Crowne Lands at Newcastle for the road to Scotland. No less than three times had they been forced to face highwaymen, or flee from border reivers, taking longer roads through open plains and across woodless hills to avoid attacks. Despite the trouble, the rider's cunning and wit, and his mount's speed and instinct, had saved them both from robbery and death.

The busy scenes around them, despite the noise, the stink of sewage and rotting flesh and desperate squalor, the dire poverty of half-naked whores and beggars amidst the gilded opulence of mansions and gaudily dressed gentle-folk therefore seemed like a half-dream, blurred images floating before them seen through their bleary eyes and exhausted minds. As they ambled along, weaving through buyers, sellers and beggars, they were rudely forced out of their dream-like stupor when a few missiles in the form of apple cores and half-rotten carrots seemed to rain upon them. The horse veered left slightly, briefly setting into a sideways canter and almost colliding with two other men on horses, finely dressed but as weary-looking as them, which forced the crowd to flee around them. There was a stench of smoke that trailed behind them as they uttered a short "pardon", and moved on. They must have come from the burning, thought Noureddine, feeling pity as the two men wearily made their way through the crowds.

A group of beggar children laughed and shouted, "The Devil, he's come for us!"

The Stranger and the horse stopped, and without uttering a word, he conjured from his cloak a few silver coins, and tossed them to the wide-eyed urchins, who, too desperate to feel fear or surprise, scrambled eagerly for the treasure as it struck the greasy cobblestones of the filthy street, before they scurried away down the dark alleyways that snaked through the adjoining tenements. The rider smiled, and moved on, a few observers raising their eyebrows in disapproval, and one commenting in well-to-do English, "Look at them, filthy mongrels, scrambling for that silver like rats! They're nothing but vermin, not worthy of God's world!"

Turning to the man, who himself looked like he was of the wealthy merchant ranks, dressed in a fine yellow silk hose and black doublet, a set of fat fingers holding the elaborate silver gilt handle of an ebony cane for which, given his youngish age and brisk gait, he appeared to have no need, the Stranger said, as he rode past, "They are of flesh and blood, like you and I, with hearts and minds, good sir!"

"Says the Devil himself," retorted the merchant, a steely mocking tone undisguised, yet a measure of fear lingered in the aftertone, as he rushed past the foreign rider quickly, wishing no further engagement with him.

But the Stranger and his horse, who were not unused to having such reactions from the fairer skinned populations of the world, simply wandered on, through the throngs that were beginning to disperse as the sun began to ease itself below the western hills in the distance.

Making their way through the Nether Bow, the two travellers could see the Canongate stocks on the right as they turned into

Leith wynd. All of the six stocks were occupied with various offenders, bedraggled looking creatures with nothing but rags for clothes—men, women and children. A young boy stood, still as a statue, with his ear nailed to the pillory, the fear in his eyes so deep that the Stranger wondered, for a second or two, whether to stop and hand him a coin. But seeing the wardens further along, he averted his gaze and carried on. Any money these offenders would take would, he knew, either end up being torn out of their hands or worse yet, their hands seeing the sharp end of an axe.

A dusting of light snow lay beneath them as the two travelers passed the darkened houses, on occasion catching a brief glimpse of a servant preparing a meal, a dog barking at the mysterious figure of the jacko-lanterns, an old man in a chair, in a sleepy stupor by the fireplace. The grand roof of the hospital church emerged as they descended further towards the suburb of the Ringers, the home of most of the city's poor folk and beggars.

There was still light above the horizon; the waters of the big blue sea in the distance glistened in the afternoon light, when the stranger and his horse passed below the tall arch of the Trinity Hospital. Disturbing screams and wailing from the Correction House opposite occasionally floated on the gusty breeze that had now picked up, blending haphazardly with the murmurings of agony and suffering that emanated from various corners of the large hospital. To the right rose the magnificent Trinity College Church.

A young boy, who seemed completely unimpressed by the unusual appearance of the Stranger, stopped when he spoke.

"Good evening, I wonder if you are able to tell me where I would find Brother Galenius?"

The boy, who could be no more than fourteen, hesitated slightly.

"Evenin', sir; Master 'Lenius is usually in the kitchen at this hour; through the yard at the end, by the physic garden, sir." A hopeful glance prompted the Stranger to produce a coin which, after dismounting, he handed to the informer.

"Thankin' you, sir, and if there's anything else I can help with...",
but before the Stranger could ask him to take his horse for stabling,
the grateful recipient had dashed off into one of the side buildings,
and disappeared in the labyrinth of rooms and maze of corridors
within the hospital. The Stranger walked slowly through the yard,
eyeing the building, which, although beautiful in its architectural
design and proportions, had seen better days. Some windows lacked
glass and were covered with shabbily patched oilskins, and where
the masonry had decayed along the walls, it had been clumsily
repaired with random pieces of stone, mud, and rubble. The patron
of this establishment, thought the Stranger, was either extremely
uncaring, or dead, to leave it in a state such as this.

They had reached the end of the yard, and following his nose,
the Stranger knew the kitchen lay in the corner building ahead
of him, beyond which he could see a beautifully kept garden, the
only part of the whole complex that seemed to receive its deserved
love and attention. All manner of scents from vibrant flowers and
aromatic herbs wafted over them with the breeze, masking some
of the foul stench of the open sewer channels running through the
streets of the Ringers beyond the high garden wall.

The dark stranger led his horse, whose name was Najd, over to
a leafless oak tree by the entrance of the garden, and left her with
a carrot there to rest, before he headed to the kitchen. He could
see that it was busy, servants and cooks rushing about, dishing out
bowls of soup and plates of bread meant for the sick and dying. He
wondered if the dying would get an added portion, or a sweet treat,
to see them out of the world, but looking at the poor surroundings,
and rationed portions, he doubted it. *How sad it is,* he thought, *to
leave this world in a manner no different from how one arrived in it.*

"Nour!" A voice called out to him, waking him from his thoughts;
his face brightened into a wide smile when he recognized his old
friend.

"Galenius- my good old friend! It has been too long," Noureddine- for that was the name of the Stranger- exclaimed, as he offered Galenius a hearty embrace.

"My dear friend- this is a surprise!" the physician uttered; the visitor noticed the redness in his eyes, and the fatigue in his voice.

"Then you did not receive my letter, Galenius?"

"I had no letter from you, dear friend! What brings you to Scotland?"

"I am on my way to the Far North; I have some... business in Sweden." He had hesitated slightly before the word 'business', but Galenius seemed too preoccupied to notice.

"Old friend- I am glad you are here!" He smiled. "Let us return to my office; there are news I must relate to you, as I am sure you have news for me."

Galenius took Noureddine by the shoulder, and the two, once brothers in arms, walked slowly towards the Infirmary offices, chatting quietly about their last encounter, and old times passed.

"What has happened here today?" asked Nouredding, peering up towards Castlehill. "Are they still burning heretics here?" He wrinkled his nose. "That is an unpleasant stench that stains the pure Scottish air!" he half-mocked. Avoiding the subject, the physician replied, as they entered the physician's quarters, "please sit, my good friend, you must be tired after your long journey; I will ask my apprentice to prepare some food and drink."

He disappeared into an adjoining room, and Noureddine could hear him giving his apprentice instructions, before his old friend returned. Closing the door slowly behind him, he took a deep breath, and said, "There is something I must tell you, dear friend."

*

Galenius, although gentle enough in his account of Margaret's ordeal and unspeakably horrible death, had done his best to console his friend, who had wept openly at the loss of his love. With a gentle hand on the shoulder, Galenius tried to soothe the anguish, and to offer some comfort.

"I was there, God forgive me," he crossed himself, "but I never heard her utter a word of pain, even at the end, she professed her innocence for all to hear," he paused briefly before continuing, "and laid a curse on those who condemned her!" He gritted his teeth in anger; that King, and the Duke, they had many deaths to answer for, many innocent lives taken so cruelly.

They had sat in silence for some time, the small dark room they had chosen in the Infirmary lightened only by the fire in the hearth, and the dim lamps that Galenius' assistant had lit, and for a while, it seemed like the flicker of the flames was the only life left in the world.

The flames, thought Noureddine, *what fickle nature; they bring us warmth and light, but condemn us to darkness!* After a while, he spoke.

"Take me to the Castle; I want to see the cursed place where she took her last breath!"

"If that is your wish my friend, of course, I will take you to that evil place," he sighed reluctantly, "but do you not think this will only add salt to your sore wounds?"

"I want to see it," he insisted, hollowly.

One resolute, the other reluctant, they set off to the Castle in the last of the twilight; as the sun gave way to night, a golden shimmer flickered like a march of fire on the horizon, and in the distance, darkness crept steadily, assuredly, over the sea.

TWO

The Lands of the Ottomans, late in 1641

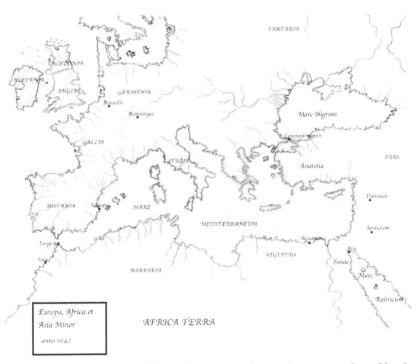

Piri Reis' Map of Europe and the Mediterranean, late 16th century, adapted by the author.

Piri Reis, Public Domain, via Wikimedia Commons

~ Thirteen ~

The Sarai-Cedid of the Sultans, Istanbul, in the lands of the Ottoman Empire; October of the Year 1641

If after death your body kept its shape,
We might hope it will be revived again,
Just as a jug, emptied of wine, could be
Refilled, as long as it remains unbroken.
But all its parts have come undone and turned
To particles of dust swept away by the winds.

Abu al-Alaa al-Ma'arri, Syrian poet, lived in the years 973-1057 of the Lord Jesus Christ

In a dimly lit chamber, richly furnished but austerely imperial, the silhouettes of two seated figures cast long shadows on the high walls; they seemed like giants, remaining motionless for some time, before one of them finally spoke.

"And you are certain he is still loyal?" asked the lady, sprawled across her divan as if discussing something as trivial as the weather, "and that he is the only one for this task?"

The man nodded, without hesitation.

"Yes, Your Majesty; he is loyal, and he is the only one I trust to fulfill this mission."

"You seem very sure of yourself, vizier; tell me why he, and no one else, should help us?"

The man hesitated slightly before replying. A fountain trickled steadily in the far corner of the vast chamber; above, the late afternoon light shone dimly through the windows.

"I owe him my life, Your Majesty; were it not for him, I would have died at the hands of the Polish at the Battle of Tutora, and the armies of our great empire would have been defeated!"

She remained unaffected in her emotion by his brief account, but raised herself swiftly from her repose; the echoes of the dripping water gave her response almost a musical air.

"That is loyalty no amount of gold can pay for, Kara Mustafa, my good vizier; show him in."

*

"The vizier," remarked the lady with the proper regal haughtiness one might expect of a mother of the Sultan of the Ottoman Empire, "holds you in the utmost high regard, Seyyed!"

She ran her eyes slowly over the man standing, humbly bowed, in front of her as if their assessment of him would confirm the vizier's high praise.

The man was Noureddine, and it was the first time he had stood face to face with a ruler of the Sublime Porte; he was surprised by his own lack of intimidation, especially considering the ruling family's infamous ruthlessness and lust for blood, even towards members of its own household.

He observed, as far as he could with his eyes cast down, the formidable lady who stood in front of him. Nour felt a mixture of admiration and apprehension; Kosem Sultan, the regent and mother of the current Sultan, His Imperial Highness the Sultan Ibrahim I, had a reputation for shrewdness, was highly intelligent, politically calculating, and unflinching in her cruelty. She was not beautiful, perhaps, but her presence, and the way she carried herself, attracted his fascination.

"I am humbled to have the good opinion of one so esteemed, your Majesty," he replied, quickly moving his eyes sideways to the vizier, his gaze fixed on the myriad of colours that adorned the tiled floor.

The Grand Vizier, whose name was Kermankes, the Archer, Kara Mustafa Pasha, was in his early fifties, and only slightly older than Nour. He was not someone to suffer fools lightly; his power stretched even beyond that of the Sultan, having ordered, and supported, the assassinations of several unfortunate souls, including members of the imperial family, who had not conformed to the ruling powers' austere vision of government.

The vizier nodded thoughtfully, almost absent-mindedly, and added:

"Captain Nour has served me well on many occasions; it was my greatest disappointment when he chose to leave my service in exchange for the mundane pursuits of civilian life....", his dark, sharp eyes stared directly at Noureddine, who could only once again avert his eyes to the floor; it was a beautiful floor, tiled with magnificent patterns of multicoloured mosaics, set amidst blue, green and white tiles, and their brightness offered Nour some welcome distraction to the stark formalities of being in the presence of royalty.

The vizier continued, in a slightly softer tone.

"But, considering the highly unfortunate circumstances, one may perhaps understand why he chose the quiet path of a landholder over the glorious but cruel treachery of battle!"

Throughout both Noureddine's and the grand vizier's conversation, Kosem Sultan had not left her intensely curious gaze on the humbled former soldier. Despite the long, thin scar that ran across his left eye and down to his lip, he was still a handsome man, not according to the usual conventions of society, but there was a presence about him that attracted her; and, she guessed, he could be no more than ten years her junior. Always considering the options of mixing pleasure with business, if he fulfilled this mission successfully according to her wishes, she would consider, perhaps, to take him as a consort. But that all depended on his loyalty, his courage, and his political canniness, for she, the Sultan's mother and regent of the Ottoman Empire, could not gain a reputation of allowing fools and failures into her inner court, least of all into her bed chamber.

Conscious of the two most powerful people in the Empire- and, it seemed to him, the whole world- scrutinizing him closely, Noureddine stood, upright and as outwardly confident as possible with eyes still directed to the floor, distracting himself by focusing on the decorative details of the grand room that was their meeting place. The walls were also adorned with ornamental tiles, broken up by an eye-catching band of blue panels inscribed with a blessing from the Qur'an that stretched around most of the grand room. A fountain gave turn to an uninterrupted, slow trickle of water, almost hypnotic and calming; set in the wall nearest to the sofa, Noureddine guessed that, rather than intending to instill calm in those visiting, its purpose was to make eavesdropping from the neighbouring rooms more difficult. The Ottomans were shrewd and masterful builders. When he had entered, he had caught a glimpse of the vast and ornate domed ceiling; it gave the effect of the room inhabiting almost the entire world in a smaller space.

So absorbed and mesmerized had he been, by the overwhelming grandeur and the regular rhythmic music of the dripping fountain, that he almost had not been aware that Kosem Sultan had begun to talk. Unfortunately, he had caught up with her words only in mid-sentence.

".....a mission of great importance, Captain, I am sure you must understand; my son, the Sultan, suffers from a highly nervous disposition, and does not always know his right mind, and there are those in the palace who would take advantage of him for their own political gain. I see it as my duty," she continued after a brief pause, "to ensure the safety of all people who live under the protection of Ottoman rule, regardless of their faith!"

"Yes, your Majesty," he replied, mentally kicking himself for letting his mind drift off, as he had no idea what the mission she had referred to, was; but his former master came to the rescue.

"Her Majesty, the Valide Sultan, I should explain, was brought up as a Christian, Noureddine; her father was a priest in the Greek Orthodox Church in Tinos, and the protection of Christians remains very close to her personal interest, as well as having politically important consequences."

The Valide Sultan had looked away on hearing the word 'Christian', as if seeking a former forgotten friend; but the grand vizier took no notice, and continued.

"The Captain, Your Majesty, was also brought up in the Christian faith."

This remark was met with in Kosem Sultan, who reverted her intense stare at Noureddine.

The atmosphere in the grand room suddenly seemed more stifled, despite the voluminous ceiling and enormous stained glass windows that let through a flood of brightly coloured evening light, a cacophony of colours between the streaks of rose and orange sunlight sifting through the ceiling windows.

A bell chimed, somewhere nearby, reminding him of his former homeland, and it cleared the thick air momentarily. The large, heavy wooden doors to the grand room creaked as they were pushed open slowly by the guards, and a train of servants followed, heads bowed, with the chief eunuch in front, carrying silver trays with dishes and cups that Noureddine recognized as the finest Iznik porcelain, a flurry of blue and white, green and red, filled with sweet and savoury dishes, some he had never before seen.

In unison, the train halted as the chief eunuch clapped his hands, the servants- all young women- doing an almost military-like 'about-turn', before they set down their trays in perfect synchronization. Once again in unison, the servants stepped back, and another grand figure strode- somewhat reluctantly, thought Noureddine- to the first dish. Producing a large finely decorated silver spoon, as if out of nowhere, he tasted the dishes one by one, waiting a few seconds between each dish, and when he had finished with the last- a mound of stuffed vine leaves artistically arranged in the shape of a large pyramid- he closed his eyes. All other eyes of the room also seemed to be upon him, to see if he, the Imperial Food Taster, had survived yet another royal tasting, and would be given the grace to live another day. After a few minutes had passed, and what seemed to Noureddine an eternity, the taster opened his eyes, bowed deeply and with some relief, before gliding out again. At a single clap from the Chief Eunuch, the subordinates proceeded to arrange an item from each dish on three separate plates; the milk pudding and baklava would be served later. A pale golden drink, faintly scented with lemon and rose, was poured into silver beakers, and placed alongside the prepared plates, which had been set on the low diwan table. After inspecting the arrangements, the Chief Eunuch- having shifted the utensils, cups and plates very slightly to ensure a perfectly symmetrical display- once again produced another loud 'clap-clap' that filled the echoing silence of the great hall, at which the train of cooks and gilt trays promptly disappeared through the doors, almost noiselessly, before they closed behind them as if a magical spirit had been in control of the whole proceedings all along.

Kosem Sultan, Noureddine had noticed, had paid very close attention to the proceedings of laying out the refreshments, watching each individual almost with an eagle eye, yet hiding quite elegantly any suspicions she might have harboured of the staff. He thought about the Imperial Food Taster, and wondered how long that man had been in that unenviable occupation. He also wondered if he had a family, and what they might feel, seeing their loved one leave them every day, and wondering, each night, whether he would return.

The regent rose slowly from her throne-like chair and with no particular grace, moved slowly over to the banqueting table, hesitating a brief second with a darting look as she passed Noureddine.

The hall, being large as it was, would have offered her ample space to avoid him, and he guessed that this was a way to assert her superiority over her guest.

She carefully let herself down on the gilt and blue velvet cushions scattered on the diwan, and the grand vizier beckoned to Noureddine to take a cushion on the floor, on the opposite end of the long table. Once again, he noticed the elaborately decorated floor tiles, hidden mostly by vast sheets of the finest woven carpets in dark reds, blues, and greens, gold threads shining through a myriad of muted colours.

The Grand Vizier and Noureddine waited silently, eyes averted, while the formidable Regent ate contemplatively and agonisingly slowly, for Nour could feel the pain of hunger in the pit of his stomach, which had become more intense and sharper with the nerves and tension of sitting face to face with the most powerful person in the Empire. After a while, having consumed almost all the items on her plate, Kosem Sultan motioned for her visitors to eat; but, not wishing it to be a relaxed or comfortable experience- particularly for Noureddine- she began to speak again, the haughty and authoritarian tone of her voice ringing out in soft echoes, dampened only slightly by the thick carpets and scattered wooden furniture that inhabited the great hall.

"My son, the Sultan," she bemoaned in an attempt at maternal concern, "suffers greatly from his nerves, as I mentioned," she paused, eyeing Noureddine, who had stopped eating, "no," she offered an inviting gesture with her hand, "please continue; you must eat while you listen to what I say- it will help your brain cells to understand the task I am about to set you." She smiled, condescendingly, as if speaking to someone of limited intelligence, sweetly menacing, revealing a mixture of pale yellow and brown teeth; it was apparent that she enjoyed the sweet delicacies that would soon follow their mezze.

"It is important that we keep the Empire tolerant- Jews, Christians and Muslims living as one, in harmony," she hesitated briefly before saying the word 'harmony'.

"There are, of course, many who might say we fail in doing this- particularly Christians- but, if you look at our fellow kings and emperors in Europe, for example, you will no doubt agree that our ways are far more just and fairer; in Europe," she emphasized, "Christians persecute Christians- the Catholics are particularly ruthless, I hear!"

Looking at Noureddine intently, she continued:

"You, Captain, must surely agree, being one who has suffered the grave sacrifice of persecution in Spain; they are not human, those who condemn their fellow brothers in such ways- separating mothers from their children, killing husbands and fathers who do nothing but live in peace, pay their taxes, ply their trade, and help the noble ranks enrich their vast fortunes- it is the cruelest of inhumanity, and, whatever else we may be guilty of as Ottomans, in the eyes of Allah," she smirked, "we shall not be like them, at least in that respect. That, Captain, you also must certainly honour, as a moral responsibility?"

The terrible anguish of Noureddine's past had suddenly gripped him, as Kosem Sultan had spoken, the reminder of that terrible day, the last image of his mother and sister burnished in his memory forever; and the gruesome execution of his father that he was forced to witness, always to taunt him. And then there was Margaret- his beloved Margaret, sent to the flames, just like his father; he touched his chest to feel the jewel around his neck, hidden beneath his shirt- her pendant was still there, and her spirit always with him.

Perhaps finding a grain of compassion in her otherwise granite-like heart, on seeing Noureddine's torment, Kosem Sultan's voice softened slightly.

"The Grand Vizier has not told me of your story, and nor do I expect you to relate it to me- but I cannot imagine what kind of anguish and pain, as a child, you must have endured; I can see that

I have brought back terrible memories, and for that I regret my careless words."

An involuntary reflex forced the grand vizier to look up at Kosem Sultan, wide-eyed, in great surprise, for he had never once heard her speak in such a forgiving tone or admit to what was usually seen as weakness in regret.

Kosem Sultan smiled wryly, amused, as he quickly averted his gaze again.

"I feel I caught the vizier off guard, Captain- I think he is not accustomed to this kind of generosity or humility on my part!"

"Your Majesty," was the hasty reply, "I assure you that I would never...", but she cut him off with a wave of her almost translucent, jewel-laden hand, and impatiently uttered, "Yes, yes.... Never mind that, vizier; we must get down to the essential business, which is what we brought your former servant here for! Please explain, as I began- I am weary and will listen to you, for a change."

She leaned back, amongst her sea of soft cushions, and half closed her small, brown eyes, as the Grand Vizier continued where she had left off.

He cleared his throat, attempting to regain composure after being caught off guard; the rasping sound echoed faintly around them, ricocheting off the high walls and disappearing into the wide expanse of the domed ceiling. Noureddine had, throughout this brief exchange, tried in vain to banish the last image of his mother and sister from his memory, and even as the vizier began to speak, their eyes, terrified and haunted, still seemed to be all around him, as he attempted to concentrate on what was about to become an unexpected adventure.

"As her Majesty mentioned, the most illustrious Imperial Majesty the Sultan suffers from an illness which subjects him to a nervous disposition, and can have rather unfortunate and," he paused briefly, apparently choosing his words carefully, "potentially unfavourable political consequences." Kosem Sultan opened her eyes very briefly, a sharp glance piercing the gaze of the vizier, who rushed to add:

"Of course, His Imperial Majesty's intentions are only ever well-meaning, and it is only his illness, which those who mean harm take advantage of, that is to blame for these political misfortunes, and not his true character, which is only beneficent and merciful, *hamdulilah.*"

As if pleased, and eased, by the vizier's comments, the Valide Sultan once again shut her eyes, her face completely blank, almost as if she had spiritually left the room.

"And as her most benevolent Majesty, the Valide Sultan, also indicated, we must protect the Empire from dissent- the harmony of our vast and varied communities must be sustained, for our own political interests, even more than out of concern for their welfare or freedoms, such as they are."

Noureddine wondered where this diatribe was leading to; surely, there was nothing he could contribute to such affairs of state?

Kara Mustafa paced a few steps back, towards the ever-trickling fountain, not, of course, turning his back to Kosem Sulttan; that would have been a crime. Standing close to its constant rhythmic flow and trickle reassured him that it would be difficult for any eavesdropper to hear their conversation.

"The Imperial Treasury has in its possession a number of items of a religious nature, which, if they fell into the wrong hands, have the danger of being used as political weapons- or even of being destroyed at the will of His Imperial Majesty, on ill-advice of some of those in his confidence."

His eyes were on Noureddine, who was curious about, but un-expectedly indifferent to, who's these 'wrong hands' might be; but he nodded, nonetheless, as if understanding and interested in the gravity of the situation. Satisfied that his servant had gained his confidence, the vizier carried on.

"One of these items is a letter penned by Mohammed, peace be upon him, now kept in the Monastery of St Catherine's; are you aware of what I refer to?"

Noureddine had continued eating, although reservedly, at the beckoning of the Regent, but stopped chewing for a moment, and nodded again. He was beginning to feel dizzy, from the rich menagerie of ornately decorated objects and furniture around him, to the thick still air, and had it not been for the soothing sounds of the fountain, his mind would most likely have betrayed his feelings of doubt, uncertainty, fear, and -yes- distaste for the other two people in this grand room. It was the kind of fear and distaste he had not felt since that early evening on the cliffs of Muela, where his mother and sister fell to their end. He shuddered, but finally spoke; it would be expected of him.

"Yes, Master Vizier, I have heard of the Deed; it was written by 'Ali and Muhammed, peace be upon them, promising protection, and privileges to Christians. It was given to the monks of St Catherine's Monastery ...", his next words had to be chosen carefully, "and removed by His Imperial Highness the Sultan Selim I for safe keeping to the Imperial Treasury here in Istanbul. A number of copies of the letter were issued to be kept for the monks in St Catherine's."

A silence followed, which Noureddine felt he needed to fill.

"That is all I know, Master Vizier and your Majesty."

"I am pleased with your informed views, Captain, which you seem to have kept up despite your leaving the higher ranks of service; it is more reassuring."

Kosem Sultan remained silent, but nodded, her expression muted.

Swiftly and elegantly raising herself from her cushions, she appeared to magically summon the entourage from the Imperial Kitchen, for the grand heavy wooden doors suddenly opened, as the caravan of servants once again performed their duties, this time to clear the enormous amount of food that was still left and replace it with pyramids of baklava and lukhum. Again, the Imperial Taster performed his duties; and again, he was allowed to live, and the trail of servants slid out as quickly and quietly as they had appeared.

"These are my favourite sweets," claimed Kosem Sultan, savouring a large plate of the lukhum, large, round sweet honey-soaked doughballs, "they remind me of my childhood in Tinos. My mother used to make them for my father every Sunday, as a treat for him, after he had given mass!"

It was almost as if she had forgotten she was now the Ottoman Regent, mother of the Sultan, in Istanbul, and now a Muslim. Sensing an awkward embarrassment which perhaps only she was aware of, she, uncharacteristically cordially, motioned to the Vizier and Nour.

"Please, eat, my vizier and captain; I dare you to acknowledge that you know of a tastier sweet anywhere in the world! They help to sustain the workings of the mind, and you will both need all your wits about you for the task you must undertake."

The men did as they were commanded. Noureddine had tasted the lukhum before, and remembered the deliciously sweet, moist stickiness of these morsels, but he had lost his appetite; he was feeling increasingly uneasy, and wished more than anything that he were back at his humble farm in Damascus, tending to his animals or in his workshop, working on his modest commissions.

The majestic tall bronze candlesticks that had been placed around the great room had been lit, somehow without Nour noticing, as had the lanterns hanging from the enormous bronze rings suspended from the vast ceiling. The light of the evening had faded almost entirely, and only the faint dark orange glimmer of the setting sun filtered through the multitude of colours in the windows.

"The deed," the vizier had resumed his speech, "must be kept in a safe place- and, things being what they currently are politically, that place is not the Imperial Treasury."

The older man folded his hands together contemplatively, fixing his eyes on a small crack in the floor tiles, reminding himself to mention the damage to the Imperial Palace Keeper.

"We have heard rumours that those opposed to the Sultan plan to steal the deed and pass it to the Holy Roman Empire; that would be a disaster for our internal political situation, and leave us bargaining with the enemy in Europe about our own interests.....", he stopped himself, as if checking his own trust in Noureddine, and continued. "The Monastery of St Catherine's has, over the last decades since His Imperial Majesty Sultan Selim I's death, asked for the safe return of the original document; we believe that this is now the most prudent course of action. The letter will be safer from our enemies at home in the desert and mountains of Sinai, than it would be here, the heart of the Empire."

Kosem Sultan had observed both men intently while pretending to show more interest in the childhood nostalgia of her sweet treats; the vizier, she had noted, was always careful to present only the necessary information, and the Captain- well, she had found him rather difficult to estimate, his countenance showing no feelings since she had seen the pain in his eyes on the mention of the persecutions in Spain. But that, she thought, was a good trait; they needed someone who would swear an oath of loyalty, reveal nothing, whose emotions and interests could be kept separate from the mission of the task.

"Your task, Captain," she finally spoke, with a cold authority, interrupting the vizier, who had begun a lecture on St Catherine's Library, "is to take the Deed of Protection back to the Monastery for safe-keeping, and to return the copies to the Imperial Treasury. This must be done before His Majesty the Sultan- or his manipulative cronies and Habsburg loyalists- discover the deception."

She gazed at him with her small, hard eyes; he nodded at the floor, wishing he were anywhere but where fate had presently taken him, and hoped, as the night grew deeper, that he would be relieved from her presence before long.

~ Fourteen ~

The road from Damascus to St Catherine's Monastery, Sinai, in the Lands of the Ottoman Empire; October of the Year 1641

From the beautiful city of Damascus, Nour's present home, the journey to St Catherine's Monastery was an arduous fourteen-day ride, taking him and his faithful mare Layla through the changing landscape of al-Sham. The pale-coloured desert and verdant, lush oases met him as he left the sandy city walls behind him, taking him along the sharp-edged hills around Umm Qays further south, down to the ancient Roman town of Gerasa, and up to the seven rolling hills of 'Amman, before the long descent into the Jordan valley, where the road would take him along the fabled Dead Sea. Once he had left the Dead Sea, the hot, dry desert lay before him and Layla during the day, with a thick, salty air, giving way to nights that were bitterly cold, before they reached the Red Sea port of 'Aqaba on the tenth day.

Feeling the strain of travel as they approached the seaport, Nour and Layla found rest at a caravanserai for the night, and, rather than continuing by road the next day as originally planned, they gained passage on a ship setting sail to the ancient seaport of Dahab, towards the southern tip of the Sinai. From there, they took the pilgrim road through the desert and red-washed valleys, which rose into great mountains and vast, desolate canyons the further inland they reached. The ride from Dahab town into the desert had been arduous; although it was a journey that normally took at least three days, Layla's eagerness and Nour's impatience meant they reached the Monastery with only a one-night stop, riding hard until, at dusk on the fourteenth day, he could see in the distance the pale maroon majesty of the monastery appearing before them amidst the waving desert dunes and craggy mountains, the snow-capped tops of Mount St Catherine and Mount Moses glistening a silvery pink in the evening sun.

They stopped briefly to admire the beauty that surrounded them. It was no wonder, he thought, that this place had been inhabited for more than a thousand years, without interruption, and had withstood the ravages of wars and politics; it was perhaps the most peaceful and beautiful place he had ever visited.

Noureddine had himself never been to St Catherine's Monastery. But his uncle had, when Noureddine was a child, traveled frequently to Egypt, and often visited St Catherine's. Looking at the enormous building before him in the distance, his childhood memories suddenly jolted him, unexpectedly, as he remembered the magnificent monastery complex commissioned for King Philip II, called El Escorial, about a day's ride northwest from Madrid. Nour had only visited it once as a child with his uncle, before the great tragedy, but it was an experience that had been imprinted in his memories.

His uncle had recounted tales of his many visits to St Catherine's, and how he had always complained that he could not describe with true justice its attributes; and now, seeing it in the distance, Nour understood why: to fully comprehend the essence of its beauty, one had to see it with ones owns eyes, just like one would have to experience seeing El Escorial for the first time. The two holy places were entirely different- St Catherine's had none of the grand opulence of El Escorial, and was less than half its size, but perhaps, thought Nour, it was being in the desert which gave the Monastery a feeling of being hewed out of another world. It carried a kind of mystery or magic which El Escorial, despite its awesome magnificence, did not possess.

As he saw the shadows widening across the mountain tops, he felt for the cylindrical scroll case slung across his shoulder and, reassured that the Deed was still with him, he moved Layla onward. He wanted to arrive at the Monastery before the darkness fell entirely. The two weary travelers descended into the valley below and reached the outer walls of St Catherine's just as the last light of the sun began to fade below the horizon. The Monastery appeared more a fortress built to defend itself, than a House of God; a monk on guard in a tower above, armed with a crossbow, signaled that he would open the large, heavy wooden gates. They were intricately carved with floral scrolls and geometric designs, which Nour recognized; many mosques and churches in Damascus bore almost identical decorations, crafted by Christians and Muslims in centuries past. As they passed through the unassuming portico, which supported a further two gates, he took notice of the thick defensive walls surrounding the Monastery complex. It had been built by the Emperor Justinian a thousand years earlier, and it had survived almost entirely the strains of centuries of passing time.

Entering the monastery grounds was like entering a small town. It was built against the steep slope of the mountain and Nour was met by a dense cluster of buildings set amidst narrow, climbing alleyways. In the three storied buildings that lined the length of the monastery walls along both sides of the gate were the monks' cells. The huge *catholicon*, Justinian's Basilica, stood before him, by far the most majestic building in the complex, flanked by a smaller, but no less beautifully constructed, mosque. Around him, along the outer walls, lay the ecclesiastical offices which were connected through several vaulted passageways to the north end of the fortification, where the refectory, library and Archbishop's quarters were located. Scattered in between, as extensions of the massive church, lay twelve smaller chapels, dedicated to various saints, used for community worship.

Despite the impenetrable fortress-like walls, the community spilled out beyond it, with further chapels, stables and accommodation nestled at the monastery's feet. It was not, thought Noureddine, as architecturally magnificent as El Escorial, but he could already feel a profound connection between the massive stones with which this sacred house was built, and those who lived, worked and worshiped among them.

"Welcome to the Monastery of the God-trodden Mount Sinai, Seyyed Noureddine," a cheerful voice said behind him, as he dismounted. A monk, old in age but not in spirit, greeted him with a curt bow. "On behalf of the Archbishop Ioasaf, it is an honour and blessing to host you as an emissary from His Most Imperial Highness the Sultan!"

Nour returned the greeting with a nod and a smile.

"I am Athanasius," continued the monk eagerly, "at your service; I do hope that your journey was unhampered by trouble- I seldom venture beyond these walls, but we hear of highway raiders and pirates along the road between the great city of Damascus and our humble corner here on God's beloved earth!"

"I thank you, Brother Athanasius, for your concern; my travels were entirely care-free! It was a long journey, but if one's destination is to be a place so splendid in its beauty as St Catherine's, it hardly matters!"

"Yes," replied Athanasius, beaming with child-like pride, "we are fortunate in our situation, both spiritual and physical! But come, good pilgrim, I will take you to the Archbishop; he is eagerly awaiting you!"

The monk waved down one of the passing novices, and gave instructions for stabling Layla; the boy, who could not have been more than fifteen years old, was in awe of the mare, who could sense a gentle soul and obediently walked away with him, but not without turning her head towards Nour, who nodded, satisfied that his most trusted friend was in safe hands.

The monastery was bustling with people; monks and novices of different orders, and, noticed Nour to some surprise, nuns, rushed about, preparing for the evening mass and meal.

"St Catherine's is a busy place, Brother Athanasius; I am glad to see it! There are many holy places- of all faiths- which have suc- cumbed to ruin, especially in the more remote parts of the world. But you survive!"

Athanasius eagerly agreed.

"We are fortunate, yes, and I am proud to say that this place of God has been inhabited undisturbed since it was built by Justinian; it has weathered the turbulence of history well. And we are a good number now, yes, and have recently joined with our God's brothers and sisters, the Benedictines of Jakobsberg in Germany, and so we have strengthened our numbers," the old man beamed; "only temporarily, you see, as they have fled the treacherous life in Germany; although they are not of the Orthodox faith, we welcome them as we do our own. The Abbess," he continued enthusiastically, "is Maria de Taye, originally from Forest Abbey in the Duchy of Brabant- but war, you know...". The old monk shook his head in sadness. "We should be brothers and sisters on this earth, and yet, we seem to make it a life's mission to destroy each other!"

Nour could see the monk's heart was, and always would be, en- tirely with the monastery, and it comforted him; what a blissful life to have to be so convinced in one's purpose and place in life and on this earth. Pushing his lamentations aside, Athanasius went on in an animated tone.

"We were so excited to hear that the Deed would be returned to us," said Athanasius, his grey eyes gleaming with a new-found hope. "It means so much to us to have the original document returned to its rightful home- it will help to ensure our safety in such troubled times!"

The two walked quietly through the narrow alleyways of the monastery complex that led to the Archbishop's house. The evening light had faded entirely, and lamps had been lit, but the shadows of darkness obscured much of the way. Noureddine wondered whether the last remarks by the monk had meant to be a quiet reference to the war in Europe and whether the blood being shed would spill as far as Egypt. As if reading his mind, Athanasius added:

"We may seem a far cry from Europe and its troubles, Seyyid Noureddine, but the persecution of some of our fellow Christians are experiences we also can relate to, and we would not wish to have such a fate visit us once again; as," he turned to look at Nour, a brief sorrow in his eyes, "you yourself would certainly understand."

Nour remained silent; he had no idea what Athanasius, or indeed the Archbishop, knew of him personally, other than that he was a messenger from the Sublime Porte, on a mission to return the Deed of Protection after nearly a century of its absence, and he was curious.

"It may interest you, seyyid, that a visiting monk hosted by the Abbess Maria de Taye, who is called Rafael de la Cruz, is also from Spain- or was it Portugal?" The old man stopped for a moment in confusion. "Anyway, he is helping us with some of our scientific manuscripts- they are difficult to catalogue without expertise- and our library is vast and full of them! There is so much to do, and his arrival is a God-send." He smiled apologetically, as if the entire fate of the world's uncatalogued manuscripts rested alone on his thin, bony shoulders.

"I see," replied Noureddine, and not being able to resist his curiosity, he asked:

"Since I came from Damascus, and am a messenger sent by the Sublime Porte in Istanbul, I wonder- why do you assume that I am from Spain?"

The old man again laughed nervously, blushing slightly, his worn cheeks a faint pink hue.

"Oh, my apologies, Seyyid Noureddine- we did receive a description of you and some other....details, as a precaution, from your master, the Grand Vizier."

"Of course," replied Nour. *They have taken precautions*, he thought, *I do not think they trust me.*

"I should also mention, Seyyid- although your master may have informed you already- that there are two.... officials sent from Cairo by the Sublime Porte on the order from the Grand Vizier, to ensure a smooth handover of the Deed, and the safe exchange of the copies?"

Nour nodded; that had been the agreed procedure, whether he had liked it or not.

"We must take all precautions with such an important document," the old man hastened to add.

"Yes, I was informed of this when I left Damascus," Nour replied quietly, before asking:

"Do you know when they will arrive?"

As if apologizing was a daily, hourly burden the monk had prescribed for himself, he said almost feverishly:

"Oh, I do apologise for forgetting- yes, they arrived a short while before you; they are already with the Archbishop, seyyid."

Nour was not surprised; he knew they would have made certain to arrive before him.

"Well, brother of this earth, Noureddine, here we are," exclaimed Athanasius, as they arrived at the Archbishop's house. It amused and, at the same time, dismayed Nour to see that a man of such high status should have his home in such a humble building; this would certainly never have been accepted in his homeland, where lavishness, opulence and the grandeur fit for kings were bestowed on the highest ranking church officials.

"I shall leave you here with Elyas, my apprentice, who will look after you once your meeting with the Archbishop is finished!" The old monk bowed, and beckoned for Elyas, a young boy of about fourteen, with scrawny limbs and large frightened green eyes, to come before them.

"Please follow me, Seyyid Noureddine," said Elyas quietly, and Athanasius disappeared down the alleyways hastily. They made their way up the steps to the Archbishop's office. "The Archbishop will see you now."

*

The Archbishop of St Catherine's Monastery, Ioasaf, who was also the abbot, was younger than Nour had imagined, although his great big black beard, greying faintly at the edges, gave him an air of ancient wisdom and, at the same time, almost a timelessness that seemed to bypass any concept of ageing.

Ioasaf, dressed in the black robes and flat hat of Orthodox bishops, with a large gold cross dangling from his neck, sat pensively in a large armchair. The two janissaries from Cairo, Nour noticed as he entered the office and bowed, bore an expression of displeasure, and he wondered if they had taken this task of supervising the arrival of the Deed upon themselves against their will.

Elyas, head bowed, and eyes lowered to the floor, spoke softly.

"Archbishop Ioasaf, your visitor, Seyyid Noureddine."

With a dismissive wave from the Archbishop, Elyas withdrew through the thick, heavy oak door, closing it gently behind him, relieved he did not have to endure the stern, cold stare of the superior visitors from Cairo.

"Seyyid Noureddine!"

Ioasaf welcomed him heartily with a broad smile that instantly transformed his serious contemplative frown into one of an easy and carefree manner. He had a square face, with narrow brown eyes extending into fine creases that stretched almost to his ears, although the rest of the skin on his smooth countenance seemed untouched by time.

"Archbishop Ioasaf, I thank you for the warm welcome, and am glad to report that I return, unharmed, to you the coveted Deed of Protection."

Nour took the cylinder from his shoulder and placed it carefully on the Archbishop's large desk. Papers and documents previously scattered across it had been neatly piled onto one side to make room for the prized possession.

The two officials, their stern stares still directed towards Noureddine, shifted slightly as they saw the cylinder before them, and the Archbishop suddenly remembered their presence.

"God forgive my rudeness, gentlemen," exclaimed Ioasaf, unapologetically, raising his arms towards Nour and the two men, "Seyyid Sinan and Seyyid Selim, from the office of the Sublime Porte in Cairo- and Seyyid Noureddine, the emissary sent by Her Imperial Majesty Kosem Sultan and the Grand Vizier."

There was a brief, cold acknowledgement, before Sinan, the taller and perhaps less suspicious of the two, commented politely and clinically:

"We are grateful for you undertaking this mission, Seyyid Noureddine," and turning to the Archbishop, he continued, "now, may we inspect the document?"

With an eagerness of a young child, Ioasaf nodded vehemently, gesturing to the unopened cylinder before him, and smiled ecstatically.

"But of course, of course," he gushed, as he backed away, inviting the officials to the desk and himself moving to stand next to Noureddine.

Night had fallen in its entirety, and with it came the bitter cold of the nocturnal desert. Through the office window, Nour could catch a glimpse of the black, star-clad skies and wished somehow that he was up there amongst them, rather than having to endure the company of two sullen officials of the Sublime Porte. The remedying factor was the presence of the archbishop, whose lighthearted chatter gently echoed through the room as the men carefully and meticulously inspected the document, one pointing on occasion to a line of the text, the other nodding, both with enormous round glass discs to magnify the small, tidy curved script that graced the page before them.

"Science is a wonder, is it not, Seyyid Noureddine?" marvelled Ioasaf, gesturing towards the glass discs. "I believe we have our

Arab brothers to thank for this invention! How different our world would be without their knowledge!"

Nour nodded and smiled genially at the archbishop, who continued his effusive praise of bygone scientists and their magnificent contribution to modern scientific inventions.

Sinan and Selim muttered between themselves quietly; through the window, which was slightly open, letting in brief bursts of cold air, an eagle or falcon could be heard above, her stunted, regular calls drifting down over the monastery in short, even intervals, as she searched for her prey. A dog barked nearby, and a cat replied with a fierce hiss as a brief spat ensued, quickly sending the poor dog scurrying away, howling in pain.

"We have inspected the document, Archbishop Ioasaf," stated Sinan with an icy formal manner, "and we are satisfied that this is the original."

"I thank you both, Seyyid Sinan and Seyyid Selim," Ioasaf bowed as he spoke, "and cannot convey to you the utmost joy I and my fellow followers feel at the return of this important Deed to the God-trodden Mount Sinai, and our humble monastery!"

Unmoved by the Archbishop's emotion, Sinan continued:

"We will need to see the copies- all of them- and prepare them for their return to the Treasury in Istanbul."

"Of course, of course," assured the archbishop, nodding and smiling, "they are safely stored in the Treasury- we will make the exchange as soon as possible," and with slight hesitation, he continued, trying to disregard the hard, watchful gaze of the two janissaries as he spoke.

"We are currently repairing the entrance to the Treasury- we had an unfortunate incident only a few days ago, when someone- an outsider," he emphasized the words loudly, "attempted to break in- for what purpose, I cannot say, for nothing was taken- but while the repairs are continuing, I feel it is best for the original copy to be kept in a safer place."

The two men seemed completely disinterested in the arch-bishop's maintenance concerns, and impatiently, Sinan almost snapped in reply:

"It is of no concern to us where the document is kept, so long as it is entirely safe and secure, and never leaves the monastery, Arch-bishop; that was the agreement," he nodded towards Noureddine, who acknowledged the situation with a faint bow of his head.

"To avoid confusion, Archbishop, I suggest the copies are kept where they are- I trust the Treasury is guarded?- and that you bring them to us tomorrow, before we depart to Istanbul."

Nour was surprised; he did not know that he would have com-pany on his return journey, and, although he could not quite figure out why, he began to feel uneasy at the thought. If he had been trusted to bring the original document unguarded, why did the Sublime Porte feel it necessary to guard the copies on his return?

"Yes, yes, that is a fine idea; in the meantime, I will place the original in the hands of Brother Athanasius, our librarian - he has a great many hiding places that no one knows of, and it will be safe with him!"

Sinan and Selim agreed to the plan and bowed to take their leave. As they departed, Ioasaf added with an unhopeful tone that was almost an afterthought:

"Will you be joining us for our evening meal, Seyyid Selim and Seyyid Sinan? Our Bedouin friends have prepared a special halal meal for us all to enjoy!"

Sinan bowed his head slightly, and Nour noticed the thick, reddish-brown hair, curled into tight bunches, underneath the jan-issary's cap. *A Cherkess*, he thought, *now that is interesting!*

"We thank you, Archbishop, that is a most kind invitation."

After the men had left, Ioasaf sat down heavily in his chair, and sighed.

"Seyyid Noureddine, I may safely say- and ask you never to repeat this to a single soul- that I hope never to encounter another janissary as long as I live!"

Nour chuckled lightly, and raising his eyebrows in muted agreement, replied:

"The janissaries have a reputation for hardness and candour, Archbishop- their purpose is to instill authority and fear, and above all, if they are given a mission to complete, they will do whatever it takes to fulfill it."

Ioasaf smiled, and looking at the document that still lay open on his desk, he commented:

"Well, we must take this to Athanasius; it will soon be time for our evening meal, and I would like to see the letter safely stored before we all sit down together. I would be grateful, Seyyid Noureddine, if you could take this task upon you, having already been the safe messenger so far? Elyas will take you to Athanasius."

As if there had been some divine communication through thought that Nour did not possess, Elyas suddenly appeared through the door.

"Archbishop, I have seen the two officials to their cells."

"Ah, Elyas, just in time; thank you, good boy. Now I must ask you to take Seyyid Noureddine to Athanasius; he has an urgent task to do before the evening meal."

Rising from his chair, Ioasaf took Nour by the hand and shook it warmly.

"I thank you once again for returning this safely to us, Seyyid Nour; and I hope that you, too, will join us for our meal?"

Nour was delighted at the thought of food; he had not eaten all day, and the long journey and strain of the meeting had left him feeling dizzy and tired, the pain of hunger gnawing inside him a constant reminder.

"I would like nothing more, Archbishop, and am very grateful for the invitation! Now," he looked at Elyas kindly, who he could see had been equally terrified of the two janissaries, and said, "let us find Brother Athanasius!"

The cylinder once again slung safely over his shoulder, Nour and the young monk bowed to the archbishop, and made their way back through the maze of dimly lit narrow lanes and damp vaulted passages that led to the Library offices.

~ Fifteen ~

The office of Athanasius was located next to the Treasury; as the head librarian, it granted him easy access to the documents he needed, as well as being easily able to supervise the apprentice monks whose task it was to care for this vast and ancient repository of knowledge and information. Nour, who had always loved to read and learn, had heard from his uncle of the great written works which had found their home in St Catherine's, and he hoped he would- despite the recent attempted theft- be able to visit the library before he left.

As they approached Athanasius' office, they could hear a heated conversation. Nour recognized Athanasius' gentle voice as he spoke to his visitor, a man with a hard and cold tone that was a complete contrast to the old monk's mild and calm manner.

Elyas hesitated briefly before knocking. He looked at Nour with a frown.

"I hear Brother Rafael is visiting again," he remarked, worried. "He has visited Athanasius almost every day in the last week!"

The young monk knocked softly, and the relief in Athanasius' voice at the interruption, as he cried "Enter!", ignoring his visitor's complaints, was so obvious it almost made Nour laugh.

Brother Rafael was a man of great seriousness. His brow appeared permanently furrowed, and as he rarely smiled, lines around his eyes and his mouth were of minimal appearance, much to the envy of many of his colleagues who, with a similar age of around fifty-five, looked in the very least ten years his senior. He was a strict culinarian; he did not partake of intoxicating drink, or any substance that slowed down the biological mechanisms of his constantly engaged mind, which, like a clock, were delicately and carefully calibrated. A diet of vegetables, water and fresh water fish kept his brilliant mind nourished and balanced, and only did he occasionally eat an apple or some berries, if they were not too sweet; sugar, he proclaimed frequently to his colleagues, who liked on occasion to indulge in cakes and other sweets, slowed down the juices of the digestive system, which caused the entire body- particularly the cerebrum- to perform at a less than optimal pace.

At first glance, Nour was apprehensive on seeing Rafael: there was something uncompassionate, and remotely familiar, about the monk's demeanor; the hard line that seemed permanently burned into the brow, and the gaunt cheeks and piercing grey eyes the colour of iron did nothing to emanate any fraternal warmth. Without warning, they brought back a dreadful feeling- the same he had felt that day his father had been taken away to the fire.

"Ah, Brother Nour!" exclaimed Athanasius. "I am glad you are come- and grateful for your help," he nodded vaguely towards the cylinder dangling from Nour's shoulder.

Rafael's mood seemed only to darken as he glared at the two interlopers who had rudely interrupted his discussion with Athanasius.

"Brother Rafael," begged the old monk, "let us continue our discussion later; I am aware of your concerns and will give them proper thought once I have settled this pressing affair."

Rafael attempted to hide his irritation by showing a faint smile and drew his thin lips up in a pursed curve.

"Very well, Brother Athanasius; I will seek you out before the dawn prayer."

He bowed, but Athanasius would not let him leave before he offered to introduce him to Nour.

"Seyyid Noureddine, this is Brother Rafael, who I spoke of earlier."

"Good evening, good monk."

Noureddine bowed courteously, but Rafael, eyes narrowed, remarked with an icy tone, barely acknowledging Nour:

"Should I be concerned that I am the subject of discussion, Brother Athanasius?"

"Oh, good man, forgive me," cried the old monk, rushing to explain himself as if he were facing a superior of his, "Brother Nour, you see, hails from Spain..originally..", he smiled, "and I thought, as you are from that part of God's great earth, you may wish to be introduced."

"But," replied Rafael, impatiently and with some anger, of which Nour took particular note, "I am from Portugal."

"Oh, yes, I apologise, Brother Rafael, I merely thought it might interest you to speak with-", but he was interrupted sharply again; Rafael's rather obvious displeasure was broken by sounds from the bell tower. The apprentice monks were marking the end of the day and the call to ablutions before the evening meal by ringing the bells seven times.

"I believe it is time for ablutions before our meal, Brother Athanasius; if you please, I take my leave now."

Rafael bowed curtly, and he passed Nour and Elyas on his way to the door as if they did not exist at all, slamming it shut in anger.

Rafael's manner had visibly deflated the old man's enthusiasm, and Nour, dismayed at how anyone could treat someone as gentle as Athanasius in such a fierce and disrespectful way, felt sorry for him.

"He is a man of few words," noted Noureddine with reserved humour. The old monk, who was somewhat accustomed to the cold and often uncompromising manner of Rafael, nodded and replied with some sadness in his voice.

"Yes, Brother Rafael is an unusual academic; he speaks little, and keeps to his own time and activities. But I must rush to ablutions; you have traveled far; I am certain you are looking forward to some nourishment other than wine! If you leave with me the Deed, I will keep it somewhere safe for now. Eat with us, and we will find a proper place for it when we return later!"

Although he could not rid himself of a lingering feeling of fore-boding, and hesitated briefly because of it, Nour could not resist the monk's invitation. He felt the weariness of the long ride settle in, and it had been days since his last proper meal. The welcome thought of a feast followed by a long sleep pushed the ill-feeling to the back of his mind, and he agreed to the old monk's request.

*

The three-storey building that made up the visitors' quarters adjoined Athanasaius' office, and Elyas had shown Nour to his cell before the young monk had rushed off to ablutions. It was a com-pact room at the far end of the guest quarters, on the uppermost floor, sparsely furnished with a bed, a chair and a small table. A large wooden cross hung over the bed, and Nour, almost instinc-tively, crossed himself; although he had become a Muslim again, he felt as connected to his Christian upbringing as he did to his Muslim roots. He cast his mind back to his childhood, the lessons at the convent, the nuns and monks who taught him and his friends before the cruel separation....and, unexpectedly, the face of Rafael appeared like a thunderbolt among those serene memories of his life before the expulsion, before the death of his parents and sister, before his return to Islam. It was the same terrifying feeling that came back, with no less frequency over the long years that had passed, of that heartbreaking day itself.

But there was something about Rafael that had brought it back with a more profound terror, and he wondered why. Was it their similar origin- although Rafael came from Portugal, the Kingdom and the Catholic power was now one with Spain- or was it the cold-ness in his manner, and especially his eyes, that reminded Nour of the priests who had dragged his father off to the stake, and driven his mother and sister over the cliffs of the Muela de Cortes? Between these visions floated the memory of his old friend Galenius, who had endured a similar fate as the son of Jews, finding a new life in England, before finally settling as a physician in Scotland.

Scotland....he thought of Margaret. Although Nour had vowed to visit her grave often, he had only been back once since her death. *Perhaps it is time for another visit*, he thought, as he touched the pendant concealed beneath his shirt. He had never removed it, and it had survived the treacheries of war and highway thieves over all those long years; having it there, he thought, was as if Margaret was always by his side.

Nour sat down by the desk. It stood beneath the window which overlooked the open passage leading to cells on either side of him, and he could see the minaret of the mosque and the tall tower of the basilica in front of him, and beyond, hidden in the darkness, he imagined the vast sea of red-washed rock and desert that surrounded them. He was so tired; his legs were heavy with the long ride, and his backside ached, but those thoughts of weariness moved to the back of his mind as that dark feeling, that foreboding once again surfaced in his conscience. He closed his eyes and tried to put into order the details of the day's conversations between the archbishop and the officials that had taken place earlier. He, Nour, had delivered the original document, and they, Sinan and Selim, would accompany him back to Damascus with the copies. Why? Why had they entrusted Nour to bring the original Deed alone, without protection, all this way, and when he needed protection to bring the copies back to Istanbul?

The thoughts stayed static in his mind, as he realized he needed to wash and dress before the meal; time was moving on. He took off his overcoat, and his shirt, and was in the process of washing his face when there was a knock at the door. It was Elyas.

"Good evening, Elyas," smiled Nour, seeing the frightened young boy before him. He wondered why the boy was always afraid. As if something had caught his eye and startled him, the boy said:

"I beg pardon, Seyyid Noureddine, but I am to bring you to the refectory for our evening meal."

"Thank you," replied Nour, "if you give me a moment or two, I will be ready."

The boy bowed and waited outside while Nour dressed in a clean shirt and mantle, and the two were, after a short time, off to the refectory.

First passing the mosque and the entrance to the basilica, the road to the refectory then took them through a long, vaulted passageway, with chapels and stores on either side, which eventually led them to a big courtyard. The three-storey building that faced them, with monks rushing about carrying out various evening duties, housed the monk's cells, with the bakery below, and the sweet and comforting smell of bread met Nour with delight, as loaf upon loaf was thrown into big baskets and carried away. He was happy to see that both the Bedouin and the monks were bakers, chatting and laughing jovially while the thick, white doughy masses were knocked and kneaded before meeting the fire of the big bakery ovens. He supposed the refectory could not be far away.

"That is a welcome smell, Elyas!" he remarked to the young monk, who had remained silent, and thoughtful, during their walk to the refectory. Elyas nodded, rather absentmindedly.

"The refectory is only a short walk away, Seyyid Noureddine."

After a few minutes, they arrived at a pair of large wooden double doors, ornately carved with birds and beasts. Above it, there was an inscription in Greek, which Nour, although once having studied the language, could no longer read.

"Elyas," he asked the monk before they entered, "I did study Greek as a boy, but the language has left me now; what does the inscription say?"

He was met with an eagerness that Nour had yet to encounter in the young boy, who replied enthusiastically:

"Oh, Seyyid Nour, it is from one of my favourite passages in the blessed Holy Bible! It says, *Blessed are those who hunger, and thirst for righteousness, for they will be contented.*"

Upon entering, Nour recognized a familiar setting: when he was a boy in the convent in Spain, the dining halls were almost identical, with long wooden tables and benches set up in rows next to each other, where the children would assemble once in the day for their communal meal before continuing their schooling. The monks and nuns would eat there three times a day, and once in the evening before retiring to their individual quarters and activities. The arrangement had been hierarchical, with nuns and monks seated according to their status within their order, but here, at St Catherine's, that did not seem to be the case. The archbishop sat at the head of whichever table pleased him that evening, regardless of the rank of those he joined.

The walls of the room, which was long and narrow but large nonetheless, were covered with spectacularly bright and vivid depictions of biblical scenes, and from his childhood education, Nour remembered them: a depiction of the Prophet Elyas being fed by a raven covered the wall to the right, and the apse at the far end of the room was graced with a magnificent scene of the Hospitality of Abraham, almost overshadowed by an elaborate painting of the Second Coming of Christ above it.

The largest and longest dining table, which spanned almost the entire length of the room, stood out from the more plainly decorated benches on either side of it: ornate angels and flowers were carved along both sides of it, and its legs- there were ten, evenly spaced, on either side- each ended in a clawed foot clasped around a ball. They reminded him of the furniture he had seen in El Escorial, and he was briefly transported back to Spain, but Nour's mind was distracted from his surroundings by the wonderful smells of food. The Bedouin had prepared a mouthwatering feast for all; roasted meat, rice and vegetables, cheese curds with herbs and thick loaves of freshly baked bread lay before them in abundance, and Nour could feel his stomach tightening in anticipation.

The monks and nuns had assembled around their designated tables, and only when Archbishop arrived, with Athanasius behind him, were they all invited to be seated. Ioasaf indicated for Nour to sit on his left, opposite Athanasius, at the large central table. Nour noted, with curiosity and great relief, that Sinan and Selim had declined Athanasius' invitation to the meal, but he was disappointed to see that the enigmatic Rafael was not among their group, although the Abbess Maria de Taye, as well as a few of the Benedictine monks and nuns, had been invited to sit with the Archbishop. Rafael was seated, slightly apart from the rest, at a table reserved for monks near the entrance to the refectory. Constantly being engaged in conversation by the monks around his table, Nour had little chance to glance across the room to observe Rafael, in the hopes that his memory might return and tell him why this aloof and cold monk seemed so familiar to him.

"Friends," began the Archbishop warmly with a big smile, as the eager chatter that permeated the refectory turned to silence, "we have cause for celebration this evening! His Most Imperial Highness the Sultan has, on this momentous day, returned to the Monastery the Deed of Protection, a most sacred deed ensuring the protection of all Christians that live in Ottoman lands!"

As the murmur of approval and relief rippled across the gathered crowd, some weeping with joy, Nour observed Rafael. His face looked disapproving and angry, in stark contrast to those around him.

"In honour of our most gracious patron His Most Imperial Highness the Sultan, we declare this day a feast, and our dear and faithful Bedouin friends have prepared a meal that is fit for sultans- let us eat!"

Ioasaf began to pray, still standing, and even Rafael joined in, quietly reciting the grace before the Archbishop gave the signal to the Bedouin to serve the food. A gracious host himself, the

Archbishop introduced Nour to those who shared his table, and the Abbess, being the only woman among them, was treated with particular deference. All ate heartily the sumptuous meal that was put before them, and Nour particularly, starved, and thirsty, was so busy filling his stomach, he did hardly speak for the first half hour. Although he had listened intently to the conversations around him, it was not until the Abbess, who had observed him with some curiosity, asked him a question as he finished his plate, that he spoke.

"Seyyid Noureddine," she began in a quiet but sharp tone, with a soft Flemish accent, "the good Archbishop tells me that you have origins in Spain."

Nour nodded in reluctant acknowledgement; did he have to go through the trial of explaining his life story once again?

Maria de Taye smiled benevolently, to Nour's discomfiting surprise. He guessed that she was about fifty-five years of age, and her white, smooth skin suggested that she had led most of her life sheltered in the dim light of a northern convent, rather than the bright and sun filled shores of warmer climates. Piercing blue eyes that almost appeared violet in the right light stood out sharply amidst the paleness of her face and the white habit she wore. Conscious of being closely observed, she gathered the rest of her table companions into her conversation.

"I should very dearly like to travel to Spain one day! I hear the convents and cathedrals are magnificent in their design and decoration.... now, of course, it is impossible, but perhaps when the war is over." She paused and looked intently at Nour.

"Tell me, Seyyid Noureddine, have you returned to Spain since you....", she stumbled briefly, realizing an insensitivity was about to come over her, before she went on, "since you left?"

Nour had to consider, for a moment, how he felt being asked this question by a Catholic, and he wondered if Maria de Taye had been deliberately cruel, or genuinely unaware of the thoughtlessness of her curiosity.

"I....left when I was thirteen, Abbess," he replied slowly and as unemotionally as he could, "and have not returned since."

A silence followed, awkward not because of the embarrassment of those around him, but rather because they expected Nour to continue with a story, which, after a minute or two, he did, but perhaps not in the manner that was expected.

"My father was sent to the fire because the-", he paused briefly, having to find the diplomatically correct word, "*authorities* believed him to be a heretic, which he was not."

Maria de Taye showed no emotion, and Nour concluded her to be as cold as Rafael in that respect; but she herself knew what the kind of loss that Nour spoke of meant to one's heart and soul. Maria de Taye knew that better than most of those around her.

The light banter and merry laughter around the table became subdued, but Nour, now that he had started his story, thought he might as well finish it, and continued.

"My mother and sister...", he stopped to close his eyes briefly before opening them again, the image of them standing on the edge of the cliff burnt into his memory, "believed death would be more welcome than a life of perpetual persecution, and so they gave their souls to the valley below the cliffs of the Muela de Cortes."

No one spoke, or ate, or drank. In shame or sorrow, most of his table companions looked away, heads bowed; but not Maria de Taye, whose bright blue eyes were fixed, expressionless, on Nour as he spoke.

"And I," he concluded, "by the mercy of God, was spared an upbringing of servitude and slavery in a 'true' Catholic family and put on a ship destined for the Barbary Coast."

Only on hearing Nour's bitterness in the word 'true' did the Abbess react.

"That is an ordeal, Seyyid Noureddine, that no child should have to endure," she spoke with unexpected passion, "and I am truly sorry that my faith has been the cause of so much grief in your life!"

"But," replied Nour, almost angrily, "it was also *my* faith, until I was forced to leave it because I was not 'pure', but a Morisco!"

The Archbishop, who had listened intently but now feared the celebratory mood was threatened, intervened, in a lighthearted tone.

"We are all God's children here and have his protection; as the Deed that you, Seyyid Noureddine, returned to us, gives proof!"

He smiled benevolently at those around him, and addressing the Abbess, who he could see had become somewhat affected by Nour's remarks, the archbishop asked:

"Good Abbess Maria de Taye, I do believe you have a good story or two about your own adventures as head of the Forest Abbey, despite the treacherous conditions the war in Europe has brought about!"

The Abbess accepted Ioasaf's graciousness with a nod and a smile and turned her attention away from Nour.

"Oh, yes, we have some stories, Archbishop; even of brother Rafael, who appears so unblemished and without fault, that he could be the Pope himself!"

No one laughed until she winked and burst out laughing herself, and suddenly, it was as if the sombre mood of the last minute had never visited the table, and as if Maria de Taye had become a different person to the inquisitorial woman who had questioned Nour; and as if his story had not mattered at all.

"My good brothers- and sister- you have not finished your meals- I pray, do continue! As we have a special guest," the Archbishop threw an inviting glance at Noureddine, "I have ordered a special sweet to have with our wine."

A murmur of excitement, as the monks took to the last helpings of the food on their plates, passed across the hall, with the exception of one: Rafael, whose specific dietary requirements had been fulfilled and forced him to disapprove of this sweet end to an otherwise Spartan meal, politely made excuses to his table fellows, bowed his head in the direction of the Archbishop and Abbess, who returned the reserved courtesy with an equally cold smile.

"He does not favour sweet things?" enquired Noureddine, half-mocking, in an attempt at cordiality. The enigma of Rafael was forming a growing curiosity in his thoughts.

"Our good brother," began the Archbishop, "has no need for such worldly gifts. But that must not stop you from enjoying possibly the most delicious sweets ever created on God's good earth!"

Plates full of small balls of dough that had been soaked in a sticky honey-like syrup were set before them, and Nour was reminded of the lukhum he had tasted at the Palace in Istanbul, the favourite sweet of Kosem Sultan. These delightful little sweets seemed to instill an extraordinarily good humour in all, and after no less than three rounds of this delight, the Archbishop finally proclaimed:

"Well, my children," the monks chuckled merrily at this remark, "I feel it is time to retire; our guest has traveled a long way, and he has a long journey still ahead of him in the next few days, I believe. I bid you all a very good night and merry dreams!"

Maria de Taye also took her leave, bowing and casting a brief, almost bemused, look towards Noureddine, who forced a quick smile out of politeness.

As the Archbishop rose, so did the entire room, and not one was seated until he and the Abbess had left the dining hall.

"It is late," said Athanasius after a few minutes, looking toward Noureddine, "and you must be very tired now, my good friend. Let me walk you back to your quarters!"

Noureddine now felt that he could hardly keep his eyes open, and welcomed the idea of sleep, however minimalist the conditions.

"Rest would indeed be very welcome, Brother Athanasius; thank you."

The two rose from the table, bid the rest of the company good night, and went in search of rest and sleep. Noureddine had, by the time he lay his body down on a comfortable straw mattress, completely forgotten that he and Athanasius had neglected to find a secure place for the letter.

Tomorrow........, he thought, drifting off into a deep, otherworldly slumber.

~ Sixteen ~

Nour felt rested the next morning, but he had experienced a sequence of vivid and eventful dreams during the night. He was not accustomed to dreaming and felt slightly disturbed by the experience.

He had been alone in his dream. He had been standing in front of a great darkness that pulled him toward it, a pull that felt irresistible. There was no light but a single sparkle that appeared to be alive and communicating to him. The pull of the darkness was so strong he could hardly resist it, but the light was keeping him fixed. A bridge appeared behind him, to which the light guided him. He crossed it and when he looked below him, there were bones and skulls floating in the water. But before he had reached the other side, he realized that the water was blood; he had crossed a river of blood. When he woke, he had felt pearls of perspiration on his brow, and the skin on his chest was damp with sweat.

Nour tried to ignore the disturbing images of his dreams and absentmindedly completed his dawn prayer in his room, rather than the mosque, before dressing in a hurry. He wanted to see Athanasius to make sure the Deed was safe before Selim and Sinan returned from the Bedouin camp. As Noureddine left his small quarters he could see the crimson light of dawn creeping over the ragged mountain tops; it was still early, and the monastery was peaceful. Walking quietly along the corridor, he tried to remember where he had seen Athanasius enter his own apartment the previous day, when suddenly a loud, shrill scream pierced the tranquility of the monastery's solitude. It happened again, and Noureddine raced along the footway, down the stairs towards the unhappy wailing, and upon reaching it, he found himself outside Athanasius' quarters. Elyas had gone to wake his master, as was his duty, but the old monk lay dead in front of them, his head separated from the rest of his body, amid a sea of crimson.

"Master.....," whispered the young monk, shaking with grief, "my master is dead.....someone has murdered my master!"

He fell to his knees and raising his hands toward the red-blue skies above them, he began to pray, rocking back and forth as if a madman, hot tears streaming down his pale, worn face. Noureddine was in complete disbelief and bowed his head; the merriment of the last night's banquet suddenly seemed a very distant past.

He glanced at the mess that remained of the old monk, laying at his feet, trying not to unload the contents of his stomach as he felt the nausea creeping in. The eyes of the old monk had been hacked out in a frenzied attack. Nour's own eyes stopped at the clenched hand of Athanasius; it was clutching something. He bowed down to inspect it, trying to steady his dizziness. Very gently he prized the item from the stiff hand of the dead man, and his heart skipped a few beats when he realized what he was looking at: it was a torn fragment of the Deed! Before he could untangle his muddled and confused thoughts, he was violently pushed out of the way by a hooded cloaked figure, speeding past him and Elyas like black lightning. It slipped in Athanasius' blood and other fluids, but seemed to fly down the lane towards the refectory at high speed. Noureddine recovered quickly, and set off after the intruder, trying not to lose sight of the whirlwind of black fabric as he chased it through the labyrinth of corridors, through the monks' living quarters, past the refectory and the burning bush, until finally Noureddine lost sight of the assailant in a crowd of monks who had appeared to investigate the commotion. "Stop!" he shouted. "Stop that murderer!" He pleaded to the crowd, as the figure, deftly and quickly weaved through the crowd with great speed, the shocked monks too slow to react; and then the figure disappeared, as if into thin air.

By the time Noureddine had found his way back to Athanasius' office, the crowd of monks had gathered at the horrific scene, and seeing what was left of their fellow brother, some wept, others comforted each other, and a few vomited at the horrific site that met them. Murmurs of fetching the Archbishop sent a young novice in search of Ioasaf, who appeared a short while later. He was visibly agitated and distressed, but remained composed, despite the horrific mess that confronted him.

"The intruder escaped," said Noureddine to the inquisitive group; Elyas nodded, and looked around the office.

"Is anything missing....?"

Noureddine was searching the room with his sharp eyes, trying to spy out the Deed, but could not lay his eyes on it anywhere.

As if reading his thoughts, Elyas said:

"It is gone, Seyyid Nour; the Deed is gone!"

In the larger crowd that had begun to form around them, Nour's heart sank as he saw the grim faces of Selim and Sinan.

"Where is the Deed?" Sinan snapped, eyes bulging with rage, as if the brutal murder of Athanasius, and the eyeless severed head that lay at his feet were nothing but an inconsequential inconvenience to him. "Where is it?" Sinan repeated sharply, his accusing eyes staring at Nour as if he was already a condemned murderer and thief.

Nour was dragged, almost by the scruff of his neck, to the court of the Archbishop, pushed and jostled through the narrow alleyways like a criminal by the bulky and almost super-human figures of the two janissaries, as bewildered monks and distressed Bedouin looked on.

Ioasaf, who had returned before them, sat at his desk, hands clasped together, and eyes closed. He did not react when the three men burst through his door. A raven, perhaps the same one that had visited the day before, perched on the windowsill, its small head occasionally peeking through the slight opening in quiet curiosity. Like Iosaf, it appeared undisturbed by the explosive entrance of the Archbishop's visitors.

"I", he muttered, weary and worn, and full of sorrow, "am so aggrieved at the death of a most dear friend." Drawing his eyes over the company of men before him- all bigger and stronger and quicker than him- he was momentarily surprised by the absence of fear or intimidation in his heart; he went on, instead, with irritation and disapproval in his voice.

"And I am also distressed at the confusion and panic this has caused in our community....never has such an act of evil been committed here; never!"

"Well," sniped Sinan, pushing Nour into a nearby chair with such force its legs considered briefly giving way to the impact, "that is the least of your problems, Archbishop!"

The old man shot a glance at Sinan, who, in the vivid imagination of Ioasaf, resembled a rabid dog frothing at the mouth, yellow teeth slightly bared, ready to tear at weaker flesh at any moment. *I trust you no more than I trust that slimy monk, Rafael,* he thought.

"What do you mean?"

"I mean, Archbishop," replied Sinan slowly, jaws clenched so tightly they looked as though they might burst through the flesh and skin at any moment, "the Deed is gone!"

It was as Ioasaf had feared; for who would murder a man as gentle and all-loving as Athanasius, unless the motive was to steal a document of such importance?

"I see."

His calm reply angered even Selim, the less hot-headed of the two janissaries, who screamed loudly at the Archbishop.

"With respect," of which of course there was none, "this is no time to be calm, Archbishop! There is a thief on the loose who has a document without which you, and your fellow Christians, would be in grave danger!"

Even the raven jumped and flapped its wings in protest at Selim's outburst. He angrily slammed the window shut, sending the bird shrieking as it flew to a nearby tree.

The Archbishop stared intently at Nour, ignoring Selim and Sinan's outbursts. His head lowered, he smiled encouragingly in a paternal pose, the old man's constant calmness a complete mystery to the two janissaries.

"We would not find ourselves in this situation if you had not failed in your duty, Seyyid Noureddine!" Selim barked, slightly calmer now, pacing up and down the office, like a lion assessing his prey.

There was a long silence. Ioasaf, who always tried to seek the way of compromise rather than conflict, attempted to soothe the anger of the officials, masking as well as he could his deep mistrust.

"Now, let us not cast blame or judgement without the facts; we could not know that there was a thief and a murderer among us here, in this most holy place! Elyas and Seyyid Noureddine both saw the presumed assassin escape from Athanasius' office, and every-one- including our Bedouin friends, who are much more skilled at tracking and finding than any of us- are searching every corner of the monastery for the culprit!"

He sighed, resigned; his demeanour and mood had become the complete contrast to the lighthearted, merry banter of the previous evening.

"At least the copies are safe," he added.

Sinan replied with a menacing grin:

"I am afraid I must disappoint you there, Holy Father," he sneered, half-mocking, "because someone has also stolen the cop-ies! We went in search of them immediately after the discovery of Athanasius, and they are nowhere to be found! So," Sinan contin-ued, hands folded behind his back, staring directly at Ioasaf, "as of now, there is no written record of the Deed among us here at St Catherine's, or at the Imperial Palace in Istanbul. What shall happen," he jeered sharply, reminding Nour of a snake, "to any of you once word of this is received by Her Imperial Highness the Valide Sultan and the Grand Vizier, I cannot imagine!"

Nour and Ioasaf glanced at each other, stunned at this discovery. Selim, pleased to have the upper hand, continued to stare at them, standing in front of them like a solid rock, waiting with folded arms for a reply he knew would not come.

"But...why?" The Archbishop thought out loud to himself, "What purpose would it serve to steal the original and the copies? I do not understand!" He looked to Nour for aid while trying to avoid the cold, hard stares of Selim and Sinan.

Nour's thoughts were so cluttered and confused; he could see no way through the mess of ideas that flooded his mind in such an overwhelming blur.

"I can find no words," he began, but was brutally cut off by Selim.

"Perhaps because it was you who took them, Seyyid Noureddine!" he growled, dark eyes flashing with anger as he stroked his thick, black beard. "You, who are neither Christian or Muslim, or perhaps both at the same time, however it suits your purpose!"

A hollow laugh echoed against the bare walls, and Nour found his own gentle self be overshadowed with resentment, fear and violent thoughts, once again throwing him back to that painful day in Spain.

"You," continued Selim, seeing he had stoked the embers of Nour's anger, "who went from Islam, to become a Catholic infidel, and then crawled back to Islam when even that rejected you! You could be a spy for anyone!" Selim considered with a tight-lipped grin and narrowed eyes. "How do we know that you are not in the service of the Habsburgs and their mission to gain power over all of Europe, and destroy the Ottoman Empire in the process?"

"I am not a spy," Nour replied, as calmly as he could. The morning sun had filtered through the window, catching the inquisitor's face. It cast Selim half in the light and half in the shadow.

"And why?" Nour went on, with a slightly raised voice. "What purpose would that suit me?"

It was Sinan who replied this time with the self-satisfied tone of someone who has solved the world's greatest mystery.

"You play neither or both sides; either way, the letter can fetch you a fortune if offered- or ransomed- to the right buyer!"

Nour scoffed loudly.

"And if that indeed had been my motive, Seyyid Sinan," he chuckled, "would it not have been cleverer of me to steal the document on my journey from Istanbul, and disappear, rather than go through the pretense of delivering it in the first place?"

The officials, for the first time since the Archbishop had encountered them, seemed deflated and lost for words. This amused Ioasaf in such a dark moment, and he took the opportunity to intervene.

"Seyyid Nour, as we all know, completed his mission successfully by delivering the Deed to me; therefore," he turned to Sinan and Selim, "the fate and responsibility of the Deed since it arrived at St Catherine's is entirely my own. I accept that, dear friends, and I must ask you to do the same."

Selim shook his head stubbornly.

"So you tell me, Archbishop, that you have complete trust in a man who knows not whether he is a Christian or a Muslim, or worse even, that he does know, but pretends not to?"

Ioasaf smiled, tired of defending that which he believed should never need defending:

"We are all God's children here, regardless of how we choose to worship," he sermoned, to the extreme irritation of the two officials, and the silent gratitude of Nour.

It was bitterly cold in the early morning air. The icy chill of the desert night still lingered as the sun continued its struggle to climb above the mountain peaks. The usual bustle of the morning's work was subdued as the monks went about caring for Athanasius' remains and arranging for his burial. The dogs howled mournfully, in synchrony, as if they marked the passing of a dear old friend; and for once, the cats relinquished their usual desire to tease them, and stayed silent, keeping watch from courtyard corners and window-sills instead.

"Very well, Archbishop," Sinan finally broke the silence, "we will respect your wish, for now; Seyyid Nour has until dusk to find the Deed and the copies. If he does not," Sinan stared directly at Nour before continuing, "he will be arrested and taken to Cairo. In the meantime, we will make use of the hospitality of our Bedouin brethren and thank you for the hospitality you have shown to us until now."

Without a bow or even a deferential nod, the two officials strode defiantly through the door and down the labyrinth of lanes that led to the main gate of the monastery.

Ioasaf breathed an audible sigh of relief as he felt the tension that had filled the room disappear with the departure of Sinan and Selim. He shifted heavily in his chair and shook his head, shuffling a few papers about on his desk as if they could help him resolve his dilemma.

The morning's events were beginning to sink into reality as Nour tried to put the sequence of events into some order, Sinan and Selim's threat looming in the back of his mind.

"They have set an impossible task, Archbishop," he remarked, exasperated, "and they do know that!"

Ioasaf peered out of the window in search of some blue sky over the monastery walls and considered the statement.

"Yes, I believe you are right in that, Seyyid Noureddine; truthfully, I am at a complete loss as to what to do now."

"With your permission," replied Noureddine, after a moment of thought, "I would like to search Brother Athanasius' office, and the library; there may be some clues, and I think if we are to start searching anywhere, that would seem the most logical course of action. And," he added, as Archbishop Ioasaf nodded in agreement, "I would like Elyas to help me- he knew the old monk better than anyone else, I think, and may hold some clues even though he may not know it himself."

"Yes, of course, all assistance you require will be at your disposal!"

"Unless you think it inappropriate, I would also like to speak to the Abbess Maria de Taye about...", but he could not for the moment find words that did not sound accusatory; the Archbishop sensed the direction of Nour's thoughts, and finished his sentence for him.

"The animated discussion between the two of you regarding your- upbringing- in Spain...I can understand how that would have left you, and the Abbess, in a state of irresolution," his frown softening as he contemplated what it must be like for a child to live in such spiritual confusion. "And, although I do not claim to know her character well, I believe that she would appreciate a reconciliation of some sort."

Nour, relieved at the Archbishop's consent, smiled and nodded.

"What do you know of Brother Rafael, Archbishop?"

Ioasaf sneered, almost haughtily, and answered with some contempt.

"Rafael de la Cruz is an enigma to us all, Seyyid Noureddine," Ioasaf mused, shaking his head softly, "at that we are all agreed!"

With a grain of resentment, not usual for his character, the clergyman continued:

"But, as the Abbess herself remarked, Brother Rafael is as fault-free as the Pope! I have seldom met a soul so steadfast in their doctrinal commitments as he, and although he appears cold and unemotional- and we disagree on many theological points- I cannot believe him to be a thief," he paused briefly with a thoughtful frown, as if to convince himself, "or a murderer."

The raven, who had dared to return to the windowsill, shrieked a melancholy moan, and both men jumped, startled. It stared at them unafraid, inclining its head inquisitively as if listening to their conversation, until Iosaf shooed it away. It flapped its big black wings in discontent as it was again exiled to the nearby rooftop of the mosque, casting a disdainful look back in his direction.

"They come begging for food," tutted Ioasaf, "and who can blame them! The cats, although I am fond of them, would eat everything here, including the ravens, if given half the chance."

Returning to the enigma of Rafael, Nour commented, as detached as possible, for he was inwardly apprehensive of the monk- although he could not yet figure out the reason.

"Your assumptions are, of course, fair, Archbishop, and I do not wish to accuse anyone of a crime without reason or proof. I suppose," Nour pondered out loud, half to himself and vaguely to the room, "I find his manner and presence unnerving!"

The Archbishop laughed gently, stroking his thick beard, twisting the ends into thin, long strands.

"In that, you are certainly not wrong!"

Somewhere, the bell chimed for the midday meal, and Nour, knowing time was against him, took his leave.

*

The plans that Rafael had so carefully laid, every detail thought out meticulously and thoroughly, as was his habit, had all gone wrong, and he was furious. All would have worked perfectly had it not been for those cursed officials from Cairo- damn them! - and the shock of seeing Noureddine- of all people- and now, that girl again!

He repented by chanting a few *Hail Marys*, but his seething blood did not cool; he had to think fast. On top of this calamity, there was a real danger that Noureddine, who Rafael had recognized almost immediately, would soon remember his own face, and that he, Rafael de la Cruz, head of the Order of Christ, would be uncovered as an impostor.

Noureddine must be distracted in some way from finding out who I am, he thought, *yes, if he is arrested....* Rafael's mind was racing as a new plan began to take shape in his mind. In his deep contemplation he had absentmindedly put his hands in his pockets and feeling the rosary he always carried with him between his fingers, he stopped with a jolt; there was another object he had forgotten about. He pulled it out. *That was very careless of me*, he reproached himself, dangling Athanasius' cross in front of his narrowed eyes. But a new opportunity had presented itself. *Yes, that is the answer,* he decided. A sly grin passed his face as he glared at the cross; to his delight, rust-coloured specks of the old monk's blood still clung to the plain, dull gold, and having slipped it back into the pocket of his tunic, he headed out of his room towards the guest quarters of the monastery. "This will mark his guilt," he muttered to himself, "and those useless Ottoman oafs will have all they need to arrest him.... and more!"

~ Seventeen ~

Elyas had been trying to distract himself from his sorrow for Athanasius by pouring all his energies into his work. He had busied himself with gardening duties in the orchards at the foot of the monastery, and helped Ali, his Bedouin friend, tend to the horses in the stables which were behind the orchards. The young monk had especially enjoyed looking after Layla; her gentle nature and calm disposition soothed his soul a little, after the recurring horrors of the morning.

Elyas had been intrigued as well as terrified by the two Otto-man officials, who had arrived at the Bedouin encampment around mid-morning, and he wondered what they had made of the affair; a murder, and two thefts had occurred soon after their- and Noured-dine's- arrival! Sinan and Selim frightened him, their demeanor always cruel and sullen, and he wondered if there ever was anything on earth that had given these two men any pleasure or happiness, but he dismissed those thoughts as he tended to the orchard. He worked methodically, pulling up weeds and wayward shrubs before planting a new olive tree, a proud young specimen with shiny leaves and strong roots. Satisfied with his work, he cast his eyes to another tree that stood a bit further away; it was an ancient but sick tree, a tired-looking mess of dry sticks that Elyas had refused to give up on, and wiping the sweat from his brow, the young monk paused for a moment, wondering what could be done to nurse it back to health. The mid-day sun was warm, and he moved to some shade by the wall to cool down and collect his thoughts. A sound, like the soft buzz of bees, hummed somewhere behind the wall, and it gave him a brief comfort; but it was not to last long. Abruptly shaken out of his tranquility, he could hear the low, sneering voice of Selim, a whisper he could barely make out, drifting over the wall. *They are so close!* He thought, quietly moving closer until he could hear Sinan and Selim in a heated discussion, voices low but biting and angry, and as he strained to hear their conversation, his blood ran cold.

"....were our orders on our return journey, anyway; the messenger was never to come back to Istanbul alive!" breathed Sinan, exasperated.

"Yes, but everything has changed now! The letter and the copies are gone! What if he has already given them to his accomplice? There was a stranger who escaped- I saw him!" snapped Selim. Elyas could hear him pacing back and forth along the wall.

"If Noureddine did take them, he will never tell us; the Grand Vizier told me enough about him to understand that he is not the sort to give up anything easily! We had orders; we have already failed in one of them- to retrieve the copies; if we want to save our own necks, we must complete the rest!"

A brief silence, what Elyas could only believe was a standoff as the two considered their position, ensued, before Selim finally spoke.

"Very well; but we cannot do it here! It would cast suspicion on us. We already warned the Archbishop that we would arrest Noureddine if he does not produce the letter and the copies; when we return at dusk, we will take him into our custody.... and do it once we have reached a safe distance!"

Sinan agreed with a grunt before adding:

"Agreed; the desert and the mountains give us no shortage of options for places to dump a body without it being discovered for a long time- if ever! It will give me great pleasure to cut that traitor's throat!"

Elyas was so horrified he gasped without thinking, and nearly dropped his rake, and although he caught it just in time, the two men were startled by the disturbance.

"Did you hear something?" whispered Selim.

Sinan frowned, nodding, and raising his voice, he asked as calmly as he could:

"Is someone there?"

The young monk hardly dared to breathe; he felt frozen despite the heat of the midday sun, pearls of sweat rolling down his temples. His heart was beating so hard he thought all the world could hear it. The shuffling on the other side of the wall instinctively made him hide, as quietly as he could, behind a large stack of baskets propped up against the ancient sick tree. As he peered through the gaps in the weaving, he could see the beady black eyes of Sinan, propped up on the shoulders of his accomplice, scouring the orchard when, as if God had answered his prayers, he heard Ali's voice.

"Seyyid Selim, Seyyid Sinan, are you looking for something?" The cheery voice of the young Bedouin, and the flustered explanations of the two officials, were almost comical and surreal.

"There is an easier way to enter the orchard, if that is your wish- the gate is only around the corner!" Ali pointed innocently to a large cedar door further along from where they were standing. Sinan mumbled something vague about wanting a view of the orchard from higher up, while Selim tried to distract from their awkward activity by asking the boy what kind of fruits the Bedouin were growing. Ali answered politely, before stating:

"It is time for our mid-day meal; my father has prepared a roasted goat and rice. Please," he continued, bowing and gesturing towards the Bedouin encampment, "it would be his honour to host you!"

To Elyas' great relief, he could hear the voices of Ali, Sinan and Selim become quieter as they walked away, Ali chatting away about the challenges and joys of tending an orchard in the extreme climates of the desert, the two janissaries grunting on occasion in accord but in reality, completely disinterested. As soon as Elyas was able to leave unnoticed, he fled the gardens through the back entrance, and hastened to the monastery. *I must find Seyyid Noureddine at once*, he panicked, *before there is another death on our holy ground!*

Elyas searched first in the guest quarters, but Nour was nowhere to be found; he only saw the tall, upright figure of Rafael stride along the corridor towards the back stairs and disappear, not noticing the young monk had seen him. Too distracted to wonder what Rafael was doing there, his next stop was the mosque, but to no avail. A passing monk told him he had seen Nour go into the Archbishop's office, and so Elyas hurried there, but, after having summoned the courage to knock on the door, there was no answer. He headed towards the library and Athanasius' office, agitated and impatient, stopping by the refectory on his way, but there also he was unsuccessful in his search for Nour. Reluctantly, and with a feeling of deep dread, Elyas made his way to his old master's office, hoping one of his fellow monks had cleaned the large pools of blood from the floor and the walls, and wiped away any trace of the morning's horrific discovery. *Time is running on; there are only a few hours until dusk, and I must help him,* he thought desperately, the beginnings of a plan starting to form in his ever-growing imagination.

*

"You promised!" Brother Rafael was standing in Maria de Taye's quarters, imperiously demanding an explanation. "You promised at Jakobsberg that it would be the first and the last time that you would help that girl!"

The Abbess replied sternly, although not able to look him in the eye.

"That girl has a name, Brother Rafael; it is Balgaire, and she is a woman now! And anyway, how can you be so certain it was her? It seems far-fetched to me!"

She cast her mind back to those misfortune-filled days and remembered well the promise she had made to her fellow brothers and sisters. Disaster after disaster had followed when they took young Balgaire in. But the child had been so helpless at the time, so desperate, so frightened, it had been impossible- even if the rumours that the girl's mother had been burned as a witch were true- for the Abbess to turn her away. Soon after her arrival at Forest Abbey, it was discovered that the girl- only twelve years old at the time- was with child. The convent, already stretched financially and in some disrepute, had neither the resource to raise a child, nor a willingness to live with the danger or notoriety of concealing an illegitimate birth. The young girl understood at first, but slowly grew bitter, and racked with guilt, she became almost incurable of her desperation. Despite being almost at the point of giving birth, she escaped one night, and all for the better for the convent, or so the majority of the holy community believed. Only Maria de Taye would not give up on her; the Abbess searched for her for months, and, when she was at the point of giving up, the girl reappeared. She had been with her family at Langenstein, the Abbess was told; but beyond that, no one ever knew what had happened in her time there, because she would not reveal anything. Only a few nights later, when a group of armed riders appeared at the monastery gates demanding her release, there was no doubt that Balgaire must have committed a grave crime.

However wrong it may have been in the eyes of God, or however right, the nuns and monks agreed that they would defend their keep, rather than give up one of their flock, and so for four days and nights, they withstood the raiders with whatever they could conjure up as weapons: nails, slings, bottles, rocks, hot oil. After almost half of the monastery building was destroyed, and the gates sure to give way at any moment, the nuns and monks realized that the only way to survive was to escape. They took whatever possessions they could carry, and fled through a tunnel passage, which ran for a few miles under the river and would eventually emerge somewhere along the road to Heidelberg.

After several days and nights of wandering through forests and across hills, the order had finally reached a safe haven: the city of Heidelberg. They found refuge in the Benedictine Monastery of Jakobsberg with the kind agreement of the Abbott and Abbbess, but only on one condition: Balgaire had to leave. The nuns had tried to plead a case for her and to convey the danger she was in- even those nuns who had first objected to helping the poor girl- but the Abbott would not concede; he had to keep the reputation and welfare of his community a priority and would not risk taking in a girl who was a fugitive.

"You cannot stay here, Balgaire," Maria de Taye had told her, as gently as possible, even if it felt as if she was banishing her own flesh and blood to ruin. Balgaire had not protested; the same night, she had packed her belongings- such meager ones as they were- and escaped, and although the Abbess had once again tried to look for her, Balgaire was nowhere to be found. And that, as Maria de Taye cast her mind back to those tragic days, had been the last time she had laid eyes on that wayward spirit of a girl- until yesterday, when the past and Balgaire had reappeared like a thunderbolt from the skies, some ten years later.

"Abbess," insisted Rafael, "your promise!"

She sighed softly, resignedly.

"Yes," she eventually muttered in reply. Rafael observed her closely; she was aware of his scrutiny and knew well how men like him judged all women. Maria de Taye, at the age of fifty-six, was still a woman whose beauty appeared in fragments underneath the habit and gown she had donned in the last forty years or so.

"I did not forget," she eventually continued, "my promise to you, Brother Rafael, and all of our other brothers and sisters!"

Irritated, Rafael moved closer to her, a waft of cold air flaring up between them as their robes disturbed the stillness of the room.

"Then why did you break it?" he sniffed arrogantly, in the firm belief that he was a superior creature to the one before him.

"That child, we agreed, would never change, and we were not mistaken! She was the Devil's making when she first came to us and has remained his follower ever since; death would be the kindest release for her, and those she infects with her ill-conceived deeds!"

The Abbess promptly snapped back:

"Only God can judge; do not be so arrogant as to think that you, a mere servant of Him, need to assist Him in His work, Brother Rafael!"

The air in the Abbess' chamber, where they were both ensconced, was dead now, stillness returning to the point where the soft breaths of the two clergy could be heard clearly by anyone else who might be present.

She turned away from Rafael's startled, and almost pained, expression, and continued, her tone less punishing but no less bitter.

"As for my promise...", she sighed again, this time a deeper and more effort-full exhale, "times are different now; ten years have passed, at least... we have all changed, for better or worse, and as the Head of this Order, I made a vow to help those in need."

"But she is a murderer, Abbess! A killer!" Rafael's eyes widened in incredulity. "Mark my words, she has done it before, and she will do it again! It is our duty to bring her to justice!"

Her back still turned, she looked out of the window; the gentle bustle of the monks and sisters going about their usual business bore no sign of the terrible events of the last day.

"Neither you nor I can make that judgement; only God can. You claim you saw someone with Athanasius, may his soul rest in peace, but you cannot prove whether she is the one who murdered him." She turned back to face him and added with an ice- cold stare, "After all, you were also there, Brother Rafael, to discuss some dispute the two of you had been engaged in, I understand; it may as well have been you that cut off his head and tore out his eyes, for all any of us know!"

For the first time since she had known the monk the Abbess saw a flash of fear and apprehension in Rafael's eyes. *I have struck a nerve*, she thought with pleased amusement, and relished driving the dagger she had taken against him deeper into his frail soul.

"Because, Brother Rafael de la Cruz, I know who you really are; who you really work for....," she smiled, seeing his eyes narrow in disbelief and anger. "You are a servant of The Order of Christ! Nothing more than a paid assassin....!"

Rafael stood, mouth agape; words tumbled out of him incoherently and frantically.

"I...I... cannot believe you, Abbess...you...of all, would say such things, accuse me, *me*! of all people....I must....protest in the strongest....it is vile, vile....and this place.....why did you bring us here! They call themselves believers but look at them!" He spluttered almost uncontrollably, trying to turn the conversation away from himself, while Maria de Taye stood calmly before him, watching him with pity and contempt as he professed his immodest superiority towards herself- which she was accustomed to in a man's world- but she was pained to hear him cast such insults towards those who had taken them in graciously in their hour of need.

"....I will take my leave, Abbess; it is clear to me that our relationship is no longer sustainable- even after all we have been through together!- that girl!- you are blinded by your maternal instincts!" he spat out at her, before concluding with such vitriolic fire it almost made the Abbess laugh, "You should have been some poor beggar's wife, then you would have been able to indulge those instincts with your twelve snivelling children, cooking, cleaning, wiping their arses, rather than sullying the good spirit of the Catholic church as the Head of the Order of St Benedict!"

With that, he stormed out of her room in a whirlwind of hate and passion, leaving Maria de Taye standing in a daze, a tear trickling down her pale, smooth cheek, for the bitter anguish of Rafael's spoken truth pierced her heart.

*

In the mischievous way that fate sometimes likes to play with people's plans, while Elyas was searching for Nour, Nour had been looking for the young monk, each missing one another by only a few minutes in the merry-go-round of fate. Nour had left the Archbishop's office only some minutes before Elyas' arrival there, when the soldier had gone in search of Elyas at the library. Not finding him there- or Brother Rafael, to his surprise- he decided to pay a visit to the Abbess first; he, too, was conscious of time moving swiftly towards dusk, and his looming arrest by the two Ottoman officials was a constant reminder in the back of his mind.

Trying to find solace in the silence of her room after her aggravating encounter with Rafael, Maria de Taye had forgotten how lonely the work of an abbess could be; she often missed the camaraderie of the brother and sisterhood, and had never really liked, or enjoyed, being the head of the Order. It had been presented to her as an honour to do God's work and lead others to do the same, which she had accepted as a duty, rather than a wish. *All this time,* she thought, *a lifetime of devotion and service to a higher purpose, but what have I achieved?* The image of Balgaire came to her, as it had done more frequently in the last weeks; was God sending her a message by bringing that child back into her life? Child, she laughed to herself; that child was a woman now, and the girl who had disappeared all those long years ago, to she knew not where, was a child no longer. *I wonder what became of her in those years,* thought the Abbess, the guilt a Catholic learns so deeply to harbour now embracing her again; *I wish I could have helped her.* Until she had seen her earlier that morning, crouched over what was left of Athanasius, Maria de Taye had convinced herself the girl to be destined for a life of whoredom, or even hoped, to ease her suffering in this world, that she was dead; but now....

Maria de Taye had been greatly disturbed by the death of Athanasius. Although she did not agree with much of the doctrine of the Eastern Church, she had found him to be one of the more likeable of his fellow monks: always in good humour and, despite his jovial and light-hearted nature, exceptionally wise. But his most admirable quality was the way Athanasius had so readily accepted her and her Order, despite the doctrinal differences in their beliefs, a charity that she, Abbess Maria de Taye, knew would scarcely be so forthcoming by the Catholic Church had it been Orthodox monks seeking protection in Europe.

She had responded to the news of Athanasius' death with silence and prayer, but it was only a brief respite; a knock on the door to her apartment shook her out of her intense fixation, and half-consciously she replied, rather sharply:

"Who is it?"

"It is Seyyid Noureddine, Abbess Maria de Taye; I apologise for troubling you, but I wondered if I could have a moment of your time."

She remembered the tense exchange of words of the previous evening, which had left her with mixed feelings of resentment and pity towards Noureddine. However, she felt no mistrust- unlike her ever-present suspicions of Brother Rafael- and wished to make peace with the convert, rather than sew the doubts of hate and anger.

Noureddine had taken the hesitation of the Abbess as a reluctance from her to speak with him, and as he stood outside of her door, offered:

"I could return a little later, if you are not inclined to speak with me at present?"

Maria de Taye crossed herself as she got up from her *prie de dieu* and opened the door.

"Seyyid Noureddine," she inclined her head politely, as he bowed in return, "I have no disinclination to speak to you; but," she continued with one raised eyebrow, "I do not think we should hold a conversation alone in my apartment, for the sake of propriety." She stepped out, closing the door behind her. She stood so close to Nour that he could smell the faint scent of almond oil from her skin. Instinctively, he moved away; but she only smirked, those big bright blue eyes staring directly up at him, for although she was not a tall lady, she commanded a presence that was larger than life.

"Let us speak while we stroll to the olive press."

~ Eighteen ~

Elyas, in the meanwhile, had tried to busy himself with library work, and although the grief of Athanasius' death, and the disturbing conversation he had overheard in the orchard, were enough to distract even the most stoically minded, he had, among the flood of thoughts and feelings, noticed the absence of Brother Rafael, who- for as long as the visiting monk's six month stay- had never missed a day at the library. So dedicated was he, in fact, that the other monks had remarked that Rafael's attachment to the manuscripts was so profound that they took priority over God and prayer. *Perhaps*, thought Elyas, *it is too disturbing even for Brother Rafael that a brother of the cloth has been murdered- oh, what a gruesome sight!* The vision of his master on the cold, hard stone floor came back to Elyas in a deluge of horrific images. He wiped away the tears that ran in a stream down his flushed cheeks, closed his eyes, and took a long, deep breath.

Amid the blood and horror that had appeared before him, his mind turned back to Rafael, and he felt uneasy, and unconvinced, by the idea that the visiting clergyman had been affected by Athanasius' death. Rafael had never liked the old monk, Elyas knew as much, and had they not had an argument? He wondered, as he opened his eyes and remembered seeing Rafael walking away from Seyyid Noureddine's room, what that argument had related to; and what had he been doing in Seyyid Nour's room?

A voice, familiar and sweet, shook him out of his thoughts; it was Ali.

"Good Brother Elyas!" he exclaimed, visibly agitated and short of breath, for Ali had run from the encampment to find Elyas as soon as he was able to leave after the mid-day meal. "I am glad I found you!"

The young monk greeted his friend with surprise, and relief; Ali had always been a good ally, a source of comfort in a place that Elyas, although he had grown to love it, had often found lonely and isolating.

"Ali," he smiled, "you startled me; I thought you would be with your father."

Ali shook his head vehemently, his brown eyes wide with worry, his hands gesturing for Elyas' urgent attention.

"My friend, please, listen! I know you were in the orchard when-", he lowered his voice, "I know you heard them- the officials; you know what they plan to do?"

Elyas was so relieved that Ali had also heard the conversation between Selim and Sinan; he had been wondering how to ask his friend for help without putting him into jeopardy.

"Yes, yes," he replied in a low voice, "I was not certain if you had heard them- I've been thinking of a plan to help-" but there he stopped; Ali had raised his finger to his lips to silence him. Someone was listening.

*

"But Seyyid Selim, Brother Rafael- this does not prove anyone's guilt!"

The Archbishop had had enough of the arrogant and impolite Ottoman official, and that miserable monk Rafael, who now stood before him, both demanding the arrest of Noureddine.

"This cross you say you found in his room- I cannot understand it; I know this belonged to Athanasius, but how did it come into Seyyid Noureddine's possessions?"

Between his thick muscular fingers, he held the cross that had once hung around the old monk's neck. It was not ornate and had no jewels- unlike the Archbishop's own cross- and in all the time Iosaf had known the old monk, he had never seen him with another cross.

"I beg to differ most vehemently," stated Rafael, imperiously, "this cross, which we found among Seyyid Noureddine's possessions, proves that he murdered Athanasius to steal the Deed of Protection! And having it in his possession, and the copies, he can do as he pleases with them- being so spiritually ambivalent, he could bid the Ottomans and Habsburgs against each other for whichever fortune of a sum he wishes!"

The Archbishop shook his head softly, with a sheepish smile, and said:

"I cannot believe that would be in Seyyid Noureddine's nature, or his plan, good gentlemen; it would make little sense, as he suggested earlier, for him to take the letter all this way, only to steal it from under our noses, when he had ample opportunity to do so as soon as he left Istanbul."

He sighed and continued in a tired voice.

"It seems a far-fetched idea to me!"

Rafael sniffed contemptuously at being told yet again his idea was 'far-fetched' but looked away in shame as the Archbishop shot him a sharp glance; Rafael's disdain for the Eastern Church had not escaped Ioasaf's notice, and had it not been for the good grace of the Abbess, he would have asked the monk to leave a long time ago.

Selim, who had been silent so far, spoke, trying to hide his irritation at the two quarreling Christians.

"Seyyid Nour had an accomplice; in the form of the person he pretended to chase after discovering Athanasius' body. We believe the accomplice has escaped with the documents, and that Noureddine's plan is to meet him once he leaves St Catherine'!"

"But," argued Ioasaf, "you said yourselves that you would accompany him back to Istanbul; would that not be difficult for him?"

It was Selim who replied this time, exasperated at the pedantic arguments of the Archbishop.

"Without any documents to take back, there would have been no need for us to travel back with him- he would have factored this into his plan. I am certain," he emphasized, "that Noureddine is the culprit, and I would have thought that you, Archbishop, would have been grateful to us for apprehending the murderer of one of your own brothers!"

A long, deep sigh followed, as Ioasaf tried to turn things over in his mind; it just did not make sense to him that Noureddine would go to such complicated lengths to be a thief- or have the cold-blooded nature of a murderer. He shot a hard glance briefly at Rafael, and thought to himself, *you, however, on reflection, are far more likely to cut the throat of someone, even for no reason whatsoever.*

"Well," he finally said, "I must be getting on with monastery business- we have a brother to bury, unfortunately. But," he asked cautiously, "may I ask that you at least hear Seyyid Noureddine's argument before you act too rashly? He told me himself he would do some investigations into the matter of the murder and the thefts and promised to come back to me at dusk with news."

Reluctantly, the Archbishops two hostile visitors agreed to his request, when Sinan burst into the room without knocking, red-faced and out of breath, pointing an accusatory finger at the Archbishop.

"Seyyid Noureddine- where is he, Archbishop? Where are you hiding him?"

Ioasaf stood from his chair, tired and angry of Sinan's childish demonstrations, and replied as calmly as he could:

"What are you asking me, Seyyed Sinan, because if you are accusing me of anything in particular, I should be very careful, if I were in your position!"

Selim intervened, trying to calm his accomplice.

"Sinan, your tone is out of ord-", but he was cut off sharply.

"Mind your own tone, Selim," breathed Sinan, "Noureddine is gone; he is nowhere to be found! And," again gesturing towards the Archbishop, he continued furiously, "I am certain the good Archbishop is hiding him from us!"

"Gone?" answered he, the Archbishop, incredulously. "But that is impossible. He was here not more than an hour ago!"

Through the open window, the cool late afternoon breeze swept in, gently, and the habitual raven had returned once again in the hopes of finding a few crumbs for his evening meal.

*

"And where do you think you may leave to?" growled Sinan. They had enlisted all the monks and as many Bedouin, poor souls weary and still in mourning after the burial of Athanasius, as they could muster, to search every corner of the Monastery for Noureddine, but to no avail, and Sinan's temper became increasingly volcanic.

"No one enters, and no one leaves, until we have found what we are looking for!" he barked, almost spitting, waving his long, thin finger at Maria de Taye in admonishment.

The Abbess, however, who was herself weary from her fair share of turmoil and disaster at the hands of men whose only way of living appeared to be by the sword, was not scared.

"I have been requested by the Bedouins to assist them with one of their young women, who has fallen ill," she replied sternly, her bright blue eyes fixed firmly on Sinan.

"And who is this?" he snapped, waving at the figure sitting next to the Abbess. Losing patience, but not fortitude, she smiled as benevolently as she was able.

"Sister Nora; she is most skilled in conditions of the female body. She will help me."

But Sinan was not convinced, and his irritation grew as precious minutes were wasted when they should be looking for Noureddine.

"I said," retorted the Ottoman official bluntly, stopping the donkey with a harsh jerk of the reins, "no one enters, and no one leaves!"

To Sinan, a woman- any woman- was an object to be owned, commanded and dealt with as he pleased, but he failed to reckon with the temperament of the Abbess, who, unflinching, slapped away his big, hairy hands and grabbed the reins back from him.

"I," she replied imperiously, not at all intimidated by the two hulking figures of Sinan and Selim standing in front of her, attempting to block her way, "am the Abbess Maria de Taye; and I do not take kindly to myself or anyone in my order being threatened by individuals such as yourselves- and nor, I imagine, would Her Majesty Kosem Sultan! Calling yourselves officials of the Sublime Porte! Have you no shame, denying sisters of the cloth their spiritual duty in this House of God? We share the same God, you and we, as your Sultan would remind you, and he would be ashamed of your actions!"

Sinan had almost lost his restraint and began to shout.

"How dare you- you are a mere woman and a guest in this country, which we command; you, and your infidel friends!" he spat, and raised his fist.

"If you speak to me in this manner again I swear, I will- ", he bellowed, but Selim jumped between them, holding back the now almost apoplectic Sinan, and laughed nervously, apologetically.

"Good Abbess, I apologise for my friend's words- please do not take them to heart; he has- we have had- a long and, er, difficult day. As the good Archbishop reminds us constantly," he attempted a reassuring smile, glaring at Sinan, waving his hand in the direction of the gate, "we are all God's children here; please, continue on your way."

Maria de Taye returned the cordiality with a brief nod of the head, and said, "Come, Sister Nora, we have a life to save....", and not being able to help herself she stared at Sinan with a hard gaze and added, "even if it is only the life of a mere woman!"

As the two pulled out of the gate, towards the encampment, she could hear Selim pulling the fuming Sinan away, yelling hysterically at his accomplice.

"Have you lost your mind, Sinan? Kosem Sultan would have your head if she knew how you have spoken to the Abbess! We are not here to play religious police! Imagine what would have happened if you had struck her- an Abbess, a Holy Mother!" he fretted, angrily. "Busy your small brain with finding Seyyid Noureddine, instead, you fool!"

*

Elyas, with Layla by his side, and Ali had been waiting in the shadows of the orchard walls, listening for the cart, hearts beating rapidly. All around them, the moonlight cast silhouettes that seemed to move and come alive. Had their plan worked? They did not dare to speak to each other, each of them contending with all sorts of thoughts and fears racing through their minds, but both surprised and grateful for the Abbess, and her suggestion to help them. Elyas, especially, had been heartened that it was she who had been the eves-dropper who heard them discussing the beginnings of their plan, and she who had now ended up being its main executor.

It was a freezing desert night. Layla's soft breath puffed out of her nostrils in faint plumes of mist, and the two young men shifted nervously back and forth on their feet, hugging their mantles and cloaks around them for warmth.

The faint sound of squeaking wheels forced their attention back to reality, and they looked at each other with apprehension. They remained silent as the cart stopped, and the quiet shuffling of footsteps through the hard dusty ground came nearer. They stood stock-still, praying silently that they had not been discovered.

"Brother Elyas? Ali?" a muffled voice whispered, and Elyas immediately recognized the soft Flemish lilt of the Abbess. Behind her, a crouched figure hid, until Ali replied in a low voice with great relief:

"Holy Mother- you came!"

She nodded, and the figure behind her raised their posture slightly, cautiously, peering around in the dark as if expecting to be caught at any moment.

"I have with me Sister Nora, as promised," the Abbess winked, with a mischievous smile, and removing the wimple and habit, before them stood Noureddine, shivering in the cold.

"I would have preferred to keep the habit, Abbess; it is a chilly night!" he remarked, with a brief chuckle.

"Seyyid Noureddine, we must hurry- they will be searching for you in the Monastery as we speak! You must leave now!" Elyas whispered, half-frantic at the thought of being so close to getting away with their plan only to be caught out.

Ali agreed.

"You must ride hard through the night, Seyyid Noureddine; the light of the moon and the star of Bethlehem will guide you to Alexandria- the road is easy to find. From there, you can claim passage on a ship to Salé; my father's friends in Alexandria tell us there is a ship, the *Ibrahim Pasha*, an Ottoman navy galleon bound for Tanja in six days' time; from there, you can take the road to Salé."

An Ottoman navy galleon, thought Noureddine, *hardly sounds safe!* But Ali had understood the reluctant response, and quickly reassured him.

"Oh, do not worry, Seyyid Noureddine- the officers are easily persuaded to take passengers if they can pocket the money, and seldom ask questions. If they do," he smiled, "just mention my father's name, and you will have no trouble! But now, it is a long journey for you and Layla. Salé, as you know, is still independent from Ottoman rule, and you may be safe from your Ottoman masters, until you recover the Deed- which I am sure you will!"

Salé, thought Noureddine with some fear; *it has been a long time since I saw those shores!* But for now, it was the only way.

"I cannot express my gratitude to all of you- but I will find a way, I promise!" insisted Nour as he took Layla, and before turning to leave, he looked at the Abbess, rather wistfully, she thought.

"Abbess Maria de Taye- may God bless and protect you! I owe you, all of you, my life."

She smiled broadly, her bright eyes shining, and asked only this of him:

"Should you visit the Duchy of Brabant.... would you touch the soil and think of me?"

Nour nodded, and bade his farewell, and he and Layla walked quietly into the desert night, the three who remained each wondering whether they would see him again, in this life or the next.

*

Nour and Layla reached Alexandria after six days. Each hour seemed an eternity; looking over his shoulder constantly, he was certain that Sinan and Selim would be right behind him. Sometimes, he was at the point of giving up, he was so exhausted; but Layla had been steadfast and faithful, even as her own legs tired, she strode as steadily and speedily as she could through the desert, until they finally entered the city of Alexandria as the sun rose on the seventh day.

There was no time to rest; Noureddine had to find the ship that would take them to Salé, and after a few enquiries, they wearily entered the port, on the northwestern edge of the city, to look for the *Ibrahim Pasha*, soon setting sail for Tanja on the Barbary Coast, later that very morning. As the young Bedouin boy had claimed, to earn extra money, some of the officers agreed to take passengers, disguising them as slaves- a custom, Nour knew, that the higher navy officials would turn a blind eye to, if it kept their ships sailing and their coffers full.

"Well, give me the money and get on the ship," a gruff and ill-humoured officer had barked at him, "we are about to raise the anchor!"

Nour and Layla were given a spare box on the lowest deck, where ammunition and cargo were kept, and for that he was grateful. He did not wish to be with the other mates, the slaves, or the officers. It was only when he looked through the port hole as they pulled away, the harbour peacefully glistening in the sunlight, the masts creaking in the gentle sea breeze, and the soft sound of fluttering sails above him, that Nour, his heart skipping a beat or two, caught a glimpse of the angry faces of Selim and Sinan, arguing with an officer, and gesturing irately towards the departing *Ibrahim Pasha*.

Safe for now, he thought, but he knew he would have to keep running at least until he had reached the Low Countries. Selim and Sinan would be sure to catch the next sailing that followed him to Europe.

He had recalled the conversation with Maria de Taye, and her suspicions of the thief and the journey of the Deed of Protection; the thief, she had believed, was a woman, who would sell it to the highest bidder in Europe. The Abbess had had no doubt in her mind that the Deed would be a desirable bargaining object for Catholics and Ottomans in their constant battles against each other for political supremacy.

After almost two weeks at sea, with a good wind in the galleon's sails and fair waters, the *Ibrahim Pasha* drew into the harbour of Tanja. It had been a mostly uneventful trip, and, apart from a brief daily stroll on the top deck, Nour had kept mainly to himself and Layla. The ship's mates and officers had paid little attention to him, apart from one, a suspicious lieutenant who had asked him where he was from and where he was travelling to on an almost daily basis. Nour had been able to avoid his persistent questioning by challenging him to a few games of backgammon, and letting the officer win each time; it always amused him how easy it was to distract someone and allay suspicions by pleasing their ego or filling their wallets.

The bright, enormous orange sun clung stubbornly to the horizon as he and Layla, rested and relieved, left the *Ibrahim Pasha*, and looking across the sea the faint familiar outline of the cragged cliffs of Cadiz appeared amid the evening haze.

We are so close to home, Layla, he whispered, stroking her neck as she, hungry after the constant rolling motion of the ship, searched his pocket for a morsel, *we can almost kiss the warm soil of Spain.* But he knew, with a deep ache in his heart, that going home would not be possible, and subconsciously felt for the salamander around his neck to lessen his sorrow. *Margaret,* he thought, *I am so glad you are still with me.*

The Republic of Salé, a recent city state formed by exiled Moriscos less than two decades earlier, was a three-day ride away, and Nour wasted no time in setting off. Safety, the Bedouin boy Ali had told him; safety from the Ottomans, yes.... and he hoped that enough time had passed since he was last in Salé for his brief visit to pass trouble-free. *Salé.... this time, who will be my friend, and who my enemy?* Nour and Layla reluctantly made their way through the crowds of Tanja's port, reaching the lonely dry dirt road to Salé just as evening slowly swallowed the sun, and the cool, salty sea breeze met the air of the on-setting night.

THREE

The Crown Lands of England and Scotland, in the autumn of the year 1641

~ Nineteen ~

He woke, dizzy, disoriented, gentle waves of freezing water lapping against his face, the rays of a bright sun warming his neck. Noureddine tried to open his sore eyes but saw only a warm blurry grayness over the shallow puddles around him. He attempted to move in the soft, wet slippery sand, but felt a sharp ache down his spine. He relaxed, briefly, tasting the salted water around him as it spilled onto his cut lips, stinging the wounds, the catastrophic events that had brought him here suddenly coming back to him in a violent flood of nightmare memories.

A panic gripped him briefly as he felt around his neck, then relaxed again, finding the salamander still with him, and Margaret, smiling sweetly, goading him gently out of his misery.

Layla, he then remembered, exhausted, but not too tired to cry. A few salty tears mixed with the sea water as if they were one element, and had been, all along. By all accounts, he, too, should be dead, consumed by the vast and ruthless sea that had taken his most trusted companion from him, along with the rest of the ship's inmates. The harrowing night came back to him, an ebb and flow of horror amidst the suffocating flood of painful recollection.

Nour braved the sharp jolt, like a dagger, that seared down his back as he turned over to face the skies above. The storm clouds had turned from ashen grey to a soft yellow-white with the sun's embrace. It was so calm, the thought of sky-high waves sweeping the helpless souls off the deck of the *Altaneen*, thrown about like sticks in a storm, and lightning crashing through the mast shattering the ship to pieces, seemed a far-away vision of a nightmare now, the kind one woke up from with the great relief of realizing that it was just a terrifying dream.

He came back to his senses. Something nudged him softly at his feet, bobbing with the waves, asking for his attention. Through the blurriness, as his eyes began to focus, Nour could see a satchel- no, two- floating near him, and the surreal horror-inducing vision of a stiff, grey hand still clutching one of them. The body it belonged to, bloated with water and shrouded in robes flowing gently with the calm waves, was that of the merchant from Venice, an unsuspecting captive of the *Altaneen* once they had set sail from Salé.

Nour raised himself gingerly to a sitting position, grimacing at the pain he felt slicing through his back; he tried to steady himself from the dizziness. He had a thundering headache, but a soft breeze comforted him a little, despite the chill of the cool October air.

The merchant from Venice had now washed up on the beach, still clinging to one of his satchels. He looked almost as though he was sleeping peacefully on a soft bed of white sand, a kindly sun warming his skin. But on turning him over, Nour choked in disgust; he barely recognized the face, its features were so bruised and swollen he could hardly make out the eyes or the nose. *He must have been thrown against the ship's anchor hole, or met the edge of the forecastle, as he was hurled overboard,* he thought. Nour kneeled down beside him, a sudden overwhelming sorrow grasping him; this man was neither kith nor kin, and apart from a few short, polite conversations at the start of their journey, Nour had no familial attachment to the merchant, but he wept for him nonetheless. He wept, because the merchant's fate would have been the same, had they met the storm or not. Rais Mourad, the captain of the *Altaneen,* one of the most notorious corsair ships on the Barbary Coast, was a Dutch convert by the name of Jan Janszoon- had enticed the merchant onboard with a promise to take him to his own merchant ship, anchored a short distance from the harbour. But Nour knew the ruthlessness of Rais Mourad, and he would have killed the merchant as soon as he had secured the goods off the merchant's vessel, for Rais Mourad was nothing more than a pirate. *I should have known not to trust that pirate*, thought Nour, cursing Janszoon, *I should have known he had not changed after all that time!*

Nour's aching back brought him back to the present. He mustered his strength and stood up, gently stretching one side of his back, then the other.

"That is a bit better," he mumbled, rubbing the bottom of his spine, before he gingerly dragged the merchant further in, onto the dry sand, pausing frequently as the occasional sharp jolts in his back began to ease a little. With the body clear of the water, he waded in and retrieved the other satchel, partly egged on by the waves, and extracted the other from the merchant's grip, placing them next to the dead man.

There was no one around. The only sound Nour could hear was the soft whistle of the wind and the faint lapping of the waves as they unfurled themselves onto the beach. He had no idea on what shores he had washed up, and there was no being or vessel on the horizon, either on land or sea; there was no sign of a wrecked ship. *I must have been carried a distance by the tide*, but judging from the *Altaneen*'s location when the storm had struck- Nour knew they had left the Middle Sea and passed Spain- he concluded he and the merchant must have washed up either somewhere in France or England.

For the first time, he diverted his attention from the dead man who lay at his feet, to himself. Nour was surprised that he himself had suffered no traumatic injuries, other than the unbearable pain of losing Layla. A sharp jolt pierced his heart; reliving the hell of the storm, he felt once again the giant wave crashing onto the deck, ripping Layla from him, her mournful scream echoing in his head as he saw her swept overboard, as he followed; that was his last memory aboard the *Altaneen*.

The shrill shrieking of a seagull, pecking at his hand in the hopes of finding a morsel, saved him from the misery of his memories.

Nour shooed it away with a weak wave, closed his eyes and absent-mindedly felt his neck. Margaret, smiling, appeared before him, soothing the bruises on his face with a soft touch and gently kissing his sore lips, so tantalizing and real was she that he wished for a long moment the sea had taken him, too, so that they could finally be reunited. The cool breeze picked up suddenly, and he felt the discomfort of his wet, clammy clothes sticking to him. He opened his eyes. His shirt and trousers were torn, but not beyond mending; not that it mattered. *Margaret*, he thought, *if the storm had also taken me, we would be together again!*

The sun had begun to warm the rocks nearby, so he stripped and spread his clothes over them, hoping, despite the cold autumn chill, they would dry a little. Not knowing where he was, he felt no hurry, other than the slow creep of hunger, which he would try to ignore as long as he could. *It must be about 10 o'clock,* he guessed, eyeing the position of the sun, *but I wonder where I am....*

He now felt so weary with sorrow, injury, and torment, that his eyelids began to feel heavy, but he tried to stay alert by turning his attention back to the merchant. He had fine clothes, almost befitting those of a nobleman, and was about the same size as Noureddine. He set to disrobing the poor dead man, placing the clothes to dry on the rocks next to his own. He had obviously been a personage of some wealth, Nour considered, pulling off the rings from the merchant's fingers, and unclasping the heavy gold chain from his neck. The horror-stricken, bulging green eyes stared back at him. *Thief!* they accused him, and Nour almost felt like a criminal. He wondered: was stealing from the dead stealing at all? He closed the bulging eyes gently; somehow, now that they were closed, the accusation had also disappeared.

Nour wondered what he could do with the body. The decent action would have been to bury him and say a prayer or two. Although he had no means by which to dig a grave, he said a prayer for the dead man, and sat down on the beach, cold but thankful for the brief bursts of warmth from the sun, and he, now naked, under an almost cloudless sky, considered what to do next.

He eyed the satchels, which he had placed next to himself, along with the jewels of the dead man. Despite the rough journey, the satchels, made of sturdy brown leather, were hardly damaged. Nour pulled one of them towards him, untied the leather straps, and pulled back the flap. Another layer of compartments protected the inner pockets, which, to his deep disappointment, contained only a small number of fine cloth samples. A fleeting smile passed his face, as they reminded Nour of Damascus. They were almost completely dry, so he replaced them and sealed the satchel, before inspecting the next one. He had no great hopes of discovering anything of value, after finding more fabric samples, and was about to bind the satchel up again when he noticed a slight difference in the structure of the inner pocket. There was an additional seam which seemed out of place; it did not line up with the rest. He searched for the pocketknife he always carried inside his left boot; it was still there, and with it, Nour carefully loosened the seams. Almost as soon as he had slit the last one, the opening gave way to a hidden compartment. Some documents popped out, hiding a thick leather folder, stuffed with notes. *A little luck at last,* he thought with relief, and pulled the contents out. He peered at the documents: they were the dead merchant's travel papers.

"Suriano," he read, as he looked over them to see who his unfortunate, now deceased, benefactor had been. There was a letter to the governor of the East India Company in London, one Henry Garraway Esq., with whom the merchant hoped to conduct business. *These could come into use; wherever I am, I have documents for travel, and money to see me through for a while. I shall be Suriano until I can clear my own name.*

The sun was shining brightly now, and the breeze had calmed. His clothes were still damp, and so he lay back down in the sand, feeling an overwhelming tiredness he no longer had the strength to fight, and fell asleep. His dreams were haunted by images of

Layla, eyes white with fear, being pulled to the bottom of the sea; Margaret, beautiful, sweet Margaret, consumed by flames at the stake; and the severed head of Athanasius, eyeless, and when he woke again, surprised at finding himself still alive a few hours later, Nour's exhaustion had been overcome by a renewed energy. *I will have justice*, he swore to himself, *I will find the Deed of Protection, for Margaret, and for Athanasius, and for all that is just in the world.* Resolute, he looked up at the skies again. *It must now be an hour or two past mid-day,* he thought to himself, *and time to leave!* The clothes were not completely dry, but comfortable enough to wear, and after dressing in the merchant's robes, he took a last look at the dead man, who had now gathered around him a company of busy flies. "The sea is where you took your last breath," Nour said out loud to the dead man, "and the sea is where your last resting place shall be!"

He dragged the body back to the shore; the tide was going out, and the merchant would soon go with it. Nour weighed the bloated body down with heavy stones, and pushed him, with a quiet deference, out to sea.

"*Bism allah al-rahman ar-rahim*...Godspeed into your next life, good merchant", he muttered quietly, briefly watching as the tide pulled the merchant gradually further out. Gathering his newly acquired belongings, Nour began to make his way along the cove, where he had spotted a path that would take him over the horizon, hopeful of finding his next destination.

I will find out where I am, soon enough, he thought to himself. He looked over his shoulder to make certain there was no one following him, the angry faces of Sinan and Selim forever taunting his conscience; but the only soul nearby was that of the departed merchant from Venice, his earthly vessel being taken gently by the tide towards the dark depths of his final place of rest.

~ Twenty ~

"I do not pretend, my dearest," snarled the tall, ghost-like apparition, her face purple with fury, "that I ignore the tricks and mischief that you get up to in this place!"

She was holding a long, wooden cane, the cracks in which were clearly visible, and ominous proof of its infamous history at this workhouse, The Poor's- or The Hospital of the Poor's Portion, for that was the proper God-sent name of the workhouse; this was the last resort for those so destitute even a squalid life on the streets had rejected them.

Meriall and Ilay- who had the misfortune of being residents of this bleak institution since what seemed to the two girls an eternity- stood with downcast eyes in the far corner of the large room. It was richly furnished with silk curtains and carpets from far-away lands the two girls had only ever heard of in stories. Around them were opulent chairs of dark, carved wood, dripping in gold and velvet, enormous, multi-coloured silk tapestries filling the bare walls between a gallery of fine paintings, ornate candelabras the size of waterwheels, all things fit to hang in the halls of Queens and Kings, rather than the office of a workhouse proprietress.

The two young girls were, however, accustomed to the riches of this otherwise uninviting part of the workhouse; they had perhaps seen its gaudy display a few times too many for their liking, and their ragged, gaunt appearance, flesh and bone starved of proper food, was a complete contrast to their current surroundings and the person to who they belonged.

Ilay was the taller of the two; she had a thick head of dark hair, tied up shabbily with a dirty strip of cloth, and despite her slightly darker complexion her face revealed an almost pale translucence, with sharp, large green eyes and a small, inquisitive nose. The hollows of her small sunken cheeks were the result of her almost life-long stay of hard labour and poor nourishment in that unhappy, unwelcome place. Despite her gaunt and feeble physical appearance, her spirit showed an iron determination, a resilience and stoicism that would rarely be found in those children who had, perhaps, seen a better life with loving parents and comfortable homes. That indomitable spirit, which never refused to be beaten, was the reason for currently finding herself in the lavish rooms of the workhouse's proprietress, Dame Druscilla West.

The other inmate, Meriall, however, was almost the complete opposite to Ilay in physical appearance. Slightly smaller in stature, she had long, almost white, hair, tidily tied back, with a round, moon-like face and large, curious brown eyes. Despite a generally starved existence at The Poor's, Meriall's cheeks were like ripe red apples, round and pink and shiny. Her eyes were normally hidden underneath a thin fringe of hair, and everything in appearance about this little girl seemed to imply a timidness, a shy and nervous personality, and yet, despite this being Meriall's first visit to Dame Druscilla's frightening room, she showed no outward fear. Meriall barely ever spoke, and to commit any tricks or mischief at the workhouse was to her not only unthinkable, but also counterproductive: as with the House of Correction which she had heard of, she believed that one day, she, like some criminals, would be released on good behaviour. And yet, here she was. It was all the doing of Ilay, whom she had never wished to befriend, but who somehow had dragged her into this mess.

"And you, Meriall," said Dame Druscilla, with an air of utter disappointment, as if betrayed by her own flesh and blood, "*et tu, Brute;*

you, I would never have expected such mischievous behaviour from you, of all the children here at this establishment!"

Dame Druscilla's back was turned to the two miscreants as she lamented her current predicament; she said the word "establishment" as if The Poor's was not a workhouse, but a thriving reputable business venture of high-class distinction, not the last and dreaded stop for those who, cast out by society and reviled by the streets, had no choice but to enter its horrors.

"I can only imagine that you were led astray by your consistently ill-behaved and mannerless friend.....".

"She is not my friend," uttered Meriall sharply; her voice was quiet, but loud enough for Dame Druscilla to hear, and offensive enough for Ilay to let out a snort of contempt.

"Well, then, if she is not your friend, my love," whispered the proprietress, moving closer to Meriall, bending down slightly so the two were at eye-level, "perhaps you would like to explain how you got mixed up in all this?"

She sniffed, her nostrils large, round and flaring like an angry bull.

"It has taken Starkey all afternoon to chase the pigs and geese out of the kitchen, and he is still not finished! And the mess!" Her voice became shrill with agitation as she continued to chastise the two girls.

"It will take days to clean it all up....".

She paused; a smirk had formed on her long, hollow-cheeked, purple face, and her eyes were narrow, fox-like, as if an idea of brilliant genius had presented itself in her thoughts.

Dame Druscilla observed with disdain the two creatures; they resembled more the ragged dolls of a poor girl than anything resembling a living being. Their dresses, the blue-and-white striped uniforms of the workhouse, were dirty and torn; they were allowed only to wash when there was an inspection by the Corporation, which happened rarely- and their boots had been ripped and mended so often that it was a miracle they had managed at all to serve their purpose for so long.

"Yes, it will take days and nights to clean and tidy the abominable mess in that kitchen..... and I know just the two little helpers who will gladly volunteer to do it!"

A gust of cool air swept through the room and the rest of the workhouse, as if fate was heaving a long sad sigh. These next days and nights would be long indeed for two already unhappy inhabitants at The Poor's.

*

But The Poor's kitchen, it would appear, saw even more mischievous activity that day the pigs had a good run through it, for while Starkey, the under-steward, had managed to chase the pigs out late in the evening and eventually maneuver them into their pen, another small and stealthy creature saw a golden opportunity to sneak into the kitchen pantry- now unlocked and very inviting to a young orphaned boy, whose plan it was to make a large picnic.

Wilfred had, to the regret of many, been ruled mainly by the desires of his stomach, ever since he was born. No meal was ever too large, no plate ever too full, and thus, as if being held captive in a godless place such as The Poor's was not terrible enough in itself, the lack of edible food was even worse. Unlike Meriall and Ilay, Wilfred was a relative newcomer to the workhouse; the burden of unloving parents who had felt it their duty, rather than their desire, to look after him, out of necessity rather than love, they had eventually decided to give him to the workhouse to spare the expense of bringing up yet another hungry child, particularly one with an appetite as voracious as Wilfred's. He had now been a resident barely three years, the entirety of which was spent attempting to satisfy his stomach. Finally, now, he had by luck and chance been given an opportunity to fill his stomach's every desire; and yet, he struggled- his discerning intestines quivered with excitement as he stood, eyes wide open and mouth agape, in the middle of the large kitchen, the fear of being discovered being completely swamped by his insatiable hunger. He could feel his taste buds tickling in anticipation: large vats of honeys, jams, stews, syrups on tall oak shelves appeared to be smiling at him, a feast of delights only reserved for the privileged few who ran the workhouse.

His senses now took complete control of him, and his brain ceased to retain the ability to reason. Wilfred found himself inside the pantry, staring at shelf upon shelf of cured meats, tasty savoury pickle, delicious dipping sauces, fat pieces of cooked chicken, smoked fish, meat pies, sweetbreads, and so much more, while he stood there paralysed, his over-excitement sending him into a trance-like state.

And then- then, as if sent by God above to make up for years and years of the culinary deprivation Wilfred had been forced to endure, he saw it: an entire corner of the pantry had been allocated for cakes, pies, biscuits, buns and all sorts of heavenly sweets he thought could only ever exist in Mr Parr's Bakery down the road, to which only the privileged few had access, so many worlds away from the bleak desolation of The Poor's.

Suddenly realizing he probably had very little time- and he had not yet heard of the mischief that Ilay and Meriall had committed by letting the pigs into the kitchen- he began to panic.

"I must.....I must take as much as I can, and hide it. Find.....somewhere...to hide it....", he mumbled, and then more luck! A large basket, peeking out from behind the pantry door caught his eye, and he grabbed it quickly. But where to begin?

"Meats," he uttered. The young boy, who was at an age where he still waited to grow in height, pulled over the nearby ladder, climbed it, and using a system of aiming and throwing from the top, he began to gather chicken, chunks of ham, cured beef steaks, taking care to take only so much as not to be an obvious ingress into the portions that already existed, or to be weighed down by its weight when he escaped. He worked his way over and down along the shelves, and to his consternation found his basket had filled up to the brim a long time before he had completed his mission.

"Oh bother," he muttered, "I haven't even reached the cakes yet...!"

Suddenly, his little heart jumped in fear as the sound of faint voices trickled into the kitchen from the distance, getting louder until he could start to understand exactly what was being said. A horrified feeling of dread and the sheer terror of being caught overcame him.

Starkey! Wilfred froze. He did not know what to do; he could still escape unnoticed, perhaps, but what about the basket he had painstakingly filled with all that delicious food?

Starkey had now almost reached the kitchen entrance, and Wilfred knew, once he was inside, he would almost certainly be caught, and then....oh no! Goosebumps crept through his skin and his heart quickened; he had only ever heard rumours of the nastiness of Dame Druscilla's punishments, never having gotten into serious trouble himself at the workhouse. But he had heard tales of the Dark Room and its horrors and was petrified in fear of being banished to it for punishment. Ruled by a strong sense of self-preservation, which also refused to relinquish the painstaking work of acquiring his new-found treasures, Wilfred now acted almost instinctively. He pushed the basket back behind the pantry door where he had found it, covered it with a large rag that had been flung into the corner, and shut the door so it was half-closed, as he had found it, before slipping out of the kitchen unseen. *I will come back for you*, he thought lovingly of his basket, and prayed that its hiding place would go undiscovered until then.

*

"I cannot think," Dame Druscilla complained, brow furrowed and hard grey eyes flashing with anger, "what to do with those troublesome children!"

She maneuvered her skeletal figure into the large velvet armchair she had placed prominently opposite the office door, her riches and power in view for all visitors to see.

Alastair, never one for long or multiple words, least not because he, now being in England, wished to diminish the reality of his Scottish origins, raised his eyebrows, and tutted softly, shaking his now hairless head, in agreement with the Proprietress' despair of those wayward children. He knew what he would like to do to them- spending most of his time either having to find extra work for them to do, a hard labour of no insignificant pain, or taking them into the Dark Room for a spell of 'correction'; or mending the cane to show them how life as a steward would be easier without them. Although only one was the main troublemaker in that workhouse: the taller one with the wild glint in her eyes. Ilay was not right in the mind, thought Alastair, not admitting to himself, even silently, that, in reality, she frightened him quite a bit, and her striking resemblance to a little girl he had once known in Scotland had utterly disconcerted him.

A pang of guilt pierced his heart suddenly when his thoughts took him back to his last days there, thirteen years previous. Effie, her body mutilated and twisted in the ice-house at Glamis, appeared before him, as she often did, to remind him: *You will never escape me, not even in death!*

"Well?" Dame Druscilla urged, impatient for some answers. "What are we to do? You must have some ideas?"

She sniffed disapprovingly, muttering under her breath just loud enough for the steward to hear, "After all, it is what I pay you quite handsomely for...!"

Effie's horrific image disappeared as quickly as it had presented itself on hearing the acidic echo of Dame Druscilla's voice, and Alastair, who had always thought his position with the Proprietress as not being one of a tenuous nature, having forged his stellar references from Glamis and thus presented himself as an illustrious steward of the highest calibre, realized now that he could quite easily be replaced and shown the door permanently. So, in an attempt to soothe his mistress, rather more desperately than he perhaps wished to sound, he offered, "I may have a solution, Ma'am."

The sickness he had felt in his stomach at seeing Effie so real and life-like before him had made him feel rather unwell, and he felt even more nauseous now at the thought of being replaced by some other lesser good for nothing, like that slimy under-steward, Starkey, constantly attempting to ingratiate himself with Dame Druscilla, even offering to do the lofty work that he, Alastair, as the former steward of a noble house in Scotland, should be doing! Alastair did not trust him.

"Yes?" she snapped, impatiently.

"But, I fear it is a solution that may need to be treated with…", he hesitated, looking up to the ceiling for words that might not naturally come to him, before continuing, "some consideration, for there may be those in the Privy Council," he cleared his throat to hide his doubt, "or, indeed, the Corporation, who may not look upon it as strictly…", he paused again, "within the proper realms of the law, as some might see it."

The Proprietress did not react particularly surprised, and replied impatiently:

"You mean to say, Alastair, in your usual roundabout Scottish way, that this scheme is illegal?"

The steward cleared his throat once again, wincing slightly at the word 'illegal', and tried hard to suppress his offense at the idea that he and his fellow Scots had a 'roundabout' way of speaking.

"While I do not, in principle, agree with the general use of the term, Ma'am, I can only say that there are those who would see it in such a light," he concurred, "if Ma'am would like to put it that way."

"It is not about how I would like to put it, Alastair," she barked back aggressively, "either it *is* or *is not* legal; and if it is not," she considered for a brief moment, "but is a good solution that will both rid me of those children as well as offer me some substantial personal profit, then I do not give a damn about this scheme's consideration within the law, even if the Privy Council do. I have no time for much of the law," she continued, now seemingly unstoppable in her tirade against a world of tiresome rules and needless regulations. "As I see it more every day, it is only designed to make life difficult for those who belong in the higher ranks of society, such as myself, while those lower creatures, which the laws of nature have given us the privilege of treading on, seem to escape its harsher punishments. They moan and complain about the cane and the stocks, the pillory and the rack and the thumbscrews, but they do not have the burdens of the tax man and the Archbishop! Although," she continued mercilessly, with a wry smile, "his days are certainly numbered, if Parliament has its way....!"

Appearing to have exhausted herself, she mopped her brow with the handkerchief she habitually had hidden somewhere within her unassuming cleavage and sighed deeply. Alastair had set his gaze to the ceiling again, and the steward in him noticed a crack in the ornately carved stone roses that decorated one of the ceiling vaults, muttering to himself, "I should get that seen to..."

"What?" Madam Druscilla's impatience returned.

"Stop talking nonsense and tell me about this 'scheme' of yours!"

She heaved herself out of the chair, and moved slowly, but somewhat regally and ceremoniously, over to the window. It was a sunny day, streams of soft light filtering through the clear glass, tiny reflections glinting in the corner of the window where the sun had not yet reached a few small particles of frost.

Her mocking tone of the word 'scheme' had given Alastair little confidence, but now that he had mentioned it, he could not retreat.

"I have heard of an...organisation", rethinking his words as he spoke, ".... rather, an *individual*, whose name I shall keep anonymous for now," Alastair mused, proud to have used such an intellectual word and in such a superior fashion that Madam Druscilla thought his manner had mutated into one that was decidedly above the steward's station in society.

"This person carries out some business with the colonies- they are low on servants and other labour there, you see," he condescended at the Proprietress' increasing irritation, "after the attacks by the Natives and the disease; plantations must be kept up for the economy," he stated imperiously, as if he had the dubious privilege of having regular conversations on the topic of the Crown's economy within the higher circles of the Merchant Venturers.

But Dame Druscilla was unimpressed with his knowledge.

"You are beginning to bore me, Alastair! Get to the point before I have Starkey throw you into the Dark Room for wasting my time!" she pompously squealed.

Starkey, he thought, *curse that slimy rat!*

"Well, Ma'am," Alastair hurried, "this individual provides a service of labour to the colonies, er, by shipping, er..," he hesitated before speaking the next word, "*volunteer*s to the Colonies for that purpose."

Dame Druscilla ignored his sheepish looks; although she was aware of official Privy Council schemes to ship vagrants and criminals to the colonies for labour, she had no reservations about the legality of shipping similar such 'volunteers' abroad without the Privy Council's knowledge; in fact, it would be doing them a favour. It would relieve them of additional painstaking work involving lodging documents and applications that would have to go through numerous offices and departments, a lengthy and surely costly process that in her mind was unnecessary, producing the same outcome that all wished for; she could merely serve as a cost-saving middle-woman.

Dame Druscilla began to see the route this conversation was taking.

"Volunteers, you say?" she mused, before adding in a slow and satisfied tone with a hint of malice that Alastair, try as he might, could not enjoy, "Volunteers, such as sniveling street children that have ended up in a workhouse?"

Alastair nodded eagerly; although he did not like the children, he was, despite its low threshold, unsure of his moral well-being by shipping them off to an unknown destination, in conditions he had no control over. They were horrible little runts, but still children, even at eleven or so years of age. But his instinct for his own survival always won above his moral conscience, and any thoughts that could perhaps have been of a kindly nature were short-lived, and quickly usurped by a fear for his own survival, in addition to the welcome prospect of a handsome compensation. And there was Starkey; at all costs, he had to prevent that odious snake from climbing the greasy pole of the workhouse office ranks.

"And, good man," Dame Druscilla said, again with that acerbic mocking tone, "what is the profit for me? Why do I put myself at the risk of the Privy Council, not to mention the Corporation, for this?"

Unlike Alastair, no thoughts of compassion for the fate of these children had even entered her ever self-serving mind; it was no wonder Dame Druscilla's self-imposed motto in life was *Omnia mihi, ipse omnia*, or 'everything for myself, and for myself, everything', which, in some long or short years down the line, would no doubt be written on her gravestone, should she ever be graced with one.

Alastair shifted nervously.

"I am not certain of the details, Ma'am, but I hear on the street that the pay for healthy young volunteers is particularly good...if you wish, I will make enquiries.... discretely, of course," he added hastily, with a forced air of superiority.

She had now moved from resembling a foul-tempered ogre to embracing a mood that was infinitely more buoyant at the prospect of profit, of which she already had plans to keep all to herself, for once, and not work hard to fiddle the books to pay the King's multitude of extortionate levies. *I will, I suppose,* she mused slightly annoyed at the thought, *have to give Alastair a cut of the deal; or, as with all men of his ilk, I am certain there is something in his past I can bargain with....*

"Find out!" she ordered, snapping her jewel-laden fingers, and dismissing him with a nod towards the door. "Find out as soon as you can; nothing would satisfy me more than to ship those filthy troublesome urchins across a vast ocean, particularly if there is a substantial profit to be made of it in the process! Ilay is nothing but trouble, Alastair, and the sooner we find a way of getting rid of that makebate- and the other one- the better! I should never have taken those children in- though, the pay for them was decent, I suppose- but they are more toil than is worth that money. Find this personage, of whom you speak; if there is a ship that can take them away tomorrow, they will be on it, mark my words!"

She smiled, her mean, thin lips pursed in satisfaction at the thought of an entire ocean between herself and Ilay.

"Fewer mouths to feed, and more coins in the coffer, Alastair; that is our aim, after all, should _I_ wish to retire with the dignity and status that _I_ rightly deserve!"

~ Twenty-One ~

Elizabeth Hamlyn was a woman for whom time was always at limited disposal, and, sitting in the waiting room of the offices of The Poor's, having to anticipate an audience with Dame Druscilla, she grew irritable. *Dame, indeed!* She scoffed quietly at what was, in the mind of Elizabeth Hamlyn, no doubt a self-claimed title so Druscilla West could worm her way into the higher echelons of Plymouth society. It was always the same with these half-wits who thought they had a higher station in life than reality ultimately proved. *She certainly does well for herself,* thought Elizabeth, looking around the corridor, where she herself was sitting on a comfortable chair that would no doubt have cost a pretty penny; foreign, too, she observed. She concluded that Dame Druscilla, who could have no honest bone in her body- or else, why would she be seeking an audience with Elizabeth Hamlyn?- must be skimming the rich cream off the surface of the Corporation's annual funds for The Poor's, so she could enhance her personal comforts and social advancement.

Her disagreeable thoughts were interrupted by the voice of Alastair, who, in his most well-spoken Scots accent, announced haughtily:

"Dame Druscilla will see you know, Mistress Hamlyn."

And here's another one, she thought to herself, *a would-be acolyte of high society, and a Scot, at that!* Smiling frostily at Alastair, she inclined her small head ever so slightly in acknowledgement, the feathers in her tall black hat fluttering gently as she moved past him and into the presence of Dame Druscilla.

For a few seconds, the two women studied each other suspiciously, evaluating each other's dress and disposition, as if assessing an opponent before a duel. The two ladies were, in fact, rather alike, both in appearance as well as in manner; they were both tall, thin and ghost-like, at forty-something of a similar age, their skeletal bodies hidden beneath a vast bundle of fine silk, and bony limbs weighed down in plain sight by gold and silver jewelry where modesty would allow it, precious gems sparkling brightly about their persons. Their main distinctions were their faces. While Dame Druscilla's iron grey hair matched the hard colour of her permanently narrowed eyes, Elizabeth Hamlyn- though not a beauty in what one might call a conventional sense- revealed a mass of beautiful, thick auburn hair tucked under her hat, and soft brown eyes that contrasted with her pale face and small, blood-red, pursed lips, which belied a cruel, heartless, and vengeful soul.

To Alastair, this mutual evaluation between the two women felt awkward, and although he wanted to leave, he knew he could not do so without the permission of his superior. Very subtly, he cleared his throat in the hopes of getting Dame Druscilla's attention, who disengaged her steely eyes from her opponent for a brief moment, and, with a dismissive wave of the hand, she ordered:

"Close the door, Alastair, and sit down."

He did as he was told, not being used to any other way of living these last thirteen years.

"Good morrow, Mistress Hamlyn; do sit down," offered Druscilla finally, as politely as she could. She had taken an instant dislike to her visitor, and was preparing herself for a long, hard negotiation.

"I thank you, Dame Druscilla," replied Mistress Hamlyn, half-mocking, but she could not help that reaction; Dame Druscilla was even more ridiculous and irritating than she had expected, with that dome masquerading as her hair sitting on top of that long, oval, horse-like head of hers, and the jewelry! She had never observed anything so gaudy and vulgar in any woman proclaiming herself to be a lady of class and distinction.

Druscilla cleared her throat, aware of her visitor's scrutiny of her, and began.

"Mistress Hamlyn, my steward, Alastair," she nodded with feigned appreciation towards him, "has informed me that you assist society in providing, er, *volunteers* to the colonies to alleviate the labour shortage overseas?"

Elizabeth pulled a snake-like smile, but her brow remained stern and hard; she could see intimidation coming her way, and she would not put up with it.

"It is a charitable occupation, Dame Druscilla, to help the countless children on our streets gain a better life through honest work in the colonies," she replied with condescension, aware of the infuriating effect this would have on her pompous host, "and to save them from the horror and squalor of the workhouse."

"I see," returned Dame Druscilla, nostrils slightly flared at the insult that had been sent her way, but remembering the distant chance for profits, she continued as calmly as she was able to, "and if I may be able to assist in this charitable cause, would you per chance be interested in a proposition that would be of mutual benefit to us both?"

The two women glared at each other so hatefully that Alastair could only look up at the ceiling to escape the tension of the heavy, thick air that beset the room. *I must get that crack seen to,* he thought, focusing on the damage he had observed recently, and imagined to his own surprise the ceiling coming down on them at any moment. A vision where the two women were buried alive, while he escaped unharmed, popped in and out of his head so suddenly and surprisingly that he let out a brief, but loud, involuntary chuckle.

Elizabeth and Druscilla shot an angry glance his way, and Alastair cleared his throat with a mumbled "Beg pardon, Ma'am", but somehow the intervention brought the women back to the purpose of their meeting.

"I am always interested in a proposition, Dame Druscilla," answered her guest slowly, with a faint menace, "so long as the terms and conditions are to my satisfaction."

But the proprietress of The Poor's had done with polite conversation, and plunged straight into her negotiating tactic.

"Mistress Hamlyn, I gather the.... *charitable* work you engage in is not, strictly speaking in the eyes of the law, seen as legal......and therefore, comes with some risk to one's personal reputation, not to mention the wrath of the Corporation and the Privy Council, should they become aware of these illicit acts of ....kindness...?"

"I can assure you, Dame Druscilla," snapped Elizabeth almost before her host had finished speaking, "that my activities benefit society greatly; and these children, they belong only to the streets, and no one else: why should anyone care, if it cleans up our neighbourhoods of begging, thieving, whoring, and murder? And," she added before Druscilla could intervene, "as for the 'legality' of my work, although there are murmurings of concern in Parliament by some of its more puritan members that children are being kidnapped," she let out a short, sharp shriek, rolling her small eyes in disbelief, "I do not think they will act; they know that the benefits of charitable schemes such as mine far outweigh any negative consequences, for, other than the unfortunate demise of some volunteers along the journey, who could complain about the prospect of streets free of clamoring vagrants, begging and thieving, or filthy whores!" She added with horror-stricken eyes, "While also assuring the continued prospering of our colonies?"

I will give her this, thought Druscilla almost bitterly, *Elizabeth Hamlyn is as silver-tongued as the Devil himself; so smooth and elegant, who could ever doubt anything she claimed?*

"I believe that you and I, Mistress Hamlyn, would have a most agreeable cooperation, if you would hear out my offer?"

Elizabeth nodded out of courtesy, but her mistrust of Dame Druscilla was so strong, she doubted very much that any agreement at all would come about between them.

"Well, I believe we can help each other, and make some profit, while also reducing the risk of discovery by the Corporation and the Privy Council....", began Druscilla, now with an air of a mother speaking to a simple-minded child.

"We," she claimed, speaking as if she were the embodiment of the institution, "at The Poor's, encourage vagrant children to find a temporary home with us for their betterment," she continued, lying, for the only children currently presently at The Poor's were the three kitchen miscreants, "and we can prepare them here for a life in the colonies, sparing you, Mistress Hamlyn, both the trouble of rounding these vagrant children up- which, even you must admit, is a risk with the eyes of the law all around us poor, God-fearing subjects," she paused to cross herself dramatically, "and, giving them an, er, *basic* education to ease the transition into their new, er, *employ*, abroad?"

Elizabeth's attention had now been aroused; as much as she loathed to admit it, Dame Druscilla had been right that the risk of her work being discovered had become more real in the last months, and if The Poor's could provide a more discrete avenue for her business, perhaps it could be an option to lower the risk of her business being shut down altogether. *But,* she thought bitterly, *no doubt this will mean a substantial cut in my own profits!*

"And, Dame Druscilla, how do you propose such an arrangement might be financially agreeable to me?"

Her host shifted confidently in her large, soft armchair, never losing eye contact with her visitor; she smirked and gestured with her long, thin fingers as if towards an imaginary idea in front of her.

"I have made some enquiries, of course," she mused, "and am given to understand that you pay a levy to your current, er, *supplier*, for bringing suitable volunteers to you; I propose to offer the same fee, with a small additional percentage to cover the, er, administrative costs of entering the children into The Poor's," and seeing the instant disapproval of Mistress Hamlyn, she added hastily, "of course, do not forget, that we offer a pre-departure preparation program, which, of course, could enable you to increase your own fees with respect to your clients in the colonies! I am certain," she smiled broadly, "they would have no objection to pay a little more, if it saves *them* time and money on any necessary, er, *education*, the volunteers will need!"

There was a silence again, and, to Alastair, the room became almost frozen in eternity. He was beginning to feel regret at ever mentioning the existence of Elizabeth Hamlyn now, and foresaw more secrecy, more work, and more sorrow in The Poor's. But it was too late to turn things back; perhaps God would one day forgive him for all of his sins...Effie....Rory.....Mistress Fionnsgoth....they all appeared before him, bowing their heads in disappointment, eyes full of shame, sadness and despair.

The shrill voice of Elizabeth tore him from his contemplation, and he almost jumped out of his chair, at the ready for any instructions.

"That is indeed an interesting proposition, Dame Druscilla; and I do confess," she admitted reluctantly, "that I have been rather disappointed with my current supplier.... the quality of the stock has gone down considerably, while he charges me more for every delivery! And what," she asked with some curiosity, "would be the additional percentage that you ask?"

"Twenty percent," snapped Dame Druscilla, "and I do not think you could argue with the fairness of that, considering the additional benefits I have offered!"

Bright rays of sunshine had flooded the room during their discussion, but the office still kept an air of sorrow or malice despite it. Alastair got up to stoke the embers in the fireplace and threw a few logs in to revive the flames. The wood crackled and spat in response. The windows were not open, so the three occupants of the office could not hear the distant sounds of the scythes reaping the fields amidst occasional cries of pain and anguish of Starkey's long cane as the workhouse inmates toiled for the profit of its proprietor.

"I will consider your proposition, Dame Druscilla," Elizabeth finally announced, "but I must discuss this with an acquaintance first and get his opinion."

Immediately suspicious, Druscilla raised her eyebrow, and attempting to keep the tranquility she had forced upon herself, stated sharply:

"I would prefer this arrangement to be kept private between the three of us in this room, Mistress Hamlyn; you must understand, the fewer who know, the lesser our chances of discovery by the Corporation or the Privy Council!"

But Elizabeth, expecting intimidation, would not bow.

"I can assure you that the person I intend to consult is one I trust entirely, Dame Druscilla, and is a man not without influence himself; and if you wish this agreement, as it were, between us to be enacted, I must insist on consulting him first."

Dame Druscilla did not enjoy being beaten at her own game, and although she would have to admit temporary defeat, she was convinced that she- a Dame, no less!- would be the true head of this scheme in very little time.

"Very well," she conceded frostily, "but, if you agree to my proposal, I must also insist on meeting your 'consultant'," she added, her ice-cold stare met with an equally frosty nod.

To Alastair's relief, after what seemed an eternity, the two ladies bade each other farewell, having fixed a time for their next meeting the following day.

Once her visitor had been shown out, Dame Druscilla sat back down in her armchair, brow furrowed in contemplation.

"Elizabeth Hamlyn is a clever woman," she offered regretfully, "but I am certain I can manipulate her, and she will make me richer, Alastair!"

The steward, unaware that Dame Druscilla had no intention whatsoever in sharing the spoils of her labour, nodded with a faint smile, not being able to bring himself to look directly at his superior. Instead he fixed his gaze at the painting of a mother and child that hung on the wall behind her; and when he had least expected it, the tear-stained face of Balgaire appeared before him briefly, as if begging him for some relief, before it slowly melted back into the painting, that child, he thought, now hanging onto her mother more fiercely, as if wishing her never to let her go.

~ Twenty-Two ~

Somewhere near Plymouth, England, late October 1641

A steep climb along rocky cliffs brought Nour to what seemed a well-trodden path, but he could see no dwellings or buildings around him until he came upon a church called St Germanus. A lonely priest, eager to see another being but mildly astonished at seeing a Moor, gave Nour directions to the nearest villages, Kingsand and Cawsand, where, if he wished, he could find lodgings.

"Or," added the priest, a not too elderly man of portly proportions, "from Cawsand, you may catch a ride on the ferry across to Plymouth," and scrutising more closely the appearance of his foreign visitor, from the tone of his skin to the clothes he wore, the priest continued, "for you, that may be a safer option!"

England, thought Nour, *it has been a long time.* He smiled at the priest, commenting on his beautiful church before heeding the old cleric's advice and setting off on the path to Cawsand, in search of the ferry to Plymouth.

The priest had been wise; Nour did feel safer once in Plymouth, being able to blend in more easily among the thick of seafarers and merchant seamen who, it seemed, had come from all corners of the world. And, looking behind him and around him as he made his way along the cobbled streets of the Barbican, there was no sign of Sinan and Selim, or any other familiar faces, to his great relief. After a few enquiries, he found an inn that seemed to be popular with foreign merchants, and he was glad to see the proprietor not giving him a second glance as he arranged for his accommodation. The young man had also been most obliging in providing Nour with options for travelling on to Scotland, for he had decided that his next destination would be Edinburgh, for a reunion with his good friend Galenius.

"London and the Great North Road would be the quickest, I reckon," suggested the landlord, "you can ask for passage on one of the coastal trading ketches- most of'em don't like passengers, but if the deal is sweet enough, they'll let you sail with'em!"

The thought of setting foot on a ship again almost made Nour vomit, and he had to fight hard to compose himself.

"Are you sick, sir?" the landlord asked, suspiciously. "Only, I don't care for sick tenants! Bad for reputation and I need all the business I can get!"

"No, no," hastened Nour, brightening up, "I am merely rather tired after my journey.... is there another way, rather than by ship, that would get me to London?"

"You'd best get a carriage or take a horse then, sir," he had suggested, "and from London I'm told there's a stagecoach that takes post all the way to York, but I hear they also accept travelers for a fare."

A horse, lamented Nour, thinking of Layla, his heart heavy; it would feel like a betrayal, and he, exhausted at the thought of another long ride, decided he would try to get passage on the coach the next morning.

"The Old George Inn, in Plympton, will see you right about a carriage to London; I can fetch a cart to take you there, if you like?"

Nour agreed, but first, he wanted to settle into his room. It was small but comfortable, not unlike his quarters at St Catherine's, although the noise from the street seemed overwhelming after the peace and quiet of the Monastery, and the long journey on the ship and the quiet of the beach. After washing thoroughly- the salt of the seawater had made him feel unwell- and feeling more refreshed, he ventured to find the Old George Inn, to secure a seat on the coach the young innkeeper had mentioned. The proprietress, an efficient and stone-faced woman in her fifties, made the arrangements and took his payment, before stating sharply as if admonishing a child:

"Coach leaves at seven in the morning, sharp; if you're late, it won't wait!"

"I thank you, Madam; I will be there in time," replied Nour as he picked up the receipt she had slapped down on the table.
"A good evening to you, Madam", he said, departing with a bow as her large, black eyes fiercely steered him out of the door.

The afternoon was fading, and the evening light set in, and Nour, feeling hungry and thirsty, took his meal at one of the many taverns scattered around the Barbican. As the evening turned into night, and the drink flowed more and more freely around him, singing sailors and merry merchants crowded in and out, and the table next to him was never unoccupied. At one point a man and woman- a change from the habitual drunken seamen- took their seats there as Nour was finishing his meal. Amidst the clamour, Nour could hear snippets of their conversation, its details swimming without interest in the back of his exhausted mind.

"This is hardly the place to discuss...", reprimanded the woman, small, brown eyes flashing in disapproval as she brushed away strands of the burnished auburn hair that peaked out underneath her tall, black hat, a bright contrast to the pale translucent skin of her face.

"We are safer here than in a quiet office," rebuked the man, and glancing briefly at Nour, who smiled in return, he added, "and the likes of him will not understand, anyway," he reassured the lady in a low, half-mocking voice. Her nerves appeared to have settled slightly. Nour turned back to his cup of wine, and the remnants of his meat and vegetable pastries, having no interest in their conversation until he had heard the word 'spies', which immediately piqued his curiosity.

The lady, now less hostile with her companion, nodded apprehensively; the room was large and crowded, sailors bumping into each other and the furniture in drunken fray, the poor tavern maids doing their best to avoid getting groped, or worse. Nour had to strain his ears to follow the conversation of his neighbouring table.

"She will cheat us; I know she will," snapped the woman in answer to a question Nour could not hear; but the man, ever patient with his doubting companion, shook his head slowly and smiled paternally at her, which only seemed to grow her frustration.

"My dear Mistress Hamlyn, she *cannot* cheat us; she must know that any attempt to do so would be to ask for trouble from the Corporation- and, worse yet, even the Privy Council!"

The sullen lady considered for a moment; there was just something wholly untrustworthy about Dame Druscilla West, and her intuition was warning against any dealings with that loathsome woman.

"And," continued the man, now in a more resigned tone, "we are facing more and more suspicion from Parliament about our activities! I hear that one of the Parliamentarians- a Scot, no less!- has brought up several debates on the matter of kidnapped children being sold into servitude! And although my influence in Parliament is such that it could be avoided, we could avoid such scrutiny entirely," he paused, as if making fictional calculations in his head, "if our supplies can be met in more discreet ways, and there, my dear, comes in the part of Dame Druscilla; if *she* becomes the supplier, it would lessen the risk of discovery for us! What is more," he concluded in a tone that perhaps convinced himself more than his companion, "it would make her bear responsibility should any investigations be ordered by Parliament- and we," he touched her hand lightly, at which she jumped and shivered, casting a glare at him that could turn iron into liquid, and he, feeling his emotions injured, withdrew, "could deny any wrongdoing! For that alone, I think it is worth a cut of twenty percent, Elizabeth!"

Elizabeth Hamlyn remained silent for a minute or two; she was beginning to feel regret at consulting with her companion but dismissed the thought almost immediately. She simply could not afford to mistrust everyone, and Martin Noell- although seen as ruthless and notorious among his fellow London merchants- had been reliable, at least until now.

"I was told she has three ready for us- two boys and a girl, about ten or eleven years of age."

Noell, relieved to have changed his accomplice's mind, grinned enthusiastically, the gold in some of his teeth glistening in the dim light of the tavern rooms.

"That is an excellent idea, my dear," he exclaimed, this time not noticing the disdainful glance Elizabeth shot his way at hearing the words 'my dear'. *He will be condescending when he pleases*, she thought bitterly, *but I know I am the cleverer of the two of us!*

"Very well," she answered stiffly, her business-like mind pushing aside any personal misgivings she harboured for Dame Druscilla and Noell, "I will make the arrangements. Oh," she added less assuredly, "there is one small condition: when I mentioned to Dame Druscilla that I would have to consult with an acquaintance- that would be you- she insists on meeting him!"

His face darkened so quickly it took Nour, who had furtively glanced at the couple throughout their conversation, by complete surprise, and the man's voice transformed from sweetness to anger in a flash.

"Why?" he snapped, taking a large gulp of his beer and slamming the glass down furiously on the table. "Why would she need to meet with me? I certainly will not let a woman such as her dictate to me my affairs- no, I shall do no such thing!"

Elizabeth smiled wryly. *This man can change his tune as fast as the Plymouth winds*, she thought, *including his commitment to my proposition!*

"Fine, Mr Noell; I shall tell her you are not inclined to make her acquaintance at present."

"Never!" he almost shouted now, forgetting where he was for a moment, then lowering his voice to a whisper Nour could almost not hear.

"I will never bow to any woman's requests, let alone someone like Dame Druscilla West!"

Still smiling, and feeling the discussion could bring no further use to her cause, Elizabeth rose, and replied sharply:

"I shall meet her tomorrow..... and I will inform you of the outcome, Noell."

"Fine," he mumbled, his small, green eyes still bulging with anger, "but I return to London tomorrow; send word by post!" he commanded, adding hastily, "But be certain to use language that is inconspicuous, should the letter go astray or be intercepted. I cannot afford questions if I am to continue my upward rise in the merchant society!"

She inclined her head in acknowledgement, curtsied briefly, and left him sitting by himself, still seething with anger.

There is a man whose good side one always would seek, thought Nour. Himself feeling weary and hearing the quiet, tempting call of his bedchamber, he left shortly after Elizabeth, the hot and thick air of the tavern briefly staying with him as he met the cold autumn night. Throngs of people from all walks of life flitted about the streets of the Barbican, like busy ants searching for sweet delights.

*

"We appear to have come to an accord, Mistress Hamlyn!"

Dame Druscilla's shrill, icy tone rang through the room with a hint of disappointment as she added, her manner vexed, "I am disappointed your consultant refused to meet me; nevertheless, I am pleased he saw the benefits of my proposition! Here," she drew out a large document from the drawer of a desk, "I have drafted the conditions of the agreement, as we discussed in our previous meeting, and there," she noted, pointing to a particular clause, "you will see details of the added benefits my twenty percent fee includes!"

Elizabeth Hamlyn glanced through the document, and having noted nothing untoward, she nodded.

"Very well; I will be delighted to sign this document," she smiled, her small brown eyes narrowed, "but I insist a person of reputation- who has no interest in our dealings- be here to witness this accord, Dame Druscilla; that, I believe, is the proper way to administer this contract."

Druscilla felt her frustration growing once again; she was so near to her goal, and now this wretched woman had to throw in yet another obstacle.

"My dear Mistress Hamlyn," she attempted a soothing tone, fighting to hide her annoyance, "in normal circumstances, I would not hesitate to agree; however, as you yourself are aware, the nature of this, er, *arrangement* is hardly what one would call within the realms of the law.... how exactly do you propose to find such a 'person of reputation' that we can trust to fulfill this obligation?"

Elizabeth, who had anticipated this rebuttal, was about to reply, when a sharp knock at the door interrupted her planned retort. It was Alastair.

"Beg pardon, Ma'am," he apologized, peeking around the door as if expecting to be assaulted by something, "but there is a visitor here; he claims to be here to witness your, erm, business dealings, Ma'am," he finished in a whisper, "a clergyman, Ma'am, and not an English one...".

His frown did nothing to hide his suspicion at the sudden and unannounced appearance of a clergyman, and a foreign one, at that; vexed and confused, Dame Druscilla shrieked:

"What? Oh, send him away; I have no time for begging clergyman at present! Tell him to come ba-", but she was sharply interrupted by Mistress Hamlyn.

"He is our witness, Dame Druscilla; the person of reputation who will confirm our agreement."

This is infuriating, thought Druscilla, *who does this impertinent vixen think she is, dictating to me my affairs, as if I am a brainless half-wit!*

"A clergyman?" asked she, half-mocking now, and further con-descended, "Is that *wise*, my dear?"

"Since, as you pointed out earlier," began Elizabeth calmly, once again trying hard to ignore the condescending 'my dear', "it would be difficult for us to find an official to do this without arousing suspicion, this clergyman has kindly offered to assist. The fact that he is foreign, Dame Druscilla, can only mean that he has no interest in our affairs, and as such, is a fact that matters neither here nor there."

"And why would this kindly clergyman go out of his way to assist us in our affairs, my dear? What does he ask in return?"

Alastair had once again felt the awkwardness of the exchange, uncertain how to proceed with the growing impatience of the visitor waiting behind him. But this visitor, having listened to the two ladies, and believing himself as a man to be morally superior, brusquely pushed past Alastair and entered the office.

"Allow me to introduce myself, madame," he said, his honeyed voice edged with a distinct acidity. "I am Rafael de la Cruz, Head of the Order of Christ, in the service of King Philip IV of Spain." He bowed ceremoniously, his long beige tunic waving with the motion as he did so.

"I believe we may be of mutual assistance to each other, respected ladies."

Alastair, feeling so ignored and emotionally injured- which he had not felt since his flight from Glamis Castle so many years before- withdrew without a word, and he, angry now, shut the door quietly. More than ever, he regretted having mentioned this 'scheme' to Dame Druscilla, and wished no further part in it, but fate, in her wry cruelty, would have other ideas.

~ Twenty-Three ~

What Dame Druscilla had not reckoned with was the endless curiosity, and insuppressible ability to sneak her way unseen through the offices of the workhouse, of the wild and fearless Ilay, who had heard every word spoken between Alastair and the Proprietress.

The girl, who had escaped the day's long travail of cleaning up the kitchen under the usual watchful eyes of Starkey, had entered the forbidden area of the workhouse, to the protest of her fellow inmate, Meriall. She knew, the young girl did, that she had committed a serious offense by doing so; but her curiosity, and more importantly, her desire to cause discomfort to Dame Druscilla at every possible opportunity, had given her something to look forward to, rather than dread. She had observed the casket of coins the Proprietress kept in her office, and was determined to steal it, and to escape, and buy some proper food. For the slop she and her fellow inmates had been subjected to in the morning had been less than edible. To say that it was vile was an understatement: it was beyond description, a muddy green sludge with brown and yellow objects of an unidentifiable nature bobbing amidst its scummy surface so life-like in their horror one might think they were alive. So vile, in fact, that a fellow inmate had vomited at the sight of it- only bile, of course, there being nothing else that inhabited the poor man's stomach, save its lining, that would come up. The only vaguely edible items were the stale bread, and moldy cheese- but these were also not to be had, after Ma Mavis and her gang of food-thieves had bullied the children into giving up these less offensive items of the breakfast bowl.

"Hand over your bread and cheese," she had snarled through blackened teeth, a thick stench of foul sour breath wafting over her, "or you'll be sure that I'll send hell your way, my lovely!"

Ilay was all too familiar with the hell Ma Mavis threatened with; she had been the victim of Ma Mavis' merciless and relentless cruelty before. She had been beaten in the fields, Starkey watching from a distance without interest until Alastair had intervened, fearing the severity of the beating would kill the girl. They had held her head in the pig trough so that she might almost drown in the slop. They had tied her to a chair and pricked her with needles and burned her with wax and fire, pretending she was a witch, with no one knowing or caring, so that she might die of either pain or exhaustion. And it was always Ilay who was the accused; Dame Druscilla hated the girl with such vigour, that Ilay became a frequent visitor of the Dark Room. But, the little girl had clung onto life despite the horror of it, although she had sometimes wondered why, if this was the treatment it thought she deserved; but she had refused to succumb to the tranquil temptation of death. So, she had learned: it was better to give Ma Mavis and her crew of satanic servants what they demanded, until one day Ilay would find her revenge, not only for herself, but for all others who had suffered at the hands of that devil-possessed woman.

"Revenge will be mine and all those you cause pain; and revenge, it will be sweet," Ilay would say to herself every night, clutching the necklace her mother had left her, before she closed her eyes in half-sleep; for she never knew when she would next suffer torture at the hands of Ma Mavis.

Ilay, now finding herself alone in the vast corridor of the offices, did not have much time, if she was to find what she needed and return to the kitchen unnoticed, so she sneaked quietly along the long, wide corridor, towards the Proprietress' office. She would have places to hide, should anyone come along, as Dame Druscilla had filled her office quarters with rich furniture and carpets, procured, without a doubt, with monies she had extorted from one of her many wealthy victims of Plymouth society. The little girl was at first startled, then enormously relieved, at the warmth that had met her once again as she had entered through the connecting door. The poor-house quarters had only one hearth, lit once a day, with sticks and sorry kindling left over from the wood shed, and she had been cold for so long, she had almost forgotten what warmth and comfort felt like.

Ilay had almost reached the office, when she jumped at the sound of voices; they were coming from inside, to her annoyance, scuppering her plan for thievery. The door was a little ajar, so she would have to sneak past it quietly. She could hear voices- the Proprietress in an intense conversation with Alastair, whose voice was rather more muffled. The girl had no interest in what was being said, until she heard her name; she stopped, heart pounding so loudly she thought they would sure be able to hear it, and held her breath.

A ship! How exciting! Her heart leapt at the prospect of finally leaving this place, the thought so welcome she almost forgot to understand what that could really mean- and, realizing as she listened intently on Alastair's explanations, she knew that it could only mean being shipped to another place of horror, with no freedom in sight, perhaps for eternity. Her heart sank.

"Well, fetch the little blighters so that I can take a look at them," Druscilla ordered, "we need to make certain they look clean and presentable for the next meeting with Mistress Hamlyn!"

Ilay froze in fear, clutching the pendant around her neck; she knew what had to be done. She darted, quiet as a thief, past the great oak door unnoticed, and back into the kitchen- the cook was asleep, half drunk, in the corner by the window, stirring gently between snores, and Starkey had gone back to the fields.

"Where have you been?" hissed Meriall, angry at having been left alone with the less than kind Starkey. "Starkey has gone off to look for you!"

"They are going to send us away on ships, Meriall, as slaves!" Ilay blurted out in excitement, eyes wide with fear as her voice shook.

"We need to escape!"

Meriall rolled her eyes in disbelief. She had become accustomed to her fellow inmate's fantasies and wild imaginings and paid them little attention.

"Don't be silly, Ilay, and help me clean up this mess before Starkey comes back! He is sore angry with you, and I'm afraid of what he'll do to you and me!"

She almost began to cry.

"I have never visited the Dark Room, or felt the cane, but I know it must be a terror!" she sobbed, fear-stricken eyes red with tears.

Ilay did not back down.

"Meriall, I am serious- I heard them; Dame Druscilla and sleezy Alastair- they are selling us to a ship bound for the colonies! We cannot stay here!"

Meriall, between her sobs and gulps, was starting to get angry at Ilay, and had it not been for the low sneeze that suddenly came from the nearby pantry, the two girls would have continued arguing; but they both stopped, frozen at the prospect of a spy finding them out.

"What was that?" whispered Ilay, her voice quivering slightly as she peered around the kitchen for an answer.

Meriall stopped briefly, between sobs, and listened, now more calmly.

"I don't know.... but I think it came from the pantry!"

Ilay, who was by far the braver of the two, sneaked quietly to the pantry; the door was slightly ajar, and she pushed it open gently until it stopped against something.

"Ouch!" a thin, frightened voice exclaimed; peeking behind the door, she saw Wilfred, huddled under a pile of muslin, rubbing his sore head, and clutching a large basket of food.

"Please do not tell Starkey!" he winced, cherishing his beloved culinary treasures with horror-stricken eyes. "I shall put everything back, I promise!"

"Right, you three!" bellowed a voice behind them; it was Alastair, and he was angry.

"You are coming with me!" he ordered in his gruff, ill-tempered tone as he grabbed Ilay and Meriall by their bony arms, dragging them out of the kitchen like rag dolls, and turning back to the pantry, he snapped:

"And you, too, young Master Freddie; and put that basket down or I'll have you doing the dishes for the next three moons!"

The Dark Room! thought Ilay, terror strangling her heart, memories of the horror of her last visit there flooding back, as Alastair paraded the children along the long corridor towards Dame Druscilla's office, *we are going to the Dark Room for punishment! But at least, I will not be alone this time...*

But, rather than the long, black terror of the Dark Room, the three children found themselves instead in the frost-edged presence of Dame Druscilla.

"Let me take a good look at you," she snarled, circling the three children as if they were her prey, "and see if we can turn you into saleable goods!"

*

It was still dark when Nour left his lodgings for the coach station, the clear skies lit only by a bright half- moon and a ceiling of shimmering stars, as he tried to find direction to the coach through the bustling and shouting of early market proprietors.

"Stone o' best beef a shilling-two-pence!......best butter three-and-a-half pence a pound!......capons, best in the market- two shillings a pair!...".

Between the noise, and the smoke, and overwhelming assault of smells, both pleasant and noxious, he did not notice two girls and a boy, clean looking but gaunt and starved.

"....and how do you suppose we get on without any money for passage, Ilay?"

Meriall, exasperated and angry, exclaimed as Nour passed them; his attention, however, was instead caught by two passers-by, travelling farriers, judging from the selection of tools that were casually slung across their shoulders.

"....the coach leaves from Eastgate, I am told, at seven this morning- it's a four-horse one, so two each....", he heard one say as they jostled past him, the other mumbling an irritated response, "well, that doesn't leave much time....".

The way to the coach, thought Nour, and began to follow them, when he felt a sudden tug on his coat pocket. Reaching in, he felt an unexpected small hand clutching a loose coin. It was one of the girls he had seen earlier; she looked at him with hateful eyes. He held on to her hand, so she could not run away with the coin she was clutching. Curiously, she did not seem to be afraid of him, and took no heed of his disapproving brow; she was only defiant, as Nour looked down on her.

"Young ladies," he said, with a smile, "should not engage in thievery!"

"Let go!" yelled Ilay, trying to wrest herself away, still clutching the silver coin; but he held on gently, and continued:

"If you had asked, I would have given you this coin."

Ilay, being a clever girl, briefly stopped resisting, and when she felt his grip easing, she kicked him very hard between his legs, leaving Nour in some excruciating agony. Unmerciful, she took off, but not before grabbing his coach ticket from him, and demonstrably waving it and the coin in front of him, sticking out her tongue in mockery; the wild, dark hair, angry face and flashing green eyes made him laugh, even as he stayed doubled over, clutching his groin. In her defiance, the necklace she had always kept so closely guarded underneath her shift slipped out from behind her open collar, and suddenly, all time and events that passed around Nour, stopped. He did not see how it could possibly be so- in this place so far removed from Glamis, and his homeland, and after so many years had passed.... but the vision of it, and the bittersweet memories, struck him like a hard punch to the gut: it was the necklace he had given Margaret, he was sure of it, for only one was ever made- and he could not believe it!

*

Having made her way back to her companion travellers, the illegally procured coin by Ilay had caused a heated argument between the three children.

"You will get us all arrested, the way you behave!" heaved Meriall, between sobs. "Don't you know they cut off hands of thieves? Or put them in the stocks?"

She clasped her hands around her round face, shaking her head, the white curls of her hair quivering along with the rest of her body.

"Ha!" replied Ilay. "Let them try- and anyway, I'm too quick for most."

She shrugged, a bit too nonchalant for Wilfred' s and Meriall's liking

"I was just a bit unlucky this time- and that man was probably afraid to catch attention on himself, anyway, with his dark skin and odd-looking clothes!"

"I'm hungry," commented Wilfred, "do you think that coin will be enough for the coach, and some food?" he wondered, hopefully; it felt an age since he had had anything to eat or drink.

"Don't be an idiot, Wilfred!!" barked Ilay. "We can't show this coin to anyone here- they will only take it from us!"

"Then why did you steal it?" asked Meriall, now getting angry at the futility of it all.

"What are we to do with it if we can't even buy food? I'm hungry, too!"

Ilay was thus faced with a small mutiny, Wilfred and Meriall standing in front of her, arms crossed defiantly, resolute eyes staring back at her.

She finally conceded.

"Alright- we can buy some food," she agreed, adding, "of course we wouldn't have to if Wilfred hadn't already eaten all of what we took from the poor-house kitchen!"

The poor boy blushed and lowered his head in shame; it really wasn't his fault that he was constantly hungry.

"Oh, leave him alone!" snapped Meriall, now finding her spirit. "I'm tired of you telling us what to do all the time! You're just like Dame Druscilla!"

Trying not to get baited by such insults, Ilay realized they had little time for arguments; they had to find a way onto that coach soon.

"Listen to me, both of you," she asked calmly, "we must get onto that coach before it leaves, without anyone seeing us! That purple monster has probably already sent Starkey and Alastair after us- we don't have time to sit around!"

She flashed the shiny silver coin and ticket in front of them.

"This is a half-crown; I've overheard enough of Dame Druscilla's conversations to know what it's worth. But if we are to pay for food, here in this market," she looked around, searchingly, "then we must pretend to be someone's servant!"

Meriall snorted. "Ha! No one would believe that!"

Ilay smiled back, with a fox-like grin, and replied:

"I have a plan- wait here!"

And before either of her travel companions could protest, the determined Ilay had disappeared into the crowds, leaving them to wait, and wonder, what fortune or, more likely, what calamity, would face them next.

*

Seeing Ilay disappear fast into the shadows of the morning market crowds, Nour had pursued her, ignoring the searing pain he still felt, realizing that he was now also without a ticket for the coach. His eyes, having to adjust intermittently to dark and light, and shadow, as the moon set and sun began to rise, searched the throngs of people, until he caught sight of a servant girl rushing towards the coach; it was her! Ilay had thieved the clothes of a servant who had met her lover behind one of the stalls, and they, in such carnal ecstasy, had not noticed the little thief absconding with the maid's clean frock and boots. So fixated on Margaret's necklace had Nour been that he had taken no notice of his surroundings, or that he had dropped his satchels, and it was not until he had almost reached the coach that two fellow merchants from Morocco had caught up with him, Nour's satchels in their hands.

"*Sidi,*" one said, "we saw you running away from your things; you must take care of them- three are so many thieves here!"

The other nodded, and Nour, trying to express his gratitude while also keeping an eye on the coach, professed his utmost thanks. The clock struck the hour of seven as he finally managed to wrest himself away from the obliging Moroccans. The coach was still standing; *I can still reach it,* he thought, forgetting that he no longer had a ticket, and perhaps it was the added weight of his satchels, slowing him down a little, and the heaving crowds of the market that saved him, for although he was cursing and yelling for the driver to wait, he suddenly froze, dead in his tracks. As if a lead weight had pulled him down, he crashed into an apple cart. In the distance, a familiar figure, now dressed in priest's robes, turned to peer in his direction. Nour's memory, amidst the heaps of apples, the clamour of the market, the horrible stench and delightful smells, and the angry curses of the apple seller waving his fists as he stood over him, finally revealed itself: Rafael de la Cruz, now stepping with calm arrogance onto the coach, was the priest who had condemned his father to the fire and sent his mother and sister to their deaths. All time again seemed to stop, the transcendental coldness of Nour's past drifting over him as the coach pulled away into the distance, a ghostly blackbird following it in flight as if it were its only keeper.

~ Twenty-Four ~

Edinburgh, *Allhallow's Eve*, November 2nd, 1641

By the large window that overlooked College Green and the many snow-dusted rooftops of Edinburgh sat John Hope. The air was one of sombre stillness, neither cool nor warm in his mind, no feeling in his heart more profound than the ache from the loss of his beloved. An outside observer could, had they been present, almost have sworn they were studying a painting by Holbein, such still, sharp clarity, ambiguous in emotion, presented itself before them.

White tufts of falling snowflakes descended in rhythmic regularity, some attaching themselves to the window and the ledge. Beyond, the bright, orange-tinged blue of the sky appeared with the rising morning sun, and no one, on seeing the beautiful optimism of the first light of day, could have entertained any notion of sorrow. But for John, having lost his wife scarcely a month earlier as she had tried to bring their child into the world, saw nothing hopeful in the room he was currently sitting in, or the world outside of it. The child, of course, a wee girl, had not survived; such was the brutal punishment God, for whatever reason, had handed him.

It was only a gentle knock at the door that caused him to move in his chair, first uncertain as to the safety of allowing a visitor-safety, in the sense that he feared losing his current state of grief to the annoyances of a trivial and inconsequential conversation; but he eventually conceded to the will of the outside world and answered.

"Come in," he spoke with no emotion, but remained seated, showing no interest in his visitor, who, after a brief silence, asked:

"John, my son....how fare you?"

Sir Thomas Hope watched his child, shift slightly, as if the words he could not find at present would somehow appear without warning. It had been painful for a father to see his son grieving so profoundly, in such an all-consuming manner, that Thomas felt he had not only lost a much-loved daughter in law, but his son with her.

"My son," he continued gently, "would your present state of mind not ease a little if you found some distraction....?" He hesitated briefly, as John flinched, a flash of anger fleeting across his face, but then went on.

"I would use your shrewd head for one or two complex questions that have arisen.... one in particular may interest you- it has resurfaced after a long time, but a time you will recall with regret, about a man you remember fondly.... Gordon MacDonald."

John started involuntarily when his father spoke that name; so much time had passed- thirteen years- since that dreadful day, and a confused mess of visions flooded his memories: the old judge being dragged off to the gallows, his frail voice protesting his innocence as the executioner readied the axe; the little pools of blood on the stone floor of his father's office after his parent had slapped him; the billowing flames and unmoving emotions of Margaret Douglas as the wretched fire consumed her; and the hateful vision of her brother, William Douglas, feigning shock at her fate, but in truth relishing his state as the hopeful heritor of Margaret's estate which could bring him further into favour with the English King.

Thomas observed his son with concern; still sitting by the window, back turned to his father, john's facial features had changed on the mention of Justice MacDonald's name, and the reserved sorrow Thomas had detected when he first entered John's chamber was now darkened with the hardness of his eyes, and the anger of his brow.

"After all this time, father, what more is there to be said about that treacherous day?"

"Aye," replied Thomas, with eyes cast to the floor in deep thought, "it was a treacherous day, and one that will weigh down my conscience until I leave this world...," he paused, considering his next words with care before he continued.

"But we may yet be able to right a terrible wrong, my son, and restore the good names of Gordon MacDonald and Margaret Douglas!"

An interest, and not a trivial one as he first had feared, crept into John's grief-stricken mind; the sorrow for his beloved- although still overwhelming- was cushioned by the blissful distraction of a curiosity.

"But how, father? Those who sent them to their deaths still carry out the offices of justice- and not just here in Scotland, but also at the Royal Court... William Douglas, for one, father...," he clenched his fist tightly as he spoke the name, "he is now in the Privy Council, the blood of his dead sister still on his hands.... and the Earl of Menteith yet exerts an iron hand in most affairs, despite having lost some favour with the English King!"

John rose and turned away from the window to look at his parent. The hard slap thirteen years ago jarred his memory again, and he glanced at the floor expecting the drops of blood to still be there. *Dear father*, he thought, *you look tired and worn. Is this what justice does to those who try to uphold the laws of Scotland when an English King rules?*

Thomas, unaware of the train his son's thoughts had taken, nodded, and raised his eyebrows in some resigned agreement, but added:

"Well, aye- there is a good point, John; but, at least we do not need to concern ourselves with the cruelty of Lord Kilcreuch any longer, now that he has retired."

John sniffed a contemptuous 'pah!' in disagreement.

"He may be retired, and some say even that he is blind, father, but I hear his grip on the College of Justice is as firm as it ever was!"

A silence pursued John's anger; he peeked out of the window, and the wintry city landscape that sprawled beneath him, beyond the hills to one side, and the vast, iron-grey sea to the other.

"There is something about winter, father," he remarked in a soft, almost wistful tone that was so completely different from the forceful ire he had expressed only seconds before, that Thomas raised his brows in confusion. *My son, my dear John; your mind is not your own at present.*

"Winter makes time seem static, unmoving; it feels so still, dear father, I fear with terror in my heart that this wretched grief shall torment me for all eternity!"

Thomas, although well-acquainted with the desperation and anger that came with loss and grief, could find no words of comfort for his son, but it seemed that John had no such expectation anyway, and instead went on, switching his tone to the business-like manner of a lawyer in court.

"It is thirteen years to this day that Margaret Douglas was burned; and thirteen years since they cut off Gordon MacDonald's head, father."

"Aye," replied Thomas sombrely; he felt the shame of his inaction all those years past creep back into his conscience, thirteen years of guilt locked behind the iron gates of paternal love and fear for the safety of his family.

"And you say that now," John mused bitterly, "after all this time has passed, we may finally see justice served?"

Thomas shifted uncomfortably. The recent revelations he had been privy to could amount to something grand and even scandalous for the Royal Court, or nothing at all, and he now felt that the fear of disappointing his son once again if the latter were to be the case, after all.

"Well, John" he summoned his courage to finally say, "it is this way, you see; I received word from Strachan, MacDonald's old steward- who has continued to serve MacDonald's widow since his execution- that she is now on her deathbed. They say she only has a few days left in this world, at most, and Strachan claims she has been muttering about murder and treason... although I think it must only be the slow fever of death that makes her produce such rantings- but Strachan says she mentions my name constantly, and is adamant there is more to it, and that I visit her before she passes."

John sighed in annoyance.

'Well, it is hardly a spectacular revelation, father!" He wondered, with the usual superiority of youth, whether his father's advancing age was beginning to take a hold of his mental faculties.

"Why should we waste our time with visiting a woman who no doubt has thirteen years of scorn and bitterness stored inside her at her husband being taken from her before his natural time! It is only to ease her soul before she dies?"

The surprising hardness of John's tone, and his blackened cynicism, did not deter Thomas from trying to convince his son.

"But there is more, John; there are documents Strachan wishes us to see- documents he claims were given to widow MacDonald for safekeeping after her husband's death; and documents that were given to her only recently that appear to be somehow connected."

"Documents? Of what?" snapped John. He was now enticed by the mystery that was starting to form, the prospect of grief lightened by his growing curiosity.

"Strachan would not give details, John, other than purporting that he believed they were to do with the execution of MacDonald and Margaret Douglas, and perhaps even a grander plot...", he stopped abruptly; he was certain he had heard a noise outside of the door, but all was still suddenly, and he continued, "involving those who were tasked with carrying out the final blows of justice...". He whispered the last few words, and John peered at him suspiciously, when both men were suddenly startled by the faint sound of shuffling feet outside the closed office door. Thomas raised his finger to his lips, motioning silence, and spoke loudly.

"We owe the lady a last sign of our respect; a visit would only be appropriate to someone who has been a devoted client for so long. Would you agree on that, John?"

"Aye, father, you are right," the son replied stiffly, a mixture of excitement and trepidation now almost completely drowning out the immense sorrow he had suffered for his beloved wife.

*

William Douglas languished, deep in thought, by the breakfast table in one of Aberdour's grand rooms. A letter lay in front of him; to its left, stood an empty mug of beer, and to the right a pewter plate held the remains of a half-eaten venison pasty. The three objects formed almost a triangle in perfect symmetry, with William's hands resting on the table edge in some apparent anticipation. The letter, written in a fine, educated hand on thick costly paper, bore the remnants of the broken wax seal of the House of Glamis, the home of his cousin Jack Lyon.

The letter, among other things, announced the visit of his cousin on November the 2nd, All Hallow's Eve- that very day, and to William's great annoyance, he had found no time to make alternative arrangements or excuses in order to avoid meeting with Jack. The two had never been friends; the death of Margaret had driven them even further apart, particularly as it was Jack, not William, who now held the custody of her estate. William felt the anger rise in him again; those lands belonged to him, by all rights, and no one else! The last thirteen years he had tried, without success, to change the will of his dead sister; but William knew that Jack was not someone who would easily give up his own honour- that much he had seen of his cousin's determination in the Bishop's Wars: if there was a principle that he held dear, Jack would sooner die than relinquish it.

Perhaps that opportunity will present itself soon, thought William, with a malicious pull on his lips; such bitterness he had held in his heart since Margaret's death and the broken promise of Matthew Hopkins to spare her soul, and the fortune he had expected snatched from him so cruelly. At first, William had felt an abysmal guilt; he had condemned his sister to death! But before long, the whispering of his wife Anne convinced him he had been robbed of his rights, and the legal rantings of the Earl of Menteith that it was all the Devil's work and the will of God, forced the guilt to ebb away, and the greed once again flowed in. So self-obsessed had William become that it had escaped his attention entirely that it was thirteen years that very day that his sister had left this world.

William had sacrificed a great deal for the King and his wars and had in the end only suffered defeat at the hands of the Covenanters. As if that in itself was not humiliating enough for him- he, the Earl of Morton!- he now had to endure the smug satisfaction of victory Jack Lyon enjoyed. *Traitor!* he thought. *The title of Lord Glamis should be stripped from you, as well as all your lands!*

A quiet but prominent voice interrupted William's dark thoughts; it was Donaldson, his steward.

"I beg pardon, my Lord, but Lord Glamis has arrived."

William made no attempt at hiding his displeasure at the announcement and answered sharply.

"Aye, let him come in!"

As the steward bowed in acknowledgement, William added, "And bring more beer and pasties, Donaldson."

A few minutes later, Jack Lyon appeared. He was taller than William, and despite the prominent scar that cut across the right side of his mouth, a handsome man, with long, reddish hair and bright blue eyes that always appeared to be amused. Unlike his cousin, war, fighting, and loss may have hardened Jack's mind over the years, but not his heart. The two men bowed to each other, though neither considering his opponent worthy of such deference.

"What an undue pleasure, Lord Glamis, to be able to welcome you to Aberdour after so long a time," spoke William, almost through gritted teeth; his voice was cold.

"Aye," nodded Jack in agreement, "it has been a long time- not," his own voice sharpened, "since my dear cousin Margaret was murdered!"

The stony silence that rose between the two men, neither of them feeling in a conciliatory mood, was relieved by the arrival of Donaldson, accompanied by a footman and a parlour maid, both carrying trays with pasties and flagons of beer.

"Leave them there, Donaldson!" William snapped, pointing to the table by the settee and waving the steward away dismissively. "I will see to it."

The servants disappeared in silence, filing out in order of rank like battle weary soldiers, and as the great oak door was closing, a small, grey-coated cat sneaked into the room. It was eyeing the pasties on the table; William picked it up and stroked it tenderly, feeding her a morsel of meat, the only sound in the room now the low, steady purring of the animal as he cradled her in his arms before he gently evicted her from the room.

What a contrary man, thought Jack, *to show such kindness to a cat, and such cruelty towards his own sister!*

"It is a long ride from Glamis, Jack; I think you must be in need of something restorative," offered William, like a well-mannered host. Jack Lyon was, in fact, neither thirsty nor hungry, but the food and drink served as a tempting pause in the otherwise hostile air of the room, and he agreed.

"Aye, I thank you, William, your hospitality is most gracious!"

"Do sit down."

The host motioned to the settee, out of habit, and it was not until Jack had sat down that William realised his guest was sitting in the same seat Margaret had sat in, on what had turned out to be her last visit to her childhood home before her death. The memory jarred William's feelings, and for only a second, he saw Margaret there,

302 ~ CHARLOTTE STORM OLSEN

smiling spitefully at him, blood spilling from her mouth, before Jack Lyon reappeared in her place. It was as if the two were somehow one; William felt on edge seeing Jack there, in the same spot.

Jack had noticed his host's unease, and though he did not normally revel in the discomfort of others, it pleased him.

"William, you look out of sorts; I hope all is well at Aberdour?"

"Never better," smiled he, briefly changing the subject to the mundane problems of everyday life- taxes, religious troubles, failing crops, until he finally asked:

"I understood from your letter that you had some news regarding my sister's estate, cousin; I confess I am most anxious to hear it."

That does not surprise me, thought Jack, *for you remain as greedy and selfish as you ever were!*

He looked at William as he took a large swig of beer; he had become harder in his eyes, and more vengeful, since the Bishop's Wars had come to an end. Jack knew William was an ardent supporter of the English King, and had thus, unlike himself, refused to sign the Covenant that would let Scotland keep its religious freedoms.

Turncoat! he thought, as he set his goblet down in front of him. *Scotland deserves better than to be ruled by men like you!*

"Aye, William," Jack replied after a short time, "there are some news that you may find of interest...although," he continued with a taunting grin, "whether you welcome them is another matter!"

Anger began to well up in William once again. He was aware of his cousin's thoughts on the question of Margaret's estate, and Jack's superior attitude inflamed William's views even more as to who the rightful heritor of her estate should be. Unable to hide his wrath, he stood up abruptly, paced to the window, and with his back turned to his guest, replied in a voice that was low, but which shook with anger.

"I have always held Margaret's best interests at heart!"

Jack could not hide his own anger and let out a contemptuous snort.

"Easy to say for a brother, now that she is dead!" He slammed the goblet down on the table, some of its contents spilling onto the bare wood, and trickling down the side onto the cold stone floor.

William turned sharply to face his opponent, who was still seated; the air was so thick one might cut it with a knife.

"Do not dare to insult me in my own home, Jack! I thought the manners of one calling himself the Lord Glamis, descendant of the Earls of Strathmore and Kinghorne, should be more couth than what I see from you today!"

But Jack only laughed at his glaring cousin; he was a fine man to talk of possessing the proper manners, the murderer of his own sister! There was a deathly calm in the room. The two men stood opposite each other as if about to begin a duel; only when the clock chimed at the quarter hour did Jack speak again.

"Before we resort to pistols, William," he smirked facetiously, "let me tell you my news, and then I shall be gone."

He rose from the settee, and as he did so, Margaret briefly appeared in Jack's place again, staring at William with sad eyes and shaking her head; she held out the scold's bridle, as if gifting it to him. *Murderer,* something whispered inside his head, before Jack's voice silenced it.

"I received word from Robert Douglas in Sweden that Duncannon, who as their son is the rightful heir to Margaret and Baron Eythin's estates- still lives; in response, I have sent a man hence, to look for him and ask him to return to Scotland!"

William for the first time in a long while, was speechless; his nephew- alive! After all this time- more than twenty years past......he could not- he would not!- believe it. *It is a conspiracy*, he thought.

Jack, amused at William's lack of response, continued, half-mocking:

"It would settle this matter once and for all, William.... but I would have thought that the news of your nephew- your sister's only son-being alive after all this time to be welcome to you...instead," he went on coldly, "I see you appear to be more concerned with having to give up your claim to an estate that you had no right to in the first place!"

"I will never give up my claim!" screamed William, having lost all reason or sense of propriety, with such force that Jack retreated a few steps towards the door, with a hand on his sword.

"The estate is rightfully mine, Jack, as Margaret's brother, and my nephew- or whoever this impostor claims to be- has no claim on it since more than twenty years have passed!"

William was seething with fury now; a storm had begun to gather over the distant sea, iron grey and dark, as if a manifestation of his own feelings. Jack remained motionless; he knew there were no words that could calm his cousin's irrational outbursts.

"And," spluttered William, eyes wide with rage and shaking his fist at Jack, "I will take it to the Lord Justice General, if I must!"

Catching his breath, he sneered, "At least he is not someone to betray his own country for a treacherous cause!"

Jack realised then that any chance of a reasonable discussion with his cousin was gone, if not entirely dead. *A fight*, he thought, *until surrender or death.... but it shall not be me!*

"The Covenant was written to protect Scotland, our home, William, not to betray it; it is a pity that this fact has escaped your understanding!"

William had lost all ability to communicate; his eyes were so black and glassy it was as if he had been possessed by another being.

"Very well, William," Jack stated, calmly, "then do what you believe you must."

He took his black hat and mantle from the settee, and with his hand still firmly on his sword, he bowed curtly as he opened the door. "But understand this, William, that the restoration of Margaret's good name is as great my desire, as the treacherous claim on her inheritance is yours!"

He turned out of the door, and as it closed, the cat slipped through once again, slinking around William's legs for attention.

All was quiet, bar the distant thunder. William observed his cousin ride swiftly away out of the gates of Aberdour, towards the vast sea that lay before it.

"If this means a fight to the end, Jack Lyon, I will have what should be mine!"

He kicked the cat away in fury, sending the poor creature flying towards the door as he left, and leaving her fleeing for nearest cover to lick her terrible wounds.

*

The home of the Widow MacDonald, Edinburgh, November 2nd, 1641

Thomas and John had set out for their visit to the widow MacDonald soon after their meeting at the College of Justice. In the back of both their minds was the prospect of a spy in the College chambers, and as they made their way towards the West Bow, they peered over their shoulders frequently, but found no one following them. The house was a short walk away, and so they had not taken their horses; the day was still fine, although cold, and the cobblestone roads were still wet and slippery with frost and snow. They passed out of the Parliament Square onto Cowgate and its lavish residences, passing Maudlin's Chapel on the left, briefly entering the wide expanse of the Horse Market, before making their way up the narrow, winding road of the West Bow.

"Justice MacDonald's house is just here, father," said John, pointing to a tall, narrow turreted house that overlooked the lower half of the West Bow. They had walked in silence until now. Thomas looked up; a cold chill down his spine made him shiver as he recognised the house.

"Is that not old Major Weir's house?"

"Aye," nodded John, "MacDonald bought it soon after the Major's...demise," he hesitated briefly between the last two words; Major Weir's passing out of this world was still a fresh memory for most of those who had lived in Edinburgh in the last twenty years or so.

"The Justice," continued John, "although kind and generous, father, was frugal in terms of living when it came to practicalities!"

He smiled, fond memories of lively conversations with this master coming back to him.

"With all the stories surrounding the Major and his sister, I believe the Justice purchased the house for a pittance- five pounds Scots!"

But his face darkened again, as his father commented:

"Aye, a bargain I should say!"

"After MacDonald's execution, the Privy Council took his home- a fine mansion, Panmure House; do you know it?" asked John; his father nodded.

"...As well as the rest of his fortune. They turfed out the widow, who could only afford to keep Strachan- and this," he pointed to the Major's house, "was the only place they could go to. They say it is cursed, and few people dare to enter the house of Major Weir!"

Thomas stopped briefly. The Major's house loomed a short distance away as they reached further up the West Bow. It looked ordinary apart from its visible lack of upkeep: there were a few shattered windows, scattered bits of broken masonry on the steps, and only a dim light and the faintest wisp of smoke seeped out from the chimney, but its sinister past hung over the house like an unshakable dark cloud.

Major Weir and his sister, Grizel, had lived in this house together. At first, they had seemed an apparently respectable brother and sister. Grizel, the story went, had taken to looking after Major Weir after the sudden death of his wife. Outwardly devout, they hosted congregations and sermons at their home, and put even those who considered themselves to be pious beyond reproach to shame. But that, it turned out, was a disguise for a terrible truth: beneath this outwardly upstanding member of society, who had even signed a petition denouncing the Five Articles of Perth, a depraved and vicious madman worked behind those closed doors. Talk of sorcery, the devil, and fornication with his own sister and those poor unsuspecting souls they lured into their mansion soon spread through all of Edinburgh's society, and before long, the Major and Grizel were arrested and taken to the Tollbooth. Then at the advanced age of seventy, Major Weir, feeling the end was not too distant anyway, confessed to all the depravity and evil: carnal gratification with his sister- who had, according to him, enjoyed the acts as much as he- heinous acts with the servants and others who came to visit, and a pact made with the Devil so strong that Major Weir believed himself to be untouchable by the consequences of the mortal sins of the common person. He became feared by all as 'the Wizard of the Bow', sightings of Satan's carriage, the horses' nostrils flaring with fire and hooves blazing in the middle of the night taking the Major and Grizel away, and all who had dealings with them are said to have met an ill fate. On the day of his execution, as the fire consumed him, he is said to have cried out, "I have lived as a beast, and now I must die as one!" And those who witnessed the burning- for there were only a few brave enough to attend- claimed the Major's flesh turned not into ash but a flock of Devil's Birds and flew away.

"Are you unwell, father?" asked John, concerned at the elder Hope's pensive silence.

"I am well, John," he replied sombrely. "But I was remembering the story of Major Weir and his sister- I was at his trial, John; and," he paused, shaking his head gently, "you know me well enough not to put too much credence to hearsay and the fantasies that people sometimes like to create, but if ever there was a man who made my blood run cold, it was Major Weir!"

John became interested; he had only heard stories and fantastical tales of 'the Wizard of the Bow'.

"I did not know you had been at his trial, father; you must tell me what transpired!"

Thomas shivered again, not from cold, but at the memory of his encounter with the Major. A few clouds, grey and snow-laden, had obscured the brightness of the sun, outlining the silhouettes of a few birds which seemed to hang motionless in the sky.

"I may tell you one day, son," he said, having no intention of doing so, "but let us first see what the Widow MacDonald, and Strachan, have to say!"

They had now entered a narrow passage off the West Bow, flanked either side by tall tenements, until they reached an open, but dark, courtyard. No sunlight, apart from a bright narrow ray that escaped as the sun skimmed the adjoining tenement roofs, brightened the gloomy aspect of the house. The air was still and frozen, and both men stopped briefly, uncertain in their decision to visit this forsaken place. Though neither of them confessed it openly, both felt as though they had entered another world.

"I will pull the bell-ring," offered John after a short silence, hesitating slightly as he stepped slowly up the stairs that led to the large double oak doors of the house. An almost mournful sound, long, and slow, and dull, but loud, poured out of the house as he pulled the heavy iron ring of the bell; no soul appeared.

"Perhaps there is no one at home," suggested Thomas after a few minutes, but then, the enormous doors suddenly creaked open, and the nervous countenance of Strachan peered out at them.

"You have come!" he gasped, almost in a whisper, as if saved from the Devil.

"I did not think you would, I confess! Please, please, I beg of you," he waved them towards the entrance, "do enter! I think you are come just in time, my Lords," and he motioned gratefully towards John, "and Lord Craighall, it is most good of you to join your honourable father in what must be a time of great grief for you, Sir! My soul was deeply wounded to hear of your wife's sudden and untimely passing...".

John, who had successfully buried his grief beneath his mounting curiosity, nodded discretely in acknowledgement, although he now found himself dismayed, and irritated at the painful reminder, and stayed silent.

'Strachan, we should get to the business at hand," Thomas interjected in a business-like manner; he needed his son's clear head, without the muddled distractions of grief.

"We do not have much time; please, tell us what you have found that you believe is of such importance."

The steward agreed vehemently, ushering the two men into a sitting room that was sparsely furnished; frayed and torn curtains remained closed, and he had lit a single lamp as they sat down on the worn settee. Next to it stood a small table with some beer, a loaf of bread that appeared to have turned to stone, and some cheese so riddled with green mould that even a hungry mouse might hesitate to steal it. The two visitors declined politely the offer of food, but gladly took a mug of ale. It felt, in the dim light of just one lamp that it was the middle of the night, and not mid-morning; that feeling of being in another world became more profound.

"Well, Sir Thomas, Lord Craighall," began Strachan, "peculiar things have been happening, and had it not been for the widow MacDonald's rantings and mutterings, I would not have requested your visit- busy and important men of state such as you are," he flattered, his grey, red-rimmed eyes wide open with anxiety. He was an aging man, well past sixty, but still in fine health, and although his children had urged him to retire from his work as steward, he had refused to abandon the widow MacDonald.

"A few days ago, a man appeared at the house- he was foreign, I believe- and called himself a physician," breathed the steward, the wrinkles on his forehead creasing as he concentrated to remember, "he carried with him a parcel... and you must understand, that since we were evicted from Panmure House after the good Justice's- er- death", he hesitated as he spoke, "we have been shunned completely by our friends, and so a visitor was most unexpected, you see!"

Strachan stared at the two men, who continued to sip their beer in silence; Thomas was maintaining his patience, but John began to feel irritated.

"The physician claimed he had been given something for safe-keeping by Lady Margaret Douglas- you remember, the noble-woman that was burned- to send to her son in Sweden! But it turned out that her son was also dead- killed fighting the Spanish, I believe- and so not knowing what to do with the parcel, the good physician hid it in his chambers- until a few days ago, when he brought it to us!"

John's impatience was gnawing at him, and he stood up from the settee abruptly that the table shook a little, cups and knives clinking as he strolled to the window.

"And what then, Strachan?" he urged the old man.

"Well, I asked him how we could help, and he said the parcel would be safer with the old Justice's papers- that they would, when the widow MacDonald passed, certainly be returned to the courts- to you, in particular, Sir Thomas!"

Thomas felt a pang of conscience; he remembered his undesir-able actions all those years ago, and how it might have sealed Justice MacDonald's fate, and swallowed hard.

"To me?" he repeated incredulous.

"Aye Sir Thomas, I believe the Justice made this a provision of his will and then," continued the old steward, "I began to wonder.... the widow MacDonald also mentioned your name....," he blushed mildly as he added, "although perhaps not in such benevolent terms.....".

Thomas cast down his eyes, and John laughed scornfully.

"But I began to think that perhaps the Justice had found things out- things he should not have known, secrets of politics!- and that was why they.....murdered him!"

He choked, a tear welling up around his narrowed eyes; he had always had such fondness for the Justice and missed his old master still.

The three men sat in silence for a few minutes; in the distance outside, the faint sound of the bells of St Giles chimed. *It must be around mid-day now*, Thomas thought, briefly distracted by the worldly sound of the church.

"What kind of things, Strachan?" John finally broke the silence. The steward composed himself and took a deep breath.

"That the burning of Lady Margaret was a conspiracy for more sinister purposes than only her brother's desire to gain her inheritance!"

Thomas and John looked at each other; both were practical and methodical by nature, as lawyers needed to be, and could only cast doubt on the conjectures of an ageing man who had lost a dear master.

"But why would you believe this, Strachan?" asked Thomas gently; he had no wish to offend the steward. Somewhere in the house he could hear something stirring.

"That will be the widow MacDonald, waking," replied Strachan, as if having read Thomas' mind.

"I was coming to that, Sir Thomas," he went on, "I looked through some of the Justice's old papers, and I was not wrong- he had been doing his own investigations! Let me show you," he offered, "but first, please excuse me, for I must see to the widow!"

He hurried, apologetically, out of the room, leaving Thomas and John alone. It was still cold, despite the small fire that burned in the blackened hearth. John noted the few logs that were left, and absentmindedly muttered:

"Perhaps we should bring them a few logs, father; it seems they cannot afford to heat this house!"

"Aye," agreed Thomas, "well, 'tis expensive these days; some wood comes from Norway, I believe, though why I cannot think- it is not as though Scotland is short of trees!"

Anyway, thought Thomas to himself, *I do not think a big enough fire exists to heat this house, nor a lamp bright enough to light it...*

"What are your thoughts, my son, on Strachan's account?" Thomas enquired matter of fact, but eager to hear his son's opinion.

John answered, staring mesmerised, into the dying fire.

"I cannot say, father, until I have seen the documents.... and this parcel; it sounds mysterious! I wonder who this physician could be?" He turned to Thomas. "Do you know him, father?"

Thomas nodded, then shook his head.

"I do not know him, John, but I agree, there is a mystery here. But," he waved one hand almost dismissively towards the fireplace, "a physician cannot be difficult to find here, especially if, as Strachan claims, he is foreign!"

After a few seconds of pondering the situation, he added:

"I do seem to remember very faintly that there was a physician who attended Margaret Douglas when she was kept in the Castle... but I cannot remember his name!"

The two men almost jumped as the door to the sitting room suddenly creaked open, and Strachan reappeared, agitated and distraught.

"She is very unsettled, good sirs; I fear she is not long for this world! She would like to see you if you agree to the visit?" smiled the steward, feebly. He seemed weary. "And then I will show you Justice MacDonald's papers!"

John and Thomas nodded, and the two men followed Strachan and his dimming lamp into the dark hallway, and up a grand staircase; the railings were unsteady, and the steps creaked and moaned some so loudly John thought he might crash through them and end back on the floor below. Two narrow corridors sprung from either side of the staircase landing, with doors along either side. Strachan motioned to the left with his lamp.

"It is this way; the third door is the Widow's room."

Strachan carefully opened the door; a freezing draft met them, and the room had no light apart from Strachan's lamp, except for a few slivers of faint daylight which had escaped through the frayed curtains.

It was so cold that both Thomas and John had pulled their mantles up around their ears as they entered the room.

"I have begged the widow permission to light a fire," Strachan added loudly, so that the widow would hear, "but she refuses!"

"I have not the money for fire, Strachan!" she spluttered angrily; from the bed, a frail figure could be made out bulging faintly from under the ragged wool blankets.

"And it is the Devil's fire, anyway, which I do not wish!"

She heaved a great exhalation, in exhaustion; *not long now*, she thought, *not long and I shall see my dear Gordon again....*

"I would very gladly bring you some wood for the fire, widow MacDonald," offered Thomas, "we have more than enough to spare at Hope Mansion!"

"It is the Devil's fire!" she coughed again, and then stopped.

"Is that the voice of Sir Thomas Hope I recognise?" she asked slowly. Her feeble voice cracked between deep, short breaths. Thomas hesitated; he had not forgotten Strachan's words in the sitting room.

"Aye," he replied softly, "it is I who have come, along with my son, John."

On hearing John's name, she began to weep gently, and reached out a crooked hand.

"John, you have come?"

"Aye, Widow MacDonald, I am here, too."

She grasped the air with her hand as if trying to catch something, until John understood it was his own hand she was reaching for; he held it out to her and she took it. He winced as she grabbed it; her grip was still strong.

"Gordon always spoke so well of you, John," she whispered, catching her breath, "you were the son he could never have!"

The old woman spluttered again, her chest gurgling painfully, until some blood spilled through her remaining teeth and down her lips and chin. Strachan attempted to wipe it off, but she slapped him away like an unwanted fly.

"Leave it!" she hissed. "This is how it ends- no fineries or etiquette, no propriety for the sake of appearance! I will die in my natural state, as I came into this world; in blood and shit, stinking like a cesspit!"

Keeping hold of John's hand, she turned to Thomas.

"Traitor!" she sneered at him; it was as if she had stuck a knife in his heart. "*You* betrayed him to his death- *you!*"

She coughed so violently the blood sprayed onto John's hand; disgusted, he tried to withdraw it, but her iron grip kept hold.

"Blood...this blood," she breathed, "is also on your hands, John!"

Thomas replied, his voice shaking, agitated.

"I had my family to think of!"

"Family!" she cried, "I had none after Gordon! Cast out from society like a leper!"

She sighed and relaxed a little with weakness; John took advantage of the brief silence by changing the subject.

"Widow MacDonald, Strachan mentioned that you had some information for us?" he nudged her gently, ignoring her attack on him. She softened the grip a little and nodded.

"Aye...aye...," she croaked, "it was all a conspiracy... Lady Margaret .... innocent! It is always the innocent females who burn! Her brother .... and the Earl of Menteith- curse that evil man! - they had a plot... gain favour with the English King!"

She spewed the last words out as if spitting on His Majesty from a distance and paused; her long greasy white hair clung to her face, the sweat pouring feverishly from her forehead, but Strachan dared not touch her.

"And, widow MacDonald," persisted John gently, "how did you come by this knowledge?"

She sneered a little, as if self-satisfied.

"Papers! Gordon's papers...", her breaths had started to become shallow and long; she closed her eyes.

"In the coffer.... Strachan knows....", she added and abruptly grabbed Thomas' hand as she let go of John's, turning to him, eyes wide open and flashing with anger.

"*You!*" she hissed, "*you* must put it right.... restore the good name of Gordon MacDonald!"

She lowered her voice. "I shall be watching you from above, Thomas Hope, and if you do not do as I ask, you will be as forsaken by God as this satanic abode!"

She coughed again, uncontrollably, blood and globs of green phlegm spraying onto the dirty blanket and Thomas' hands, her arms flailing and her ashen face contorted in pain.

"The Minister!" she pleaded. "The Minister...!"

"I must send for the clergyman," Strachan announced, "I think she will not live out the day!"

The three men left the room, and Thomas, still shaking from the Widow's angry condemnation, and feeling nauseous at the blood and phlegm, was eager to be released from this dark place, and offered to help.

"Allow me to call for the Minister; I shall return promptly!" He turned to the door before Strachan could protest, leaving John alone with the steward.

"Well, Lord Craighall, I may as well show you the Justice's papers while we wait for your good father to return!"

He led John down the stairs and into a study opposite the sitting room. It was quite dark, save a dimly lit lamp on a small writing desk.

"I do not recall lighting a lamp in here," he exclaimed, scratching his head, "but then, I may just have forgotten with all these strange events!"

John felt a chill again; it was an odd sensation, unnatural- not the kind of chill one would feel when walking in the winter air, but rather a coldness that clung to the soul.

"There it is," Strachan said, pointing to a coffer on the writing table, "I put everything in here, including the physician's parcel!"

John nodded and opened the coffer carefully. A thick plume of dust shot up at him, and he coughed.

"This house," regretted the steward apologetically, "I clean it daily, and yet it is still full of dust!"

But John had already begun to look at the documents, and almost forgot the old man was still there. He leafed through the box carefully, until one page in particular caught his attention.

"Well," he mused, eyebrows raised, "there is an interesting idea!"

He waved towards Strachan.

"Bring your lamp a little closer, Strachan," he begged, "the light is still too dim, and I must take a closer look!"

The steward obeyed, glancing curiously over John's shoulder; his eyesight not being the best at his age, he could make out only a few words as John read the note in silence.

"Bishop Laud's love for the Duke and his hatred of Scotland.... Spanish assassin... William Douglas.... sister's estate.... aid to the King...."

John folded the note and laid it aside and leafed through the remainder of the documents in the coffer. He had almost given up searching for something relevant when he spotted a faint slit in the bottom of the box.

"Strachan," he asked the patient steward, "are you aware if the Justice ever felt the need to hide any of his papers?"

"Aye," replied he eager and wide-eyed, "he was always talking about spies and had little trust in people, did the Justice, particularly before he was....", he stopped, and gulped at the painful thought of his master's last few days on earth, "so he always had papers hidden about the house! How he remembered where they all were, I cannot think!"

John nodded absentmindedly. He felt the bottom of the coffer again and knocked it gently. It sounded hollow. He felt around the outside, pushing at various parts to see if it would release a catch that would reveal a secret compartment, but nothing moved. Frustrated, he closed it, and stared at it. *There must be a release somewhere,* he thought, *I must find it!*

A sound from the hallway- perhaps the front door opening- distracted him briefly, and Strachan, ever aware of the widow's waning time on earth, asked anxiously:

"I beg pardon, my Lord, but I think that must be your father returning with the Minister! Please, let me go to them- the widow...".

"Of course, Strachan, but could you leave the lamp?"

John, now alone in the study, folded the document he had laid aside and slipped it into his pocket, along with Margaret's parcel. But the coffer still intrigued and irritated him; he was convinced there was something hidden beneath its bottom.

He looked at it again. A story his father had once told him leapt into his memory; it was a story of ingenious devices used by emperors of the Orient to hide their secrets, like boxes with hidden compartments.

The box itself was unusual. It was made of oak, stained in pitch, and had a date inscribed on either side of the lock- 1603. *A fateful year for Scotland,* regretted John, wondering briefly how life would be for Scots had there been no union of the crowns. Casting his attention back to the mysterious coffer, he noted its detailed decoration. There was a thin panel of carved bone plaques around the outside along the bottom edge, yellowed with age. He felt with his fingers, pressing as he moved along each plaque, but again, nothing moved. As he became more irritated, he simply repeated his actions, convinced at some point that the secret would be discovered; but nothing moved. An anger suddenly overcoming him; John shook the coffer and slammed it down onto the desk, and suddenly, as if his frustration had finally won, the left corner of the panel moved! He pressed harder, but instead of pushing in, it gave way to the pressure and slipped out. A button! John pushed it in, and a tray slipped out not from underneath as he had expected, but from the side. *At last!* he thought and began to remove it when he heard raised voices from the entrance hall.

"Who are you?" Strachan was shouting. "You are not welcome! Put that sword away- you do not frighten me!"

Danger, thought John, *and no time to delay!* He grabbed the paper from the secret tray, pushed it shut, and closed the coffer.

"Give me what is mine!"

It was the voice of the stranger, cold and thin; sword drawn, John threw open the door, but he was too late. Poor Strachan lay dead on the floor, throat cut like a lamb to the slaughter, and before he had time to react, a figure pushed him violently out of the way as it flew past him into the study. The memory of failing Justice Gordon rushed back; the guards taking him away to his death, and he unable to stop them, and anger overtook his fear. John bounded after the assailant, who had reemerged with the coffer.

"Leave that; it does not belong to you!" screamed John slipping in Strachan's blood as he ran out, but the assassin was deft with his sword, and a lightning quick scurry between the two left John only able to inflict a gash on his opponents face before he escaped down the narrow lanes of West Bow. John pursued him briefly, but the killer had disappeared. Out of breath, he returned to the house, and seeing Strachan again, he vomited twice, still doubled over in pain and exhaustion when Thomas and the Minister arrived, only a few minutes later.

"John!" Thomas rushed to his son, concerned he was injured. "What has happened? Are you injured?"

John exhaled, still dizzy and out of breath.

"No," he replied, wiping dribbles of vomit from his mouth, and feeling sick again, "but Strachan... poor man, he has been killed!" He steadied himself on his father's arm and continued.

"He took the box, father, the assassin took the box!"

Thomas and the Minister, shocked at the sight of the murdered steward, butchered like an animal, were lost for words. John added quickly:

"But I think I saved what we were looking for!"

The Minister, a small and sickly-looking man who's most exciting adventure in the entirety of his fifty-odd year long life had hitherto involved chasing a pig out of his garden, became unwell at the sight of Strachan. He stood for a moment, unable to move, until from above, as if the horror of Strachan's bloodied remains- his eyes still open, dumb-struck- were not enough to send the fear of the Devil into one's hear, the widow MacDonald began to wail violently.

"The Devil! He is here! I will not go with you- you cannot take me! Be gone, you wretched creature, be gone from this house! God will save us! God will save Scotland!"

She paused, catching the last remains of her breath.

"Give me Scotland, ere I die!"

A gurgle and a violent spate of coughing followed, seemingly unstoppable; the Minister, now somewhat recovered and having found the courage to close the steward's eyes and pray for him, muttered:

"I must go to her, my Lords; I think she draws her last breath now!"

He hurried up the stairs, but stopped mid-way, and turned to Thomas.

"Would you be so kind as to wait for me?" he asked, embarrassed. "I know God is on my side, of course, but in this house.... I fear the Devil!"

Thomas and John nodded, and the Minister hastened on; it was only a few minutes later, after incoherent and crazed screams, a deathly silence followed, and that they could hear the faint voice of the Minister.

"I am the resurrection, and the life saith the Lord,

He that believeth in me, though he were dead yet shall he live,

And whosoever liveth, and believeth in me, shall not die forever.

We brought nothing into this world, and it is certain we can carry nothing out.

The Lord gave, and the Lord hath taketh away. Blessed be the name of the Lord. Amen."

~ Twenty-Five ~

Rafael de la Cruz was annoyed. *I should have finished off the other one, too!* he thought to himself, as he inspected the long cut down the side of his face. But it had been too risky already; he had seen Sir Thomas leave the courts and did not know there would be some-one else with him- someone younger and more agile. No matter; he had the coffer, and they would never be able to find him. He had made certain to cover his face, and even with his fresh scar, it had been too dark in the hallway for anyone to recognise him, and in daylight, he wore his cowl.

The monk was still angry. He stood over the basin, dabbing the open gash with a cloth, dipping it in the ice-cold water, method-ically, and almost rhythmically; his blood mixed into the water in artful swirls of crimson turning to a soft pink, and it gradually turned the clear water a dusky rose colour, as he reflected on the events of the last month.

Nothing had gone according to plan. He had not expected to see the girl in St Catherine's- or that she worked for the enemy! Nor had he anticipated the shrewdness of Maria de Taye, who had found out his real identity; had he not been so pressed for time in pursuing the girl, Rafael would have cut her throat, too.... or worse, perhaps a repeat of his dealings with that servant girl at Glamis all those years ago.

But now, he had one more task. *I must take more blood today,* he thought, smiling to himself; it pleased him to rid the world of sinners and false believers. *One day soon,* he thought with euphoria in his heart, *the true faith will be restored across the world*, and he kissed the gold cross around his neck, a tear rolling down his cheek as he looked up towards God. It stung the open gash that John Hope had branded him with, but it was worth that sacrifice.

*

Galenius stood by the window of his small apartment. The evening light was beautiful, a golden sun lighting up the distant hills and sea and it seemed as though a great march of fire had lit up the horizon. But behind it, a storm rolled in; dark clouds, heavy with snow and rain, waited for a night of thunder and lightning. He thought back in time; it was thirteen years to that very day that Margaret Douglas had been burned, and for thirteen years he had held onto the promise of finding her son. And now, it was no more- for he, too, was dead, Galenius had found out.

The physician wondered if he had been right to return the parcel to the old Justice's widow. He would have taken it to the courts himself, but he was afraid; it was easy these days, with the war in Europe, as a foreigner to get arrested- and he might be accused of theft, or treason, or God only knew what else. *God,* thought he, *why should God have to be loved so differently by all of us? Are we not all the same- of flesh and blood, and vile excrement, all that will decay and end over time?*

Strachan the steward had seemed understanding and sensible, despite Galenius' status as 'foreigner', and he had promised to help. Reassured, the physician turned away from the window as the first flashes of lightning cut through the distant sky. A roll of thunder followed, and heavy drops of sleet began to descend and stick to the window. He shivered; the cold had gotten to his bones, and he moved to the hearth to stoke the dwindling fire.

Twenty-seven years he had lived in this city, and although it was his home, he would always feel like an outsider- not because of the people: most afforded him the respect and honesty he, as a physician, deserved after years of honest work- but because he had always longed to return home, to Spain. Galenius looked around his rooms; they were nicely furnished, not richly but all his possessions were of good Scottish craftsmanship and above the scale of decency required should a client of the upper ranks of society wish to seek his advice. The chambers, which were now his home as well as his practice- his work at Trinity now infrequent- were on the second floor of a tall tenement, near enough to the hospital for him to walk to, but far enough away so that he might forget the day's constant flow of human tragedies. For it seemed that it was only ever the dying, those beyond all earthly help, who came to Trinity to see out their last days.

But there was nothing in his home that reminded him of *home*- he carried only a small token in the inner pocked of his cowl which took his memories back to Spain. He would have worn it around his neck, but the cross of Christ had taken its place for so long now, he dared not. Galenius felt for something in his pocket, and took it out- his hand shook a little; he was afraid, for he never removed it for fear of losing it. It was a beautiful gold pendant, in the shape of a tulip with five thin long petals that resembled each finger of the hand. *Hamsa*, he thought, and kissed it, *you have kept me safe and patient for so long!*

He glanced at a letter that lay open on his desk; it was from Noureddine. He longed to see his old friend again. They had seen each other only once since the tragedy of Margaret's burning, and now he was in England. *Perhaps this time*, thought Galenius, *I will leave this place with him; leave this home, and return to where I belong.*

He was shaken out of his thoughts by the loud clatter of what sounded like stones being thrown at his windows and looked up. From out of the dark small hailstones were being hurled violently around by the stormy winds. He moved to the window to close the shutters when he saw the shadow of a figure walking in the street below. It stopped, and looked about, and then disappeared out of Galenius' sight.

Brave to venture out in this storm, he thought, and closed the wooden shutters. But amidst the noise of the storm, he had not heard the figure enter his chambers, and when he turned to be faced with him, his heart nearly stopped in shock; not because he was afraid of the tall man brandishing a long, sharp dagger in his hand, but because he recognised his face.

"Galenius," the figure said, "at last we meet again! And I see," he exclaimed bitterly, pointing with his dagger to the *hamsa* in Galenius' hand, "that you are still a Jew at heart!"

The physician was unmoved; in some ways, he had longed for the day he could finally see the murderer of his parents again, even if it meant that it would be his own gruesome end.

"And you," he replied mockingly, "Rafael de la Cruz, you are still nothing more than a paid assassin, I see!"

A crash of thunder bore down from the skies, shaking the windows and shutters. Bright lightning struck in successive flashes, before all, it seemed, turned to a dead calm.

*

It had taken John and Thomas some time to find anyone willing to come to Major Weir's house to remove the mutilated remains of Strachan, and the withered, stone-cold body of the widow Mac-Donald, not because blood and death were unpleasant, but because no one wanted to set foot in Major Weir's old house for fear of the curse. But as human nature finds itself all too often willing to favour fortune over fear, once John had offered enough coins, two men eventually appeared at the house and took the dead away.

"Come home to your mother, John," begged Thomas, "she will see to your children; you should not be alone in your grief."

John's heart sank again; he had entirely forgotten about his dead wife during their visit to the widow MacDonald. Neither did he know, to his great shame, if he felt any guilt, and it unsettled him.

"Father, I am well- truly," he said, half truthfully, "but we should speak alone together of today's events- and you must take a look at the papers I rescued before the thieving murderer got away with the coffer!"

"Aye," agreed his father, as they made their way back along the Cowgate; it was coming onto late afternoon, and beyond the setting sun, storm clouds- black, expansive, and ominous- crept in over the golden shining sea.

"I should not be surprised if we have thunder and lightning to-night, John," he muttered, looking up at the distant horizon, "and more snow!"

Hope Mansion was one of the grandest homes in the city, with two entrances and a large courtyard as one entered; it had been John's childhood home, and he often missed it. Going back to it took him back in time, to fond and carefree memories of childhood. *What complications we create for ourselves as we get older,* he thought, *would we could all stay as children forever!*

The grand sitting room of Hope Mansion waited for the two with a large warm fire, enormous bright windows, and the sound of chat-ter and laughter as John's children, young Tom and Archie, scurried about the house, having no understanding that their mother had died and left them in the incapable care of their father. Hearing him and their grandfather enter the house, the two boys bounced down the vast staircase and flew around them in a whirlwind of excitement, urging his father to play a game of hide-and-seek or to inspect the child's horse and carriage, which their kind grand-mother had gifted them that morning. But it was all too much for the elder Hope, who called out in frantic irritation to his wife:

"Eliza! Eliza!"

She eventually appeared with Mildred, the nurse-maid.

"Please take these wee rascals away ere my head explodes!" he begged, and the two boys, only momentarily disappointed at the old man's lack of interest, disappeared as turbulently as they had come.

"Let us go in here," urged Thomas, indicating towards the sitting room, "and let us have some beer and food first of all! I am famished!"

He rang the bell, and a very short time later, they were alone, eating and drinking, and contemplating the bizarre and disturbing day that had passed.

John had laid out on the table in front of them the items he had managed to save before the murderer had entered Major Weir's House; a few torn and hastily scribbled notes, and the parcel delivered by the physician, whose name they had discovered was Galenius, and who had claimed Margaret Douglas had entrusted him to pass it to her son.

"This took my attention, father," remarked John between mouthfuls of pasty, handing the elder Hope the first of the notes. Thomas peered at it, skeptically at first, but his eyebrows slowly lifted as he read on.

Duke of Buckingham- paid assassin: not Jack Felton! Privy council-Scotland

MD- convenient but innocent

E of M- and B. L.- aid from W.D.

Royalist traitors!

Letter from L. K.- Spanish plot?

These were some odd abbreviations of names, but Thomas quickly understood who MacDonald made reference to; he was unable to speak at the shocking revelation, while John continued.

"Aye, father; it would appear that we have traitors in our midst-traitors in the College of Justice!" he said bitterly and pointed to the next document. Tomas picked it up, glancing apprehensively at his son.

"In truth, I am not certain that I wish to know any more, my son;" he began, "when Strachan- poor dead man, God rest his wretched soul- contacted me, I did not realise the extent of MacDonald's investigations!"

He closed his eyes; thirteen years of guilt flooded back to him in an avalanche of memories.

"Read it, father," demanded John, his voice hard and unyielding, "you owe that much at least to Gordon MacDonald!" And so the old man dared do anything other than what his son commanded.

W.D.- letter from B.L.; hidden with D.D. It is all about Parliament and K.C.!

Thomas read on; the note mentioned a further letter, from E.M to MacDonald; but there was no sign of it.

"This letter he mentions-it is not here?" asked the father of his son, hopefully. "Tell me you found that also, John?"

John shook his head, dismayed.

"No, father; I regret I did not. I searched the coffer- there was nothing else of significance, and no letter from this E.M.... who I presume is the Earl of Menteith?"

John stood up and walked slowly to the window. The breeze had turned into a strong wind, and the last of the evening light was fading as the storm marched in. In the distance, he saw faint streaks of lightning followed by the low, slow rumble of thunder.

"I believe, father, that Margaret Douglas was an innocent victim of a grand political plot! The Duke and his disastrous diplomatic and military efforts were too embarrassing even for his most devoted adherents- but I confess," he sighed, weary of human folly, "that I find it even harder to believe that our fellow Scots- loathsome as some may be- would work with the Spanish to.... 'remove' him!"

Thomas suddenly felt the weight of the shock; he remained speechless for a minute, and concluded vehemently:

"We must find that letter, John- these notes are meaningless otherwise!"

He joined his son by the window. It was now completely dark, and only the light of a few jack-o-lanterns lit for Allhallows Eve broke through its blackness.

"And I fear that whoever it was you encountered at Major Weir's house will also be looking for it-", he stopped, snapping his fingers: the parcel!

"Did you take a look at the parcel, John? Is there anything there?" he asked eagerly. Thomas returned to the table; the parcel lay there, neatly wrapped, and he picked it up, but hesitated. He felt uneasy opening something that was intended for someone else; it had kept its secret for so long. John joined him, and the two stared at it, uncertain as to what to do.

"We must open it- we do nothing wrong, father; Strachan told us that the parcel was never delivered because the physician had learned that Margaret's son was also dead- that is why he kept it for so long!"

Thomas nodded feebly; he was still uncertain, and puzzled, as his thoughts went deeper.

"But why did he return it to MacDonald?" he wondered and found his curiosity pushing aside his uncertainty as he carefully slit open the wrapping. It was a book, to his surprise.

"A copy of George Buchanan's *De Jure Regni Apud Scotos*....", mumbled Thomas, perplexed, glancing at John, "what an unexpected find!"

John took the thick tome from his father; this had been George Buchanan's most controversial work, lauding Scottish sovereignty, and dismissing the divine right of kings.

"It is still banned," he commented, with a smile, "it is still a crime to possess this!"

He opened it carefully; it was a fine copy, almost completely unmarked, with an unassuming leather binding that neither bore the work's title, nor had any other decoration: plain, as expected of its Presbyterian nature. He was about to shut the cover when he noticed that the corner paper on the inside of the cover had loosened. It gave way when he pulled it gently.

"There is something hidden!" he exclaimed, heart pounding with excitement; he could feel something under it with his fingers! It was a paper of some kind; John slid it out slowly and gingerly, and unfolded it.

"What is it?" demanded Thomas, seeing his son's wry smile as he read. "Is it the letter to MacDonald?"

Again, John shook his head, but this time, there was no dismay.

"No, father," he mused, holding out the paper to the elder, "not the letter we were looking for... but you had best read it yourself!"

My loyal and esteemed friend William,

It has come to my attention that, as the Earl of Morton and ardent supporter of King Charles, you desire to advance your status by aiding His Majesty financially, and that the possibility of doing so is hampered by your sister's unwillingness to relinquish her claim to a disputed inheritance. It will comfort you, William, to know that both I and the Bishop have laid out a method to persuade your sister to yield to your request, due to a combination of events, one being the unfortunate but necessary murder of the Duke of Buckingham for which she will find herself a complicit culprit unless she acquiesces to your request- in which event, no harm will come to her bar the possibility of a brief appearance in the courts. Understand, of course, that neither myself nor the Bishop are involved; but you will be visited- and I ask you to host him at your home- by the renowned English Witchfinder General, Matthew Hopkins, whose life mission it is to root out all Devil's work; including your sister's unnatural power over you and the inheritance that should, as the elder male, be rightfully yours.

I have been reassured that your agreement to our scheme shall bring you great societal powers, including, I have good reason to believe, the procurement of the Barony of Orkney and Shetland, which is also currently in the possession of your sister.

Your visitor will be with you by the end of the first seven-day of October, and I trust you, as the Earl of Morton, will show him the true heart of Scottish hospitality.

Your faithful friend,

Lord Graham, Earl of Menteith

Thomas' jaw had dropped as he read the letter; it was unbelievable!

"This is... this is most extraordinary, John... I can hardly believe it!"

John nodded, staring at his father's incredulity; he had been right in his instinct, and John felt sorry for having such doubts in him that same morning.

"But how did this come into Margaret's hands- and why is it tucked away in this book?"

He frowned at the confusing cacophony of the day's events. John had no answer; he had wondered the same himself, and the two were now so enthralled by the mysteries they were faced with that neither had noticed the lightning and thunder, and the thick, hard hailstones that had begun to descend onto the city.

"We must find this physician- Galenius, was it not?- and hear what more he can tell us.... he may be able to help!"

John agreed enthusiastically, the happy prospect of distraction from grief in the back of his mind, and before long, they had begun the long ride to Trinity, reminders of All Hallows Eve all around them as they battled thunder, hail and an ice-cold wind.

*

Rafael de la Cruz had not anticipated a fight from Galenius, believing the physician to be a natural coward, but he had put up such resistance that the monk once again found himself standing by a basin, still in the physician's chambers, washing the blood from his face and hands. The sharp blade of the long dagger made a tinny sound against the copper bowl as he tried to scrub the blood from it, and he was so deep in concentration that he had not heard the door opening.

"We meet at last, Brother Rafael," a rasping, calculating voice said, "after thirteen years!"

Rafael spun around, dagger in hand, but was met only with laughter.

"May I say your work concerning the Douglas case was truly formidable! Your trail of destruction created such distractions it would have been impossible for anyone to know who really ordered the murder of the Duke... most admirable!"

Rafael remained silent, still poised to strike, while his visitor continued.

"Although, I do question your ready willingness to murder fellow members of the cloth...," he bowed, with a grin, peering at the body that lay on the floor.

"Master Matthew Hopkins, Witchfinder General, at your service!"

Rafael lowered the dagger, still dripping with water and blood, and stared at the General.

"I work only in the service of God, Master Hopkins, and should that work involve the need to take the blood of unbelievers to fulfill my duty, then so be it; it is the will of God!"

He wiped the knife on his cloak and slipped it back into a sheath concealed inside. Galenius lay at his feet, his throat slit and tongue protruding from the cut orifice; both men glanced down at the body with disdain.

"Anyway," sneered Rafael, spitting at the remains, "he was only a *converso*- a Jew pretending to be a Christian. He deserved nothing more!"

He scowled at Galenius' remains; Matthew Hopkins nodded fervently in agreement, but his eyes narrowed, and the tone of his voice hardened.

"Do not forget our agreement, Brother Rafael- we must find the missing letter you failed to retrieve from the widow MacDonald! There is much still to do, and time will wait for no one!"

Rafael replied, with menacing scorn, for he did not like to admit failure or defeat, nor did he appreciate the excessively irritating manner of Matthew Hopkins.

"*And* we must retrieve the Deed of Protection from our enemy, as we also agreed!"

They left the bloody remains of Galenius, leaving only a black cat that had come in through the open door sitting, statuesque and mournful, by the dead physician, as if on guard. Amid the thunder, lightning, and hail, the clock of the Grey Friars struck the hour of nine, ringing in the departed of All Hallows Eve.

HISTORICAL AND FICTIONAL CHARACTERS

Historical Characters

John (Jack) Lyon, Lord Glamis, Second Earl of Kinghorne.

Born 13 August, 1596, at Glamis, to Patrick Lyon, 1st Earl of Kinghorne, and Lady Anne Murray. He was an ardent supporter of the National Covenant, formulated in 1638, and spent most of the vast family wealth to finance the Covenanter Armies against King Charles I. In reality, he died in 1646, in St Andrews, but I have fictionalised parts of his life for the purposes of this story.

Charles I, King of England, Ireland and Scotland

Born in Scotland in 1600 into the House of Stuart. His parents, King James VI and I and Queen Anne of Denmark, moved to England when James was made King of England and Scotland in the Union of the Crowns after the death of Elizabeth I in 1603. He married Henrietta Maria, the sister of King Louis XIV of France, in 1625. During his lifetime, it appears that Charles I made only one brief voyage to Scotland in 1633 for his Scottish coronation; his interest in Scotland remained mainly in his desired alignment of religious practices in England and Scotland, which would soon be a serious cause of conflict. His marriage to a Catholic, and proposed religious reforms, aroused suspicions that Charles I would take Scotland back to the Catholic faith. Believing in the divine right of kings, Charles I clashed frequently with Parliament regarding the levying of taxes, who sought to curb Charles I's powers refused his requests to raise taxes. This clash with Parliament eventually resulted in the dissolution of Parliament in 1629, and the start of eleven years of 'Personal Rule' by Charles I. Facing bankruptcy after the Bishop's Wars against the Scots in 1640, he was forced to bring back Parliament, but further quarrels in 1641 resulted in the start of the First English Civil War, and the Wars of the Three Kingdoms, which lasted from 1642 until the beheading of Charles I in 1649.

William Laud, Bishop of London and later, Archbishop of Canterbury.
Born in 1573 to William Laud, a clothier, and Lucy Webbe, the sister of William Webbe, the Lord Mayor of London. Laud studied divinity at Oxford, and was ordained in 1601. Subsequently, he rose through the ranks of the clergy to become Bishop of London in 1628, when he was also a close confidant of George Villiers, 1st Duke of Buckingham, before ascending to the position of Archbishop of Canterbury in 1633. He became a staunch advocate of Charles I's religious reforms, which were by many political opponents considered to be closer to Catholicism than Protestanism, which caused controversy and mistrust in England and Scotland. Although Laud was arrested in 1641, and beheaded in 1645, for the purposes of this story, the latter part of his life has been partially fictionalised.

George Villiers, 1st Duke of Buckingham.
Born in 1592 to a minor gentleman, he rose through the ranks of society and became a Gentleman of the Bedchamber during the reign of King James VI and I, who it was rumoured took George Villiers as his lover. He remained King James I's closest confidant until his death in 1625, and continued to be a close advisor and confidant to King Charles I until Villiers was stabbed to death in 1628.

William Douglas, 7th Earl of Morton.
Born in 1582 to Jean Lyon, Countess of Angus, and Robert Douglas, Master of Morton. He was Treasurer of Scotland and a staunch supporter of the Royalist cause, often seeking favour with King Charles I through raising funds for the King's numerous failed military endeavours. He died in 1648.

Lady Anne Keith, wife of Sir William Douglas
Born in the 1580s to George Keith, 5th Earl Marischal and Margaret, Countess Marischal. She married William Douglas, 7th Earl of Morton, in 1604, and they had nine children. Their son Robert, who would succeed his father as the 8th Earl of Morton, married Anne Villiers, the niece of George Villiers, Duke of Buckingham, in 1627.

Matthew Hopkins, The Witchfinder General
Matthew Hopkins existed in real life, although he was born at a later date (ca. 1620). For the purposes of this work, he was born in England around 1600. His father was a Puritan minister in Suffolk, and the younger Hopkins became a zealous witch-hunter at an early age, whose activities flourished during the English Civil war. Although it does not appear that he visited Scotland during his life, his remarkable impact on English society made him the ideal character for extending his pursuits there, as Scotland went through several periods of intense witch trials during the 17th century. He died in the late 1640s.

Sir Thomas Hope, 1st Baronet of Hope of Craighall, Lord Advocate

Born in 1573 to Henry Hope, a wealthy Edinburgh merchant, and Jacqueline de Tott, a French- Swedish lady. He studied law and was admitted as an advocate in 1605, and after defending a series of high-profile case, he earned himself a reputation as one of the most eminent lawyers in Edinburgh. In 1626, he was appointed as Lord Advocate under King Charles I, and was created Baronet of Novia Scotia in 1628. Thomas married Elizabeth Bennet sometime before 1605, and they had fourteen children, eight of whom died young. He died in 1646.

John Hope, Lord Craighall

The eldest son of Sir Thomas Hope, John was born around 1605 in Edinburgh. He followed in his father's footsteps to become a lawyer, and was admitted as an ordinary lord of session in 1632. John married first wife, Margaret Murray of Blackbarony, with whom he had eight children. Margaret died in childbirth in 1641, and in 1643, he married Dame Rachel Speir, Lady Currichill. Fiercely loyal to Scotland and her religious freedoms, he joined the committee that was established in 1640 to provide defenses for Scotland against England and King Charles I, and remained loyal to the Covenant cause throughout the Civil War. John Hope died in 1654.

William Graham, 7th Earl of Menteith, 1st Earl of Airth, Lord Justice General

Born around the year 1591, William Graham inherited his title and lands in 1610. A staunch supporter of King Charles I, he was appointed to the Privy Council of Scotland in 1626, and made Lord President of the Court of Sessions in 1628. That same year he also became Lord Justice General. King Charles I recognised Graham's loyalty by appointing him to the English Privy Council, but this was somewhat short-lived, when, in order to try to claim the title Earl of Strathearn, Graham claimed his bloodline to be of Robert II, and more pure than that of Charles I. Despite loss of favour with the King, Graham remained a fierce defender of Charles I, and never signed the Covenant. He died in 1661, leaving the remainder of his estates to his seven sons and four daughters.

Sir Alexander Seton, Lord Kilcreuch, Senator of the College of Justice

Born ca. 1576 to to James Seton, 5th Laird of Touch, and Eline, daughter of Andrews Edmonstone, Alexander Seton acquired Culcreuch Castle in 1624 due to debt owed to him by his brother-in-law. He took the title Lord Kilcreuch in 1626 upon his election as a Sentator of the College of Justice, and was knighted by King Charles I in 1633. The Seton family were Roman Catholic, and Lord Kilcreuch remained loyal to King Charles I. With his wife, Marion Maule, they had one son, Alexander Seton of Graden. There are different accounts as to the date of his death, but here it is set around 1645.

Kosem Sultan, Valide Sultan (Queen Mother) of the Ottoman Emperor Sultan Ibrahim

Kosem Sultan, the mother of Sultan Ibrahim I, was born to a Greek Orthodox priest on the island of Tinos around the year 1589. She is said to have been kidnapped in 1604 by Ottoman raiders to be brought as a slave to an Ottoman governor, who sent her to Istanbul to be trained in the harem of Sultan Ahmed I. She became mother to several of Ahmed I's children, including Murad IV, who would rule from 1623 to 1640, and the last of Ahmed I's heirs, Ibrahim, who succeeded the throne in 1640. Internal Ottoman politics were fractious and bloody, and Kosem Sultan became shrewd at navigating the unpredictable politics of state, often exercising ruthless orders in order to protect herself and her sons. Ibrahim was known to be mentally unfit to reign, and was eventually deposed in 1648 so that his youngest son, Mehmed (then aged 7) would take the throne. Kosem Sultan remained Regent until she was accused of plotting against her grandson Sultan Mehmed, and brutally murdered in a palace coup on the orders of Mehmed's mother, Turhan Sultan, in 1651.

Kermankes Kara Mustafa Pasha, Grand Vizier of the Ottoman Empire

An Albanian Ottoman military officer and vizier, Kara Mustafa Pasha was born in 1592. He became Agha of the Janissaries in 1634 and became Kapudan Pasha (Grand Admiral) of the Ottoman Navy in 1635, before being appointed as Grand Vizier- the highest post after Sultan- in 1638 by Sultan Murad IV. During the reign of Ibrahim, Kara Mustafa Pasha became the de facto ruler, with Kosem Sultan as Regent; this eventually caused friction between him and Kosem Sultan, who, together with Ibrahim's consort, Turhan Sultan, eventually dismissed Kara Mustafa Pasha in 1644. He was executed that same night.

Iosaf, Archbishop of St Catherine's Monastery, Sinai

Little is known about Ioasaf that can be found in accessible historical sources. He was Archbishop of St Catherine's Monastery from 1617 to 1661, making him one of the longest-serving Archbishops in the history of the Monastery. We can guess that he was born sometime in the 1580s or 1590s, probably in the Levant region or Eastern Mediterranean, as the Monastery belongs to the Eastern Orthodox Church, and the Archbishop is ordained by the Greek Orthodox Patriarch of Jerusalem.

Maria de Taye, Mother Superior and Abbess of Forest Abbey, Duchy of Brabant

Maria de Taye became the 25th Abbess of Forest Abbey, a Benedictine abbey, in 1609. She became notorious for excessive spending of the Abbey's funds, apparently purchasing a *refugium* (safe haven) in Brussels, and commissioning paintings from Hieronymus de Orlay. Forest Abbey is said to have fallen into disrepute under her stewardship, with rumours of a loose discipline among the nuns. The connection with the Benedictines of Jakobsberg in Germany is fictional, and although she died in reality in 1637, in this story, she lives well into the 1640s.

Elizabeth Hamlyn, entrepreneur, 'Spiriter of Children'

Elizabeth Hamlyn, probably born around 1620, carried out her work as a 'child spiriter' in London, rather than Plymouth, where she operates in this story; her exact dates of birth and death are unclear. The 'spiriting' of children was common in the 17th century, where opportunists seeking to increase their fortunes took vagrant children from the streets, and sold them onto slave ships bound for the newly formed colonies in the Americas. Although this was considered a criminal act, the level of corruption among court and parliament officials was such that these activities largely went undiscovered- even justices and court officials were known to take bribes to turn a blind eye, believing that in reality these illegal schemes cleansed the streets of unwanted individuals that were a burden on the state and society. Hamlyn was eventually caught and convicted in 1643, and was sent to Newgate prison in London.

Martin Noell, Financier, Merchant Venturer, Slave Trader

Although his exact date of birth is unknown, Martin Noell was the son of a Stafford mercer, and had already established himself as one of the plantation owners of Barbados by the 1640s, profiting greatly from the sugar boom and the Atlantic slave trade. A member of the radical Parliamentarian faction that brought about the execution of King Charles I, he became a favourite of Oliver Cromwell, gaining lucrative government contracts that made him one of the wealthiest merchants in England; so wealthy, in fact, that he became Oliver Cromwell's de facto bank, lending him money both privately as well as for the running of state business. He was accused of trading in white slaves with the colonies, deemed a violation of liberties that tragically did not apply to their black brothers; but he also fought off these accusations without much trouble, and continued to influence government and trade until his death in 1665.

Fictional Characters

Hamish MacNair, stable boy at Glamis Castle

Born 1613 in the Highlands, orphaned, and taken in by Maldouen MacAdam as a stable boy at Glamis at the age of 9. He is staunchly faithful to Glamis and Jack Lyon, and will sacrifice everything for his Master. Later in the story it seems that Hamish's connection by blood to Glamis is much closer, and more important, than anyone could know.

Margaret Douglas, the Baroness Eythin

Margaret Douglas, born around 1588 as the only daughter of Archibald Douglas, the 7th Earl of Angus, and Jean Lyon, Countess of Angus and daughter of John Lyon, 8th Lord Glamis, did exist, but died young at the age of around fifteen. I have fictionalised her past for the purpose of this story. She married James King, Lord Eythin, at a very young age, and gave birth to a son, Duncannon, around 1603. After receiving news that her husband had been killed fighting in Europe in 1620, she sought relief from her grief with Noureddine Elamin, and in secret, gave birth to a daughter, Isobel Balgaire Douglas, who she claimed to be a niece from a distant cousin in Orkney. She has two half-brothers; William Douglas, Earl of Morton, with whom she falls into dispute over her mother's inheritance; and Alexander Lindsay, 2nd Lord Spynie, who commanded a Scottish regiment in Europe. Both of her brothers were ardent supporters of King Charles I, but it is William who eventually betrays Margaret. She is convicted of witchcraft and murder and executed in 1628.

Maldouen McAdam, Coachman of Glamis Castle.

McAdam (fictional) was born on the Isle of Arran in 1597. His father was a farmer, and his mother a laundress. McAdam left Arran in 1611 after a dispute with his father and brothers, and eventually found employment as a stable boy at Glamis in 1613. His hard work and loyalty earned him the title of Coach Master of Glamis in 1619. His fierce loyalty to the House of Glamis spurs him to protect Lady Margaret's niece, Balgaire, from the Witchfinder General by taking her to Germany, where he remains to fight for the Protestant cause against the Habsburgs. A case of mistaken identity in battle gives him the opportunity to eventually return to England with a new name and title that outwardly supports the Royalist cause, but gives him a cover to seek revenge on those responsible for Margaret's death.

Fionnsgoth Hardie, handmaid to Baroness Eythin

Fionnsgoth (fictional) was born in Braemar, in the Highlands west of Aberdeen, around 1580. Little is known about her life before she became Lady Margaret's handmaid in 1607. She claimed to have been widowed at an early age, and that she bore several children who all died soon after they were born. Fionnsgoth has dedicated her life to serving Margaret and Balgaire, Margaret's alleged niece, but the mystery around Fionnsgoth's past provoked the people of Kirriemuir to speculate that she was born a witch, and was consequently scorned by the local villagers.

Alastair Noble, Steward of Glamis

Alastair, one of seven sons, was born in Dumbarton, east Scotland, around 1590. His father was a ship-builder, seldom sobre and able to work, and his mother worked as a weaver and cook to keep the family alive. After Alastair attempted to kill his father, he escaped, first to Orkney, but his brothers followed him there; eventually, he avoided capture by returning south and first finding employ with the Duke of Atholl at Blair Castle as a stable boy, before he moved on to Glamis Castle, where he became Lord Glamis' steward. Alastair keeps his past a secret; he lives in fear of his family, and his violent tendencies have often landed him in trouble with the law. Despite this, he is faithful to Lord Glamis and his master's political cause.

Effie Campbell, parlour maid to the House of Glamis

Born in Glasgow around 1613, the only daughter among eleven children of Stuart and Morag. Her father had no interest in work and spent his time drinking; her mother supported his habit by selling her only daughter, Effie, to men by the hour or night. Effie eventually escaped the horrors of her family with the aid of her eldest brother, Thom, who found her work as a maid in Fife, before she found her way into the House of Glamis, and the employ of John Lyon, Lord Glamis. A good-natured person at heart, all she wants is a secure life free from violence and fear; but the abuse she suffered as a young girl has left her so bitter and broken that she becomes vengeful and spiteful, even towards those who care for her.

Isobel Balgaire Douglas, secret daughter of Margaret Douglas.

Isobel, or Bal (short for Balgaire, meaning fox in Gaelic), was born around 1621. Although she is presented by Margaret Douglas as her niece by a distant cousin from Orkney who died in childbirth, Bal is in reality Margaret's daughter. Bal is unaware, or indifferent, to her own past, believing that her mother died in childbirth, and that Margaret has taken her into her care. Bal's real father is Noureddine Elamin, a soldier from Syria who fought with Margaret's cousin Robert in Europe, and who accompanied him as a visitor when Robert returned to Scotland to give Margaret the news that her husband, the Baron Eythin, had been killed.

Brother Athanasius, monk, St. Catherine's Monastery, Sinai

Athanasius was born on the island of Tinos, around the year 1582. His parents were killed during a raid by the Ottomans when he was a child, and he was subsequently brought up in an Orthodox orphanage. The orphanage was run by the priest Theophilos, who was the father of Anastasia, later known as Kosem Sultan. Athanasius and Anastasia were in love, and planned to marry, but she was kidnapped by Ottomans and taken to Istanbul. Athanasius could not come to terms with his loss, and left Tinos to join the priesthood, first in Jerusalem, before he was taken in by the Archbishop of St. Catherine's Monastery in Sinai.

Rafael de la Cruz, Benedictine monk, secret Head of the Order of Christ

The enigmatic Rafael was born to a cobbler and weaver in Madrid, around 1590. He was one of eleven siblings, and his parents, being poor, had no love to give any of their children; they were brought up in the harsh cruelty of child labour and destitution. For Rafael, this became unbearable, and when there was a chance to join the priesthood, he took it. He quickly rose through the ranks, joining the Inquisition at the age of seventeen, and by 1609, he had become one of the main advocates of expelling the Moors from Spain, a program King Philip III of Spain decreed between 1609 and 1614. Rafael had by the end of this gained such a reputation as a fanatical advocate of the Catholic faith that King Philip III offered him the position of Head of the Order of Christ, a clandestine and secretive group of assassin monks tasked to fight anti-Catholic sentiments across Europe. Rafael will stop at nothing to preserve the Catholic principles he was taught, and eventually met a treacherous end as a result of his fanaticism, a poetic justice for all the horror and cruelty he inflicted on the innocent throughout his life.

Dame Druscilla West, Proprietress of The Hospital of the Poor's Portion, Plymouth

Little is known of Dame Druscilla, or how she received her title of honour. Rumours say that she was born out of wedlock to a prostitute and nobleman, around the year 1580, somewhere in the south of England. She claims her father was an earl, hence her entitlement to the honorific of 'Dame', and that her wealth came from his estate; in reality, the truth is much darker. Druscilla has cheated, betrayed and even murdered to reach the higher echelons of Plymouth society, and will do everything to protect her status and her fortune.

Islay, Wilfred and Meriall, parentless children of the Poor's, Plymouth

The three abandoned children all come from an obscure background, all having been given up by their parents early in life, a memory of which they have only fragments. Islay, it is said, came from Germany, where she was abandoned in a monastery; Merriall's parents were apparently poor cotters who had come from Scotland to seek a better life in England, but had soon realised that life was as cruel as it had been; and Wilfred, he was always told, had been given up by his parents in London as they could not afford to feed his excessive appetite. All three are of similar age, born around 1631 or so; all three have an unexpected past that they discover along their journey.

Galenius of Maryburn, physician at the Trinity Hospital, Edinburgh

Born in Valencia, Spain, in 1596 to *conversos*, Jews who converted to Christianity to avoid the brutal persecution of the Spanish Inquisition, Galenius grew up as a Catholic in Valencia, along with his friend Noureddine, the son of morisco (Muslim converts to Christianity) merchants. Galenius also came from a prominent merchant family, but his parents were persecuted by the Inquisition, and killed, in 1609, when moriscos were also systematically killed or expelled from Spain; Noureddine, aged 11, was sent to North Africa. The trauma of losing his family, and his best friend, forced Galenius to flee Spain; he sought refuge first in Germany, where he studied to become a physician near Nuremberg, and spent some years practicing in a small town called Mariabrunn. But he soon found that it was easier to be a Christian than a Jew, and still a Jew at heart, Galenius left Germany and eventually settled in Edinburgh around 1620, where he took the name Galenius of Maryburn, an anglicised form of Mariabrunn.

Noureddine El-Amin, retired soldier of the Ottoman Army

Like Galenius, Noureddine was born in Valencia, Spain, in the year 1599, the son of prominent merchants. Although he was also raised as a Catholic, his family were Moriscos, Muslims who were forced to convert to Catholicism by the Spanish Crown. His childhood was happy, until, at the age of ten, his father was taken away by the Spanish Inquisition, and executed; facing the systematic expulsion of Moriscos by the Spanish Crown, his mother took him and his sister to the Muela de Cortes, a last Morisco stronghold in the mountains. Facing capture, she could not bear the thought of servitude and torture, and with her daughter, threw herself into the valley below Muela de Cortes, as Noureddine was dragged away by Inquisition officials. He was put on a ship destined for the Barbary Coast, where he was taken in by a family in the Republic of Sale, near Tangiers. A dispute when he was twenty forced him to flee, and he joined the war in Europe as a mercenary, before becoming an officer in the Ottoman army. When he was twenty, he accompanied the Scottish General Montrose to Glamis to inform Margaret that her husband had been killed; during the one night of his visit, she took solace in his kindness, and later gave birth to his daughter, Bal, who she passed off as daughter of a cousin. Noureddine had no knowledge of Bal's existence, and only made the discovery when he returned to Scotland to visit Margaret in 1628, but to find that she had been burned at the stake as a witch. Noureddine, whose surname means 'honest, loyal and faithful', vows to seek revenge for those he has loved and lost.

Gordon MacDonald, eminent judge at the College of Justice in Edinburgh

Born in Aberdeen in 1567, Justice MacDonald gained a reputation as a fair and level-headed adjudicator, being able to leave his own religious and political views out of his legal judgements during a time when politics and religion influenced every aspect of social fabric in Scotland. Considered a thorn in the side by members of the Privy Council, and Charles I's Royalist supporters in Scotland, MacDonald is subject to a plot that sees his downfall when he is assigned the case of Margaret Douglas. He is executed on the same day that she is tried and burned as a witch.

Milton Keynes UK
Ingram Content Group UK Ltd.
UKHW012310011223
433579UK00003B/42/J